⋅MOUNTAIN⋅
Grown

·MOUNTAIN·
Grown

Johny Weber

Hildebrand Books

an imprint of W. Brand Publishing

NASHVILLE, TENNESSEE

Hildebrand Books an imprint of W. Brand Publishing
j.brand@wbrandpub.com
www.wbrandpub.com

Cover design by designchik.net

Mountain Grown / Johny Weber — 1st Edition

Available in Paperback, Kindle, and eBook formats.
Paperback ISBN: 978-1-956906-50-9
eBook ISBN: 978-1-956906-51-6

Library of Congress Control Number: 2022922057

CONTENTS

To my children, Amanda and Shane,

and their precious families.

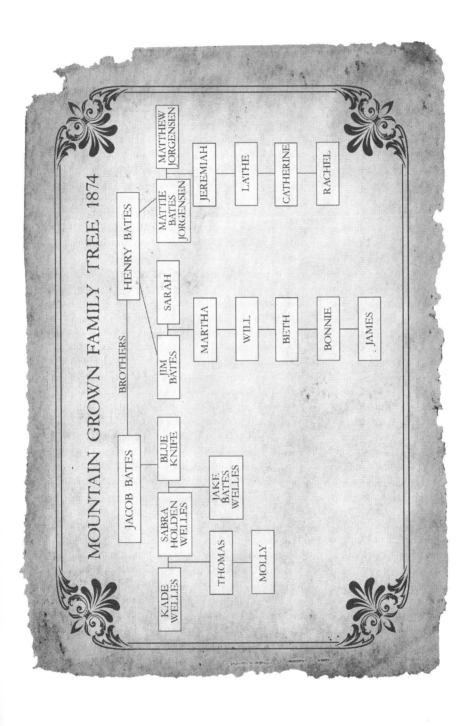

MOUNTAIN GROWN FAMILY TREE 1874

CHAPTER 1

Cheyenne Village – July 1874

Jake was glad to be leaving the fort. Too many white folks made him nervous. Hell, too many people made him nervous. But the two nights he spent on the outskirts of the fort had been fun. There were some Shoshones camped around the fort, and he visited them. He found a willing young Indian woman to lay with while he was there. He left her smiling with baubles and beads and a new skinning knife. Rested, stocked up on supplies, and talked out, he was ready to move on.

Jake found he was accepted better by the Indians than the whites. At twenty-five, Jake was a well-built man, fully muscled and filled out. He wasn't a big man, but not small either. Hidden under his long-sleeved buckskin or homespun shirts were massively muscled shoulders. On the small side of average height, it wasn't until one noticed his eyes, his intense look that demanded respect, that people took notice. He had huge palms and short fingers that gave him great strength in his grip or his fist. He had the Indian ability to show no emotion at all in his face. His eyes could bore into a stranger who crossed him. He didn't often start a fight, but he wasn't known to back down either.

His features easily showed his Indian heritage. Jake's father was a mixed-blood Indian, with a Ute mother and a white mountain man father. Jake, on the other hand, was the product of his Ute warrior father, Blue Knife, and Sabra, his white mother. Still, he showed more Indian features than white. Dark-skinned, he was not mistaken for anything but a man of Native American origins. But he was handsome too, having the high chiseled cheekbones of his Indian ancestors and the fine features of his white mother.

The young girls on the wagon trains they traded with would stream out with their fathers to see the dark-skinned trader's son who ignored them. Occasionally, one would try to talk to him but would find him polite but taciturn, not inclined for conversation. And, although they didn't know it, it wasn't because he couldn't speak well. Instead, Jake knew these people were wary of him. He saw the fathers hustle their daughters away. Messing with these white girls was just asking for trouble and Jake didn't go looking for trouble. But it had a way of finding him anyway.

It was much the same at the fort. People who didn't know Jake were wary of him. While there were usually few white women at the fort, there was often someone itching to pick a fight over nothing. He'd never been to the fort when he hadn't gotten in a fight of some degree, but he fought fair and usually won, and those who knew him understood that. Jake grew up "play fighting" with his stepfather, Kade, who taught him moves and tricks for fighting. Then as his half-brother, Thomas, grew older, the two boys, along with Jake's cousins Jeremiah, Will, and Lathe, were always tumbling about. Jake never saw anyone really fight mean or fight mad, until he went on the trading trips, but he knew how to handle himself when the time inevitably came. He knew what to do.

At first, his reputation was only as Kade's son. Jake had traveled to Ft. Laramie with his stepfather since he was a young boy. Kade had been a regular at Ft. Laramie, first as a trapper, then as a wagon scout, and finally, as a trader. Kade had been patronizing the fort, in one way or another, for longer than Jake had been alive. Kade was trusted and respected by all who knew him or had heard of him. Now Jake had his own reputation. He started few fights, did not drink to excess, gambled well but little, and rode the best horses. His money and his word were good. These traits alone garnered Jake respect from everyone who knew him. Unfortunately, there was always some passing white man or soldier who thought it made him a big man to bait a man with Indian blood. As Kade once told Jake, a man could only take so much.

On this trip, the fight, such as it was, had been in the sutler's store. The sutler knew Jake, and they were putting together the trade goods Jake wanted. A white settler, full of himself, had come in and wanted the sutler's attention.

"Sutler, I'm in a hurry," he snarled. "The damn half-breed can just wait."

The sutler looked up mildly. "I'll be with you in a minute. Wait yer turn."

The settler elbowed between them, pushing Jake's pile off the counter with the sweep of his hand. "Git boy," he said. "Git yor stinking ass . . ." He didn't get another word out. Jake came unleashed like a wild animal, lethal and deadly. Turning, Jake grabbed the man by his shirt front, propelling the surprised settler backward. The next thing the settler knew, the wind and most of his senses were knocked out of him as he was slammed up against the far wall, head bouncing against the lumber walls. If Jake hadn't been holding him upright, the man would have slid to the ground.

"My name is Jacob Bates Welles, mister," Jake's words came out low and soft. "You want to refer to me, you use that name. Until then, you wait your turn," he said, using surprisingly good English. Then Jake let go of the man and let him slide down in a heap. *In retrospect, it was a pretty easy fight this year,* he thought, but because of it, word spread to leave the "mixed-blood Indian who spoke good English" alone.

Jake was glad to lead his string of horses and pack mules farther away from the fort. He was heading to the mountains, and for much of the next month, he would be alone, except when Brown Otter came to meet him. For the past nine years, he had met his half-brother at his grandfather's cabin. The first two years, Kade or Old Tom traveled with him, but at eighteen, Jake was considered a man and no longer needed a guide or a companion, so he had gone alone to the fort and alone into the mountains to spend a month at the cabin. Now at twenty-five, Jake always went to the high mountains alone.

Other than his family's home, Jake's grandfather's cabin was the place he loved the most. Secluded in a small mountain valley, it was the place he was born. Although his mother and Kade had moved the year after his birth, they had taken Jake back before he was grown. There, Jake first met his half-brother when he was eight. Brown Otter was twelve years Jake's senior, already a man, but he was interested in knowing Jake. They shared the same father, a father that Jake never knew. Blue Knife was the son of old Jacob Bates and his Ute wife, and Blue Knife was dead before Jake was born. Brown Otter filled that void, telling Jake stories of their father. Brown Otter taught Jake the stories of their tribe too and helped him master the Ute language. Sabra and Kade had felt that Jake needed this connection to his Native people. Jake had a foot in both worlds. Before he could know where he was going, Jake needed to know where he came from.

Kade had taught him what he knew about the Utes and their language, as well as the universal sign language of the Plains Indians, but Brown Otter filled in the gaps. Most summers, if Brown Otter's village was nearby, Jake spent some of the month in the village as well as the cabin. Preferring the solitude of the cabin, Jake also found it rewarding to be accepted by the tribe. Visiting the tribe also satisfied the young man in him; there was always a young woman in the village who was willing.

His trade goods also came in handy. After helping his pa with the trading along the Oregon Trail, Jake went to Ft. Laramie to get his mules loaded with trade goods. Then he went to the mountains of his birth. If the village was close, he would also go there to trade and visit Brown Otter.

Jake figured it was about five days before getting to the cabin, but only two days to the mountains. Like Kade, his stepfather, he yearned for the cool crispness of the mountains. The higher he went, the better he liked it. The cabin was at a higher elevation than the valley his parents lived in now. In the middle of summer, it was cool and refreshing after coming off the prairie.

He wore new buckskins, traded for at the Shoshone camp. His long hunting shirt with new fringes hung below his waist. He wore it belted, skinning knife in its sheath attached to the belt. He had a small knife on a leather string hanging from his neck; the little blade was handy for small jobs or for eating.

His rifle was a new Winchester 1873 model. Using cartridges, he needed no powder horn and shot like his pa had to carry in the old days. In addition, it was a repeater rifle, so it could shoot several times before being reloaded. He had a small knife in a leather sheath hanging from his neck by a string. If he had to quickly exit his horse, his gun, which he rode with over his saddle in front of him mountain man style, and his ammunition always went with him.

This was his mountain outfit. When he returned home in late summer, he would don the shirts and trousers his mother made that were more suitable for the lower elevations and the late summer heat. But like his pa before him and the Indian father he never knew, his buckskins were his clothing of choice when he went to the high mountains.

It was nearing mid-morning when Jake spotted the lazy wisps of campfire smoke ahead. It was still too far from the mountains to meet Ute warriors at this time of the summer. They would come out to hunt buffalo in the early fall, but he thought this was still too early. It might be a Cheyenne village. He had heard at the fort that there were some bands this way. He was too close to Ft. Laramie to encounter any on the warpath. He had plenty of trade goods. It would be good to stop. The

Cheyenne didn't often come into the mountains by his home, but if they occasionally did, it didn't hurt to have them think kindly of him and his family. He would trade with them if they were interested.

He looked behind him at the pack mules and the two mares he had purchased at the fort. Both mares were nice horses. Not flashy but big-boned, they would fit into his mother's band well. She wanted some new blood in her herd. Other than her family, his mother's one love was her horses. The Ute called her Woman with Many Horses. *That pretty much explained his mother,* he thought, smiling as he thought of her. So many times as he grew up did they eat cold supper because his mother had spent too much time with the horses. She was happiest out riding with Kade.

Jake approached the village slowly, waiting for the dogs to herald his arrival. He saw several braves come out from the lodges and watch his approach. Taking out a pipe, Jake held it up and made the peace sign. When he was answered in kind, Jake dismounted and approached, leaving his string to graze. It was a Cheyenne village. He did not know their language, but the universal sign language was sufficient for his purposes. Jake went to his packs and taking down one blanket wrapped parcel, he laid out some trade goods. Other members of the tribe came out, examining his goods. *Let the bartering begin,* Jake thought.

After the exchanges wound down, Jake packed away the furs he had taken in on trade when an old man, who Jake assumed was a chief because of the deference the others showed him, invited Jake to come to eat. Sitting before the fire next to the old man's lodge, Jake saw two middle-aged women working, one cooking and one working on a hide. Jake and the old man took their knives and cut meat from the haunch on the spit. While he chewed, Jake tried to explain, as best as he could, that he was headed to the mountains.

The youngest of the two wives went into the lodge, and Jake heard her start screeching. Suddenly, a girl or young woman was shoved violently outside by the older woman. Losing her balance, the girl fell to the ground on her rump, her back to Jake and the old man. The older woman was on the girl in an instant, grabbing a handful of her hair and violently jerking the young woman up. The young woman was sent tumbling toward the nearby creek. The older wife threw water containers toward her, screeching orders.

Jake glanced at the old man and saw he seemed not to have even noticed what had gone on. Apparently, this treatment was not a new thing. As Jake watched the retreating figure, he took in her matted hair, black as a raven, and her torn and tattered dress. From her back, Jake could see the left sleeve of the leather dress was completely torn off. And were those her toes poking through her moccasins? She was a slave girl; he knew right away. She would be from another tribe, but he couldn't tell which one from the rags she wore.

By the time the slave girl came back with her containers of water, Jake was almost ready to get up and take his leave. He still had a whole afternoon to travel, and he wanted to move on. Jake watched the girl approach, head down submissively. That didn't appease the older Indian woman, however. When the girl got close and set the water down, the old woman struck her again, knocking her down. This time though, her back was not toward Jake. As she climbed to her feet and scuttled away, she glanced up at Jake and the old man. With a start, Jake saw that she had blue eyes. *What the hell,* he thought, *she's a white girl!* Jake studied her face. It was sunburned dark and covered with dirt. Without those blue eyes, she would pass for an Indian if one didn't look too hard, but he could see by the shape of her face now that she was a white girl. She was not of mixed blood either but a full white girl. She scurried away as the Indian woman approached her again.

Another thought rose unbidden in Jake's mind. If his father, his blood father Blue Knife, had not taken his mother as his wife, this would have been his mother's fate before Jake was born. His mother never spoke of it, but Brown Otter had told him the story. Blue Knife's village had been pillaged by white trappers, the women and children killed or abducted while the braves were on a hunting trip. Jake's mother and grandfather had come upon Brown Otter, then a young boy, and two small children who had survived the massacre. Jacob and Sabra had buried the dead and taken the children home with them. Blue Knife and the braves turned up months later after trying to get back the surviving Indian women who had been abducted. Some of the braves had lost sisters, some had lost wives. Blue Knife's wife had been killed. The braves were angry. They wanted revenge against the white men and intended to take it out on this white woman who was now alone in their mountains. They would have taken her back to the village as a sex slave, but Blue Knife, thinking she was his late father's wife, intervened. He would take the woman as his wife. It was his place as Jacob's son; it was his right. And so, Jake's mother had become wife to a Ute warrior, against her will. Yes, Jake knew this white slave girl wasn't his business, but he also knew he had to make it his business.

Jake sat smoking, thinking. Then with signs and gestures, because he didn't know all the words for what he was asking, Jake made the chief understand that he wanted the girl. The old man grinned and grabbed himself in the crotch, making an obscene gesture. Jake grinned and nodded, for it wouldn't do to offend the old man. But he also shook his head and tried to explain that he didn't want to take the girl once, he wanted a woman to go with him. Jake gestured at the old chief's wives. He hoped he was saying what came to mean that the old chief had two women and a slave girl.

"I need a full-time woman to do for me. I buy your slave girl," he signed, waiting while the old man thought.

After a pause, the old man nodded toward Jake's horses. He wanted the two mares. Jake shook his head, holding up one finger. Jake would pay one horse for the girl. He signed that she was just a slave girl, not a daughter. She was not worth two horses. Jake hoped this would work, because he knew he would pay far more if it took that to get the girl. The old man thought about that. Finally, he nodded. The old man would sell the girl for one horse. Jake rose and went to the horses. He untied one of the mares and brought it to the lodge. He looked at the old man but nodded toward the girl. The chief barked something at her, and she jumped to her feet. Jake saw her look at them both, sheer terror rising on her face, but she came to them as ordered.

Jake signed to the chief to tell her to get her things. The old man laughed, replying that she had no things. Jake went to the other mare. Taking some skins that he had just traded for, he tied them with long leather thongs to the back of the mare, making the girl a saddle of sorts. When she hesitated to approach, the older Indian woman struck her on the back. Stumbling, the slave girl came, and Jake helped her onto her horse. She sat rigidly on the mare and wouldn't look at him. Then mounting his own sturdy gelding, Jake took the lead line for the mare and the mules, and they made for the distant mountains.

They must have ridden a couple of miles before Jake began to relax. He didn't think any of the village would come after them. He didn't think they valued this girl that much to change their minds, but he wanted to put distance between them and the village. It never hurt to be too cautious. He glanced back now and then to check on the girl and his mules. She rode as if in shock. Jake knew she was scared. The fear of the unknown is sometimes worse than the fear of the known, no matter how bad that was. Jake felt for her, but there would be time later to ease her fears. If the girl had been with the Indians a short time, he knew that he looked like just another Indian to her. She didn't look like she had been treated very well by Indians so far. Going off alone with him had to be scary. If the girl had been with Indians a long time, he wondered if she could even speak English or if she remembered her white life.

When they had been traveling for about an hour, he pulled her mare up so that she rode beside him. Jake watched her face register alarm as he drew her horse close to him, but she didn't resist. They were moving at a nice slow jog, and she sat the horse easily. She had been on horses, at least, and was comfortable in doing so.

"What is your name?" he asked softly.

Her eyes were on him, but she made no indication that she understood his words.

"Do you speak English?" He waited. "Talk white man language?" There was no reply.

Jake tried to sign the question, saying his name first. "Me, Jake Welles," he said out loud, then gesturing to her with a questioning look. Again, there was no reply. Jake searched for another way to ask this question. Where does he go from here? He didn't know the Cheyenne words.

"Anna," her voice was soft, and it startled him.

"Anna," he echoed. "What is your last name? Anna, what?"

She did not answer. Finally, Anna shook her head, her eyes wide. Jake realized she didn't remember her last name.

He tried again. "Do you speak English?"

It was like pulling teeth to get anything out of her, but finally she held up one hand, her thumb and first finger very close together, and said, "Talk white."

He thought about that and how she used her words. She had used "talk" and "white". He had used those words. She had indicated a very small space between her two fingers. How long had she been with the Indians? She was picking up words that he said. She couldn't yet pull up words from her past.

"You talk the white language a little," he used more of a complete sentence, letting her hear the words. She nodded. "You don't remember what your last name is." He spoke carefully, enunciating each word. Then he waited, and again she nodded, only this time she didn't seem so sure. Maybe that was too many words thrown at her at once.

"My name is Jake, and my last name is Welles," he said. "You say, Jake." He pointed at her.

She studied him. He repeated his name and told her to say it. "You say my name. Say, Jake."

"Jake."

"That is my name. Your name is Anna?" he prompted. "Say it again."

"Anna . . . Anna," she hesitated, thinking, "Anna Costis . . . Anna Currs . . ."

Jake stared at her. Her last name was like Costis or Currs. "That is good, Anna, to remember," he said. He saw that talking and thinking had helped her relax some. Well, maybe relax was too broad a term, but at the moment, she did not have that look of sheer terror on her face.

Jake studied her. Under all the dirt and mangled hair, she might be pretty. She was young but not that young. She looked about the age of his sister Molly, but no, this girl was more filled out, woman-like, than Molly. His sister was fifteen. This girl was older than that. Her dress must have been a hand me down from one of the chief's women because it was much too big for her and was terribly tattered. To his chagrin, he couldn't help noticing that her torn sleeve left a big gaping hole on the side. If the girl leaned forward at all, the dress top hung away from her. When that happened, he could see the small, rounded breast through the ripped armhole. If she knew that, she didn't care. The thought came to him that maybe she was beyond caring about her appearance, but only trying to survive. He also noticed that she was painfully thin. That might make her look younger than her years. This girl was also taller than Molly. If Anna grew no more, she wouldn't be a tall woman, but she was not short. *Perhaps it was because she was so gaunt that she looked so young,* he thought.

They rode in silence while thoughts swirled in Jake's head. He needed to talk to her, so she heard more words. Maybe she would remember then and understand more of what he said.

"Do you remember how long you have been with the Cheyenne?" he asked finally. Then he tried to sign those words as well. He could see her thinking.

She held up three fingers and made the sign of the moon. He was surprised. She should not have forgotten the English language in three months.

"You have been with the Cheyenne for three moons? Three months?" he signed the words as well. She nodded.

"How did you come to be with the Cheyenne?" Again, he signed the words as best as he could remember.

He could see her thinking. She came up with a word, not a Cheyenne word but a Pawnee word. It was the name the Pawnee used to refer to themselves, and Jake knew that word. He was surprised.

"You were with the Pawnee?"

"Yes," she came up with the first English word he didn't think he had used himself first.

"How long were you with the Pawnee?" he spoke slowly so his words fit the signs he used. He could see her thinking. Finally, she used both of her hands, holding them far apart from each other. He understood then that she had been with them a long time, a long enough time to forget the English language.

They camped that night by a small stream that gave the animals a place to drink, and for them, a bit of lowland where they could be below the skyline. The fear ramped up on Anna's face when they stopped. Jake could see it as she took in the place, the loneliness of it. He knew she was afraid of him. Jake figured he could tell her again and again that she was safe with him, but she wouldn't believe his words. He had to show her. He stripped the saddles and packs off his horse and the mules. He saw Anna watching him, and then she searched for the knots that tied the skins on her horse and took them off. She started to gather firewood, but he stopped her.

"No fire tonight," he said, shaking his head. "We will make a cold camp until we get in the mountains." He didn't care if she understood him now but just wanted her to hear more words. He searched through his pack and, finding a cake of homemade soap, he handed it to her. "You go wash," he gestured to the creek.

She stared at the soap and looked up with questioning eyes to him. "Wash?"

He pointed to the soap, then to her face, and tousled her hair, seeing her flinch away from him. "Wash the dirt off. You know soap?" he waited, watching her study the soap. Suddenly it was like a light went on in her head.

"Know soap," Anna said, wonder in her voice. She turned and made her way to the creek.

Jake searched through his packs for jerky and hardtack biscuits. He went to the supply packs and found a tin of peaches. He wasn't comfortable here so exposed on the open prairie to chance a fire. Better to eat tinned or dried food than to get ambushed by some roving Indian band or a group of renegade white men. The camp was below the skyline along the creek, well-hidden unless someone stumbled upon them. As darkness came on, he could not see any movement on the prairie. Campfire smoke now or the light of a fire later would only alert Indians or other travelers on the prairie of their camping spot. They didn't need the fire.

Jake tried not to look at the girl in the water. He tried to stay busy. Maybe it wasn't in his nature, he finally decided as he glanced a second time toward the creek. The girl had shucked her dress and was partially submerged in the shallow water. But the part of Anna above water showed he was right; she was not a child. She was woman developed, although maybe her womanhood was still emerging. She was so damn thin it was hard to tell. Jake saw the line of her backbone and the outline of her ribs as she turned away from him. Her arms were like sticks. He saw her lean over the water, getting her hair wet and soapy. *He might have to check her head for lice,* he thought. *God, what had he gotten himself into?*

Anna donned her tattered leather dress before she came back, and her face and hair were scrubbed. Jake had been right. She was quite pretty in a scrawny way with the dirt scrubbed away. Jake had found a comb in his trading pack. He handed it to Anna. She looked at it wonderingly.

"Talk this?" she asked.

Jake grinned. She had the word "talk" down, even if she used it wrong. "It is called a comb. Its name is comb. You know what it is for?"

Anna reached up to her tangled mess of hair, grabbing it and putting the comb to it. Jake just nodded. He watched her try to comb through her hair. She was able to unknot some locks near her face, but a big tangle on the back of her head was a struggle for her. He pulled out his small neck knife and, untangling his legs, he rose and went to her.

"Here, let me help," he said, reaching out with the knife. Anna saw the blade coming toward her and gave a little scream, scrambling away. Jake cursed himself silently for moving so quickly at her with the knife. He saw her shaking as she watched him. He tipped the point of the knife away before speaking, quietly but firmly.

"I won't hurt you. You are safe," Jake said softly, then repeated, "I won't hurt you. Let me help." He advanced on her slowly this time as if she was a spooked colt. Anna was on her knees, and Jake knew she was ready to bolt, but he kept speaking softly to her as she held her ground. Kneeling to her level, he gently reached out for her hair and turned her head away from him. She sank on her rear, facing away from him. He could feel her trembling. Taking the tangled mess of hair at the back of Anna's head, he ran the blade of his knife through the worst of the tangle, slicing some hair off, but breaking up the mass. Carefully, Jake did this twice more, then he reached out, took the comb from her, and worked it through. Slowly the hair came loose and lay over her shoulders. It felt soft to his fingers. He searched through her scalp for lice and was relieved to only find a couple. How she wasn't infested with them he wouldn't know, but he knew he would have to check again another day, just to make sure. Finally, when he was satisfied, he handed her the comb. This whole time, Anna had been rigid, not moving at all. Her wide eyes showed confusion while she searched his face. Apparently, no one had been kind to her for some time.

Jake laid out an ample supply of the hardtack and jerky. He opened the tin of peaches with his small knife and took out one plump ripe fruit, popping it whole into his mouth. Then he put the tin and knife down in front of Anna. He could shoot some game tomorrow afternoon. Tomorrow night in the mountains he would make a fire and get some good food in her, but tonight this would have to do. Jake took some food and ate, gesturing to her to eat too. But Anna just sat there, staring at the food.

"You are hungry. You eat now," he said again.

Anna seemed to be thinking of words before she replied, "You eat." She pointed at him and then touched her chest. "Anna eat . . ." she was at a loss for the words. Gesturing with hands and signs, he realized what she was trying to say. She was allowed to eat the scraps that were left. Anna had been made to wait until the others were finished and then was allowed only what was left. By the looks of her, there hadn't been much left. She had probably been beaten many times for taking food before she was allowed. Jake reached for some of the food and put it in Anna's lap. He handed her the peach tin.

"Eat now," he said, using sign language to emphasize his words. "With me, you eat when I eat. You eat all that you want." He put more food in her lap. "You eat," and Jake used her sign for a lot, putting his two hands wide apart, "a lot."

The girl carefully picked up the peach tin, examining the contents. Taking the knife, she fished out the remaining peach and bit off a big chunk. It didn't take her long to finish the fruit and then tip the tin up to drink the juice. Then she took a jerky and tentatively took a bite. When she saw that Jake did not react to her taking the food, she ate with relish, as if this was the finest of food. Jake had no doubt that she was hungry. She devoured it all.

After eating, Jake got out his pipe. He sat watching her as he smoked. *There was something peaceful about having a pipe,* he thought. From as early as he could remember, he had seen his pa or old Tom pulling out a pipe in the evening. Tobacco was one of those items he brought back in large quantities, not only for trading but also for home. For every visitor that stopped by, be he white trapper or red, the pipe was the first to come out.

Anna combed her hair over and over, and then finally parting it in the back, she began to braid. She might not have braided her hair recently, but she was skilled at it. When she reached the ends, she searched her dress for a fringe long enough to pull off, but there was none left on the old leather. Jake took his knife and sliced a fringe off his sleeve, handing it to her. She threw him a quick glance but took the fringe. He cut another, and leaning over her, placed it in her lap for her second braid. It was almost dark and with no fire, she was just a silhouette now.

Jake went out to picket the horses and then on the way back, he stopped at his packs. He took his blanket, and from his trading pack he took out a new one for the girl. They wouldn't need much in this prairie heat, but it was cooling down some as the sky darkened. If nothing else, when the mosquitoes found them, a blanket was good to pull over one's face for protection. He handed a blanket to Anna, and then turning he found a spot that looked level and lay himself down. He watched her out of slitted eyes to see what she would do.

At first, she just sat there, looking at the new blanket, then at him, and back to the blanket again. Finally, she got up and he saw her move a little way off and her profile got low to the ground. He knew what she was doing and pretended to sleep. When she returned, she came hesitantly. She picked up the blanket and spread it on the ground where she had sat before. She waited. When Jake didn't stir, she finally lay down on the blanket, pulling it over her as well. In the silence of the prairie, he could hear her breathing. It was some time before the slow deep breathing of sleep took over either of them.

The next morning Jake was up early, the girl coming awake with a start when she heard him moving. He put out cold food again and gestured for her to eat. He took a jerky, chewing on it as he went to bring in the horses and mules. When he went to gather the blankets, he saw that Anna had rolled them up in readiness to be tied onto the pack mule. He nodded his thanks to her. She hadn't eaten much. He picked up more jerky and, putting it in her lap, he told her to eat. She didn't need to be told twice. She almost attacked the food. They watered at the creek before they mounted their horses and headed toward the mountains.

Jake wanted to question her more to find out how she got to be with the Pawnee and for how long she had been with them. But the language barrier was too tiresome for that now. Instead, as they rode, he told her many things and had her repeat them. Occasionally, he used sign language to help, but mostly he would point and speak and have her repeat what he said.

"This is a horse." He would point. "Say, this is a horse." He would command Anna.

"Those are the mountains." Again he would point. "Say it." Then he would wait for her to talk. This went on for hours. Jake wasn't sure if he had ever talked so much in one day, but words were coming back to her. By afternoon he could ask her questions, and she started to answer him with remembered words. Sometimes she would use a word that he knew he had not said, so he knew that the English language was coming back. Maybe tonight, he could get her to talk about how she came to be with the Cheyenne.

The other thing he noticed about her was that she wasn't as fearful this day. She seemed to forget her fear while intensely concentrating on trying to talk. She had gone almost twenty-four hours without being screeched at or struck. That had to be a first, at least in the last three months. The last thing he noticed was that she had no idea that she half fell out of that godforsaken sleeve hole in that tattered rag of a dress. He took to riding on the side of her where she still had a sleeve down her arm. It wasn't that he minded the view from the tattered side, but he had a distinct feeling that coming at her with a god-awful hard pipe sticking out the front of his pants wasn't going to make her feel safe. After seeing the old chief's first reaction when he offered to buy her, he had no doubt she had been sold before for a night's roll. Every time he thought of that, his mind went to his mother and how close she had come to that life.

They reached the foothills of the mountains by mid-afternoon. Just before beginning their climb, Jake shot an antelope. Going to it, he quickly bled it, gutted it, and hung it over one of the mules. They weren't far to a camping spot now and he could finish skinning and cutting it up there. When they reached the first heights where they could see far out on the prairie, they pulled up to look back on the way they had come. For miles and miles, they saw nothing except some antelope grazing. There was no one out there. Jake felt it would be safe to start a fire when he got a little deeper into the slopes and in a more secluded spot.

After finding a suitable camping spot along a small brook, Jake dropped the packs, antelope carcass, and saddle and went to hobble the horses in the grass along the edge of the brook. The girl gathered wood for a fire and stood waiting for him. She gestured at the antelope.

"Skin it me?"

"Yes, you can skin it if you want," Jake replied, smiling. He went to his trading packs and found a new blade and gave it to her. Anna attacked the antelope expertly, folding back the skin as she went.

Jake got a fire started and found some sticks the right size to spear chunks of meat to prop up over the fire. It would be good to eat fresh meat. Then he sorted through some of the cured skins that he had traded for and selected some he thought would be right. He was tired of seeing Anna's toes sticking out of the pieces of leather that passed as moccasins on her.

After filling up on fresh cooked antelope meat, Jake put on more to cook. They could take it cold with them tomorrow and eat during the daytime. While the meat was cooking, he took the skins he chose and went to the girl. She seemed relaxed as she skinned the antelope and while she ate, but now as he approached her, he could see Anna tense up. He held up the skins.

"Can you make yourself some new moccasins with these?" Jake asked. He pointed at her feet.

Anna's eyes widened, but she nodded. He gave her the skins and moved to a spot not distant from her, but not close enough to threaten her. Maybe while she worked, he could get her to talk.

"How did you get with the Pawnee?" Jake asked.

Anna wrinkled up her brow, trying to remember not only events but words. "Ma, pa, brother, sister, baby come wagon. Wagon broke. Other wagons go. Pa say go." Here she used her arm to mimic her father signaling to the other wagons to go on without them. "Pa fix. Pawnee come. Kill ma, pa, brother, sister," she paused, in her mind probably seeing that day. "Baby with me. Ma say watch baby. I reach hatchet, hold up. Braves laugh at me. Raise knife at me. Chasing Hawk say no. Bring girl to old grandmother. I go."

"What happened to the baby," Jake asked softly, fearing what he probably knew.

"Kill baby," Anna's voice betrayed no emotion. Jake imagined all her tears were shed then, and now it was too long ago to mourn anymore. She had been through too much since then.

"Who is old grandmother? Were you a slave girl?" he asked.

"Old grandmother was mother. Mother . . . Chasing Hawk. Live Chasing Hawk tepee. Old grandmother daughter die. I old grandmother's daughter. Old grandmother teach Indian ways. Old grandmother good to me."

"How did you end up with the Cheyenne? Were you stolen?" Jake decided to let her words flow as she thought of them rather than correcting her with better grammar. This was not the time for an English lesson.

"Old grandmother old. She die. Chasing Hawk squaw not like me. She mean to me when old grandmother not look. Old grandmother die," she repeated. "Chasing Hawk start looking me. I big girl now. Not little girl. Big girl with these," Anna cupped her breasts. "Squaw not like Chasing Hawk look me. Cheyenne come. Old Cheyenne chief want young white girl. Squaw tell Chasing Hawk sell me."

"That was three months ago, three moons?"

"Three moons," Anna shrugged, not sure. "Sell me after the snows melt," Anna answered.

Yes, thought Jake, *that would be at least three months, maybe four even.* Jake thought he would take a different approach for a bit. He thought it might give her a break from hurtful things. "What was your Indian name?" he asked.

"Pawnee name or Cheyenne name?" she asked.

"Pawnee."

"Pawnee, call me White Bird."

"What did the Cheyenne call you?" he asked.

Anna turned away from him. For a minute, she didn't answer, then she hung her head. Very softly she said, "Cheyenne call me Ugly Woman No Make Man Hard."

Sweet Jesus, Jake thought, *it just gets worse and worse.* He didn't even know where to go after that.

Indians could be very crude sometimes. This was one of those times. He knew exactly what this name was talking about, and it wasn't good. Silently they sat. After a bit, Anna continued the story on her own, without his prompting.

"Old chief want young girl. Say he want to see white skin. Chief got two squaws. They no like me. Old chief lay with me but it," she stopped, and he could see she was searching for a word. She started again, "He lay with me . . . do things but his . . ." again, she searched for a word. Finally, she pointed to Jake's crotch, "What called?"

Shit, Jake thought, *what the hell do I tell her?* She didn't even realize no white woman would ever ask that question. He tossed about in his mind a proper word to give her.

"Manhood," he couldn't think of anything else better to use.

"Yes," she said, "yes, manhood. He couldn't make manhood hard. He couldn't make it go in me. He angry. He beat me. Old squaws laugh at me. I get name."

Her matter-of-fact telling shook him, but Jake found he felt a little better knowing she hadn't actually been raped by the old man, try though he had. His relief was short lived.

"Old chief let other braves take me," Anna continued. "Their manhood got hard, but they never told old chief. They only say ugly girl no good. They hurt me with teeth . . . with fire. They laugh at me."

Anna quit talking. Jake looked into the fire, keeping all emotion from his face. Right about now, he wished he'd never asked. But not asking and not knowing wouldn't change what had happened to her. The one thing to be grateful for in all of this was that she was apparently taken as a child and hadn't a good handle on the shame of it. If Anna had been raised for any length of time with the Indians, she would have heard a lot of talk of, if not seen, the ways between a woman and a man. Both men and women in the tribes were a lot more open with what happens under a robe.

It was not uncommon for an Indian woman to be "shared" with others, and if the woman received gifts, she was usually more than accommodating. Jake knew that from first-hand experience. He had been trading for nights with Native women for years and never felt that any of the women ever resented sleeping with him. They came willing, sometimes more than willing, asking for him. With Anna, however, she had been raped, but the act was not the same in her mind as it would be in the mind of a white woman who was abducted after she reached womanhood. Anna had to have been young when the Pawnee captured her to not understand rape. But no one is too young to understand being abused or ridiculed. Everyone understood those things.

"How old were you when the Pawnee took you?" he asked finally.

Anna thought about that. She stood up and held her hand below her shoulder a good way. "Little. Not baby."

"Do you know how old you were?"

Again, she thought about that. She closed her eyes and thought. Jake suddenly realized that what he heard her whispering was a tune. It was the children's birthday song. "Happy birthday to you . . ." she sang softly to herself. Then she looked up at Jake. "I was eight."

"Do you know how long you were with the Pawnee?"

But Anna just shook her head. She had no idea. She held up her hands, "Maybe this many?" She held up seven fingers. "Maybe this many?" She held up all her fingers. "Don't know."

Jake thought about what she had told him. He was missing something. Something from his memory stirred in him. He tossed back in his mind to his first year trading along the Oregon Trail with only Pa and Tom. It was a trip when his mother didn't go. He was sixteen and proud to be on the trading trip with the men. A wagon train had come in and told them a single wagon was left behind because of a broken wagon. There was another train one day behind them, so the family in the broken wagon sent them on and would come on with the second train after making repairs. But when the second train arrived the following evening, they came with sad news. They had found the broken wagon and the family. They found the family slain, the livestock stolen, and the bodies scalped. Jake's pa had been angry. Stupid pilgrims, Kade had fumed. You don't go off and leave a family alone out here on the plains. But the wagon train that had left them had already gone on. The members of the second train had found and buried the bodies of the parents and three children. There was a picture of the family in the wagon, and there were four children in the picture. It had been assumed that the fourth child had died either before the trip began or along the way. They had not found any evidence of the fourth child. That was nine years ago. Jake knew what happened to the fourth child now. She would be seventeen now and her name, if Jake remembered correctly, was Anna Curtis.

CHAPTER 2

Going Home – July 1874

T he sun was past its zenith and heading down toward the western horizon, but there were still many hours of daylight left. Kade watched the familiar rise of the mountains take shape before him. He wanted to move the livestock faster the closer they got, but these animals were in poor shape and moving them at a faster pace was out of the question. It always took him double the time to return home as it did to head north weeks earlier with fresh livestock. He wanted all these animals to make it home to eat, rest and grow fat on the land.

Twenty-three years he had made this summer trip to meet wagon trains along the Oregon Trail. Twenty-three years ago, he made the first trip with Sabra, little two-year-old Jake, and old Tom, who now, at nearly eighty years old, pretty much stayed close to home. That was the first year of a lucrative trading business which was now a dying business. Twenty-three years ago, the wagon trains along the Oregon Trail sometimes numbered over one hundred wagons in each train. Some days more than one train would pass them as they waited to trade. Now the trains were fewer, smaller, and often better equipped for the trip.

Tom and Kade knew the Oregon Trail well. They had guided two wagon trains west along the Trail in the 1840s: one in 1846 and one in 1848. They were familiar with the country from the earlier years of hunting and trapping in the mountains and these western ranges. Now their business wasn't guiding wagon trains but rather it was trading with them. They brought fresh oxen, mules, and cattle, to the Oregon Trail and traded them for worn out livestock owned by the pioneers. It took them about a week to reach the Oregon Trail near Independence Rock from home. They gauged their arrival somewhere near Independence Rock in late June to catch the early trains. These trains had a greater chance of hitting wet or inclement weather, wearing their livestock down trying to pull wagons in wet conditions. It also afforded the best grass to graze their own animals on before the livestock of the wagon trains ate it down.

It was a rule of thumb that the wagons should reach Independence Rock by the 4th of July. Kade wanted to be there before the first trains arrived. Here they would wait for the trains to come. Faced with losing livestock to exhaustion, the settlers were willing to trade for fresh animals at a rate of two or three worn-out animals for one fresh. The exhausted livestock, mules, oxen, and breeding cows, were brought home where they could rest for a year before being driven back the following year to be traded again. And each year, Kade and Tom had more livestock to trade until finally, they left extra cows at home to raise calves and increase their own herd; these had multiplied over the years to create the foundation. There was a sizable cattle herd now at home, grazing the high slopes above their mountain valley in the summer.

Now, they had to stay along the Oregon Trail a week longer to get all their livestock traded since the wagon trains were smaller and less frequent. And with the completion of the rail line that spanned the western territories in 1869, there was a significant drop in the number of wagons that made the trip. Kade expected that his business would soon be doomed. But he reckoned he still had a few years left if he wanted them. The heyday might be over, but the wagons wouldn't quit rolling yet. Wagons were cheaper for families to bring all their worldly goods west in than to transport them by rail. Kade, however, was ready for the end. He and Sabra had a cattle and horse herd to live on now. They were starting to take the older steers to Ft. Laramie to sell occasionally. Kade found he wasn't looking forward any longer to the trading trips. He was ready to leave the trading to the boys or quit altogether.

They lived close enough to Ft. Laramie or to the new towns springing up along the railroad to sell their extra stock when it came to that. And as much as he hated the thought, Kade knew this land would not last as a wilderness. Changes had come already with settlements reaching farther and farther west. They got more visitors coming through their valley these days, and soon some of them would stop somewhere along the way. He heard that Jim Baker, a mountain man he used to know during his trapper days, built himself a two-story log cabin a couple of days ride west of them. Settlers would follow. Hell, weren't he and Sabra, the Bates and the Jorgensens settlers? Life, as he knew it in the mountains, was coming to an end, whether he liked it or not. *Adapt or die,* he thought. Well, he was adapting.

Kade watched the animals slowly advancing through grass not yet yellowed by the midsummer sun. The animals were tired, having come from St. Louis or Independence. He let them poke along, grabbing mouthfuls of grass. It was slow traveling, but he didn't want to lose one now. They were almost home. It was mid-July, and heat had come to the prairie. He was anxious to be back in the mountains.

He surveyed his help. His youngest son rode toward the lead. At just twenty-one, Thomas was a handsome young man, showing signs of wanting to step up and take on more responsibility. Kade was ready to let him. On the other side of the herd rode the cousins, Jeremiah Jorgensen and Will Bates. The oldest sons of Kade's two partners, Jim Bates and Matthew Jorgensen, they were responsible and reliable. There also were younger brothers who would soon be able to step up. Kade knew he had good help coming up. Hell, he might just stay home soon and let the boys take over.

Kade glanced at the other riders, fanned out around the slow-moving livestock. The community, or ranch as it was beginning to be called, centered around three families. Kade and Sabra were the ones who were in the mountains first. Kade had wandered these mountains since he was fifteen, traveling with his father and two older mountain men, Jacob Bates and Tom Grissom. On a visit back east to his brother's family, Jacob met Sabra and helped her escape a forced marriage by bringing her to the Rockies to live in his mountain cabin. There, Sabra had a child with Jacob's son, Blue Knife. But both Jacob and Blue Knife died before the baby was born.

Kade married Sabra when the baby was only three months old. So Kade and Sabra and their children were the first of these families to settle on this ranch.

The other two families were the Bates and the Jorgensens. Mattie Jorgensen and Jim Bates were siblings and were niece and nephew to old Jacob Bates. Mattie was Sabra's friend growing up. The two families were heading to Oregon on the Trail, one in 1849 and the other in 1850. On Sabra's suggestion, they ended up in these mountains instead to farm and ranch with Kade and Sabra. Now with their children, the ranch had built up a herd of horses and cattle. They had vast fields to cut for hay, and the two farming families kept fertile gardens of produce that were shared among them all. It was a partnership that had lasted over twenty years.

The one rider who was missing on the homeward end of this trip was Jake Bates Welles. Jake was Kade's first son, his adopted son. Named for his trapper grandfather, Jacob Bates, Jake was Sabra and Blue Knife's son. On this day, Jake was somewhere between Ft. Laramie and the mountains. Jake went on his first trading trip when he was two, riding horseback with either Sabra or Kade. Sabra went on many trading trips then, and the children came with them. When Jake was sixteen, he went alone with Kade and Tom. But after trading along the Trail was finished, Jake now went on to Ft. Laramie to replenish their trade goods. When the rest of the crew broke camp the last morning on the Oregon Trail and headed for home, Jake would take pack mules and head to Ft. Laramie. He would spend the next month living in the high mountains, trading with the Utes and any other travelers he might come upon.

Every year, first Tom or Kade, and now Jake, went to Ft. Laramie and stocked up on trade goods, ranging from tobacco to beads and trinkets prized by the Indians, as well as blankets and knives. These were traded liberally with their Yampatika Ute neighbors and other whites or Indians they happened across. They traded fairly with the Indians, sometimes even taking a loss on some goods by undercutting the prices the Indians would have to pay at the fort. But it worked well both ways. The Indians considered the families in the northern reaches of their territory friends, and every year, these same families sported new moccasins, hunting shirts, and tanned skins. After decades in the mountains, Kade still felt most comfortable in his buckskins, only going to the lighter shirts and trousers his wife made him for the little time he spent in the heat of the plains in the summer. Even Sabra and the children wore moccasins all year long, having lived in them so long. They only wore heavy boots in the winter, ordered through the Post store. What skins they traded for and did not use themselves had value at the fort trading post. Trading animals or goods was a lucrative business, and they had built it up well.

In addition to trading, Jake went to the high mountains to visit his half-brother, Brown Otter, in the Ute village, and stay at his grandfather Jacob's cabin. Brown Otter was twelve years Jake's senior and taught Jake the Ute ways and the Ute stories. Jake was considered part of the tribe. While Kade was "pa," the only father Jake knew, he learned about his biological father through the stories he was told over the years by Brown Otter. Jake was accepted by the Utes as one of their own. After all, he was the son of a Ute warrior.

Kade could see the cabins of Matthew and Mattie Jorgenson and Jim and Sarah Bates now coming into view. Their cabins lay at the edge of the river valley. Behind these cabins, another vast valley rose gently toward distant peaks. The farmlands, mostly hayfields, surrounded the cabins and lay on both sides of the river. A good-sized creek bubbled and gurgled down from the upper valley and fed into the river. Because they had followed the river for miles, they didn't need to stop to let the animals drink. Instead, they skirted the fields and headed toward the valley behind the cabins.

As they came closer, Kade could hear Jim's dogs starting to make a racket. Kade knew that he had been away longer than usual, so he knew that those left behind would be watching for their return. Mattie and Matthew's son Lathe, fifteen-year-old daughter Catherine, and thirteen-year-old Rachel would be saddling up to help move the herd up the valley. Jim and Sarah's younger daughters, sixteen-year-old Beth, and thirteen-year-old Bonnie, along with young James would be saddling horses, making ready to move the livestock on its last leg on this journey. The girls, Lathe, and James, along with Kade and Sabra's fifteen-year-old daughter Molly, would be ready as soon as they caught sight of his herd. In these families, all the children learned to ride at an early age.

When Kade got the livestock past the farming fields, they would start the ascent up the valley floor for three more miles. After the first half mile, Kade, Thomas, Will, and Jeremiah would peel off. Their job was done, and the youngsters would take the livestock up the valley. Will and Jeremiah would return to their homes for a well-deserved rest and to visit with their parents.

Thomas would suffer a hug from Sabra and then would go to visit "Grandpa" Tom. Crippled by rheumatism, Tom would be anxious to hear how the trip had gone. Named for Tom, Thomas had always been close to the old man and his wife, Clara. They were "grandparents" to all the children. But to Thomas, they were special. Thomas would go there for the evening, sharing their fire and the food that Clara would have ready.

Kade could leave the final two and a half miles to the teenagers. It was a slow but easy drive the rest of the way. The kids would push the cattle to the end, where there was good grass and water. There they would watch the livestock bed down for the night or lower their heads to graze. At the slow pace the weary animals maintained, it would take a good hour to push the cattle to the resting place and more to settle them there. Then the girls, James, and Lathe would race home, unsaddle their horses, and burst into the cabins to hear stories of the trip. It would take the kids at least an hour and a half, or maybe closer to two hours to finish the task. It would be enough time for Kade's plans.

Kade raised his hand to the far hillside across the valley floor toward Tom's cabin. He saw Tom and Clara sitting in front of the cabin and raised their hands in greeting. He knew they wouldn't expect a visit with Kade until the next day. They knew the drill by now. Ahead of him, Thomas was greeting his mother, who stood smiling in front of their cabin. Kade watched, letting mother and son have their moment. He pulled his horse up by the barn and stripped the saddle from him, turning him loose. It had been an easy ride back for the gelding, pushing such weary and footsore animals before him. But still, the horse was hungry and ready for a rest. Recognizing home and his familiar band of horses, the horse trotted off to join them.

"See you later, son," Kade said as Thomas came riding down from the cabin. "Tell your grandpa we did pretty well this time."

"I will, Pa. I tole Ma I'd probably take food there iffen she don't mind. Be back after dark."

Kade nodded in agreement. That was the plan and pretty much had been every year that Sabra stayed home from the trip. He smiled inwardly, wondering if his children, now mostly grown, knew what he planned. For what pulled at Kade now was not a well-needed rest, but a hunger for Sabra. *How could a woman pull at a man so for twenty-five years?* Striding up the hill to his cabin, with Sabra standing smiling in wait, Kade could already feel the blood rushing in him. He had been away for almost four weeks. *Damn, they had only two hours of an empty cabin,* he thought. He had no time to waste, and scooping up his wife, they swept laughing into the cabin.

CHAPTER 3

Another Name –
July 1874

I t felt good to be in the mountains. The first day for Jake and Anna was the most difficult as they were climbing a lot. The second day, they crossed North Park, an expansive high mountain valley surrounded by majestic peaks; a wonderland of wildlife could be found in this valley, making fresh meat easy to come by. It was the moose that interested Anna the most since she hadn't seen many of them. Jake didn't want to pack that much meat, so he settled for a young elk late the second afternoon; that would be more than enough meat to get them to the cabin. In one lowland creek, they skirted around a bear fishing in the waters and saw buffalo several times in the distance.

When the going was flat and easy, Jake made a point to ride beside Anna to keep her talking. *Nine years without a white man's word would be hard to come back from without some practice*, he thought. He was starting to form a plan for her. He bought her simply because when he saw her, scrawny and beaten, all he could think of was, this could have been his mother. The stories he had heard from Brown Otter and others came to him then. He hadn't thought through what he would do with Anna after they left the Cheyenne village. But riding for several days gave him time to think. He was pretty sure that her name, Anna Curtis, was correct. It sounded like what he remembered from that summer nine years earlier. Pa or Tom would remember.

After he spent time at the cabin with Brown Otter, he would take Anna home with him. They could write a letter and send it to Pa's brother in St. Louis. Uncle Joe was a lawyer and would know how to search for this girl's people. Her immediate family was all killed along the Oregon Trail, but surely there was family left behind who were still living. She had the right to know her people. It would take time, maybe a couple of years, but she seemed a good girl. He knew his mother would have no problem with her coming to live with them. She might be just a bit too "Indian" right now anyway to send her back to white civilization. She would never yearn for the Cheyenne and the treatment she got there, but she seemed to have good memories of most of her years with the Pawnee.

Anna finished one moccasin the first night when Jake gave her the deerskin. The second day she rode with one new moccasin and one old. He caught her looking at her feet at a water stop and giggling at what she saw, one old and one new. She had been taught well in leatherwork, and she had done a nice job. When they got to the cabin, he would find some beads in his packs and give them to her to adorn the moccasins. But the evenings were just too short on the trail, and the light left the sky too soon for her to work very long. At least her toes weren't sticking out.

When they got to the cabin, Jake would give her all the skins she needed to make herself another dress. Or maybe Anna would make a blouse and could refashion some of the dress into a skirt. He never really thought too much about what clothes the Native women wore; he was far more interested when they weren't wearing them.

Jake had told Anna to keep the knife the night he gave it to her and fashioned a sheath to put it in to tie around her waist. Her eyes had widened with surprise that she could keep it. Jake noticed her touching it at her waist several times during the next day to make sure it was still there. When he shot the elk, Anna went right to work skinning it. She made signs that she could do it herself, but Jake told her that he would help.

"We've got some miles yet before we camp," he told her. "We will take the hide and as much meat as we can carry with us and keep going. It goes faster if we both do it." Taking pieces of canvas from his packs, he wrapped the good chunks of meat and secured them on the mules. There were still two more days of riding before they reached the cabin, and he didn't want to ride into the dark either day.

The second night in the mountains, they camped at the west edge of North Park, having made it across in one day. While the meat cooked over the fire, Anna started on her second moccasin. Jake pulled out his pipe and watched her. Her fingers flew over the leather, finding the places she wanted to cut and where to sew the pieces together.

"Old grandmother taught you well how to do that," he commented after a while. "What else did you learn to do?"

"I cook, I fish, I hunt berries, roots, wild things," Anna spoke without looking up. Jake nodded, thinking, then put all her words in complete sentences and threw them back at her. *Hell*, he thought, *he was speaking better English than he usually did.* His mother had been a stickler about all her kids speaking good English, but it was easy to fall back into the easy language that often came out of Pa's mouth and the pure trapper language that always came from old Tom.

As a kid, he had resented being made to speak well, but it had often served him well as an adult, especially when he was around whites. It always startled the whites that he met, both soldiers and settlers, when he could speak better English than they could. It gave him a bit of an upper hand at times. He often heard the whispers: "Don't mess with the Indian that spoke good English."

Of course, there were some that just couldn't take a hint. They felt Jake thought he was better than them with his "good talk". Well, maybe sometimes he did think himself better than some of them. He would never have made an issue of it though, not until they did. Then he finished it. He hadn't lost a fair fight since he was sixteen. Jake might have been smaller than most men, but he was quick and strong. He was smart too and could outthink most of his opponents. But unlike many who were good at fighting, he didn't enjoy it; he just wasn't going to be pushed around. He might be of mixed blood, but as his mother told him, he was from good stock on both sides.

"We go to your home in mountain?" Anna was looking up from her leatherwork at him.

"Not my home, really," Jake answered. They had gone over this ground before, but he thought that she didn't quite grasp all the English words before, so this was the second time she had asked since they left the Cheyenne. "It is an old cabin. It was my grandfather's cabin. My mother lived there when I was born. I go there this time every year and meet my brother. Sometimes I visit my people too. My father's people."

"Who your people?"

"My father's people are Utes," Jake answered. "Yampatika Utes. They live in these mountains. The village is sometimes close. When the village is close, I visit there too." As he spoke, Jake could see she was troubled.

"You Ute?" she asked.

"Part Ute," Jake explained. "My father was half Ute. My father had a white father, my grandfather. My mother is white."

"You more white than Indian," she said. It was a statement rather than a question. She wasn't dumb, he could see. She studied him. "You look more Indian than white. I white. You look Indian."

Jake grinned, "Yeah, I have been told that. Many times, for that matter. Guess the Indian part is stronger medicine."

Anna was silent for quite a while as she worked the leather. He caught her giving him little glances like she was thinking of more to say. *Maybe she couldn't formulate the words*, he thought. Finally, when he thought maybe he was wrong and she didn't want the conversation to go on, she softly spoke.

"You sell me Utes?" She wouldn't look at him.

"No," he was surprised at her thoughts. "No, I am not going to sell you."

"What you do with me?" This time she glanced up at him quickly then looked back to her work.

Jake thought about how to tell her his idea. She had so few words yet.

"I thought I would take you home. Take you to my home where my ma and pa and brother and sister live. Then we can send word back east," here, he used sign language to indicate the direction she had come from with her family so many years before. "We can look for your people."

"My people all dead. My people all killed by Pawnee."

"Your family was killed, but you might have other people that were left behind. Aunts and uncles." Did she understand aunts and uncles?

"I no remember other people."

"Well, it is something we should find out."

"You sell me to my people?"

Jake was a bit frustrated by her lack of faith. But he supposed she had been let down enough to have no faith. Her dead family left her in a way. Her Pawnee old grandmother died and left her with people who didn't care for her. They sold her to the Cheyenne, who raped, ridiculed, and abused her. In her memory, all her people had left or abused her in one way or another. He shook out his pipe and rose to go out into the night before turning in.

"I will not sell you to your people, Anna. We find them, and you can go to them if you want," and with that, he was gone. He picketed the horses and mules up close where they wouldn't stand out on the skyline. When he returned, he saw she was rolled up in her blankets. He pushed dirt over the campfire coals and lay down. Just as he was drifting off, he heard her softly murmur, as if to herself.

"Everyone sell ugly woman."

The next afternoon, as they came out onto a small clearing on the mountain slope, they could see a deep green valley far below them. It was a long way down. It would be well into evening when they got there. Jake saw the river, sparkling as it wound through the valley floor. Tom still referred to it as the Bear River, but Kade said he had heard people refer to it as the Yampa River, named after the yampa plant that grew in this area. The roots of the yampa plant were good eating and Jake had eaten them often when he had been with the Utes. His people were known as "Yampatika Utes" or "root eaters."

As Jake looked down into the valley, he felt like he was coming home. Kade had told him that Jake stood with a moccasin in each world, the Ute world, and the white world. Jake knew that was true. But among strangers, he was accepted more in the Indian world than the white world. This was his ancestral land. In a way, he would always be coming home when he came here, just as certainly as he would be coming home when he returned to the valley to the north where his white family lived.

"We will camp when we get down there," he told Anna. "It will take many hours, but I hope we will get there before dark. Then tomorrow we follow the river that way," he indicated the south with his hand. "If we get down to the valley tonight, we can make the cabin tomorrow afternoon."

She nodded that she understood. "It is pretty. River is shiny."

Jake grinned. She was starting to stay in a conversation a little longer each day. She seemed more comfortable answering questions than thinking up things to say off the top of her head. But he was seeing her make comments here and there as she thought of the words by herself. He had no experience with this language teaching, but he thought he was doing a pretty good job as her teacher.

That is what he gets for buying her without thinking things out. But in his heart, he knew he couldn't have left her there after he saw those eyes. His mother's eyes were brown, not blue like Anna's, but he knew that they would have been just as desperate if his mother's situation had been the same as Anna's.

From Brown Otter, he had learned that his mother had been very different when Blue Knife first took her for his wife. Brown Otter had only been a boy then, but he knew things were different. He knew the white woman was afraid and sad. Brown Otter told how his mother had struggled before she laughed and sang again. It took a long time for her to be the woman Brown Otter had first known. It took her a long time to learn to care for Blue Knife. Now, seeing Anna and her situation, Jake had a much better understanding of his own heritage. Kicking his horse, he started the descent. It was a long way down, so they better make tracks.

They reached the bottom of the slopes and came out of the trees in heavy dusk. Coming off a mountain in the dark was not such an easy thing to do, so Jake was relieved when they broke from the trees and saw the river. They watered their animals and made a cold camp, eating cooked meat from the night before. They were both tired, so they went quickly to their blankets.

In the morning, Jake was up and gathering the horses before the sun brimmed the mountain ridge. When he got back to the camp, Anna had their blankets rolled, meat set out to eat, and was ready to leave. They ate as they rode this morning. Jake wanted to get to the cabin long before dark. It had been a year since he had been there, and unless Brown Otter had stopped by at another time, the cabin would be dirty and needing an airing before they stayed the night.

They pushed the horses most of the day. A horse could trot a long time before it needed to be rested. Despite the pace though, the ride along the valley was an easy one. All the mountain slopes were behind them now. They crossed the river once to be on the west side, and then they just followed it until mid-afternoon. When a sandstone cliff rose off to the west, Jake turned and rode for it. At first, it looked like they would ride right into the cliff, but when they got closer, there was a small gorge with a small creek gurgling out through it. Following this creek through the ravine, they rode between the cliff and a heavily wooded slope until they broke through the trees into a small valley. At the near end of the valley sat an ancient beaver pond, clear blue water sparkling in the late afternoon sun. At the far end of the valley sat a small log cabin, and behind it a little lean-to log barn and corral. Winding its way from behind the corral to the beaver pond was a small brook, maybe twelve inches across. The whole length of the valley had water for man and beast.

"This is it," Jake told Anna. "This is as far as we go for now."

He felt the relief of making his destination. He glanced at the girl thinking she too would be relieved that the trip, for now, was coming to an end. But her face held that troubled look that she so often had. Jake wanted to ask her what she worried about, but he let it go. She probably had nothing but worry going through her head. He saw the worry leave her as she rode each day of travel, but it came back at each campsite. Thinking about it, he wondered if Anna feared what he might do to her. She hadn't had many men in her life that treated her well, he reckoned. Well, he couldn't make her trust him, she'd have to learn that on her own.

They piled the packs in the cabin and turned the horses and mules loose to graze. The meadow was lush, and the horses were tired. They wouldn't wander far. Jake hung the hunks of elk from the rafters and then went in search of firewood. It was hot during the day, but the evening chill of the mountains was settling on them. A fire and freshly cooked meat would taste good. He saw Anna go outside, and when she came in, she had more wood with her. Jake found the old homemade straw broom behind the door and began to sweep out the mouse droppings and leavings from scavengers that used the cabin the part of the year he was gone. Anna came to him and took the broom.

"Woman work," was all she said. Jake didn't figure he even wanted to argue that point. He didn't relish cleaning, but he did like it to be clean. Old Tom told a story about when his mother first lived with his grandfather Jacob, and Kade had come to spend Christmas with them. On Christmas Eve, Sabra had made the men bathe in a little washtub she had brought west with her. Tom could tell a good story for sure, and Jake grinned, thinking of the two astounded mountain men being faced down by his little mother standing over a tiny washtub. *Well, that is my world,* Jake thought. *I grew up with her for my mother.* Many a time, he had hauled water to fill a tub for himself and his brother and sister. Seldom did anyone cross his mother, especially about being clean.

By the time they had finished eating, it was full dark, and Jake could see that Anna was tired. He had one buffalo robe that he had used to cover the extra foodstuff carried on a mule. He would take home much of that food. He had a good supply of flour and sugar. The mule carrying trade good packs had a canvas covering over the goods. Jake took the buffalo robe and a blanket and handed them to Anna.

"You can have these," he said. "I don't need more'n a blanket." He turned away from her and spread his blanket on one side of the fireplace. Through hooded eyes, Jake watched her. Anna stood, gripping the heavy buffalo robe, watching him. When she saw he ignored her, Jake saw her shoulders relax. She looked around the small cabin, then spread the robe and blanket on the other side of the fire.

They spent three days lazing in the meadow. Jake went off hunting early one morning and brought home a fat young buck. They had plenty of meat. He also took an extra rifle from his packs. Jake had purchased a couple of rifles that he could use for trading if the need arose. Otherwise, he would take them home. It never hurt to have extra guns. The gun was a Ballard Carbine, .45 caliber, that was used a lot during the Civil War in the states and now was often sold in war surplus outlets, of which the sutler's store in Ft. Laramie was one. The Ballard was a breach-loading gun, making it much easier to load than the old muzzleloaders and lighter than the old Hawkins that Tom still carried. Calling Anna over the first afternoon, he showed her how to load it. Going to some fallen logs on the edge of the tree line, he had her practice firing the gun, reloading, and practicing again.

"If I am away," Jake cautioned Anna, "you never leave without this with you. We will practice again until you are good with it."

Anna had nodded at that. She wasn't afraid of the gun, Jake noticed. Like the knife he had given her, he watched her often touch the gun that first day, like it would disappear from her sight. Then he had brought out some tanned skins he had traded for with the Cheyenne before he had bought her. Laying them down in the corner of the cabin, he motioned to her.

"Think you can make yourself new clothes?" he asked. He touched Anna's torn off sleeve. "You need more on you. Can you make a dress? Or," he tugged on his own shirt, "a blouse?" He went to his packs and rolled out one blanket filled with goods. There were needles, awls, and heavy thread. "Use what you need. You pick." Finally, he unrolled the trade beads. "Take what you want. Make it pretty."

She was clearly overwhelmed. "For me? Use pretty beads? New clothes?"

Jake nodded. Embarrassed to see Anna so overcome at his gesture, he turned and left the cabin. When he returned later in the day, she was busily working the leather. But he was glad to see that, as she sat in the sun in the doorway, she had her new rifle laying beside her.

The fourth day at the cabin was an unseasonably hot day for the mountains. Jake had gone fishing in the river and had brought home four fish for their supper. It would be a nice change from the elk and deer that they had been eating. Anna had gone out and found ripe berries and roots she knew about to flavor their stews, but the fish would be welcome and tasty with only the fruit.

The walk back up from the river had Jake sweating. Pulling off his hunting shirt, he threw it in the corner of the cabin. Anna was sitting in the shade in the front of the cabin, working on her clothes. She was adding beads. The clothes looked finished to him, but she hadn't put them on yet. Without trying to look too hard, it appeared she had made two pieces of clothing. Jake went inside the cabin to his pack and pulled out a breechcloth. He was going swimming. A breechcloth would be cooler to walk back in and let the air dry him. He spoke to Anna as he went by her.

"I'm going to the pond," he said. "I'll be back in a bit." Taking his rifle, he went down the meadow, feeling the mountain breeze tickling his bare chest.

The water felt marvelous. It was cold like mountain water always is, but it had warmed some in the day's heat and was not frigid. After he got used to it, the water was refreshing. He could see why his mother loved this place so much. It was secluded. It was beautiful. It had everything she wanted when she first came to it. But it was small. It would not sustain the livestock or farmland the Twin Peaks families had amassed.

Five or six days north, where they now were settled, made for a shorter trip each year to the Trail to trade. The mountain valleys where his parents and cousins now lived was closer to Ft. Laramie, where they could replenish supplies, mail letters to Pa's brother in St. Louis, and get news. It was enough that he could come here to his grandfather's cabin for a month every summer. This land was his private place, his other world.

Jake came out of the water and put on his breech-cloth, dripping water. He had unplaited his hair, letting it fall over his shoulders. Like his pa and Tom, he wore his hair long and in braids most of the time.

As he started up the meadow toward the cabin, he saw one of the mules throw up his head, looking intently into the distance behind Jake toward the mouth of the gorge. Jake checked his rifle and looked to see what the mule saw. Now the other animals were intent as well and began to mill. A lone rider came through the opening between the trees.

Jake was alert but not yet concerned. Most of the visitors he got in the meadow were Ute. As the rider emerged from the trees, he could see that this was no exception. The rider was a Ute brave, but not Brown Otter. Jake waited for the man's approach. He recognized the man as Iron Wing, a brave from his brother's village who was on his way back to the village, he told Jake when he got close. Jake motioned to the cabin, offering a meal, but Iron Wing wouldn't stop to eat; he wanted to get home that day. Iron Wing knew that Brown Otter would want to know his brother was back, so the Ute had come into the meadow to see if Jake was there. He would tell Brown Otter that Jake had arrived.

Jake watched Iron Wing drift out of sight, then turned and made his way to the cabin. The cabin had one small window and the door to let in light. In the summer, the door stood open most of each day. Anna was not outside anymore, so she must have gone in. Entering, Jake had to let his eyes adjust to the dim light. He saw Anna standing by the fireplace. She had on her new clothes. He saw that he was right that she had made a two-piece outfit. The blouse hung long over the top of her skirt. She had sewn beads along the neckline of her blouse and had a leather thong around her waist where she carried the knife and sheath. She had done a good job making the clothes. He felt relieved that she was completely covered now. He wouldn't have to watch his eyes so much or suffer his reaction when they wandered.

"That is a pretty outfit, Anna," he commented softly. "You did a good job."

"You sell me now to that Ute?" her voice trembled. That was when he saw that her eyes were wide with fright. She was rigid with tension.

"Anna," he said firmly, "I am not going to sell you."

Jake could see that the girl apparently didn't hear his words. She was near terror at the thought of being sold again. He guessed that Anna had seen him gesture toward the cabin as he talked to Iron Wing. She must have thought he was offering to sell her.

"I make pretty clothes. You give me much food. I wash, you don't beat me. I look better. You get two horses, three horses, for me!" Anna's voice rose as she spoke. She was losing control.

"Anna!" Jake spoke more sharply than he intended, frustrated that he couldn't get through to her. "I will not sell you!" He turned away from her, trying to breathe calmly. He knew now where she got this thought about him selling her. One of the days they traveled, he told her how he and his pa would go to the Oregon Trail and trade one of their strong animals for two or three head of the settlers worn out livestock. Then they would take the worn-out animals home where they would fatten them up before selling them the next year. This was their business he had told her. This was how they made a living. Now, she thought that was his intention with her. Oh, Lord, how can he get through to her. He looked out the door to the meadow. All was peaceful out there. It was inside that the storm brewed. He heard movement behind him, heard the rustle of leather. He took a deep breath, willing himself to speak more calmly, trying to ease her fear.

"Anna," he said softly, turning toward her. "I will not . . ." the words faded. She stood before him without her new clothes. She stood stark naked. His eyes drank her in. He had known there was a woman under there, but to see her, all of her, took all thought from his mind. He just stood and stared.

"You take Anna. Anna take manhood. Anna don't mind. It don't hurt much. You don't beat Anna," she spoke quickly, trying to get all her thoughts out. "You keep Anna. Anna do for you."

Jake had the brief thought that he was not winning this battle. He was fighting a woman who couldn't reason through her fear. He was also fighting his own desire. Just seeing her like this had his blood pumping. *Shit, there are some things a man just can't control.* He felt very out of control at the moment, standing near naked himself in his breechcloth.

Anna came closer, reaching for him. He shuddered as her hand brushed his breechcloth. "Your manhood," she said simply, "hard. Anna take. It don't hurt much." She sank down on the buffalo robe, looking up at him. "Anna don't mind. It don't hurt much."

Jake finally registered her words. "It don't hurt much." Her whole experience with men had hurt. They had treated her roughly, but she was willing to lay with him because she thought it would hurt less than being beaten, that it was a better alternative to being sold.

"Anna," he said softly, "You don't have to do this. I am not going to sell you."

"You take Anna. Anna don't mind," she was only a fraction less hysterical than before.

He knelt beside her, knowing despite himself that his desire was taking over. He reached for her braids and slowly untied the leather and unplaited her hair. He ran his fingers through the softness of it. Her hair was raven black against her tanned but fair skin. She reminded him of a wild thing with her wide eyes. But she lay still as he touched her gently, brushing the hair off her face.

"Anna don't mind. Jake don't beat. Manhood don't hurt much," she was becoming calmer now. Instinctively, and probably without realizing it, she was using her sex to get a better situation for herself. *Hell,* Jake thought, *how can he fight both her and hims*elf?

He bent and kissed her, first her forehead, then her cheek, and finally slowly moving to her mouth. She lay completely still. His hands reached out to her, gently feeling her curves. He dropped his mouth to the tender skin of her neck, sucking gently but firmly. *She would have his mark on her tomorrow,* he thought vaguely. He caressed her breasts, trying ever so hard to stay gentle. And it was then he felt it; he felt her small moan of unconscious pleasure. His heart swelled with desire. He released her and looked into her eyes.

Speaking so softly she could barely hear, he murmured, "It shouldn't hurt. It should never hurt."

It was nearly dusk when Jake woke. Anna slept curled into him. He watched her sleeping. She was untroubled in her sleep. Jake wondered if Anna would wake up untroubled or if her fear would come back. *He shouldn't have slept with her,* he thought, feeling like a heel. Then he drove the thought from his mind. He wanted this and it was good. He wouldn't cast her off. He wasn't her first, after all. Yet Jake felt like he was her first. Anna's whisper when they were finished said it all, "Is this how white people . . . Ute people feel? Feel good?"

He had just smiled at her, caressing her cheek. Then he closed his eyes and relaxed. He felt her snuggle close and eventually they both slept. Now, watching her sleep, he wondered how she would wake.

This wasn't the way Jake wanted to find a wife after all. He didn't imagine himself going out and buying a wife, but essentially that is what he did. And this woman lying with him now had been so abused. Jake hadn't bought her to be his wife, but after this day, he knew he couldn't abandon her either. Jake didn't see that he had much choice, and he wasn't sure what he felt about that. Did he love her? He desired her, but love? That was different. He didn't know about love.

Jake had had his share of women, Indian women, since the first time Tom had set him up with a Shoshone woman when they made the trip to Ft. Laramie when Jake was seventeen. According to his pa, Tom wasn't always a good role model. But hell, old Tom was a damn good adopted grandpa and knew what a young man needed.

But Jake never wanted to stay with any of the women he had slept with after the night was over. He had seen some comely Indian women that turned his head, but he wasn't ready to take one as a wife. Jake had no desire to live in an Indian village with Indian relatives. And he lived too close to the Utes to take a Ute wife. He would have half the village visiting every year if he were to take a Ute woman home.

Then there were white women, but they were scarce for a man of mixed blood. White women were almost unknown to him. Jake had been trading along the Oregon Trail with his family his whole life, both when his mother went, and when, at sixteen, he went with only his pa and old Tom. He saw many white women on the wagon trains. He saw daughters who smiled shyly at him and saw their mothers or fathers pull them away just as fast. To them, Jake was just another Indian, or "half-breed", as many white men referred to Jake. He knew better than to harbor thoughts of those white girls. His white aunts and uncles had daughters, but those girls were relatives.

He never thought of Catherine or Beth or Bonnie as more than cute girls he had grown up with. They were cousins, distant cousins, but still relatives.

Last year when he was at Ft. Laramie, Jake heard talk of the "hog ranch" that was about three miles out. A tumbled-down establishment that sold whiskey to the enlisted men when they could get away, it was said that there were white women there that were more than willing to lie with the men for money. He had taken a woman there for an afternoon. At first the proprietor was going to run him off, thinking he wanted whiskey. When Jake had replied, in his good English, that he didn't want any rotgut whiskey but would take a woman, the man had looked at him and said, "Yore the half-breed that speaks good English. I've heard of you."

There were no soldiers there so early in the afternoon when Jake walked in, but two women were at a table. They wore gaudy dresses, low cut and tight. They didn't look particularly clean or young. One stood up.

"Come on, honey. I ain't never done a half-breed."

He had left shortly after his needs were fulfilled. The woman had been homely but willing. Her cheap perfume was strong in his nose and not pleasant to him. It wasn't a particularly memorable experience. To her, it was a job. The Native women he laid with were far more satisfying. Until today, that prostitute was the only white woman he had ever had.

Jake looked now at Anna, curled up beside him, white skin against his dark skin. The thought flicked through his mind that this was what his father had seen when he laid with his mother, white skin against dark. For Anna's skin, protected by clothing was almost pale white, soft, and milky, but she was all bone, elbows, knees, and backbone; even her hip bones protruded. Here and there were scars, bite marks it looked like, and burns, many were recent. Anna had been abused in more ways than one, and it showed.

Jake felt Anna stir. Her eyes fluttered and opened, focusing on him. He did not see fear in her eyes. Instead, it was more like curiosity, or questioning. Maybe it was waiting to see what came next. Maybe it was hope.

Jake caressed her side, lingering over a scar on her left breast. "What is this?" he asked.

"Bite," Anna said matter of factly. "Old chief gave me to man for night. He bite me, make me cry. Laugh at me."

"And this?" Jake's fingers gently traced a spot on her shoulder.

"Old squaw burned me with a stick. I no run fast enough."

Jake thought about this. There were other smaller scars. He didn't want to pursue them. In time maybe, but now she should start to forget those things. He studied this naked girl beside him, gently moving his hands along her sides. She needed to think about other things.

"You need a Ute name," he said to her. "You had a Pawnee name. You had a Cheyenne name. You have a white name. Now you need a Ute name."

"What name I have? You give me name?"

Jake stroked her hair. "Your Ute name is Beautiful Bird." His finger traced her face. "You forget your other Indian names. They are gone. Never say Cheyenne name again. Cheyenne name bad. You are Anna Curtis, and you are Beautiful Bird."

She murmured the name, rolling it over on her tongue. "I like that name."

Jake lay there, content to just be still. There was more to be said, but he was trying to work out in his head how to say it. After several minutes, he spoke again.

"With the white people, when two hearts come together, they make a vow to stay with each other," he searched her face. "You understand vow? Like a promise?"

She nodded her head slowly. "Like say something and not change ever."

He nodded. "I am Ute, and I am white. Outside, I am more Ute, but inside I am more white. When a white man wants a forever woman, he asks her if she will stay with him, never leave him."

She nodded again, not sure where this was going.

"Anna, will you be my forever woman? Will you be my wife?"

She looked at him wonderingly. "Jake want Anna to keep? Not to sell?"

He laughed at her. "Yes, I want to keep Beautiful Bird. No other man ever take my Bird away," he used her pigeon-English. "Bird lives only with me. Now you tell me what Anna wants. Say the words, so I know."

"Anna wants to stay with Jake. Anna wants to be forever woman."

He smiled at her. "It is good," he said. Then giving her a gentle shove, he told her, "Get your pretty new clothes on, and we will make vows to each other. Then we will have a wedding feast of fish and berries."

Because of the heat, Jake made a fire outside in front of the cabin. Anna cleaned the fish and set the kettle in hot coals to cook slowly. It was too hot for his leather hunting shirt, so he took a cloth shirt out of his pack that was clean. Then Jake took Anna's hand and by moonlight, led her down the meadow to the pond. They stood close together, hearing the night sounds around them. Jake pulled her back against him and rested his chin on her head. He felt the hard bones of her back pressing into his chest. He found it easier to say what was in his mind if he wasn't looking at her.

"Anna, my Beautiful Bird, I will be your husband for all our lives. I will never hurt you or sell you. I will take care of you," he briefly thought about adding love, but he wasn't sure what love was. No sense promising what you can't give. Right now, he only knew that he wanted her and that he would stay with her. "Your white name will forever be Anna Curtis Welles," he hesitated. "Now you speak," he finished.

Anna stood silently for a few moments. "I will be your forever woman," she said after a pause. "I will lay with you. I will do what you want. I will be your woman. I will be only yours."

They stood, standing close, watching the pond in the moonlight. They didn't speak more words. Jake just stood holding Anna against him. Finally, he turned her toward him, and gently kissed her. Turning together, they started back to the cabin. Jake had a fleeting thought, wondering if there was time before the fish was cooked to go back to the buffalo robes. He pushed the thought from his mind. Anna was so thin. They would eat first.

CHAPTER 4

I Remember Bread – 1874

Sabra rode through the trees, coming out onto the valley floor. She could hear the others crashing through brush and trees up and down the hillside as they descended the steep slope. Kade and Thomas were each riding three-year-olds for the first time outside of the corral. The Welles didn't start the colts until late in the summer of the young animals' three-year-old year. Then the young horses were only ridden sparingly. As four-year-olds, the young animals began their advanced training. Kade, Jake, and Thomas rode all the young horses now.

Sabra gave up training eighteen years before, after she had a fall from a young horse on a slippery slope. That fall caused the first of two miscarriages that Sabra underwent, and she and Kade had despaired that they would ever have a third child. Other than the fall from the horse, Sabra had no idea why she had trouble after that carrying a baby to full term, but she lost the next baby early in the pregnancy. She remembered that her mother had many miscarriages and was often sickly. Maybe Sabra would be like her mother. Then six years after Thomas was born, Molly finally came along.

Sabra and Molly rode five-year-old geldings. Next year, these same five-year-olds might be the ones taken off to sell or trade. They would decide in the spring which horses to keep and which to sell at a fort every couple of years. The army paid well for horses of the quality that Sabra and Kade raised.

Molly came out of the woods first. The older horses knew best how to handle the weight of a rider on the steep slope. The men would keep the young horses moving more slowly and carefully. Molly rode a big bay gelding that she had taken a fancy to when it was just a weanling colt. Molly called it Rascal because it had been such a meddlesome colt when it was young. Sabra had a suspicion that this colt would not be sold in the spring. Molly was as good with a horse as Sabra and, along with Sabra, gentled the young animals before they were taken from their dams.

At fifteen, Molly was filling out and turning into a beauty. Taller than Sabra, she still resembled her mother in looks, with dark brown hair and big brown eyes. She would turn heads for sure, and it would be soon. Next year, they planned a "family" outing to trade along the Trail. If a train didn't come along on the Oregon Trail, they would go on to Ft. Laramie, or maybe to Cheyenne, a town that had grown up along the new railroad line. It was time Molly saw more white people. Molly only saw their ranch partners, the two other white families, and Tom and Clara. Occasionally a trapper, an old friend of Tom or Kade, might stop by, but never people that were not "mountain people."

That was the one thing about being so isolated. Who would her children find to share their lives with? Thomas now was showing some interest in Jim and

Sarah's girl, Beth. Beth just turned sixteen that spring. Sabra had noticed a difference in how Thomas was starting to treat Beth. The children of all three families had grown up together, climbing trees, playing in the creek, and roughhousing. They treated each other like brothers and sisters, or at least as cousins, which Jake was to the Bates and Jorgensen children. But lately, Sabra detected a difference in Thomas and Beth. She hoped so. Those two would be a good match, and the valley would not lose either one that way. *But for their other children, where would they find mates?*

The confines of civilization didn't quite reach out this far. They had made up their own rules for how they lived. Sabra knew her lifestyle would be frowned upon if she were back in the settlements. Sabra saw a woman on the first wagon train they traded with back in 1851, wearing the most surprising outfit; many men and women thought it scandalous, but Sabra had loved it. The woman had on high top boots and wore a pair of knickerbocker pants, the short blousy type that came down and covered the top of her boots. Over this, she had a modest but short dress that reached her knees.

Sabra loved this idea. The pants would give her the freedom of working with her horses without long skirts to get in the way. She had started making herself a similar outfit as soon as they reached home. It was the one time she and Kade really argued. He didn't feel the outfit was proper. She wouldn't budge, though. Whenever she worked with her horses or rode, she wore this. Molly did the same as she grew up, and eventually, Kade had to admit it was more appropriate for the outside work that Sabra liked to do. The only significant difference that Sabra had in her outfit was that she wore high-topped moccasins. After all, she spent more time outside with the horses, moccasins on her feet, and an old floppy hat on her head than she did inside on most days. No one in the family even owned a pair of shoes. They all had a pair of serviceable winter boots, but those were put away as soon as winter was over. It was a wonderfully free life, but there was still a worry. *Where would her children fit in the world that was coming?*

Kade and Thomas emerged from the trees, heading toward home. Sabra and Molly rode to meet them. This was enough for the colts' first day out. It was the second trip out that the women had made that day, but the fourth trip for Kade and Thomas. Each time they had all ridden different horses. Good horses weren't made by sitting in the corral. Unless other chores needed to be done, the men rode several horses every day. Sabra and Molly rode most days, although usually not all day.

Next month, they would all head to the high country with pack mules, to camp and gather and push the cattle down off the slopes to the valley for the winter. It could take them days or weeks, depending on how much the cattle had scattered, but the cattle that had been on this land several years already would know the routine and might just be starting to wander to the lower elevations on their own. Still, they would not all come home by themselves. The fall gather was a big affair for the family.

Sabra could see their cabin, a mile distant, sitting nestled on the east side of the valley against the trees. Across the meadow on the west side was the small cabin of Tom and Clara. The valley was narrow there, about 200 yards wide. In front of Tom and Clara's cabin was a beaver pond glistening in the sun, fed by a brook coming out of the wooded slopes behind the cabin. Throughout the whole valley ran a clear cold mountain stream, and from the surrounding hills, little brooks fed into this stream. The valley had ample water for man and beast the entire length and breadth of it.

Sabra couldn't see the cabins of Sarah and Jim or Mattie and Matthew yet. Mattie Jorgensen and Jim Bates were brother and sister. They were also niece and nephew to Jacob Bates, Jake's grandfather, which meant they were kin to Sabra's firstborn, Jake. Those two cabins lay at almost the mouth of the upper valley before it merged into the river bottom. These cabins stood a mile farther south from Sabra and Kade's cabin. Matthew and Jim were farmers. Out in the river bottom were the farming fields and hay fields they tended. It was a small community that the Bates, Jorgensens, and Welles families formed, along with old Tom and Clara. They relied on each other for the success of their livelihood as well as their friendship. Sabra knew it had taken Kade a while to get accustomed to living in one place when they were first married, and it had taken the farming families time to adjust to the solitude of this mountain existence, but in the end, they all adapted. This isolated mountain with its valleys and river was home for them all.

But change was on its way. Civilization was pushing its way toward them. Six years ago, in 1868, the United States had signed a treaty with the Utes. By ceding the eastern slope of the Rockies to the whites, the Utes were guaranteed a permanent reservation on the western slopes. The Utes were also promised yearly annuities of food and supplies. However, the food and supplies were sometimes late, or not delivered at all, and the Utes were often hungry. They left the reservation frequently, looking for better hunting grounds or going to white settlements on the eastern slopes to get supplies.

Kade and Sabra's valley was just north of the reservation. They had not had any trouble with the Utes, because they were considered friends. Several times, Kade and Jake drove some of their cattle or older oxen to the reservation to meet Brown Otter at his village, giving the animals to the hungry Utes. But tensions were rising, and more whites were intruding. Sabra and Kade watched the white advancement with almost as much apprehension as the Utes did, but Sabra and Kade also knew that they could adapt to the inevitable encroachment. It wouldn't be the same for the Utes.

Sabra scanned the horizon to the south. She was looking, as she had been for the last week, for Jake's return. He had been gone almost six weeks now, first trading along the Oregon Trail with Kade and then to Jacob's cabin and time with his half-brother, Brown Otter. Jake was due back, and Sabra missed him. He was her firstborn after all, and there is a special bond with your first child.

Every year Sabra feared he would come home to say goodbye. She feared Jake would take an Indian wife and only come home to tell them he was going to live in the village. It wasn't that Jake ever gave her the feeling he wanted to live with the Utes, but every summer, he was drawn away to be with them and live in his grandfather's cabin. *If he took an Indian woman for a wife, would he bring her here, where the woman might be unhappy? Or would Jake stay with her and her people?* If he chose a

Native woman for his wife, Sabra would welcome the woman with all her heart, for she feared for her eldest and the limitations of his choices. Sabra knew the stigma his mixed heritage gave him. But she didn't want to lose Jake either. She didn't want him to move away.

Jake might not be Kade's blood son, but he was more like Kade than Thomas. Ten years of going to the mountains to meet Brown Otter, living in the mountain cabin, trading with the Indians, and fending for himself during that time gave him the confidence and skills that none of the other boys of their little community had. Thirty years earlier, Jake would have followed Kade into the mountains, trapping beaver and living the free life that the early trappers enjoyed. Now he just went to his ancestral home every summer.

There was no approaching horseman though. Sabra caught up to Kade.

"He should be back soon, right?" she asked.

Kade looked south, scanning the horizon, knowing whom Sabra worried about. "He should be soon," Kade agreed. "But you never know just what might keep him. I wouldn't worry yet."

"I am a mother," Sabra said shortly. "I'm allowed to worry."

Kade just grinned at her and urged his young colt faster. "I'm hungry. Let's make tracks." Kicking his colt into a rolling lope, he caught up with Thomas, and they led the way home.

The horses were turned out, grazing on the valley grass, and Sabra was in the cabin heating stew for supper. They had a cookstove now which made mealtimes a lot easier and allowed Sabra to be outside longer.

"Sabra," Kade called. "Someone's coming. Might be Jake."

Sabra hurried outside and scanned the distance, looking for what Kade saw. There in the distance was a rider coming. It was just a dark spot at first, but then it separated, and it was two spots.

"Two riders," Kade commented.

"You think Brown Otter is coming back with Jake?" Sabra asked. "Or maybe it isn't Jake at all." She knew she would be disappointed if that were the case, but it could just be some mountain travelers. They had men stopping over sometimes. Old mountain men who still wandered the mountains and plains knew where Tom and Kade lived. Some stopped every few years, smoking their pipes and drinking whiskey around their fire or with old Tom. The stories flew then of times gone by. Sometimes Brown Otter or another brave from his village would stop, too. Sometimes they stayed a day or a week, but they always moved on.

By the time the figures reached the Jorgensen and Bates' cabins, Kade and Sabra could recognize Jake. Or maybe they knew him by his horse. In any case, they knew he was home. Sabra rushed into the house to look after the meal, then leaving instructions for Molly, she went out again. The figures were getting closer now, and they could clearly see Jake, but the other figure was smaller and unfamiliar.

"I think he has a woman with him," Kade remarked finally. "An Indian woman, I think. She's in buckskins."

But on the final ascent up the slight rise to the cabin, Kade and Sabra both saw he was wrong. It was a white girl who rode with Jake. She was dressed all in buckskin, decorated with beads. Her hair was jet black and hung long in front of her shoulders, tightly wound in twin braids. She rode a good-looking mare comfortably without a saddle.

"Who's that with Jake?" Thomas asked as he and Molly came out to wait with them.

"I reckon we will find out soon," Kade replied mildly. "Mind yer manners."

Jake and Anna rode up to the cabin, followed by the pack mules. When Jake dismounted, they saw him motion to the girl, and she got down as well. Sabra saw that the girl was pretty but terribly thin. She didn't smile, and her eyes were wide with apprehension. Jake went to her side and touching her arm, he urged her to walk with him. Jake went to his mother first, hugging her, then shook hands with Kade.

He looked at his family, "Guess I'm needing to build a cabin. This is my wife, Anna," he said. "Anna Curtis Welles," he hesitated a moment and then added, "she's been with the Cheyenne."

Sabra thought that one sentence might have more meaning than just the words. She smiled at the girl.

"How wonderful!" she exclaimed. "Welcome to our family." But she did not go to Anna. The girl's uneasiness was apparent to them. Anna stuck to Jake like a shadow, almost hiding behind him.

Anna's eyes remained wide and her body tense, but she softly replied, "Hi," and nodded slightly.

It was an awkward moment. No one knew what to say or do. Kade wanted to welcome the girl as well, but he knew he shouldn't. He didn't want to spook her; she looked close to bolting. It was Sabra who thought to speak again.

"You must be tired. Let's get your things off those horses and mules and get some supper in you. Thomas, help your brother carry their things inside."

"Ma," Jake interrupted, "if it wouldn't hurt your feelings none, Anna and I have been camping out so much lately, I think we'd be more comfortable setting up camp yonder by the trees until we get a cabin up."

"Of course, it won't hurt my feelings, son. You go get settled and then come back. We can talk and eat then." Sabra had a feeling there was going to be a lot to talk about tonight. This bringing home a wife was pretty sudden, and something was off.

Sabra saw Jake touch Anna's arm again and leading their horses, they made their way off a distance. Before they got too far, Jake turned back to them.

"It's kind of warm tonight," he commented. "Reckon it would be sort of pleasant sitting 'round the fire outside eating if that would suit you?"

There was some hidden meaning in those words too, Sabra knew. She smiled at him. "That is a wonderful idea," she replied. "I should have thought of that. Yes, you come back when you are ready, and we will make a fire outside to sit by. Supper will be ready when you are."

When Jake and Anna were out of earshot, Molly turned to her mother. "What is wrong with her?" she asked. "She never said a word but 'hi' and she looked scared to death!"

"We will just have to wait and see," Sabra replied. "All we know at the moment is that she was with the Cheyenne. Something has happened to her. Whatever it is, we need to be kind."

When Jake and Anna returned for supper, they all sat mountain man fashion around the fire. They had done this a lot over the years, especially when they went on the fall gather, but also when it was hot in the cabin. There was something pleasant about being outside and watching the dark descend upon them around a crackling fire.

Sabra and Molly brought the food out, the stew in a kettle, radishes, and onions from the garden along with bread, fresh-baked that morning. Sabra dished up each plate and Molly passed them out. Sabra surreptitiously watched the strange girl. Anna took the plate and just stared at it. Then, setting it in her lap, she picked up the bread, running her fingers over it, feeling the soft inside. With wonder in her face, she turned to Jake, and very softly she spoke.

"I remember bread," she was unaware that they all stared. "My mama made bread." Then picking up the spoon and fork, she asked him, "Jake, what is this called?"

He told her, and she replied, "I remember spoon and fork. You don't use fingers." But the family could see she wasn't sure how to hold them.

"Jake," Sabra said, drawing the attention to her. "Did your trading go well?" While she spoke, Sabra picked up the fork slowly, positioned it in her fingers, and speared a mouthful of meat. Then while she waited for his answer, she carefully placed the food in her mouth. Anna watched Sabra's actions, then slowly picked up her fork and, mimicking Sabra, started to eat.

The rest of the meal was pleasant, with Jake being plied by questions about his travels, whom he saw, and how the trading at Ft. Laramie went. Anna was quiet, and when her plate was empty, they saw Jake lean over and get her more from the kettle. He snagged her more bread too, and she cleaned it all up. Sabra could see that Anna was more relaxed now, but she didn't enter into the conversation at all.

After eating, though it wasn't late, Jake touched Anna's arm, and they got to their feet.

"I'm going to get Anna settled and then I will come back with some of the things you ordered from Ft. Laramie. You going to be up still?" he asked, looking at his parents.

"We'll be up," Kade replied. "I reckon it's mighty pleasant to just sit by the fire a mite."

Sabra and Kade exchanged glances as the couple left. They didn't need the supplies tonight that Jake brought back with him. It was his way of saying he would come back and talk to them. They would maybe get some answers then.

The family still sat around the fire when Jake came back alone. Jake and Kade took out their pipes, and Sabra could see her eldest son relax as he sat with them. Jake said he had told Anna she should get some sleep and he would be back. Jake knew Anna could see him sitting by the fire so she would not be alarmed that he was far away.

"I came onto a Cheyenne village a couple of days out of Ft. Laramie. Thought I might get a little trading in, so I stopped," Jake started. "Sat by the fire of one of the elders, and here came Anna out from a tepee with an older squaw beatin' the tar out of her. Hell, I didn't even realize she was white until she came back from getting water," he stopped, remembering that time.

"Ma," he said, looking at Sabra, "she looked up at me after the old woman knocked her down, and I saw her eyes. All I could think of was you." Jake looked away for a minute before going on. "I know you have never said a bad word against my father, but Brown Otter has told me what it was like, at least at the beginning. All I could see in Anna's eyes was you."

"Jake, your father never beat me. Never. I learned he was good. It just took some time."

"I know, but I kept thinking, too, what it might have been like for you if Blue Knife hadn't taken you for his wife. I knew right then I couldn't leave Anna there," Jake paused. "I owe you a horse. I traded one of the mares I bought for you to the chief for Anna."

He stared in the fire, silent for a while before going on, "She was so thin. She's still thin, but she was nigh onto starving when I got her. They only let her eat the scraps left over."

"How did she survive all that?" Molly asked. "How long had she been with them?"

"She had only been with the Cheyenne three or four months. Before that, she was with the Pawnee. Pa," Jake turned to look at Kade. "Do you remember the first year I went with you to the Trail without ma? Remember that train that came in and told of finding that wagon with the family all rubbed out?"

"Yeah, that was what, nine years ago? You tellin' us she was from that family?"

"She remembered that her first name was Anna but wasn't sure of her last name. She tried some partial names that were close to Curtis, sounded near to that. I am pretty sure that was the name that family was called. Remember there was a picture of the family that was found in the ransacked wagon? The picture had four children but one of the kids, a little girl, was never found. That would be Anna. The Pawnee took her to be a daughter to an old grandmother. They treated her well for most of that time, pretty much eight or nine years, until the old grandmother died. Anna was pretty grown up then, and the brave's wives got jealous of him looking at her, so when they met up with some Cheyenne, they got him to sell her to them. The Cheyenne didn't treat her good."

Jake was quiet for a few minutes, smoking and thinking back on the last month. "I talked to her a lot. She couldn't pull English words out, couldn't remember, but the more I talked, the more she picked up. She was only eight when the Pawnee took her, so English words are coming back. She's pretty much talking good now. But there is so much she doesn't remember or maybe was too young to know. Every now and then, she remembers something. Like she did with the bread tonight."

Jake stretched and got up. "Anyway, that is pretty much the story. I first sort of worked out a plan in my head where I would bring her back here, and maybe we could get a letter off next spring to Uncle Joe. Maybe he could find out if she had some people somewhere that she could go back to. But then, well, after a couple weeks together, we figured to stick together. So that's what we did," he finished. He looked at Kade. "I brought back some skins I traded for with the Cheyenne and Utes. Reckon I should put them in the barn for now." He picked up the sizable pile, hoisting it to his shoulder, and made for the barn.

"I'll walk along with you, son," Kade got up, and together they made their way down to the barn.

Kade knew Jake's story wasn't finished; he understood
this adopted son of his. There was more to this story, but
Jake couldn't talk about it in front of his mother and sister. If Jake needed to talk about it, it would be man to
man only. They piled the skins into the dark barn and
then went back into the moonlight. They could see the
fire dying in front of the cabin. Sabra, Thomas, and Molly had gone inside.

"Pa," Jake started, leaning back against the barn wall,
"that isn't all of it."

"Didn't reckon it was, son."

"She wasn't just a slave, but she was passed around
some, not with the Pawnee, but when the Cheyenne
got her," Jake started hesitantly, thinking through his
words. "The old chief was first, but he couldn't get it
up. Gave her a bad, disgusting name. Said it was her
fault, and the women ridiculed her. Then he let others
take her. Anna was beat up pretty good, both by other braves and the chief's wives. She was pretty scared
when I rode off with her. Took her a long time to start
to trust me," Jake stopped then, thinking back. "I don't
actually think she did really trust me, but for about ten
days, she didn't get beat up, and she got all the food
she wanted so she figured I was better than anyone
else that had her. I gave her some deerskins to make her
clothes. She was about falling out of her rags. I told her
about how our trading business was. Shit, I tried to talk
so much that trip that I ran out of things to say. Anyway,

after we got to the cabin, Iron Wing rode in one day, and Anna saw me motion toward the cabin. We were down by the beaver pond, and I was just inviting Iron Wing in for food, but Anna thought I was trying to sell her," Jake looked at Kade almost beseechingly, wanting him to understand how it was.

"By the time I got back to the cabin alone, she was like a wild thing. She was panicked. I couldn't reason with her. And then suddenly, there she was, her clothes flung to the floor, and she was offering herself to me. Just so I wouldn't sell her," Jake moved away from Kade then, turning away, ashamed. "Pa, I should never have bedded her then. She didn't know what she was doing, but I did. But damn Pa, she was just so . . . woman. I tried, Pa," Jake took a breath. "I did. I told her she didn't have to do that, but she just kept saying, 'it don't hurt much' over and over. Everyone had hurt her, ceptin' me, I guess. She was just so fuckin' desperate. And hell, it seemed I couldn't calm her any other way."

Jake turned back to Kade, "I didn't hurt her, Pa." Jake stopped, looking off toward the glisten of the pond in the moonlight across the valley. "But I did take her. I'm not too proud of that, but there you have it. I can't abandon her now. We went to the beaver pond that same night, and we said our vows to each other in the moonlight. I owe her that much," he finished gamely.

Kade studied this young man in front of him, guilt-ridden for not being able to resist a woman, a naked woman crazed with fear. Jake was right that Anna probably felt she had no other options, that she was spooked beyond thinking. But would her living in fear be better at this point?

"You ever think maybe you did the right thing?" Kade asked. "She was afraid. In her mind, you did the only thing you could to make her know you would not sell her or abuse her. You reckon she is still afraid of you?"

"No, I don't think she is, but still . . ." Jake hesitated, in thought. "Damn, I never thought I'd be so desperate I'd have to buy a wife."

"Well," Kade said mildly, "as long as you did, you sure got a pretty one." He saw Jake smile in grateful agreement as they turned and together walked back up the rise.

CHAPTER 5

Shivaree – Early September 1874

A s soon as they had eaten in the morning, Jake and Anna set out walking up the valley. It was a crisp, mountain morning. The creek, bubbling down the valley, sparkled; the grass, summer grown and tall, waved in the mountain breeze. As they walked, two deer came cautiously out of the trees across the valley and watered at the creek. Jake pointed them out to Anna, and they watched the animals bound back into the aspen forest as they approached.

"Where are we going?" Anna asked finally.

"We are looking for the spot to build our cabin on," Jake replied. "We need our own cabin."

"For us?" Anna asked. "A cabin just for us?"

Jake laughed at her. "You don't think we are going to live in a canvas lean-to all winter when the cold and snow comes, do you?" She amused him. She really had no idea of living together outside of an Indian tepee. Anna probably still saw tepees as a home. Her childhood memories were slow to come back until she saw something that triggered them.

Taking Anna's hand, he pulled her to him and tickled her, making her smile. She smiled more now, especially when she was sure that she pleased him. But new things still scared her, like meeting his family last night. Anna had been Old Grandmother's adopted daughter, but the rest of the family had not liked her. In some Native villages, just like in white society, jealousy could raise its ugly head. The outcome of a brave looking at her had not been good without the old woman's protection. Especially when the brave had jealous wives. Tossed off like refuse, Anna had become a slave to an even worse fate. Now Anna was learning a whole different culture, one that lived down deep in her memories. Jake knew it would take time for her to heal the wounds in her mind. Anna might never completely assimilate to white ways, but then again, had he?

Jake had a spot picked out in his mind to look at first. It was about a half-mile up the valley from his folks on the same eastern side. A spring fed into the creek at this place, and the slight rise from the valley bottom would put their cabin just high enough that the early spring run-off would not flood around the site. This knoll was heavily forested with aspen, spruce, and pine trees above it, and a small meadow bowed out eastward from the valley. Here, Jake could eventually fence off a pasture and put up a barn or lean-to for his saddle horses and extra plunder.

Now, any horses not turned out into the horse herd were behind Kade's barn below his folks' cabin. Behind Kade's there also was a big enough meadow to keep several horses in all summer and have grass. With aspen and pine poles secured to trees, it was fenced enough to keep the horses from wandering. Jake wanted the same set-up. It was always important to have a horse close at hand, whether to gather the herd, or for needed transportation when danger presented. He wouldn't want to have to hoof it a half mile down the valley to Kade's corral for his horse.

"Here, Anna, do you like this spot?" he asked, pulling her up the gentle slope. He looked around, surveying the view, the meadow off to the side, the protection of the trees, and the spring trickling down toward the creek. It was as he remembered.

"Yes, it is pretty," she replied. She gazed around her, seeing it for the first time.

"Well, do you want to look farther, or do you think this will do?" he asked her.

"If you like it, I like it," she said.

"We could go farther if you want," Jake told her. "But I was thinking that the cabin could sit here." Jake motioned to a flat area up against the trees. "It will be protected here, but we can see out and onto the valley too. What do you think?"

"If you like it, I like it."

"Bird," Jake started impatiently. "We would live here. Always. You don't have to like it because I like it. What do you like about it? Is there something you don't like?"

But it was not possible for Anna to voice her own opinion. "If Jake happy," she spoke as she had on the mountain, something Jake noticed her doing when she was unsure of herself, "Anna happy."

Jake knew it was no use. Maybe when she had been with him and with his family longer, she would be able to have an opinion. Right now, her whole life was just trying to please him. While there certainly was something in that to be happy about, he wasn't used to a woman who had no opinions. None of the women in this little community of family and friends were afraid to give their opinion. It just didn't seem right.

He took her hand again and led her around, telling her what he envisioned as the future building site. Pointing up the slope, he told her that his pa and brother would help him cut logs and bring them down for the cabin. They would start that afternoon maybe or the next day. It was almost a month until they would start the fall gather, so this was a perfect time to start. Jake wanted the cabin ready well before the winter winds began to blow.

Anna nodded at his words, offering no more but not looking displeased either. In about six weeks' time, this was a big life change for her, going from slave girl to wife, Indian woman to white woman. Jake watched her as she looked about, wondering if she was envisioning what he described.

"We will put the corners of our house here and here and . . ." he said, indicating the four corners of the cabin. "Someday, we may have to build on another room," he added, wondering if she thought any of children. "We can gather rocks from the creek and build a fireplace here," he pointed to where the back wall of the cabin would stand.

"Where will we lay our sleeping robes?" Anna asked.

"Where do you think it would be best?" he asked her, hoping she would have an idea.

"Where you think is best," she answered, again leaving the decision up to him. But then she surprised him with a suggestion. "We could try a place," she said, and turning, she came to him. Her hands touched his shirt shyly, pulling the tail from his trousers. Jake felt her hands reach in and move up his sides and to his back.

Damn, Jake thought, almost immediately feeling his body respond. That was a good idea. He was a randy sort, for sure. They tried a spot in front of the future fireplace.

In the afternoon, Jake took Kade and Thomas up to the site he had picked out. They walked off the area to find the best level spot. They walked into the trees to look for just the right size for cabin walls. Deciding that it was too late to get started that day, Kade suggested that they spend the evening with the family and get started early in the morning.

Sabra had gone to the Jorgensen's and the Bates that morning and Kade had walked over to Tom's cabin, so everyone in their little community heard the news that Jake had brought home a wife. Sabra and Kade told the families enough of Anna's situation for them to understand Anna's circumstances and how she was learning to adapt to her new life. Sabra had invited them all to come for supper that night. Sabra had baked bread and had chicken and elk meat on the fire. She had tinned peaches, and Molly made a pie. The Bates and Jorgensens would bring more desserts, and Clara and Tom would bring rice pudding. This was a time to celebrate. Anna needed to know the others and be welcomed. Jake deserved a wedding feast. He was a well-respected son in their little community. He was also the first son or daughter to get married. That he had done it before coming home was of no difference to them. This was indeed a time to celebrate.

Sabra and Molly had also been busy trying to put together a wedding present for the occasion. If she had had time, Sabra would have loved to make something special for Anna. But one day wasn't enough time. So instead, she went through her things, looking for something that would suit. Finally, in frustration, she gave up. It just wouldn't do to give her new daughter-in-law hand-me-downs for a wedding present. Then she had a thought.

Going through the trade goods and the supplies she had ordered from the fort she selected some material that she was going to make into clothes for herself and Molly. There were plenty of choices, so instead of giving Anna a finished product, she would have Anna pick out what she liked. Then Sabra and Molly could offer to help Anna make new outfits. Coming of age in a tribe would not have given Anna the experience to know the variety of clothes she would need as a white woman. She might remember wearing other garments as a child, but even they wouldn't be the same as a grown-up woman's clothes. Sabra had a sneaking suspicion that Anna had no clothing other than the deerskin blouse and skirt. She would need night attire, and dresses or skirts, and even the things a woman needed under her outerwear.

Sabra laid a selection of materials on her bed. Then she hung out several wardrobe options to show Anna the type of clothes she could help Anna make. This would be a fitting wedding present, but it might also be a way to get to know her new daughter-in-law better.

When Sabra took Jake and Anna into her bedroom before the rest of the guests came, Anna stopped at the door, wide-eyed. They all noticed that she stared at the bed, but they weren't sure why. Was it all the things piled on top of it? Then Anna spoke in a soft voice.

"I remember ma and pa had a bed off the floor," she said, not talking to anyone. It was more like her thoughts were coming out of her mouth. "When ma had baby," she went on, "she and baby were in the bed, and I brought her soup. 'Let yer ma sleep,' pa told me. They had a room all to themselves, like this."

Tears welled in Anna's eyes but didn't fall. Sabra had a feeling that the memories of the things her family had before they were all killed were sparking a feeling of loss that Anna had banished from her mind while in captivity.

Jake drew Anna to him, comforting her with his presence, and Sabra waited patiently for her to come back to the present in her mind. Then she showed Anna the type of clothes that she would need and the material that they had.

"Molly and I would love to help you make some clothes," she said. "While Jake is building a cabin, maybe we can do some sewing if you'd like."

Anna looked to Jake for his opinion, and when he nodded to her, she shyly spoke, "I would like that."

It was settled then. The women would begin sewing the next day. And as the other guests came, the future sewing party grew larger and larger. Each woman would come when they could and help, just as all the men promised to help with the cabin as they found time from their other chores. It would be a busy September for all of them.

The party was a success. Jake was touched that everyone came to share in the feast. He could also see that while Anna had been timid and clung to him the whole night, she had also enjoyed the festivities. She was overwhelmed by the variety of food, but it triggered memories as well. She remembered pies. She remembered that she liked pies as a child and that her mother made apple pies, getting apples off a tree in their yard.

Each family brought them a present. The Bates brought canned peaches and a quilt that Mattie had just finished. The Jorgensens brought a homemade straw broom for the new cabin and a small side table that Matthew had just built. He had intended it to be used beside their own bed, but he could make another one. Tom and Clara brought a chair that together they made from branches of trees. Every family had chairs or benches constructed by the old couple. Tom and Clara were always puttering around making more. Tom told Jake that they would make a matching one so he and Anna would each have one.

As they sat outside on stumps or on the ground eating, Tom got into the storytelling mood. Everyone enjoyed Tom's stories, and this night was no exception.

"Reckon you got married in them thar mountains just to get out of being shivareed, Jake," he said, addressing the young man.

Anna looked at Jake, questioningly, "What is shivering?" she asked.

"Not shivering, Missy," Tom answered for Jake, not sure if Jake himself knew what shivaree meant. "A shivaree is sort of a surprise party people give to married folk, the first night they git themselves hitched," Tom went on. "I recollect a shivaree way back before I ever left my pa and ma an' headed to the mountains." Tom paused, looking around. "Why the neighbors and friends of this married couple all came back after the festivities were over, an' the young couple had retired to their wedding bed. These uninvited guests made an awful racket, pounding on the walls with pots and pans and yelling until the couple opened the door," Tom grinned, remembering. "Then they picked up the little bride and put her in a wheelbarrow. Had the groom push her all the way to town to the local establishment." Here Tom looked around with more meaning in his glance than his words, "And buy a round for every man with 'em and celebrate through the night afore making him push his bride all the way home. Reckon it was about sunrise before they got home, an' all tuckered out to boot. It was a hell of a party." Tom finished, then realizing he had used a curse word, he added, "'Scuse me, ladies."

Kade looked over at Jake. Grinning, he commented, "See what you missed by getting hitched in them mountains by yourselves?"

"I think I can live with that," Jake grinned. "Some things just have a way of working out."

The party didn't last late into the night. Matthew, Jim, and their boys were trying to get their crops harvested and wanted to get that done so they could help with Jake's cabin. Jake, Kade, and Tom wanted to get an early start in the morning to begin felling trees. There was a lot of work to get done before the fall gather.

Kade and his two sons worked well together. Both boys, mountain grown, were skilled outdoorsmen and no stranger to hard work. Together they chose which trees would work and chopped them down. Tom, stiff and sore from rheumatism and arthritis, brought a stool and, perching beside a tree, he methodically sawed off the branches. When the others had downed many trees, they helped Tom with that task. When the logs were ready, they hooked a mule to them and hauled them to the building site. There was an endless supply of trees, so they did not have to go far to get logs.

As the week went by, though, Kade watched his eldest son grow quieter and quieter. Gone were the first few days of jovial camaraderie where the brothers joshed and wrestled with the logs, competing with each other at times. Gone was the easy smile as Tom told his stories. It wasn't that Jake seemed to be brooding, but more like he had a weight on his mind. Kade wondered if there were already cracks in this new marriage. He hoped not. He liked Anna and felt that she was a good addition to the family as well as suitable for his son. More and more Anna seemed to fit in. He wondered if Jake was just now thinking that this thing that he and Anna did was permanent. Kade certainly could relate to second thoughts about settling down. He had been there once himself.

"Son, you seem like you have something on your mind," Kade said one afternoon when the two of them were alone, trimming off branches on a tree. Thomas had gone with the mule dragging a log down to the cabin site and Tom was working down the slope where it was easier for him.

Jake glanced up but didn't reply right away. Kade knew that was the way of them, his boys and himself. It took some time to put the words together. By Jake not denying it, Kade knew something was up. He could wait.

"Pa," Jake finally said, "I reckon I do. It's been over seven weeks since I took Anna from that village." Jake struck savagely at a branch, then left the ax where it struck. "I told you how it was for her. With the bucks, I mean."

Kade nodded. He knew Jake had to get this out. With only the beginning of this conversation, he already suspected what it might be about.

"Well, damn, I didn't grow up in a small cabin with a mother and sister without having some idea about what went on . . . you know, private woman stuff." Again, he hesitated before continuing, "Anna should have had her time, you know, long before now. But she never. I know that for sure," Jake eased himself down to sit on the log.

"I reckon that is probably right," Kade spoke slowly. This was what Kade had thought was bothering Jake. "Course she was pretty starved out, you know. That could change things, maybe. Does with animals sometimes."

"I have been hoping that too," Jake replied, "but seven weeks? And," he paused. "Here's where I get all mixed up in my thoughts. I'm worried she carries another man's child, and I'm 'shamed of those thoughts. The way you took me for your own, you didn't have to do that. I never have felt you treated Thomas or Molly different from me. So why am I thinking like this?" he finished and looked up at Kade, confusion in his eyes.

Where the hell does a man go with that, Kade thought. *Maybe with the truth?*

"When your mom was carrying you," Kade began carefully. "I couldn't accept it. I walked away. Then she got took back to St. Louis, and I couldn't accept that either. I went for her and set her free, but her being with

Blue Knife haunted me, and I was ashamed of that. It took Uncle Joe's wife, Aunt Katie, and her angry words to get me to look at myself. Bless her heart, if I could kiss her now for those words, I would. So, I found your ma back at Jacob's cabin, and we worked it out. Took time, but we did it."

Kade lowered himself to a log across from where Jake sat. "Look, son, when I married your ma, you were just a baby. A man can't hate a baby, an' you were a cute little thing. But I never really gave you much thought at first. That first winter at Jacob's cabin, if you were fussing an' your ma was busy, she'd hand you to me, an' I reckon I just kind of got used to you. When you started crawling, you'd climb over your ma an' me as we lay on our robes. You were a busy little shit. You walked early, an' one day, just before we left the mountain, I came 'round the cabin, an' you saw me, an' your little face broke open with a grin, an' you came running to me with your little arms up," Kade smiled at the memory. "I reckon when we married, I figured I would try to be a good father, even though you were another man's child. But Jake, that day you came running to me, you weren't Blue Knife's son anymore. I never reckoned to love you like that, but I do." That was a long speech for Kade. "Sometimes, just between you an' me, I think we are more alike than Thomas an' me even. Blood don't always mean a thing."

Jake thought about this and nodded. "So, just wait and see then?"

"I don't reckon there is anything else you can do, is there? Unless you are fixin' to turn Anna out."

Jake was startled by this thought. "Hell, no, I won't turn her out," he exclaimed. "I just was . . . shit, I don't know. It just was bothering me, is all."

Kade grinned at him. "We seem to find a lot of things to be bothered 'bout when we set up with a woman," Kade laughed. "But this thing, well, you can work through it. I remember your Aunt Katie's words to me that day, just as surely as if she said them today. She stood up straight and stamped her foot she was so mad at me," Kade chuckled remembering. He drew himself up and imitating his sister-in-law, he said, "'What difference does it make what she was. It is what she is that is important. She is a good woman, and she loves you. That is the only thing that should matter. You are feeling sorry for yourself, Kade Welles. I always thought you were a better man than that,'" Kade smiled in the remembering. "An' then she flounced off to the house leaving me standing in her yard feeling pretty foolish an' small." Kade picked up his ax. "So, consider your Aunt Katie standing here now. She'd say the same thing to you." Kade turned back to his work on the tree.

"Pa," Jake asked as he too rose, "you knew Ma loved you, right? You think Anna loves me?"

"Boy, you ask the damnedest things. All you have to do is look at Anna when you walk in our cabin in the afternoons to tell her you're back," Kade chopped at a branch for a while before continuing. "And you love her too. Any damn fool can see that."

They got the cabin raised before the end of September. Matthew and Jim came with their sons for several days to help get logs. Sabra, Molly, and Anna took the light wagon and hauled rocks in from the creek. Tom, with Lathe's help, began laying the rocks for the fireplace. Then they all came to help on the day they raised the cabin walls. Sabra, Molly, and Anna brought up dinner so the men could eat and keep raising the walls. When the walls were up, it was only a matter of days before they got the rafters in place and the roof laid.

The logs still needed to be chinked on a couple of sides, and a loft added inside. The fireplace was started but it was far from finished. Late in September, the whole community stood there on a late afternoon and watched as the front door was attached. A cheer went up. The cabin was far from done, but it was enclosed enough that Jake and Anna could move in.

It was a one-room cabin with the fireplace across from the front door. The cabin was designed so Jake could eventually build a short half wall to create a small bedroom on one side and a kitchen-sitting room on the other side. But that would come later. Some of the work could be done in the winter. The chinking, the north and west wall done by the women as the men worked on the roof, would have to be completed before heavy winter set in, but for now, it would suit.

Jake and Anna walked back to the campsite with the others. Thomas and Molly helped them gather their things, pack them on a mule and take them up to the new cabin.

"You want help putting things away?" Molly asked. "Are you coming back for supper?"

"Thanks, but no," Jake answered. "We are tired tonight. I know Ma and Pa are too. We have some leftover meat from breakfast we can chew on, and then when we get organized, we'll just go to bed. Think we all need a good rest. It has been a long month."

Molly and Thomas smiled their goodbyes and headed home. Jake and Anna surveyed the cabin. They carried in their few house belongings. They had Tom's two chairs, a little table, and the broom, and some packs of food and clothes. Jake had his cook skillet, and Sabra had given them a couple of plates and silverware. They used the new kitchen utensils to cut up some meat and eat. Soon Jake would make some shelves to store their things. For now, they just stacked the extra items on the floor. The sun went down, and they lit a candle. Jake took the buffalo robe they had been using for a bed, and their blankets and looked at Anna.

"Where are we sleeping?"

Anna looked around. "Maybe we try some places?"

Jake shut the door and put a bar across it. He wasn't expecting trouble, but there were bears about still, and he didn't want to have one busting in his cabin. They had no fire yet. He laid the robe down right in the center of the room.

"Beautiful Bird," he said, peeling off his shirt, "you look awful pretty in your new clothes." His fingers worked through the buttons on the new dress she and Sabra had made. When it fell to the floor, she now wore frilly underthings too. "But it was a lot easier getting to you in buckskin," he laughed. "Now you have more layers on."

"Good for you," Anna smiled up at him. "Make you work."

Jake leaned over and blew out the candle as they sank onto the robe. His hands went under her new chemise, "Tomorrow night, you can put your new nightdress on first," he said. "But tonight, let's just take things off."

Anna giggled and wiggled her way out of the clothing. Jake pulled her to him, feeling her curves and nuzzling her neck. She was filling out, and the first thing he touched wasn't just skin over bone. He liked the feel of her as she filled out and her body softened.

And that is when the racket started. Pots, pans, bangs, catcalls, and war hoops resonated outside. The banging was on the walls and along with the clanging of pots and pans against each other, the noise was deafening. There were some shots too, exploding outside and breaking through even the sounds of the clanging.

"Holy shit," Jake whispered, grabbing for clothes.

"What . . ." Anna began, "who?"

"Bird, get some clothes on before they climb in through the windows," Jake told her hurriedly. "We are being shivareed."

Everyone was there. The young men had hitched a mule to the light farm wagon and loaded Sabra's piano. As Jake opened the door, Sabra played a rousing tune. Anna and Jake were swept into the waiting hands of the men and women of the four families. They were whirled between people, laughing and stumbling. Tom and Lathe were building a big fire and when the song ended, and everyone stood laughing, Mattie and Sarah set out food on the wagon box. Tom brought a jug and the men and boys, even young James, had a nip. Matthew brought out his fiddle, and he and Sabra took turns supplying music, and the dancing continued. At first, Jake was afraid that Anna might be frightened by the doings, and indeed she had been right at the start, but Jake saw that Kade captured her first and talked to her as they danced. He heard Anna say once, "I don't know how to dance!" to which his father replied, "Honey, you are dancing right now."

They didn't quit until the glow of the dawning sun began to highlight the upper ridges of the mountains. By then, there wasn't a man among them that hadn't drunk too much, eaten his fill, and blistered his feet. The women were just about as bad off, with feet aching from dancing. Kade hitched up the mule, and they all piled in and left Jake and Anna smiling and waving at them, Anna pretty much supporting her sagging husband as he watched his family, all of his family, going home.

"Bird," Jake slurred, "I think I am not going to get them clothes off you this morning. I think I just need to sleep this off." And with Anna's help, Jake stumbled into the cabin. This time, Anna barred the door and, turning, found her husband already fast asleep on the buffalo robe.

Three days later, the chinking was done, at least for now. There may be touch-ups to do later or repair work, but now Jake would work on the fireplace. The nights were getting cold, and already they would like to have a fire in the evenings. Anna had been arranging things on the shelves that Jake hammered up the night before, but when Jake returned with a load of rock, Anna was not in the cabin. Jake set to work on the rocks, selecting the sizes he needed, remembering Tom's instructions. He hadn't built a fireplace before.

After quite some time, Jake began to be concerned when Anna hadn't returned. He thought she had probably just stepped out for the necessary things that needed the privacy of the woods, but when he got up from the fireplace, he saw Anna's dress hanging on a hook on the wall. *What the hell,* Jake thought, *did she wear leather?* He went out looking for her.

It didn't take him long to find her. She wasn't really hiding; she was just sitting wrapped up in a blanket at the edge of the woods. But as he approached her, he saw a look of apprehension flicker across her face. He slowed his pace. She hadn't looked at him with anything near to fear since they had said their vows. *What the hell was going on?*

"Bird," Jake softly called to her. "What are you doing out here alone?"

"Stay away," she said. "I am dirty."

Jake was confused. "Anna, you are not dirty. Come here to me."

Anna shook her head, not rising. Jake advanced slowly, not wanting to spook her but needing to know what was scaring her.

"Tell me," he said firmly. "Why are you scared?" He was close now, and she shrank back.

Anna pulled the blanket completely over her head, gripping it tightly to her. From within, he heard her say softly, "Woman go away when it is time. They beat me when the blood comes. I go live with the horses, fight with dogs for scraps. Sleep out of tepee."

Jake knew how distressed she was by the way she spoke. Gone were good sentences. But suddenly, he knew what she was talking about. His heart soared. She wasn't carrying a Cheyenne baby. When a baby came, it would be his baby. He knelt beside her and pulled her curled up into his lap.

"Beautiful Bird, you do not need to go away. Look at me," he commanded gently and pulled the blanket off her face. "I love you, Anna. I am happy your woman time comes. That is a good thing."

"I don't know what to do," she said softly, looking down. "What do white women do?"

He laughed at that. "You ask the damnedest things. I have no idea. But I'll get my mother. She will know." And lifting her in his arms, he carried her to the cabin.

CHAPTER 6

Looking Back – June 1875

Tom shuffled out of his cabin and surveyed the meadow. He could see across to Kade and Sabra's cabin and the activity there. They were organizing the supplies needed for this year's trading trip to the Oregon Trail, getting them ready for the pack mules. It would be a family affair this year, the first for all five of them to go. No, six now with Anna. This would be Molly's first trip off the ranch, and she was excited to go. She had never been out of the valley, except for hunting with her pa or brothers or going on the fall gather. So, this was something different for Molly and for a sixteen-year-old girl, it was a big thing.

Old Tom loved that little Molly girl, just like he loved her mother, Sabra. But he loved them like a pa or a grandpa. All those years trapping, sprees in St. Louis or Independence, and a warm woman in his bed at times, he never would have believed he would end up with a family. Not a blood family, but still an honest to goodness family. That's what happens, he reckoned, when he hooked up with good men, men who stuck, be it to good friends or to a woman.

All of those years ago when he met Jacob trapping with the Rocky Mountain Fur Company, and they hooked up, that was the beginning. Even then, despite the newness of it all, Tom knew he didn't want to stay with the fur brigade for long. But he was green to mountain ways. He had much to learn. And then came along Jacob, and Kade's pa, Jonah. Both men were a few years older than Tom, and sure enough mountain men already, having trapped in the northern woods together. After that one year in the fur brigade, they all wanted to branch off from the company. The three of them worked well together, Jacob steady and calm, Jonah serious, and Tom fun-loving.

When Jacob took a Ute wife and made his home in the mountains, Jonah and Tom would bring Jacob's furs with them to rendezvous or to St. Louis. When Jonah married a young neighbor girl to his folks' farm and began to spend half the year near the growing city, Tom bounced between Jacob's cabin, sprees in St. Louis, and some welcoming Indian village. But always, the three came together when the weather turned cold, and the pelts would be prime.

Kade was fifteen when Jonah brought him west to join them. A scrawny young'un at the time, but he had the mettle for the mountains. He fit in well. Kade, a wild one at home, was a bit more like his serious father when he came west. But, over time, a bit of Jacob's calm and Tom's fun rubbed off on the boy.

How many years had Tom wandered and trapped in these mountains? It took some thought. *Well over thirty years maybe, forty even, figuring before and after Kade joined them,* Tom thought. Eventually, the beaver led them higher and higher into the mountains for a catch until they finally become so scarce it wasn't worth it to hunt for them. Then the price of pelts dropped to pennies.

Jonah gave up the mountains for the farm. Jacob pretty much stayed at his cabin, so soon it was just Kade and Tom, almost a generation between their ages, rambling around the mountains, doing what they could. They would occasionally stop at Jacob's cabin. Jacob's Ute woman and his girl children got rubbed out, Jacob had thoughts of quitting the mountains and going back east to his brother's place. That didn't last more than a winter, and when he came back, he brought Sabra with him. *Waugh!* thought Tom.

Now Sabra and Kade and their brood was his family, bound together by years and some bond none of them could explain. But the bond was there. Now here Tom was, grandpa to all the young'uns in this valley and he was with a good woman, too. It was a good life. This was a good place to live and a good place to die. A right smart better place to die than alone in the mountains the way so many of his kind went.

Tom had long outlived most of the old trappers he knew. He must be well into his mid or upper 70s now. The rheumatism had gotten bad these last years, and his joints ached and troubled him, but he could still get around. He could heft that old Hawkins, although he hadn't had need to put it to his shoulder for several years now, but he kept it close. It was part of him. If trouble came to this valley, Tom would be ready.

Clara came out of the cabin to stand beside him, watching the activity across the valley.

"You wishin' you were going with?" she asked Tom.

"I reckon I hate to see 'em go without me," Tom smiled at her. "But I cain't say I want to go. My days of ramblin' are over. I kin sit here an' cry 'bout days gone by, er I kin jest be glad I'm still breathin'. Hell woman, I got you now. What I need with another journey?" And he pinched her ample rear.

"Quit that, old man," Clara punched him gently. "You will be the death of me!" But she didn't look upset. "I am going over to give them this hunk of cheese. You want to walk over with me?"

"You go. My knees are hurting today. Think I'll set a spell in the sun an' jest watch from here. Tell Kade I'll see him before they leave."

Tom watched Clara, basket in hand, heading down the gentle slope. She made good cheese. She didn't keep her own cow anymore but got the milk from the Jorgensens. It was a cow that brought them together. *How long ago was that? Little Jake was three years old that year so that would be twenty-three years ago now.* His mind went back to that trip as he slowly lowered himself into one of his homemade chairs. *Damn, he was stiff today.*

It was 1852, and Tom, Kade, and Sabra were making the second annual trip to trade on the Oregon Trail. Their herd was twice as big this second year, and Sabra had brought one of the colts she had raised to see if there was a market on the Trail for a fine horse. Kade thought that good horses like those Sabra raised would be of more value to the army, so this was just a test. The rest of the herd consisted of all the oxen and mules, and half of the cattle, traded along the Trail the year before. They kept the better cows that had calves at home. Those were the seed herd that would be the foundation for a future business. Trading along the Trail wouldn't last forever. Settlements would eventually come. When that happened, there would be a market for beef.

Little Jake was three years old that summer, and he rode his own Indian pony. Kade had traded for the little mare with a passing Ute. It was a cute little thing and just gentle enough for the little boy. Little Jake had just about been raised on a horse, and he sat up like a hand already. When Sabra or Kade noticed the little tyke getting sleepy, one or the other would ride over and pluck him off his horse, and he'd sleep, cradled in his parent's arms.

Now, in the late afternoon, they started to sight the Platte. They would be along the Trail now and could find a good place to bed their livestock down and wait. It shouldn't be long as it was nearing the end of June. The earliest of the trains should be moving into this area any time now. If they had to wait a few days, it just gave their livestock a chance to rest and fatten on the untouched grass. Once the trains started rolling, the grass would thin. But they would be long gone by then.

Kade scouted ahead and found a spot to camp, signaling Tom and Sabra to bring the herd. They had no wagon with them, only pack mules hauling their supplies. Kade found a spot not too far from the river where there were some trees for shade.

Sabra began unpacking their things, turning the mules loose as she took their packs off. Soon, she had a fire going and some meat cooking. Sabra was a good traveler, tough, efficient, and uncomplaining. For the moment, if you just pointed Sabra at a horse, she was happy. She didn't care how long she rode. Tom wondered how much longer she would go with them. He was surprised that little Jake didn't have a brother or sister on the way yet. Just from watching the young couple, Tom had no doubt it wasn't for lack of trying.

They only had to wait two days for the first wave of pioneers to appear. The first wagon train was big. There were almost eighty wagons and a huge herd of livestock. Kade and Tom pushed their own herd back along some river hills to keep them separate from the train's herd. Then finding the captain of the party, they explained they had fresh livestock if there were some on the train that were getting along poorly. By this time of the trip, a lot of the animals were spent. Many settlers traded or bought fresh livestock at Ft. Laramie, but a lot kept on going, bullheaded, thinking the animals would make it. Some wouldn't. The trail was littered with the bones of dead animals. And so, the trading would begin.

After the settlers got their wagons set up, a steady stream of men would come out to talk business. Some walked over, some rode their horses over. They would eye the former mountain men and the pretty woman with the half-Indian child and mostly keep their thoughts to themselves. Usually, the train would lay over a day so the exchanges of animals could take place. The women always used the time to try to wash. They were camped along a little stream that had some clean water, so it was a good spot for everyone.

Toward evening that first night, Tom sat under the tree smoking his pipe and telling stories to some of the pioneers. There was no disguising Tom as anything other than an old mountain man in his leather breeches, even though he sported a shirt that Sabra made for him. Leather hunting shirts were too hot for the plains in summer. His stories were good entertainment, and he usually drew a crowd once the evening was upon them.

This night was no exception, and the ring of men around Tom enjoyed his humor. On the outskirts behind Tom sat a woman, perched upon a log. She listened and watched and smiled every now and then at the stories, some of which were off-color. It was well past dusk when the group broke up, heading back to the wagons. The woman got up then too, but she didn't follow the men. If one of them was her husband, she didn't show it.

"Kin I ask a question?" she asked of Tom as she approached. She was what one would call a "buxom" woman, heavy chested but not fat, just sturdy. A pleasant but plain-looking woman, she was somewhere in the middle age of life. Her graying hair was tied up in a bun, but her eyes were direct and unashamed to be there alone talking to strangers.

Tom was startled. He hadn't noticed the woman before. She had been sitting too far behind, out of his range of sight. "Ma'am?" he replied.

"I reckon you is a mountain man. Am I right?" she spoke directly to Tom rather than to all of them.

"Ma'am, I was that oncet," Tom answered.

"You ever run acrost a young man by the name Samuel Tenbrook?"

Tom got to his feet, uncomfortable sitting before a woman who was talking to him. He looked over at Kade, questioning. Kade shook his head.

"No, ma'am, don't reckon I do. You thinking he was in the mountains?"

"I know he was maybe four or five years ago. I haven't heard from him in the last few years, but the last letter I got from him was sent from Ft. Hall. He was traveling with some old trapper, and they were hunting for the fort at that time."

Tom thought a moment, then looked to Kade. "Weren't there some young feller there hunting when we went through in '48 by the name Sam Tenny? He was riding with old Calvin Hotten. Could that be him?" he inquired of the woman.

"Yes, friends called him Tenny a lot as a kid," she was excited. "I'm sure that is him. Did you see him?"

"Heered about him, is all," Tom continued. "He was off on a hunt when we went through. The bourgeois thought well of him, though. Said they were eatin' good."

"You never heard where he went from there?" the woman asked hopefully. "Last letter I got from him, he said he was moving on. I haven't heard more'n that."

"No, ma'am, never got over that way again. He a friend?" Tom was curious now.

"He's my son. He run off nigh onto seven years ago, but he tried to keep in touch with me. Jest his pa he had no truck with," she turned to go, then as if thinking of something else, she turned back.

"I got me this sweet little milk cow," she said, still addressing Tom, although it was Kade that had all along been doing the trading. "I'm feered she may not make it to Oregon. You interested in a milk cow?"

Again, Tom looked over at Kade, but Kade was making himself busy with little Jake.

"Ah, not sure of that," Tom said, "we don't have any milk cows with us to trade with, and not a heap of cash money."

"I am more worried about the cow," the woman replied, "as she's getting footsore. She won't bring me any money dying along the trail. Won't do anyone good then. I wouldn't be too hard to bargain with if I decide to sell her. She's a nice cow."

Tom looked again at Kade but got no help. Kade had moved off away from the fire. "Reckon I could walk over an' see her tomorrow in the light an' we could talk then," he said.

"I'd like that," she said, "I surely would. She's gentle; I could even walk her over here tomorrow since we are laying over." The woman turned to go then hesitated, seemingly just then realizing how dark it had gotten. The light of the fires from the distant wagons flickered, but the dark swallowed everything else up.

"Ma'am, it appears your husband has gone off and left you," Tom spoke. "I could walk you back."

"That would be right neighborly of you," the woman replied. "It gets powerful dark out here." As they walked off together, Sabra heard the woman continue, "My name is Clara Tenbrook. And I ain't got no husband."

Tom was late coming back. Kade had gone out to night guard their herd. That was the hardest part of this trip, with only the two men guarding the herd at night. But Sabra was an early riser, and most mornings she went out and spelled whoever was on at dawn if little Jake stayed asleep. This night, Sabra was already wrapped up in her blankets with little Jake snuggled up beside her. She didn't rouse when Tom came back.

As Tom lay himself down, he knew that he was short a couple hours of sleep this night already. But the woman, Mrs. Tenbrook, was good to talk to and in no hurry to chase him away. He had learned a lot about her as they walked. Then she had coffee simmering on her fire, so he stopped and had a cup. Other than Sabra and the wives of the other two couples in the valley, it had been a long time since he had had a conversation with an honest to goodness white woman.

Clara came from the Missouri country. She'd been married, but her husband had died the year before. When he offered his condolences, she had replied, "Don't be sorry, I'm not. He was a sour old man at thirty. He didn't get better as the years passed."

"He drove our son away when Samuel was fourteen," Clara spoke matter of factly, but Tom could see she had a lot of bitterness in her about that. "Sam wanted me to leave too, but a woman jest cain't do that. I made my bed."

"What you goin' to Oregon for then? You got some kin out there?"

"I reckon I'm jest going to be going. I had these two mules and this here little farm wagon," Clara indicated her wagon. "I figured I could outfit myself and go. Thought maybe iffen I get out into this western land, I might run acrost my son. I'm leaving word at all the forts we go through, telling him his pa is dead, and his ma left the settlements. When I settle somewhere, I kin post a letter and iffen he ever gets through any of them places again, he will hear from me where I planted myself."

"Ma'am, this is a right hard trail fer a man alone. You goin' alone cain't be easy."

Clara laughed at that, "Since when is going any-where easy?"

"What you figure to do when you get to Oregon? How you goin' to live?"

Clara looked at Tom thoughtfully, as if wondering what to tell him. "Well, there seems to be a shortage of women out there, so maybe I can catch a husband. My age works against me there, but you never know. Lots of older men lose wives and need someone to keep house for them. I can sew, and I used to make a lot of cheese for our community. That is why I brought my cow. Figured I could maybe sell cheese. I don't know, but maybe I cain't make it on my own, but I jest need-ed to try. Maybe I wouldn't dare, but that somewhere out here is Samuel."

Tom looked at Clara appraisingly. "You got gump-tion, for sure, ma'am," he commented. Rising from the fire, he handed her his cup. "I'll watch fer you to come over tomorrow, or iffen you need help, you jest come find me." Touching his hat, Tom moved away on silent moccasin clad feet. Clara sat and watched him fade into the night.

Clara brought the cow over midmorning before the day got too hot. Kade and Tom were both out cutting livestock from the herd for prospective trades. She sat and visited with Sabra, playing patty-cake with Jake, and pretending that things went missing, getting the little boy to hunt the grounds until he came back with a prize. Sabra enjoyed her time with the woman. Sa-bra had not had many women friends over the years, so the morning passed pleasantly. Clara never once commented on Jake's obvious heritage, nor did she shy away from the little boy.

When the men came back, Kade looked at the cow and told Clara they couldn't pay much, but they could give her something for the cow, as fair a price as they could afford that year. Clara asked if they minded if she were to think about it. She did hate to give up her little cow. Sabra insisted that Clara stay and share the midday meal, and it was mid-afternoon before Clara bid them good-bye.

Tom and Kade went back to check on their livestock. With new livestock added and some they brought now traded away, they needed to watch the herd more closely until the animals settled. Kade doubted they were done for the day, anyway. This train had gone through some rough stretches. He figured there would be more men over later in the day to see if they could make better trades before deciding what they wanted to do. It was a gamble for the pioneers. Could they reach Oregon with the livestock they had, or were they better off trading for fresh but fewer animals that could make the trip? Kade was hoping that he would get their rested livestock traded yet today. If so, they could head for home in the morning.

The trading began again in earnest in the late afternoon. By suppertime, Tom and Kade came in to eat and rest a bit before the sun set. Tom pulled out his pipe and settled, but after a few minutes, he stretched and looked at Kade.

"Reckon I might jest wander over and see if that lady decided on her cow," he commented, not meeting Kade's eyes. "Walk'll do me good."

Kade looked questioningly at Sabra as Tom moved off toward the wagons, but Sabra only smiled and shrugged. "She seems a nice lady," Sabra said. "But I have no idea what's happening there."

Tom came back just after dark. Mrs. Tenbrook would decide by morning, he said. But he had shared some coffee at her fire. She had wanted him to tell her about the mountains and what it was like trapping. He reckoned she was interested in knowing more about her son's life in the mountains. In any case, Tom found it pleasant to sit by her fire, smoking and talking.

But as the day dawned, Mrs. Tenbrook did not come.

"I suppose she can't part with that cow," Kade remarked. "I'm not surprised. She seemed pretty taken with it. I hope it makes it to Oregon."

"How soon you fixin' to head out?" Tom asked, for they had traded all the stock they brought. Now their herd had tripled, but the condition of the animals would make the trip home slower than the trip coming out. Most of these animals needed food and rest, so they would push them slowly when they traveled.

"Think I'll let the animals graze until the train is out of sight, then head ours south," Kade answered. "I best go out and make sure we don't have any of ours following the train."

"Kin you make out without me fer a bit?" Tom asked, looking off toward the wagons. "I could jest wander down there, jest to make sure."

Kade grinned and sent Tom off. Whatever was going on with Tom was fun to watch. He thought Tom might be getting a bit interested in the Tenbrook woman.

Tom made his way to the train. Twice now, he had been to Clara's wagon, so it didn't take him long to get there. The cow was tied to the tailgate, and the woman was hitching up her mules. She had a light wagon with not much for plunder, so she only had two mules. They seemed in reasonably good shape, and he could see she expertly set the harness upon them.

"Ma'am . . . Mizz Tenbrook," he said as he came near, "you want fer us to go on then?"

Clara turned to look at Tom. "Well, I just was going to drive out to your campsite," she said.

"You decided to sell then?"

"Well now, I jest don't know," Clara said sadly, shaking her head. "I jest sure hate to part with this cow. And for that matter," and here Clara stood up straight and looked directly at Tom, almost challenging him, "I reckon I just hate to take another step west after you told me all about your mountains and your valley."

Tom studied her. She stood up tall, proudful, unashamed at what she was so obviously saying to him. Tom might not have had a lot of experience with white women, but he was not clueless. He caught her meaning, and now he had to make a step, one way or the other.

"Ma'am," he started slowly, thinking through his words, "I have a little cabin in that there valley. Nothing big nor nice, but it is sturdy. Money never much meant anythin' to me, but I get some from Kade for when I need. Iffen you want, you could come back with us. We could see how it goes between us. Iffen you don't like it there, I could bring you back here next year, and you could go on your way. I got nothin' much to offer to you, but I ain't no sourpuss neither."

Clara smiled. "I don't have much myself," she said, "and I won't have to sell my cow. I'd like to see your valley."

And so, it was decided. Tom returned to the camp-site where Sabra was busily packing their things. Kade was out with the herd, but he had staked Tom's horse nearby, and Tom went to the horse and saddled it. Just as he was ready to ride out to the herd, he turned to Sabra.

"Mizz Tenbrook is going to come along with us'n iffen you don't mind," he told her. "She was almost hitched when I left, but she was posting a letter to her son so's someone could leave it at Ft. Hall." And with that, he rode off. Sabra watched him go. She liked Clara already. She still wasn't sure what was happening between the two, but she was glad another woman was joining them.

The return trip, although taking longer, was quite pleasant. Sabra enjoyed Clara immensely. Clara would watch Jake and start supper while Sabra helped the men settle the weary animals. Kade would not let Sabra take a night watch, but he would allow her to come out just as dawn was breaking, relieving whichever of the men was on duty. Now instead of chewing on cold meat, Clara had something warm on for them at dawn, and they could have a bit of breakfast before breaking camp. Clara had a variety of food along in her wagon that she would cook. She could cook up some mean biscuits, and she had some homemade jam. She just seemed to be as comfortable with them as if she had been with them all along.

Sabra and Kade still had no idea what was happening between Clara and Tom. And they weren't sure Clara and Tom knew either. The two never sought each other out nor did they wander off together. In the evenings, the four of them sat around the fire, telling stories, and visiting before a nightguard went out and the rest turned to their blankets. So, when the Jorgensens' and Bates' cabins came into view, Sabra thought it might be time to make an offer. While the herd was bunched at the river drinking, she rode over near Clara's wagon. Tom was sitting on his horse by Clara's wagon, pointing out how far up the valley the next cabins would be. Clara was nodding, although Sabra knew Clara couldn't see that far up the valley yet.

"Mrs. Tenbrook, I am not sure what you have decided to do, but if you would like, Kade and I could surely find room for you in our cabin."

Clara looked at her and then at Tom. "Me and Mr. Grissom here, well, we thought we would take some time and see how it goes between us. I don't reckon we could do that iffen I am living across the valley with you. I thank you much for the offer, but reckon I best go to his cabin and we kin make out. I don't have much with me but a mattress and foodstuffs. Should be room for that much," with this, Clara looked to Tom.

"We start at my place," Tom echoed, nodding solemnly. "Then we see."

It was late afternoon before Tom and Clara got to the cabin by the beaver pond and began unloading her wagon. Clara had taken one look at the little room and remarked that they could make it work. Together they carried in what Clara would need for the moment, finding a place here and there for her things. Some kegs and boxes of food and supplies they left in the wagon for now. Clara thought she might want to do some deep housecleaning and organizing before she unloaded everything. It got dark quickly in the mountains when the sun went over the peaks, and it was getting dark fast. The last thing Tom reached for was her straw tick mattress. "Where you think you want me to put this?" he asked, not looking at her.

"Oh, just put it anywhere," she said, "and we can decide on that later. It is hot, and I am so sweaty and dusty. That beaver pond looks awful inviting. You ever swim in there?"

"I been known to wade out in it some, to cool off. But swim, no. It's a might chilly."

She turned to him. "Let's go then. I'm needing to cool off."

Off she went down the slope to the pond. Reaching the water's edge, she sat down and took off her lace-up boots and stockings. Tom followed, compelled to see what she was up to. She sat on the edge of the pond and dabbled her feet into the water.

"It is chilly!" she exclaimed. "As hot as it got today, I didn't think it would be this cold."

"It ain't usually so warm here, an' this pond is fed by mountain creeks," Tom explained. "It don't usually warm up much. You have to be tough to swim in mountain water," he grinned at her.

Clara took his challenge. Rising, she waded into the water until she was in almost to her knees, her skirts flowing around her. "Well, maybe I spoke too soon," she said. "I reckon a swim is a might too much, but I was hoping to wash the dust off. I can't make myself go farther. How do you make yourself get in all the way?" she laughed.

It was fully dark now, but the moonlight glistened off the water. Tom grinned back at her and pulled off his moccasins. He waded out near her and stopped. Then holding his arms out straight from his body and turning to face the shore, he stiffened his body and fell back into the cold water. The water splashed up onto Clara, and she shrieked while Tom splashed and sputtered in the water.

"Now you!" he grinned, struggling to stand. "See iffen you kin do it."

And she did. Holding her arms wide, she fell backward, the cold knocking the wind out of her. They both laughed then, and like little children, they splashed water on each other. Clara came up out of the water first, shivering.

"Oh, my," she said. "That is cold! But I feel good."

Tom also stood, letting the water drip from him. He looked over at Clara, staring into the distance, and she became quiet. After a few moments, she turned toward Tom and started to speak.

"I ain't told you the all of it, what my life was like," she spoke low. "I mean 'bout me and my man."

"It's yer business," he replied mildly.

Clara looked away, and taking a breath, she started to talk.

"I was married to my husband, Ezra, when I was sixteen. I thought my man was good and, well, he was then. He was older than me by almost ten years. We started off happy. In the first three years, I had a miscarriage, and two more children, but both died before they were a year old," Clara turned to look at

Tom then as she continued. "We had our son, Samuel, seven years later after many miscarriages."

"It did something to Ezra. He got more and more silent. Sometimes he was angry. It was like he was searching for something, and he couldn't find it," she stopped thinking. "I thought when Samuel came and grew up strong, it would help, but Ezra got mixed up in a religious group before then. He had this notion that losing our babies was God's punishment. We started going to this church, and one day Ezra came in and said we were moving. He had sold our farm and donated it to the church. We moved to this community of believers. Everyone got the same kind of house. There was a bedroom on each side and a sitting room with a stove in the middle. When we first got there, we had one bedroom, and Samuel had the other." With this, Clara reached up and took the hairpins out of her hair as she talked. She sat down in the water again, gasping at the cold but lay her head back, letting the hair float on the water. She didn't stay in long though; the cold drove her back up to stand. She shook her hair out and it hung long below her shoulders.

"I hated it there, but I thought maybe it would give Ezra peace. It didn't though. Then I really got to hearing the preaching, really paying attention, and how people were changing. The families that had been in the community a long time started moving into the bigger buildings when their children grew up. Men went to one house, women to another, and the older children to a third. I refused to move. That was the one thing I wouldn't budge on. But Ezra . . . well Ezra, he wouldn't share my bed anymore. He said that pleasuring ourselves was evil." Clara worked on the buttons of her wet dress, slipping it off. She stood in the moonlight in her chemise. Tom could see her in the moonlit glow. She knelt to the water and worked the dress in the water, washing it as well as possible without any soap. She walked to the edge of the pond and threw the dress onto the grass. She turned back to Tom.

"I got so lonely. I was lonely for my old home and my friends and for him. I just wanted him to touch me again. So, one night I went to his bed. I caught him unawares, and before you know it, he was there with me, loving me. I thought I had him back. I thought he would realize what we had, but he never. He got up the next morning and moved his bed into Samuel's room," Clara stopped, as if thinking how to go on. When she began again, her voice was low. "When Samuel ran off a few years later, I thought to try again. I was even lonelier when my son left. He and I understood each other. When we were alone, we still laughed. We still saw the beauty in the world. I was so lonely with Samuel gone.

"So, one night, I went to Ezra agin, and this time, too, I got him to respond. I hoped it would change him. But in the morning, he wouldn't speak to me. That Sunday, when we went to church, he took my arm and marched me right up to the preacher. Right there, in front of the whole congregation, he told them I was a temptress. The whole community shunned me. That was when I began to hate Ezra. I still wouldn't move into the women's house, so he couldn't move either. That was the spite I had in me. I was not going to give him that after how he shamed me."

Clara looked at Tom, still standing knee-deep in the water. "When Ezra died last year, I waited until the community buried him. That very night I packed everything I still had in that little wagon, and I left during the night. If that community thought they deserved my cow and mules and wagon, they could just come and find me. They got our whole farm a long time before that. I worked as a seamstress that winter, pinching every penny I could, and this spring, I headed out. I wasted twenty some years there and I ain't goin' to waste anymore."

Tom waded closer to her by the shore. "I reckon I understand why," he said. "Cain't say I blame you a bit."

"Tom," Clara used his Christian name for the first time. "I ain't been touched by a man in a long, long time. I am forty-four years old. I have passed my childbearing years. When I sat that first afternoon and listened to you telling stories, I set my cap for you right then. I said to myself, 'This ain't a man to mind pleasuring a woman. This is a man who would laugh and play the fool.' I reckon I tried to trap you by coming over and asking for you to walk with me and talk with me. But there you have it, that's what I did. Maybe that does make me a temptress."

Tom studied her in the moonlight. Her chemise was dripping wet, clinging to her. He saw her nipples standing out against the thin fabric. She had a magnificent bosom, he had to give her that.

"You are a handsome woman, Clara," he said, coming close to her. "You deserve better'n me, an' you deserved better'n your Ezra. But iffen you still have yer cap set, I am fifty-five years old, or there 'bouts.

And I would sure take pleasure with these," he ran his hand over her breasts.

She reached out hungrily for him, finding him in the moonlight. They kissed, then pulled back and looked at each other again. Clara spoke first.

"I reckon we know where to put my bed now," she said, and they splashed out of the pond and headed for the cabin.

Kade went to close the door as the chill was coming in. Sabra had Jake asleep in his corner and was making ready for bed. It was good to be home. Then Kade stopped, listening. He called to Sabra.

"Sabra, come here."

"What is it," she asked, going to the door.

"*Shh*, just listen."

Then the sounds he heard came again. There was a splash and a shriek and laughing and giggling.

"What is going on down there," Sabra asked, smiling.

"I think that Tom and Clara are getting to know each other," he said with a grin, pulling Sabra in front of him, feeling her curves.

"I get the idea," she said. "You don't have to illustrate. But they're in that cold pond? I would think that would . . ." she let her thought drift off.

Kade laughed outright at that. "I reckon, but it might be a good place to start, iffen you weren't in a hurry." He pulled her inside and shut the door. "I think I am better off starting in here. Maybe we can work on making the next baby."

Sabra came into his arms, feeling the hard muscles along his back. "Well, we can practice," she said, "but the next baby is on the way." She smiled up at him. "I am carrying your child this time."

"When?" he asked, pulling her close to him. "How long have you known?"

The baby should come in January. I was pretty sure I was pregnant," she said, "about a month ago."

"You little sneak," Kade exclaimed, "if I had known that I would have made you stay home with Mattie instead of coming out on the drive."

Sabra grinned and pulled her nightdress over her head. She leaned over and blew out the candle and stood before him in the firelight. "Well, why do you suppose I waited to tell you?" she asked. "So now you can pout about it, or you can just come to bed."

Kade opted for the bed. Sometimes he just couldn't control this little woman, but damn, he loved her.

CHAPTER 7

Pirates – Late June 1875

The mules were all unpacked, but Kade told the boys to picket the saddle horses nearby. They would need them to settle the herd if the animals wandered far. They were within a quarter of a mile of Independence Rock, and by the looks of the grass, there had been no early trains through yet. Kade was willing to wait there a day or two, letting the stock rest and fatten. Then if no wagons appeared, they would start east on the Oregon Trail toward Ft. Laramie. Kade knew he could sell the cattle at the fort for sure and probably the oxen and mules as well. It was a gamble to see if any wagons would still make this trek. But there were small trading posts and new forts along the western reaches, so he knew he could get a good price for his animals; it would just mean traveling farther.

The whole family was along. Molly and Sabra, in their godawful knickerbockers, were busy setting up the cooking supplies. Sabra had promised that the two of them would change into their respectable dresses in the morning or at the first sight of any white man. Over the years, Kade had gotten used to Sabra's "work" outfit, but he still felt himself becoming hot with desire seeing her legs sticking out from her short dress. He didn't cotton having other men see his wife and daughter in such an outfit. The boys were setting up tents, one for Sabra, Kade, and Molly and one for Anna and Jake. Thomas and Lathe would sleep under the stars unless a rain blew up.

Kade strolled up a slight rise, scanning the horizon to the west. The trains would come from the east, but he had a stinking suspicion there might be something coming from the west. He realized that he was uneasy with the women along this time. He had traveled with his wife in the past enough that it surprised him that he was anxious on this trip. Maybe having a daughter and daughter-in-law with them was what triggered his concern.

"Pa." It was Thomas. "We got the tents up. Ma said she doesn't need us, so can I take Molly over to the rock?" There were still a couple hours of daylight left, and Kade knew that Molly wanted to see the names chiseled in the rock. They were laying over at least one day, but the young can't wait. She wanted to see it today.

Kade turned and walked down the slight slope to the campsite. "Take your rifle with and keep it handy," he said, adding, "and ride over, don't walk."

"Sure, Pa." Thomas gave him a curious look, but Kade just nodded slightly toward the women and Thomas left the topic alone. He called to Molly and Lathe, and they went for their horses.

"What did you see?" Jake came up to Kade to ask. Sabra looked up from her fire to listen as well. She had lived with Kade long enough to pick up on his worry.

"The herd crossed tracks a few miles out," Kade replied, looking toward the west. "I was on the lead side of the herd and saw the tracks before our cattle covered them. The tracks were heading west."

"Shod horses?" Jake inquired.

"Shod and by the shape of 'em, no tracks of mules, I think. Might be nothin' but a small party heading west, but you'd think they'd be needing pack animals. I heard tell of pirates along the trail last year causin' some trouble with the small caravans," Kade looked west. "Iffen they be pirates, they've seen our dust and will circle around to the west and come from that way. Iffen they be California bound, then I am worryin' fer nothin'."

"Never hurts to be cautious," Jake replied. "I was going to take Anna to the rock, but I can wait until tomorrow, too."

"You go, son, but take your gun and keep your ears open. I'll let you know iffen I need you."

Jake looked toward Sabra, then back to Kade. "Anna remembers this place. She said her brother climbed the rock with a bunch of other boys. She wants to search for his name, maybe. She isn't sure that he chiseled it in, but she'd like to look."

Sabra and Kade watched the young couple mount up and head to the massive turtle shaped rock sitting in the middle of the plains. They had climbed it themselves when they came on their first trading trip together. Sabra slipped her hand inside Kade's shirt, running her fingers up and down his back.

"You remember climbing up there that first year?" she asked, looking up at him.

Kade grinned down at her. "Jake was sleepin' an' Tom said he'd stay an' watch him," Kade drew her close to him, "but iffen I remember just right, we didn't do much sightseeing up there."

Kade kept a watchful eye out. He saw the young folk going up the rock, disappearing over the top. They had their horses tethered to scrub brush out of sight. The afternoon was beginning to cool when, just as Kade thought that he was worrying for nothing, he saw them. Riders rode toward them from the western skyline. The sun was starting to set and would soon be in the Welles' eyes. Kade watched the approaching riders. First, they were just tiny dots, but as they got closer, he could count seven.

"Sabra, get on your horse and bring me mine," he ordered, his eyes never wavering from the distant figures. The riders were now about a mile away. Kade had chosen a decent place to see approaching riders, but not much in the way of protection. The area was flat other than the big rock. Kade cast around for banks to lie behind.

"It might be nothing," he told Sabra. "But we are going to be ready. I am between the riders and the cattle, so if they fancy them, they have to go through me," Kade looked toward the rock. "But I reckon they might try for the horses. With horses, they can travel fast."

Kade cast his gaze around the land. "Start the horses toward the rock. If they are up to no good, they will split, send some my way an' some after you an' the horses. They probably will think it is just the two of us." Kade paused, thinking. "If they split, I will fire a shot. That will alert the boys. We can catch them in a bit of a crossfire if the boys come out from behind the rock. You get to the girls an' get them mounted an' help you drive the horses. Get'em the hell away from here."

"You want us to find a place to shoot from too?" Sabra asked, for all the women in the family were familiar with a rifle.

"No, you take the horses way off, an' you can see how it goes. I think I will be fine with the boys." Now Kade turned from watching the approaching riders to looking directly at Sabra. "If it don't go well, you take the girls, leave the horse herd, an' ride like hell," Kade was as serious as Sabra had ever seen him. "You understand what I am saying? There ain't horses alive that can keep up with ours. If it goes wrong, you get the girls out."

"But Kade, we . . ." Sabra didn't get any more out before Kade cut her off.

"Sabra," he said levelly but with dead seriousness, "get the girls out of here. I mean it." He paused. "Hell, probably some lost pilgrims an' we are worrying bout nothing. But jest in case." He let his thoughts drift off. "Let's jest see how their stick floats before we worry too much. Go now," he finished.

Kade saw Sabra reach the horse band and get them moving, pushing them into a long trot. The horses were enjoying the grass and the rest, and it took a little to get them started again. The riders were closer now but still a half-mile distant. Kade got his horse in position, watching what the riders would do. Sabra was halfway to the rock when Kade saw the riders split. Kade's rifle barked, and he saw that Sabra pushed the horses harder, wanting to reach the horses near the kids.

Kade watched the riders advance. Three came toward him, and four went after the horse herd. They had kicked their horses into a gallop and were now advancing more quickly. Kade lay his rifle across his horse's saddle, taking a bead on the lead rider. This was one of those times he was glad for a well-trained horse. It would stand stock-still while he fired.

Kade waited until he was sure the rider was in range, then carefully squeezed the trigger. The lead rider fell from his horse. The remaining riders split, and finding a swell to get protection, they were off their horses and disappeared from sight. Kade slapped his horse on the rear to get him out of the way of bullets and dropped behind a small cut bank. Crawling along it, he peeked up from a different spot. Kade glanced toward the rock and saw Jake appear at the top alone, rifle in hand. Jake stood, taking aim and Kade heard the shot, then saw one of the four riders advancing toward the horse herd fall also. Two down, five left.

Kade saw Sabra had made Independence Rock with the horses, and the herd disappeared behind it. He thought he could see the girls mounting, then heard shots coming from the brush at the bottom of the rock. Thomas and Lathe must be there now. The three pirates pursuing the herd were off their horses now, returning fire. Suddenly, Kade saw Jake, who was descending the rock stagger and fall. Kade knew Jake was hit but when Jake fell, Kade saw his son roll, gripping the rifle as he fell. There was some relief there; dead men don't keep their guns with them.

Kade wanted to watch to see where Jake ended up, but he knew he had to watch his hair. Instead, Kade looked for the two outlaws on the ground closest to him to pop their heads up. It was a waiting game, pinned down as he was, while he knew his son was probably bleeding at the bottom of the granite. Kade heard gunfire break out from below the rock and saw two riders, skirts flying, heading out after the horses. That would be Sabra and one of the girls. There should be a third girl and after a few minutes and a volley of shots, he saw the third ride out. The women rode to a distant hillside where they could hold up and watch.

Just then, one of the two outlaws closest to him popped up to fire. Kade was ready and squeezed off a shot. It was short, spitting up dust in front of the outlaw who disappeared again. There must have been some decisions made then by the pirates because Kade saw the outlaws break cover and run for their horses that were ground tied behind them. They kept the horses between them and Kade as they mounted and made their retreat. Kade had a fleeting thought of shooting the horse, but he hated to shoot a good horse. It wasn't the horse's fault he had scum for an owner. But when the pirates mounted, Kade got off one more shot and thought he might have winged one rider.

Kade stood up to get a better view of what was going on in the distance. He saw the other three outlaws also getting on their horses. It appeared one needed help, but they all got mounted and fled. A shot rang off at the retreating figures, and one of the three jerked, then spurred his horse. From the way he was riding, Kade suspected the outlaw might have an arm or shoulder wound.

Kade wasted no time in gathering his own horse and heading for the rock. He saw that the women, seeing the outlaws heading out, were coming in on a run. Kade came upon Lathe and Thomas first as they were hurrying on foot toward Jake. Kade spurred his horse ahead of them.

Jake lay at the bottom of Independence Rock and sat against it, cradling his rifle in his lap. As Kade approached, Jake looked over at him and grinned. Immense relief washed over Kade, but concern remained. Jake's shirt was soaked with blood. His face was cut and bleeding where he had bashed it on the rock as he rolled toward the plains.

"I'm alright, Pa," Jake started. "Just a scratch, I think. Hurts like a bitch, though."

"They always do, son," Kade returned. "Let me look at it."

Kade had just gotten the shirt cut off Jake's shoulder when Sabra and Anna rode up. They were both near frantic with worry. Sabra calmed first, but concern was still written all over her face. Jake had a clean-through shot below his shoulder bone. If he didn't get infected, it would heal, but he was losing a lot of blood. Sabra tore part of her skirt off and began pressing it to the back of Jake where the bullet exited, and Anna did the same under his shoulder in the front.

"Pa, are we just going to let them go?" It was Thomas who spoke, although he watched Jake as the women worked on him.

"I think I might just track them some an' make sure they keep going," Kade said thoughtfully. "I think there is two sprawled out there in the grass dead, an' three that might be wounded. You see anything different from your angle?"

Thomas thought a moment. "You got one and Jake got one and I haven't seen them move. I think I got one in the arm. Then Lathe and Molly both were aiming at that one that had to be helped on his horse. At least one of their shots found their mark."

"Molly was shooting?" That must have been why there were only two of the women riding off at first.

"I told her to get her horse and follow," Sabra said over her shoulder. "I thought she was behind me."

"Pa," Molly spoke up defensively. "You didn't teach me to shoot just to run away, did you?"

Kade just closed his eyes a minute and took a breath. Women were going to be the death of him yet. He had to remember that she did leave as ordered, only not right away.

"Pa, as soon as Anna and ma get me wrapped up, I'll ride out with you to track those hombres," Jake spoke from the ground. That is when the storm broke.

"You will not!" Anna demanded, her distress that Jake was injured overcoming her reluctance to make decisions or give orders. "You will stay."

"Anna, I am all right," Jake spoke soothingly to her. "We won't be gone long." Jake tried to struggle to his feet, but the effort was too much for him.

Fear and fury were clouded on Anna's face. "You will stay here." Anna stamped her foot. "You will not go! You will not!"

Confused, Jake stared at his wife. He had never seen her like this. Never had she even given her opinion to him much less an order. Yet here she was so mad she was stamping her foot.

"But . . ." Jake looked to Kade for support but only saw a slow grin appear on his father's face.

"Son, I reckon when a woman speaks to you in that tone of voice, you'd best listen," Kade turned to Thomas. "Get your horse, Tom, an' we will trail those bandits a bit an' make sure they keep going." Then turning to the rest, he continued, "Lathe an' Molly go gather the horses an' cattle. Get them bedded down. We will lose the light soon."

Kade turned back to Sabra and Anna. "You need help getting Jake back to camp?" he asked.

"Pa, I don't need . . ." Jake started, but Anna cut him short.

"You will stay down until we get you a horse and you will ride it back. Now sit!" And this time, Anna shook her finger at him and pointed to the ground. Jake stayed put.

Kade rode off then. He had a feeling Anna had things pretty much under control.

Kade and Thomas rode in after dark. They had rounded up the two horses of the dead bandits and led them with them to save time. They trailed the outlaws a couple of miles until they came on a third body. This man had been gut shot, had a hole through his arm, and then also was shot squarely between the eyes. Kade was pretty sure this was the man that Lathe and Molly shot. They must have both hit the man, who either was slowing down the retreating pirates or had begged them to put him out of his misery. A gut shot was not something he was going to recover from. In any case, the man was now dead. Thomas helped as Kade loaded the dead man on one of the spare horses. Kade was pretty sure the four outlaws that retreated would keep going. Two, for sure, were wounded. They wouldn't be back.

Kade and Thomas found the two dead men that were slain near camp and brought them back as well. They laid canvas over them for the night.

"We'll plant them in the morning," Kade commented mildly to Thomas. "I don't feel like diggin' a grave tonight. We kin do that at first light before they get to stinking in the heat." Then turning, Kade went on to their camp.

"Molly, you and Lathe did a good job of shooting," Kade told them as he came into the firelight. "Your man had two wounds on him, so you each found your mark. Then the fatal shot came from his friends when they left him. Live and die by the gun, I reckon."

Kade went to Jake and Anna's tent. The flap was open, so he stooped to look in. Jake was lying on the ground with Anna fussing over him. Jake looked up at Kade.

"Think maybe you all was right about me staying back. I am feeling some poorly," Jake said. "I should be up and around tomorrow."

Kade grinned, "Well, we will wait and see about that. Right now, you get some rest. We have no reason to hurry. We can stay put a few days and let you heal." Then just before turning to leave the tent opening, Kade said, "Good shooting, son."

⚜

The following morning, Kade and Thomas dug one grave and rolled the dead outlaws into it.

"Guess it is the Christian thing to do," Thomas commented. "But I'd almost just as soon see the buzzards pick them clean."

"Reckon I could feel much the same way," Kade replied, "but for our womenfolk. Packing women makes us civilized, I reckon. No sense fighting it."

Kade had gone through the dead men's pockets, finding little except a few dollars. The two horses, though, wore good saddles, and in the saddle packs were some plunder worth keeping, blankets, and powder, and shot. The dead men's guns were with them, and Kade gathered them up. These could be traded. Kade would keep the saddles. Anna was riding a borrowed saddle of Jim Bates' on this trip so she could have one. The other would be a spare when they needed one.

Jake was feverish in the morning, and his shoulder was inflamed, but Sabra hoped that was normal for this kind of wound. They washed and bandaged it again in the morning and made Jake stay in bed. This time he didn't argue. There was healing in sleeping.

Thomas came in about noon and said that one of their pack mules had thrown a shoe. He decided to fit a new one on since they were just lying around anyway. Kade took over the herd watch, and Thomas caught the mule. Tying it to a tree, he began the process of nailing the shoe on. But the old mule was not one of the easiest mules to work with. Just as the last nail went in, the mule pulled his foot away, and as quick as lightning, he whirled and kicked Thomas squarely in the thigh, knocking him down.

Cussing the mule, Thomas dragged himself up. His leg hurt, and he had trouble standing. Riding in from the herd, Lathe saw it all and was there to help Thomas hobble into the camp. Sabra examined Thomas and didn't think the leg was broken, but it was sorely injured. He, too, was sent to his bed.

When Kade rode in later, he found both of his sons laid up. Lathe and Kade would share night herd duties, with Molly and Sabra watching the herd in the early evening and the early morning to give the men a break. *Yes,* Kade thought, *this was a good place to layover.*

CHAPTER 8

Visitors – 1875

B y late afternoon, it was evident that Jake's injury was giving him problems. The fever continued, the wound was red and angry and painful. Sabra and Anna tried cleaning it with some of the whiskey they carried and put clean new bandages on it. All they could hope for was that they could keep it from getting infected if it wasn't already. Jake lay in the shade of a scrub, feeling helpless as the women fussed with him. Kade, Lathe, and Molly took turns riding on the herd and keeping watch, not only for more bandits but also for a wagon train. If a train came along, they would want to make sure their herd was distant enough not to mix.

Sabra had the fire going and supper on when Lathe came riding hard in from the herd.

"Kade," he called as he approached, "riders coming in from the east."

Kade stood up and looked to see what Lathe saw. The camp came alive as all eyes watched the distant horizon. Kade searched for what Lathe had seen, finding the dots moving toward them. As they came closer, it appeared to be seven riders and they were leading pack animals. They were not coming fast.

"Think it may be traders or travelers," Kade spoke, thinking out loud, "probably pilgrims, but after yesterday, we better be ready." He looked around the camp. "Molly and Sabra, you better get on the horses. Anna, too."

"No," Sabra said firmly. "I have two sons here that are hurt. I am not running. I can shoot."

"Me too," Molly said. "Pa, you taught us. You know we can do it."

Kade took a deep breath to calm himself. Damn women. "Go get the two saddled horses and have them with you. If I say go, you go, you hear?" he spoke firmly, looking at Sabra. "Lathe, give Anna your horse."

"I will not leave Jake," Anna was firm as well. "I will stay."

Kade studied Anna for a minute before nodding. He wasn't going to win this battle. "Lathe, spread out that way," Kade indicated to the north. "Molly and Sabra stay behind me."

"Pa, I can shoot. There is nothing wrong with my arms," Thomas said. "Molly, help me, and we will go out south a bit." Kade studied the two, then nodded. Thomas, leaning on Molly for support, spread out south of the camp.

Jake was struggling to his feet. "Anna, get my gun," he said.

"No, Jake, you lie down," Anna insisted. But this time, Jake just shook his head, climbing to his feet.

"Not this time, honey," he replied firmly. "You need to help me now. Get my gun." She gave him a hard look but turned and went for his rifle. When she returned, she helped him to a scrub tree. Here he stood leaning on Anna and propped the gun on the crotch of the tree, using his uninjured shoulder and arm.

Kade looked at his family, spread out in a line, waiting. They were ready. He hoped this time it was a false alarm. He had two sons hurt already. He didn't want more trouble. It weighed on a man to have family with him in times of trouble. Silently, they watched the approaching riders. As they came closer, Kade stepped forward to meet the lead riders and waited.

The first rider looked to be a mountain man by the buckskin pants and moccasins that he wore. He looked about forty, give or take some years, and was sporting a mustache and trimmed beard. Kade had a suspicion he was a guide to the others. Behind him rode three men together in a line. They were well-dressed in store-bought hunting clothes. In the rear rode an Indian and two more men, who were not as richly dressed as the first three. The closer this group came, the better Kade felt. He did not think these were bandits. Still, he waited.

"Kin we come to yer fire?" called the mountain man, pulling his horse to a halt.

"Come slow then," Kade answered, "and leave your hands free."

The riders came forward until they were near the camp. The oldest of the well-dressed threesome rode forward with the guide.

"You expectin' trouble?" the mountain man asked, looking up and down at the line at the family standing ready and unsmiling with their firearms.

"We have had trouble," Kade replied, nodding toward the mound of the grave in the distance. "Don't reckon we want more. Jest being careful. What's yer business?"

"I'm guiding these gents, doing some hunting," the man replied. "We're just passing through, looking for game. Saw your smoke."

"Is that grave some of your party?" the older gentleman asked. He had an English accent. "Have you had Indian trouble?" he spoke with refinement and was stately and aristocratic.

"Bandits," Kade replied. "There are three under there. Jest my son hit," Kade nodded toward Jake, who was starting to lean heavily on Anna. Sabra, lowering her rifle, went to help get Jake back to his blankets.

"Was he shot then?" the gentleman asked.

"Shoulder wound, in and out," Kade replied. "Not sure it's healing right."

"One of my men has a medicine chest and some medical training. I could send him over later. Mind if we camp near?" the older man asked. "We have traveled far enough today."

"We would appreciate having your man look at Jake," Sabra spoke up, coming to stand beside Kade. "We are worried about Jake but don't have any medicine with us. And you are welcome to share our meal. We have plenty of meat." Kade saw the Englishmen look at Sabra with surprise at her clear and precise diction.

The guide nodded to Sabra at the offer, then turned and rode off a a short distance, searching for a good spot for a camp. Leaving the three Englishmen visiting with Kade, the rest of the party followed the guide to make camp.

"I am Richard Crowden," the older gentleman said, "and this is my son, Jackson, and my nephew, Rudolph. We are touring your great American west."

The three men dismounted their horses and stood visiting. There was a family resemblance among the three men. Of average height, they held themselves straight as they stood. All three sported reddish-blond hair and ruddy complexions. They were handsome men. Richard and his nephew had mustaches, but the younger man was clean shaven. Both of the younger men were in their twenties, Kade judged, but the nephew appeared older than the son. There the resemblance ended. Richard and his son had open friendly faces, interested in their surroundings and the people they were speaking with. The nephew, Rudolph, didn't crack a smile or a word. He looked disdainfully around the camp with its fire and kettle resting in the ashes.

The Crowdens were from England, and it was apparent from their dress and manners that they were from the aristocratic class. The Crowdens had heard of the American buffalo and the great herds of them roaming the plains. While the actual classification of these animals was bison, the animals were known across North America as buffalo, and had been since the 1600s. The great herds were becoming scarce these days, overhunted by both aristocratic hunters, plainsmen, settlers, and buffalo hunters. The Crowdens were hoping to be able to hunt these animals, as well as the variety of wild game found on the western prairies and in the mountains.

The mountain man was the party's guide, the other two men their servants, and the Indian was hired to help with the animals. The Crowdens had some fine horses they were riding, blooded stock. Richard Crowden was curious about coming upon a family and herd of livestock in this place.

Kade also offered the hospitality of their food and fire. "We have plenty of meat and biscuits, not fancy fare, but you are welcome to join us," he said. "Thomas brought in a nice young antelope yesterday, and Lathe got a deer, so there is variety."

"Thank you for the invitation, but ours is probably in the making," Richard Crowden answered. "However, we will come back with our man when we get settled." With that, the three men led their horses off to join the rest of their party.

Kade sent Molly to the herd. She was reluctant to go, not wanting to miss the activity going on in the next camp, but Kade was firm. Lathe needed rest before taking a night watch. The rest of the family all watched the preparations being made in the new camp. The workmen were stripping equipment and packs from the mules. The Indian took care of the animals after they were unsaddled. The two servants unpacked the mules and then set up tents and a table.

The guide came back first, striding silently on moccasin-clad feet with a ground-covering walk. He was a plain man, carrying no extra weight but thick muscles rippled under his linsey-woolen shirt. His eyes roamed the countryside as he walked, watchful. He carried a jug with him.

"I'd sure take you up on the supper invite," he said, grinning at Sabra. "I am hankering for some plain food, and when you said meat, well, I reckon I have had enough of the fancy fare that is served over there."

"You are most welcome," she replied, smiling at him. "We have plenty."

The guide looked at Kade, "You seem a man who would take a nip with me. My name is Sam."

Kade nodded, "Kade Welles," he said, offering his hand to Sam. Then gesturing at his family grouped around him, he named them all. Lathe and Thomas joined them, and they all sat and cut strips of meat from the roasts hanging over the fire. Sabra brought out a pan of biscuits, but she didn't sit with the men. She and Anna were too worried about Jake to rest before the fire. He lay feverish, propped up against a log. The effort of standing had taken its toll on what little energy he still had.

"Seems I have heard of a Jake Welles," Sam commented, looking over at Jake. "He trade at Ft. Laramie some?" he asked, looking back at Kade.

"Jake started going with me about ten years ago. He makes the trip there every year now," Kade replied, thinking back over the years, "I've traded at Ft. Laramie for nigh onto forty years or more."

"I pulled into Ft. Laramie a few years back, and the soldiers were still repairing things from a fight," Sam grinned at the remembering. "Seems some half-breed took offense at something said to him. Talk was it was three against one until the sutler came along with a shovel and knocked one of the three over the head." Sam looked over at Jake, who was following the conversation, "That mixed-blood must have been you."

Jake grinned weakly, "I remember that fight. I didn't start it, though."

"I asked the sutler why he stepped in to help," Sam went on, smiling. "Sutler said it jest wasn't right three against one, and he hadn't finished trading with you yet. He said your money was good."

"That is one reason I go there every year," Jake said. "I can trust that trader."

From the other camp came a shout, "Tenny, you going to eat?"

"No," Sam replied, turning to call back, "I'll take my meal here." When he turned back to the Welles, he noticed Kade watching him as if surprised.

"You are Samuel Tenbrook," Kade remarked. It was a statement, not a question.

Sam studied Kade before replying. "You know my name," he said warily.

"Your mother is Clara Tenbrook?"

The wariness left Sam's eyes. Instead, he became very still before asking, "You know my mother?"

"She married my old partner," Kade answered. "They live across the valley from our cabin." Kade hesitated before adding, "She's been searching the skyline for you since she came west, hoping to see you come riding up."

"Hell, man, I thought she was in Oregon. I got a letter at Ft. Laramie years ago from her saying she was going to the Oregon Country," Sam drank from the jug and then passed it to Kade. "I been out that way twice over the years but never came on anyone who had heard of her. I figured she may not have made the trip alive, being that she was alone."

"We met her wagon train about this same time in '52," Kade explained. "She and Tom came to an understanding, and she came home with him. She sent a letter on with the train to be left at Ft. Hall for you. It would have told of her intentions." Kade took a drink before adding, "They been living together right at twenty-three years. She's happy with Tom."

"She deserves some happiness," Sam said. "She sure as hell didn't get any of that with my old man." Sam seemed deep in thought for a while, puffing on his pipe. "When I get through with these Englishmen," he said, "I'd like to find your valley. I'd like to visit her."

Richard Crowden and a man with a small wooden box walked up then, followed by Richard's son and nephew. Kade got up and joined Sabra, who led them to Jake. Jake was dozing but came awake as he heard them approach. He was pale and hot with fever. The man knelt beside Jake and opened his box. Taking out scissors, he told Jake he was going to cut off the bandages to see the wound. Jake just nodded. He knew this bullet hole was trouble.

"I worked for years with a military doctor," the man said. "Hopefully, I can help."

The man poked and prodded the wound, then turned Jake on his side to look at the back. The lesion seemed to be draining from the back but not from the front.

"I think the wound is infected here in front," the man said. "I am going to have to take the scab off and see if there is any drainage. It's going to hurt some."

"Hell, it hurts now," Jake spoke softly. "Go to diggin'. It ain't going to get better this way."

Just watching, Kade knew it hurt. He knew his son too. There was no outward expression of pain, only a twitch in his jaw and the closing of his eyes. He lay silent as the man scraped the scab, and then pressing out pus when he had it open. The man put some powders on the wound that burned. Jake never moved, but his breathing became slight and shallow. Anna sat beside him, holding his arm, helpless to do more. Finally, it was over, and new bandages were going on.

"We can see how that looks in the morning, but I have seen this work for other injuries that looked like this," the man said, packing up his supplies. "I'll come back after breakfast."

"Thanks, doc," Jake whispered weakly. The little man just waved his thanks away and headed back to the adjoining camp.

It was then that Kade noticed the three Englishmen who had come over from their camp. He invited the men to sit at the fire and took out a pipe. "I don't think we have done introductions," Kade said. "My wife, Sabra," he gestured toward the fire, "and my daughter, Molly, is out with the herd. My son, Jake, there who was shot yesterday, and that is his wife, Anna. Then this is our son, Thomas," he pointed his pipe toward Thomas, who was reclining against a log, sore leg stretched out before him. "He got kicked by a renegade mule. It was not a good day yesterday for the Welles', but reckon it could have been worse," he said thoughtfully.

"Better a mule than a bullet," Thomas interrupted, smiling.

"I do believe you are correct, young man," Richard Crowden smiled. "And you have a third son?" Richard indicated Lathe.

"This is the son of friends of ours who are in business with us," Sabra explained. "Lathe enjoys these trips more than farming with his folks," she laughed, winking at Lathe. "His great uncle was a mountain man, and I think Lathe would follow in his footsteps if he could."

"We live four or five days south of here," Kade told the visitors. "Been building up a herd there an' raising some horses. We been bringin' fresh stock to the trail to meet the wagon trains for twenty-four years. Any year now, I expect the trading business to dry up. If no trains come through soon, an' when both of my sons can travel, we will head to Ft. Laramie an' sell our cattle there." Kade offered the jug to the visitors, but they politely turned him down. "I planned to start east to-morrow, heading toward Ft. Laramie, but we're a might worried about Jake. Think we will lay over until he is on the mend. We got time."

The men sat and smoked, talking quietly, while Sabra bustled around, and Anna sat with Jake, who thankfully slept. When it began to get dark, Kade sent Lathe to the herd to relieve Molly. Kade didn't like Molly out with the herd after dark, and he also knew she would be anxious to come in and see the visitors. She met so few people outside the valley, and most of them were just old trappers still drifting through the mountains.

Sabra had a plate of food ready for Molly when she came to the camp, and Kade called her over to sit by him as she ate. "This is my daughter, Molly," he told the men. "She was here when you first came, but she had to go out to the herd right away."

"If I remember right," Richard commented, smiling at her, "she was carrying a rifle and looked like she knew how to use it."

"Pa insisted that we know how to shoot," Molly said, wanting to be part of the conversation. "I'm a fair shot."

"She does well enough," Kade said, with not just a little pride in his voice. "She and Lathe sighted on the same outlaw yesterday, and they both found their mark," he grinned at Molly. "You two need to talk to each other more and not waste a bullet."

Molly just grinned back and then turned her attention to the visitors. She looked across at the man she remembered as being Rudolph.

"If I remember right," she said, "you are Rudolph? Do they call you Rudy then?" she asked politely.

The Englishman looked haughtily at her for a moment before answering stiffly, "They call me . . . Rudolph," he emphasized the name.

Surprise came into Molly's face, then a flash of anger. She looked up and down Rudolph before replying with sarcasm, "Yes, I can see that now." Then she turned away from him as if dismissing him.

It was Jackson who lightened the moment. "Perhaps you remember my name?" he asked politely.

"Jackson," Molly replied cautiously.

Jackson winked at Molly before adding, "But sometimes I'm called Jack."

He was rewarded with an impish smile from Molly. Her smile lit her pretty face and her eyes sparkled. "Yes," she said to Jackson, looking him up and down, "I can see that now." The words might have been the same, but the tone of voice was completely different from what she had used with Rudolph.

Kade looked at the two young people, smiling at each other. He knew this day would come when his daughter would spar with a young man. He had hoped it wouldn't come so soon. At least this young man was not long in their territory. England was a long way away. Kade wouldn't lose Molly soon.

The evening passed quickly. Jake had drifted off to a restless sleep with Anna sitting guard beside him. Kade commented that he had night duty in a few hours, so the visitors took themselves away. Before they went, they arranged for both Sam and Kade to take them on a hunting excursion the next day. The Englishmen were hoping they might see a buffalo. Kade mentioned that buffalo were getting scarce now, but they might find some since no wagon trains had come in yet. He had seen some buffalo sign along the trail.

The next morning dawned to new hope in the Welles' camp. Sabra went out before the sun rose to watch the herd, and Kade came in to get another hour of sleep. They were relieved to see that Jake's fever was down. He wanted to sit up so Kade dragged a log closer into the camp so Jake could lean on it. The best indication of Jake's recovery, though, was that Jake was hungry. That had to be a sure sign he was mending. Anna, preparing breakfast, was beginning to smile again. The camp woke slowly as the sun rose in the eastern sky.

Eventually, Lathe went back to the herd, and Sabra came in. Kade was up and had spitted some meat over the fire to eat as they got hungry. As both camps came awake, the man with the medicine chest returned and was happy with Jake's improvement. He felt the bandages could stay on until evening, and so saying, he took himself back to his own duties.

It wasn't too long afterward that the Crowdens returned. As the older gentleman stood talking to Kade, Rudolph strolled over to look down on Jake. When Anna met his eyes questioningly, Rodolph spoke, disdain in his tone, "How is it a white woman is with a half-breed?"

Anna might not have much experience with white people yet, but she recognized the insult in this man's tone. She bristled but glanced down at Jake.

Jake looked up with hooded eyes at the man, then said flatly, "I bought her."

Anna picked it up from there, "I was only worth one pony then. Now I am worth three ponies, or four." She held her head high as she turned her back on the man. Not knowing what to say to this, Rudolph simply stared, then turned and joined his uncle.

Kade and Sam decided that they would take the three Englishmen out for a hunt before the day got too hot. Thomas felt good enough to watch the herd for a while, but he chose the easiest horse to ride to avoid being jostled. Lathe decided he was going to get some extra sleep. The hunting party went to gather horses and guns and were soon on their way.

The hunt went very well. Jackson shot an antelope. He was a good shot, Kade admitted, and he listened to direction well. Rudolph, on the other hand, was impudent and belligerent, and only wounded his antelope, even though the animal was not moving when he made his shot. The antelope took off at a wild, staggering run, and Kade quickly brought rifle to shoulder, sighted, and shot. The antelope fell dead.

"He would have died soon," Rudolph said angrily. "No sense wasting shot."

Kade looked at him with disgust but only said mildly, "We hunt here for food, not sport. And we don't leave an animal to suffer if we can help it." Then he turned his back on the man and went to help Sam skin and gut the two animals.

When they came on a small herd of buffalo, Kade pointed out a yearling to Richard. "Reckon it is your turn," he said.

Richard asked advice, listened, and then began to sight down his rifle. Softly he whispered to Kade, "I'm not the shot my son is, but hopefully better than my nephew. Would you back me up, just in case?"

Kade grinned and nodded. He had the distinct feeling that there wasn't a lot of love between uncle and nephew. He wondered why Richard had Rudolph along on this trip.

Richard got the buffalo. Rudolph wanted to shoot one too, but Kade put a stop to that. "There are not many of these animals out here because of wasteful hunting like that," he said angrily. "We don't need more meat now than what we have. You want more hunting, you do it with someone else," Kade could see that the man was angry at his words, but Kade didn't care. He just about had enough of this pompous Englishman.

When the hunting party got back to camp, Kade helped the women rig up a rack to smoke some buffalo meat on. Since they were laying over anyway, they could take the time to preserve the meat. There was a powerful amount of meat to be shared between the two camps and eaten before it spoiled. It would spoil fast in the summer heat.

In the early afternoon, Molly went out to get Blue. They had brought the five-year-old blue roan stud along to get more training and experience. Blue would hopefully be used as one of their herd studs in the future. But they wanted to know the horse was worth his salt before they turned him in to breed mares. They would ride and use the animal for another year before they would put him out to stud, if he lived up to their expectations, that is. Jake or Thomas did most of the training on the stud, but Molly rode him often when the boys were busy. She liked the horse, and with no mares along on the trip, he was tractable and willing.

"I can ride Blue on the herd tonight, Pa," she commented as she picketed him close. "He hasn't had much work since we got here."

Blue was a fine animal. He had the breeding of Sabra's original blooded mares that she had brought from the east more than twenty years ago. Those mares, mated with tough Indian ponies, and then with animals Kade or Jake purchased at the fort, were the bloodlines of Blue. He was a sturdy stud, without being heavy. He had good bones, strong and well-made, and a deep heart girth. He had a fine head with wide-set eyes. Smaller than the Crowdens' royally bred thoroughbreds, Blue was quick and sure footed. And best of all, this horse could flat out fly yet was easy to handle.

As the afternoon sun lowered in the sky, Sam and the three Englishmen returned to the Welles camp. It was hot but not unbearable, and the family and visitors sat comfortably in the shade and visited. Even Jake was awake and sat leaning against his log. His fever was gone, but he had no strength yet, so he was content to just listen to the conversation around him.

"That is one nice looking horse picketed there," remarked Jackson, noticing Blue. "He's a stud?"

"He'll be our herd stud next year," Kade replied, looking over at the horse, "iffen he lives up to our expectations. He's home raised. His breeding goes back to the original four mares Sabra brought west with her nigh onto twenty-eight years ago. She mated them to an Indian pony stud. They make strong, fleet animals."

"I suppose for here in the west, he is considered fine," Rudolph sniffed, "but he sure doesn't hold a candle to the fine animal I brought with me."

"I wouldn't count Blue out," Kade said mildly. "He isn't as big as your horse, but he is quick and has endurance."

"Would you like to put a wager on that?" Rudolph asked belligerently. "He couldn't touch my horse for speed."

Kade looked at Rudolph, sizing him up. "Iffen I had a jockey for that horse, I would," Kade replied, "but it appears both my sons are laid up at the moment."

"I'll ride him, Pa!" Molly was intent on the conversation.

"Now, Molly girl," Kade soothed, "I know you'd like to but not in a race."

"I can do it, Pa!" Molly insisted, "You know I ride Blue all the time."

"She can," Sabra interjected. "She is as good a rider as either of the boys. You know that."

Kade looked at his wife and daughter and just shook his head. Strong-willed women seemed his lot in life. "Maybe I should just ride him myself, or Lathe," he suggested.

"Pa, you are too old!" Molly was adamant. "I would do a better job. And Lathe doesn't ride our young horses. You know that."

Kade looked over at Sabra. "I am not that old, am I?" he asked her with a quizzical look.

Sabra smiled fondly at Kade. "Well, no, not really, but you don't ride Blue, and Molly does. She can do it, Kade. Let her fly."

Kade knew he was beaten. He knew Lathe was not yet the horseman his sons and daughter were. He knew his daughter was capable, but damn, he hated to see his little girl grow up, and he really hated seeing her take part in things that could hurt her. This would be a grown-up man's race, and she was just a girl. But Kade nodded and looked over at Rudolph.

"Iffen you want a race, you got it."

Rudolph was ecstatic. "I will wager you twenty-five American dollars that my horse will win. Easiest money I will ever make."

Twenty-five dollars was a lot of money to the Welles, but Kade didn't hesitate. This English bastard had gotten under his skin. He had faith in the horse and Molly. He nodded agreement at Rudolph.

It was decided then. The race would be in an hour, before the sun set too low in the sky. It would be run from camp for a half-mile east to a small grove of trees. The riders would curve around the far side of the trees and return the half-mile to camp. Kade and Molly mounted and rode the course to look over the ground. Rudolph was going to have the Indian ride his horse. The Indian, too, went over the course, Rudolph riding along.

"Molly girl," Kade cautioned as they rode around the grove of trees, "you stay clean clear away from the other horse behind these trees." Kade was serious and Molly sensed it. "If there is trouble, it will be here, out of sight from us. I don't trust that English snob. He'll promise the Indian something to get this win any way he can. I don't trust Rudolph to play fair. So, whatever you do, don't go around these trees side by side with him. I'd rather lose the race than see you or the horse hurt."

Molly nodded. She understood what her father was telling her. If she rode next to the Indian as they passed out of sight, he could try to unseat her or run into her horse to trip it. If they lost because of it, it would be her word against his, and Rudolph would claim they were sore losers. She had faith in her horse, but she would be careful.

At the designated time, Kade had the stud saddled waiting for Molly. Anna had helped Jake get up to watch the race, and Thomas had limped over to stand by Sabra. Kade looked for Molly and then groaned when he saw her. She emerged from the tent in that knickerbocker riding outfit she had.

"Molly girl," he said, "there's people around!"

"Pa," Molly countered, "you don't expect me to ride in a race with my skirts flying! I will change as soon as we are done."

Kade looked helplessly at Sabra. He knew Molly was right, but in his mind, the outfit was scandalous. Sabra remembered a time, long ago, when she first came out west with old Jacob. Kade had objected violently to her being in the mountains. When she asked Jacob why Kade even cared since at the time, he had just met her, Jacob had answered, "Some men are ruled by what they thinks is right an' wrong, an' Kade be one o' them men." Kade was still a lot like that. Sabra just smiled and patted Kade on the arm.

"Breathe, Papa," she soothed, "this is not civilization, even if there are Englishmen here."

The riders mounted. Rudolph's horse was a big, rangy thoroughbred that he had shipped from England. The horse danced with anticipation. The Indian rode without a saddle and sat easily upon the horse.

"This is my daughter riding," Kade cautioned Rudolph, "I don't want any rough stuff. Let the horses win fair."

"Of course," Rudolph agreed amiably. "There will be no need for that. Your horse won't ever be close enough."

Sam was the starter for the race. He waited until both riders had their horses facing forward. Blue was still, waiting for a cue but the thoroughbred whirled once then straightened, facing forward. Sam dropped his arm, and the horses bolted forward.

Molly and Blue leaped ahead, but in four strides, the thoroughbred came up beside her. She kept Blue at a steady gallop, not pushing him for more yet. There was a long race to be run, and Molly didn't want to lose it by pushing her horse too fast too early. But as she approached the trees, Molly asked Blue for a bit more speed, trying to pull ahead. As her father had cautioned, Molly didn't want to go around the trees with the other horse on her side. But the Indian, sensing her intent, let his horse out too. They raced head-to-head. Molly knew that Blue still had more speed to give but coming up on the trees with too much speed could cause the horse to overshoot the turn.

So, this is what they intended, just like Pa said, Molly thought quickly. Blue was so well trained. She instantly had another plan. She asked for a bit more speed, and the horse beside her increased its pace too. Just as they almost made the trees, Molly cued Blue for collection. While the animal was running too fast to completely shut down, Molly was able to slow him drastically. It is hard for a running horse to collect and slow suddenly, but that was part of Blue's training. Molly gloried in his response. He went from a flat-out run to a collected hand gallop, dropping drastically behind the long-strided thoroughbred. The Indian, seeing her suddenly fall behind, began sawing at the reins of the big thoroughbred. But the long-legged animal could not respond as quickly. As the Indian and his horse swung wide, overshooting the trees, Molly reined Blue behind the big horse, cutting close to the trees as she rounded them, saving precious ground. The thoroughbred was a length beyond before starting to make his turn. She emerged from the trees a full two lengths ahead. She was too far away to hear the Welles camp explode with cheers.

The last half-mile was anticlimactic. Molly never let the other horse regain the lost ground. As she approached the last quarter of a mile, she leaned over Blue, asking him for even more speed. He responded with a burst of speed, and they raced over the finish line a good four lengths in the lead. The Welles camp celebrated with cheers and catcalls.

Rudolph was livid, but Richard and Jackson were smiling and clapping at the performance. They came over to congratulate Molly, who slid from the horse but prodded by Kade, she made a beeline to the tent to change. As she went, though, she was jumping with excitement.

"That's my sister!" Jake laughed, leaning against Anna. "I knew she could do it." Then he winked at his mother, "I taught her everything I know."

Rudolph looked at the exuberant Sabra, smiling as Kade walked off with Blue to cool him off. "I suppose, madam," he growled insolently, "you must have been in very bad straights to marry a squaw man."

The camp went deadly silent. If Kade had been in earshot, there would have been blood spilled at that remark. But Kade was too far off to hear. Jake did hear, and leaning on Anna, he stiffened. Shoulder wound or no, he turned toward the offensive man, but Anna grabbed him before he could make a move.

"Rudolph!" Richard exploded. "Enough!"

It was Sabra who drew herself up and looked at the offensive man. "My husband never had a squaw," she said evenly. "Jake is his adopted son. Jake's father was a respected Ute warrior and a very good man." Sabra looked Rudolph up and down. "Something no one will ever say about you." Then she looked at him defiantly and added, "Jake's father was my husband. Jake is my son."

"Pay up your wager," Richard commanded Rudolph, "and go back to camp. You are not welcome here." He was so angry his voice shook. Then turning to Sabra, he said, "I hope you will not judge us too harshly because of my nephew. I am truly ashamed of his behavior here."

Rudolph reached into a pocket and came out with the twenty-five dollars. He dropped the money on the ground with an insolent sneer and turned stiffly, retreating toward his camp. It was Jackson who picked the money up from the ground and handed it to Sabra.

"I am so sorry, ma'am, for my cousin's words," he said sincerely. Then he turned to Molly as she emerged from the tent, dressed respectably again. "You ran a great race!"

The dark mood was broken. Not having heard the exchange between Rudolph and Sabra, Molly was still flying high with her victory, and her family and the men from the other camp shook her hand and patted her back. Sam picked up the surprised girl and swung her up onto his shoulder where she smiled and laughed. By the time Kade came back from putting the horse away, the celebration was well underway.

Sabra had supper ready with a buffalo roast cooking all afternoon, biscuits in the kettle, and chokecherry jelly for supper. There was enough for both camps, minus Rudolph, who never ventured over again. The English cook brought over tins of food that were sampled by all. He also brought a fiddle, and as the sun went down, the party went on. Lathe, Kade, and even Thomas took turns riding out to the herd, watching that the animals bedded down for the night, but they all wanted to take part in the festivities.

It was Sam who pulled Molly to her feet and started the dance. Then Kade and Sabra joined in. When Jackson claimed Molly, Sam pulled Anna out. At first, Anna shook her head no, but Jake pushed her away and told her to go and have some fun. He would dance with her the next time, he told her. The three women were passed from arm to arm as all the men claimed them for a dance until they finally had to call it a night. The fiddle grew softer, playing slow sounds. The party calmed down, with everyone sitting around the fire in quiet camaraderie.

"We will be heading toward Ft. Bridger tomorrow," Richard told them. "My nephew is going to meet a trader there and travel with him to the California country. From there, he will go to the coast and take passage on a ship home," Richard looked thoughtful. "I will be glad to be finished with him. He is a pompous man. My brother insisted he come with us on this trip. Now I know why. My brother can't stand him either!"

They all laughed at that, and then Richard continued, "If our guide will stay on with us, and if you are willing," he looked at Kade, "we would like to come and see your ranching operation. I am interested in doing some investing in this country. Maybe the cattle business would be a good place to start. Would we be imposing if we visited you in your valley?"

"We would be glad for your company," Kade answered. "And I think your guide would be obliging, too," he said. Then grinning at Sam, he remarked, "Reckon you might want to come for a visit?"

It was decided. The two Crowdens, guided by Sam, would visit the valley after leaving Rudolph and the servants at Ft. Bridger. Kade noticed that his daughter looked particularly happy about that as she sat basking in the attention she was getting. This would undoubtedly be a summer for her to remember.

CHAPTER 9

Change of Plans – 1875

Thomas shared night duty shifts with Kade and Lathe so neither Molly nor Sabra had to go out. Jake wanted to take a shift as well, but Kade and Anna both vetoed that.

"I can ride," Jake protested. "I'm healing."

But Kade was firm. "Get a good night's rest, son," he said. "We need to make some decisions tomorrow, and I'd like you to be rested and be part of them. I'm thinkin' we will need all of us healthy in the next few days."

The morning sun rose with Sabra and Kade enjoying a cup of coffee while most of their camp still slept. Lathe was out with the herd and the rest of their camp were still in their blankets.

"How long has it been since we got up early and could just sit and have a cup of coffee together?" Sabra asked.

Kade sipped his brew before answering, "A long time, it seems. I'm glad the boys are both mending." He grinned at Sabra before adding, "I'm just about done with family outings. It weighs on a man."

Sabra smiled fondly at Kade, "You raised them to take care of themselves, even Molly. We always knew this land could be dangerous. It isn't just you who worries, but I wouldn't let worry rob us of being here together. It's our choice to be here, too."

While they sat, they watched the visitor's camp come alive and begin to tear down tents and pack. As the activity increased, it wasn't long before Richard and Jackson walked over to join them.

"Jackson brought up something last night that I hadn't thought of," Richard began. "There is no reason for the two of us to go on to Ft. Bridger. Sam will guide the rest there, and then he can head back and find your valley. If it is acceptable with you, Jackson and I would like to accompany you to either your next destination or your home." Then he added, "I would not like to impose on you. We would be more than willing to help along the way."

Sabra looked at Kade and very slightly nodded to him. Kade smiled before answering, "We would be grateful for any help, iffen we need it. You are welcome to join us." Kade glanced around his sleeping camp. "We have to make some decisions today on how long to stay here," he said. "That is, when my crew wakes up. Must have been a party last night," he grinned, then paused and grew serious, "We've been here far longer than we planned already. If Jake is up to it, we need to make tracks soon."

So, it was decided. The two Crowdens would stay while the rest of their party went on. Sam came over and talked to Kade, getting directions to find the valley. Then shortly after full light, Sam led the others to the west. Rudolph never came over to say goodbye, which did not bother any from the Welles camp.

Jake and Anna were the first up, followed by Thomas. As they sat around the fire, nursing coffee, Kade brought up what was on his mind.

"We got to decide how long we want to wait here for a wagon train, or if we just want to strike out for Ft. Laramie and see if we can meet one on the way," he paused, thinking. "You know we ordered a wagon an' supplies sent out on the first train Uncle Joe could find, but if there ain't no train, then our wagon an' supplies will go by a hired freighter to the fort 'n wait fer us there. I was hoping it would come on a train as that would save many a mile. It has what we ordered for the farm families an' ourselves an' also all the trading supplies we need. But how long do we wait here for a train?" he paused, then looked at Jake. "How you feelin' this mornin'? You think you can travel soon?"

"I can travel whenever you need me to," Jake replied. "I am feeling like I am getting my strength back."

Anna looked worried and voiced her fear, "If he tries to do too much, he might just open that wound."

"I'm fine, Bird," Jake protested. "I'm feeling pretty good."

Kade looked at the two of them and then came to a decision. "Let's stay today and maybe tomorrow, then head toward Ft. Laramie if there hasn't been a train through by then. You take a turn with the herd today," Kade nodded to Jake, "and see how you do. Then we can talk about it in the morning."

So, they spent a lazy day. Richard and Kade rode together watching the grazing animals so that Thomas, Lathe, and Jackson could go hunting. Jake took a shift and seemed no worse for wear for doing so. And late in the afternoon, a train finally came rolling in from the east.

It was a small train by standards of past years. There were twenty-seven prairie schooners and assorted mules, oxen, and cattle being herded alongside. They rolled up to Independence Rock and made preparations to camp for the night. The captain and a couple men came over to talk to the Welles.

This train had the ordered wagon, so the driver brought it over to the Welles' camp. Joe had found a man going to California and hired him to drive the wagon to meet Kade. The man would go on to California with his own horse and mule as soon as he delivered the wagon to Kade. The extra money for bringing the wagon this far would help him make the goldfields with money for supplies.

The captain circulated through the train and let men know that fresh livestock were available for purchase or that trading worn-out animals was an option too. The captain mentioned to Kade that there were several wagons with footsore and tired animals. Kade knew there would be a few men over later.

The Welles party made ready. Lathe, Molly, and Jackson brought the herd up closer to their camp. Kade, Thomas, and Jake waited for prospective buyers to come. It didn't take long. The first man wanted to buy fresh mules, and while he and Kade dickered over prices, Thomas walked off with the second man to look at the oxen. A couple came up next, and Jake went to them and offered to help. The man, distrust in his voice, shook his head at Jake's approach.

"I ain't dealin' wit no Injun," he said belligerently.

Jake looked at him mildly, "I would guess then that you will not do any trading with us." He always was careful to speak clearly and carefully when insulted.

Kade, hearing this exchange, was not so selective with his words. "He's right, yer done trading here," he said, looking over from where he stood. "Git your ass back to the train," he said coldly.

They could see the man was angry, not expecting this treatment. He hesitated but Kade turned back to the settler he was dealing with. It was the woman who eased the situation. Moving up beside her husband, she took his arm and gave him the lead ropes to the two thin mules they had led with them.

"I'd be obliged if you would trade with me," she said to Jake. "My man has no more sense than a chicken an' cain't think before talking."

Jake looked at the woman, middle-aged and weathered. She looked back at him, her gaze direct, and offered her hand. "I am sorry for my man's words."

"Ma'am," Jake said, making a decision and taking her hand in his, "I would be pleased to trade with you."

The woman smiled gratefully at him. He examined the two thin mules while the husband stood silent and brooding. Then Jake and the woman started for the herd, leaving the husband behind holding the mules. Anna came to join them.

Jake introduced himself and Anna, and if the woman was surprised to see a part blood Indian married to a white woman, she didn't voice it. She looked at the mules the Welles had to trade. Jake offered her one mule for her two, and the woman had enough money to buy the second mule. Lathe cut some mules out of the herd for the woman to consider. The renegade mule that kicked Thomas caught her eye, and she asked about it.

"Ma'am," Jake responded politely, "that mule laid my brother up for a couple of days when he put a shoe on him this week. I would be glad to sell you that mule, but

I am warning you he is not safe. We felt the fort might fit his disposition better. We are pretty tired of him."

"Your brother?" the woman inquired.

Jake indicated Thomas, helping the buyer choosing oxen.

"That is your brother?" she asked, surprised.

Jake just smiled. "That is my brother, yes, and that is my sister," he gestured toward Molly on the outskirts of the herd on horseback. "And," Jake went on, "that was my father who spoke in camp, and my mother was by the fire." Then he grinned and added, "I'm a throwback to a different ancestor."

The woman laughed then, "Young man, I reckon you get lots like my man. I am sorry 'bout that. But you seem fair an' smart, an' I am glad to meet you both. I'll trade my two mules for this one," she pointed to one of the mules that was driven up, "an' buy that next one. You can keep the kickin' mule."

The trading went on for a little bit, but the train was small. It wasn't long before the Welles campsite was quiet again. A man came walking from the wagon train to the Welles camp. He was a gangly, wiry young man wearing the pants of a soldier and a store-bought shirt. He looked in his early twenties. He walked up to Kade and Jake.

"There is a woman at the camp that says you are Jake Welles," he said, smiling at Jake. "If that be right, then I owe you a big thanks."

Jake grinned back and struggled to his feet, protecting his sore shoulder. He offered his hand to the stranger. "Well, I have no idea what I did for you, but that is a better greeting than I usually get from strangers," he commented.

"You ran a compact little bay horse against our Colonel's horse in a match race two years ago," the young man told Jake, "and I bet big time on your horse. I won a lot of money on that race. Never got a chance to meet you then and say thanks."

"I remember that race," Jake said, then looking at Kade, he told him, "I was riding that little bay gelding that we sold last summer. I figured he would win over the ground they wanted to run on. He was a sure-footed horse and ran like the wind." Then looking back at the stranger, Jake asked, "Were you a soldier at the fort then?"

"Yes, just starting there. My winning didn't make me a lot of friends at the time, but made me a lot of money," he laughed. "I mustered out just as this wagon train was going through. Thought I'd just ride along with them until something else touched my fancy. Eventually, I reckon I will have to get a job. The army don't pay enough to live long on."

"What's your moniker?" Kade asked.

The young man grinned, "Armond," he said. "Armond Talbot. Ain't that a name? Wasn't my choice, I can tell you."

"What are you good at?" Kade asked him.

Armond thought about that. "I worked in the stables at Ft. Laramie when we weren't out on a trek. I like horses, raised on a farm. I sure as hell don't want to go to no town or back east, but I don't want to follow a plow all day neither. Just thought I'd wander and see what comes up."

Kade exchanged glances with Jake and then looked back at Talbot. "We got a lot of horses needing riding, and the boys are all heading out for a few weeks. Then we are also into a hay harvest now, and we gather our cattle out of the high country in the fall. I could give you a job through then for sure if that interests you. After fall, we kin jest see how it goes."

Talbot didn't think about it long. He stuck his hand out to Kade and said, "I think that would be great, especially if your horses are like that bay he raced," Talbot nodded toward Jake.

"Well, you got yourself a job then, Army," Kade grinned, renaming the young man. "Throw your bedroll over here if you want. We will be leaving here either tomorrow or the next day, I'm thinking."

Jake and Kade introduced Army to the rest of the family, who were all grouped around the fire. The young folk, less Jake and Anna, decided to walk over with Army to the wagons and visit awhile. Army would collect his gear and return with them to the Welles camp.

"Thomas, take care of your sister," Kade called after them.

"Pa!" Molly was indignant. "I am sixteen!"

Kade looked after his daughter. "I believe I knew that," he said mildly. Then giving Thomas a look, he repeated, "Thomas, look after your sister." Kade chuckled as he watched the young folk move away, Molly with her back up trying to regain her dignity. *Molly was maybe getting too big for her skirts*, he thought.

Dusk was falling when suddenly there were shouts of alarm from the wagon train. Kade stood up to see what was causing this. Toward the south, riders were coming. It was Indians; Kade could see that right away. They skirted the train and rode up toward the Welles camp. Jake stood up and went to meet them.

"It's Brown Otter," he said to the rest as he moved away. "I didn't expect him. He knows I'd be coming to him. I'm thinking this may not be good."

There were four braves and Brown Otter. Kade did not know any of the others, but Jake knew them all. They took care of their horses and came to join the Welles around the fire. Sabra had meat roasting over the fire and put out biscuits for them as well. After they ate, the men took out their pipes and sat smoking.

"Our people are hungry," Brown Otter started. He spoke good English. Most of the Utes could speak some English now since there had been such an influx of whites in the mountains, but Brown Otter was taught English as a child. As Jake's half-brother, Brown Otter had a similar build but was taller, and his features showed more of Blue Knife's native blood. Though the brothers shared the same father, Brown Otter had a Ute mother.

"We signed the treaty and gave up the eastern mountains. Then the white men came digging in the ground for the metals that the white man prizes," Brown Otter spoke slowly, searching carefully for the English words he needed. "Much of our hunting lands have been taken from us, and what we have left is being hunted out. And now the promised supplies do not arrive. We came to the prairie to look for buffalo, but they are not here. The big herds are gone. So, we came to talk to my brother."

Jake knew that Brown Otter would not ask him directly for a handout. Jake knew that it was not good on the reservation if Brown Otter came to him. He was not surprised about this situation. Jake and Kade had talked about the latest treaty when it was signed in 1873. At the time, Kade had wondered if the government would keep the promises. Over the last two years, when Jake had visited Brown Otter in the mountains, there had been worry in the village about the infringement of whites on their land. Now, only two years later, it was looking like the promises were only on paper.

"Brown Otter," Kade spoke up. "We will send some oxen back with you. We will talk in the morning about it. Tonight, we will smoke and talk about old times," he finished seriously.

They sat around the fire as the early evening turned to dark. Sabra and Anna went to their tents, and after a while, Brown Otter and the others moved away to bed down. Jake and Kade sat by the fire. Kade was waiting for the young people to come back. He didn't have to wait too long. The wagons would leave early in the morning, so bedtime came soon after dark. As they approached, Kade called to Thomas to join them at the fire. He sent Lathe out to the herd, Molly to the tent, and Jackson went to join Richard in their tent. When they were alone, Kade began to speak to his two sons.

"This is not a good thing that's happening to the Utes, but I seen it comin' years ago," he started. "Now, without talkin' it over with you two, I promised Brown Otter some oxen. I figure this business we do is not jest mine anymore. You are both grown men, doing the work too. So, it jest don't shine for me to make all the decisions," he paused. "I figure it this way. This trading on the trail is getting tiresome. We don't get the big trains now, so we wait longer. We may have to go on every year to sell our extra cattle somewhere else anyway. For me,

I am done with the oxen an' the mules that we don't need to keep for ourselves. I am done with these trading trips. If you boys want to keep on doing it, it is up to you. If you do, you will need oxen an' mules to meet the wagons. For me, I am satisfied to just keep on with horses and cattle. We have a herd of both built up now an' can take them on to one of the forts every year. So, my third of the oxen can jest go to Brown Otter. It is up to you what you do with your share."

Thomas glanced at Jake before answering, "I'd rather just stick with the cattle and horses, too, Pa. Brown Otter can take my share of the oxen."

"Mine too," Jake spoke. "I am with you on the trading trips. I'd rather just handle the horses and cattle. I can trade other goods on the side like I always have."

"Well, that settles that. I can take home the thin mules an' oxen, an' maybe cut out a couple yokes of good ones for use at home. We can always use a few head there. The rest of the fat ones can go to the Utes," Kade took a puff on his pipe before going on, "Jake, you feel good enough to pull out with Brown Otter tomorrow? We can sort the oxen off in the morning an' send you on your way."

When Jake nodded, Kade looked at Thomas. "Now we got the four-year-old steers we brought with us to sell, either here or at the fort. I was thinkin' of taking Army with me home to help with the hayin', but maybe he an' you an' Lathe could take the cattle on to the fort."

"Pa, I got a suggestion," Thomas cut in. "Jackson was telling me how they came through Cheyenne and Laramie City, and both towns had stockyards, and they were buying cattle. It would be closer to go to Laramie City and maybe a better place to head. I was thinking

Lathe, Jackson, and I could get our herd there and give it a try this year."

Kade thought this over before replying, "I've heard that Cheyenne is booming, but Laramie City is said to be pretty rough yet. I ain't never dealt with buyers in a town, Thomas, but if you want, you could try it. You'd get to Laramie City first so if you think best, you could ride in and see what buyers there are offering. Go around and head for Cheyenne if you feel you need to," Kade paused. "But might be Richard won't want Jackson going off without him."

"Jackson already said he would like to go if we decided on it," Thomas replied. "We were talking about that tonight. He is twenty-one, you know."

"I'll talk to Richard in the morning, an' if it shines with him, we can cut you out the fat cattle an' send the three of you off." Kade looked at his sons, grown men, responsible and steady. He and Sabra had raised them right. "Your ma, Molly, an' I, along with Richard an' Army, will head home an' take the thin an' extra stock an' the wagon. We will pull out after you all get going in the morning then."

Anna was awake when Jake came into their tent. As Jake sank to their blankets, she sat up and helped him off with his shirt. His shoulder was pretty sore yet, so he appreciated her concern. He felt she worried too much, but that wasn't all bad either. He was getting restless, though, and ready to make tracks.

"We will sort off most of the oxen in the morning," Jake whispered to her, "and head out with Brown Otter toward the agency. Can you get our things packed up in the morning and be ready to travel by the time breakfast is over?"

"Do you feel strong enough," she asked.

"Bird, I'm fine. I'll be careful, and I can't hurt my shoulder on a horse," he assured her.

Anna sniffed but said, "You think you are strong. But you might be wrong."

"Well, if I am wrong, we will just stop," Jake said. "You worry too much."

Anna lay down and turned her back to him. "I just don't want my baby's father to die before it is born."

Jake sat staring at the dark form of her back, the words registering on his mind. He reached out and turned her toward him.

"My baby is here?" Jake asked, placing his hand gently on her stomach. He felt rather than saw her nod. It had been a year since he and Anna first came together. He had begun to think that there would be no children. The happiness he felt at her words surprised him. "When?"

"I will give you a Christmas present," Anna whispered. "I talked to your mother. She thinks this baby will arrive in the Christmas month."

"Are you sure you want to make this trip now with me?" he was suddenly concerned about her welfare. "You could go home with my folks."

Anna laughed, "I am fine. I need to stay with you so you will not go and do something stupid like standing on a big rock shooting at bad men."

Jake lay down beside her on his good side, spooning her into him. "Anna, my bird, I am going to remember that the next time," he whispered in her ear. He felt her relax against him and knew that for now, all was right in their world.

Dawn broke, and the men were already out with the livestock. Sabra and Molly were cooking breakfast for everyone while Anna was packing together what she and Jake would need for the next few weeks. They would travel with Brown Otter to the White River Agency, where the village was camped. Then if Anna still felt good, they would travel on to the mountain cabin and spend some time there. Jake would take trade goods with them and do some trading along the way.

When the oxen were cut off from the cattle, mules, and horses, Richard rode the outskirts of them, letting them graze but keeping them together. Jake brought the Utes to camp for breakfast before leaving. He brought a couple of mules in to pack his and Anna's belongings. When the Indians finished eating, they left to take over the ox herd, but Brown Otter lingered, going up to Sabra.

"You married a good man, white mother," he said solemnly. "You raised good sons. My people thank you."

Sabra smiled up at the man before her, seeing instead the boy from her past that she had loved like a son. "I married two good men," she replied gravely, then she smiled and added, "and I am proud of all three of my sons. You come to us whenever you can."

Brown Otter just nodded, but a hint of a smile touched his lips. Then he reached out to Sabra and touched her arm gently. She smiled up at him, wanting to hug him but knowing she shouldn't. He did smile then, and turning, he walked away. Sabra watched him leave, sadness welling up in her. *Such a good man*, she thought, *but from a dying culture.* This land was being settled, and no one could stop it. She and Kade watched the coming of civilization with trepidation, but she knew that they would adapt, and they would thrive. The Utes would not. And there wasn't a thing in the world that she could do about it.

The cattle sorted from the horses and mules. Sabra and Kade chose the horses and extra mules they would send with the boys to sell and tethered them together. They left Army watching the animals that would return with them to the valley, and Richard and Molly began moving the cattle on the slow trail to the east while the boys came in to eat. Kade and Sabra rode in with them. There were flapjacks, eggs, and biscuits waiting. As they ate, Kade talked with Thomas and Lathe.

"When you get to Laramie City, Richard said there are big stockyards on the outskirts. Get the herd in and get a good count. I counted as we cut them out, and I got 120 head. Richard thinks there are several buyers there. Ask around and see, talk to them all," Kade sipped at his coffee, thinking. "We should get between $45 and $50 a head if we went to the fort. If they want to steal them in the towns, you can take them on to the army."

Kade looked at the two men, his son, and the son of one of his business partners. "You get paid, you find yourself a bank. Go in an' put that money in the bank. Pay Jackson a dollar a day for his help an' pay yourselves the same but start from when you left home.

That will be your "spree" money. Jest be careful, an' stay together."

"You mean like at all times we stay together?" Thomas asked innocently. "We always got to stay together?" He glanced over at Lathe, and they grinned.

Kade gave the boys a quick look, knowing what was on their minds. "Jest watch each other's back then," he said dryly, "an' remember you ain't in some Indian village."

They finished eating and rose, but Kade had more instructions, "Put the money in the bank in both your names."

"Kade, you want my name on your money in the bank?" Lathe was surprised.

"Lathe, this money is as much your family's as mine," Kade answered. "It may be my cattle, but they were fed on your hay. We will settle accounts as we can, but until then, we will have more names than one on the paper. Safer that way." Kade reached out and shook Lathe's hand before turning back to Thomas. "When you are ready to leave town, go to the bank an' bring home maybe half of the money. Split it up between you two to carry. Leave the rest there. We don't have much use for money at home, but I'll need wages for Army, an' I'd like to pay Matthew an' Jim some too. Never hurts to have some cash on hand," Kade reached out his hand to his son. "See you in a couple weeks."

The trip home to the valley was uneventful. With both Army and Richard to help drive the animals, Sabra and Molly took turns driving the wagon or riding, with Richard relieving them both at times. As the days passed and they drew near their settlement, Sabra waved to Richard to come and join her on the wagon box.

"If you follow the river, you will soon see the two cabins just ahead," she said when Richard got settled on the wagon with her. "The farthest one is Matthew and Mattie Jorgensen. They have four children. You know Lathe; he is their second oldest of the four. They have an older son, Jeremiah, but he is more farmer than traveler," Sabra smiled at that. "Lathe is more like his great uncle, Jacob, who brought me west. Jacob was an old mountain man, and his son was my first husband, Jake's father," she added. "Mattie and Matthew have two younger girls too. Mattie was my best friend growing up."

"Then, on the right is the cabin of Jim and Sarah Bates. Jim is Mattie's brother, and he used to pull my hair when we were kids. I used to spend a lot of time at the Bates' farm as I grew up," Sabra paused, thinking back to those bygone years. "Sarah and Jim have five children. The oldest is Martha, who is Sarah's daughter with her first husband. He was killed in a wagon accident when they came out with a wagon train in 1849. Martha was about three or four then, I think. Jim was on that same wagon train, and he helped Sarah after the accident. He married her a year later. Then they have Will, who is home farming, and two more daughters and a younger son. Their next oldest daughter, Beth, is seventeen now, and I suspect our Thomas is sparking her," Sabra smiled at this. "Their youngest son, James, is thirteen this year, and he is going to be sorely disappointed that we won't be making any more trading trips. He has been counting the years until he can go with us. I think he will take after his great uncle Jacob, too."

"These people have been with you all these years then?" Richard asked.

"The Jorgensen's came west in 1850 and met us out here," Sabra answered. "Kade and I had gotten married the winter before. Jim and Sarah came to join us the next year, in 1851. It was Kade and Tom's idea to find a larger mountain valley and begin trading with the wagon trains. We had a couple of wagons and stock brought out with Tom that first year, and of course, Mattie and Matthew had stock, so these were our start-up for the first year. Both Kade and I have investments in St. Louis with Kade's brother, so over the years, we have had more cattle bought and sent out. We have a good-sized herd now. What we brought with us this summer is only a portion of what we could sell."

As they approached the cabins, Sabra could see some of the girls and young James come out on horseback to help push the stock to the end of the valley. The men were in the distance in the hay fields along the river. Sabra waved as they went by but didn't detour to the cabins to visit. She would see everyone after they got settled. She would drive the wagon home and she and Kade would unload the supplies they had ordered, then take the wagon back tomorrow so the Bates and Jorgensens could get the things they ordered.

As they left the river and drove past the cabins, Sabra pointed ahead. "About a mile farther up, you should see a cabin on the left side of the valley and one on the right," she said. "Tom and Clara Grissom live on the left. That's Sam's mom," she added. "Kade and I and the kids live in the cabin on the right side. We have that barn built below the house. And finally, if you go another half mile farther up, there is a new cabin that is Jake and Anna's. You won't be able to see it yet."

"You have your own settlement here then," Richard commented.

"We do," Sabra agreed. "And I guess Kade and I never minded having these people around us. We like them so much. But more are coming. An old trapper has a cabin up the river two or three days from here, and there are mining towns springing up not too many days away. Little settlements are springing up all around us, it seems," Sabra thought about this before going on. "Neither Kade nor I look forward to this country getting filled up but guess we can't stop it. Maybe it's for the best, with our children growing up now. But we have enjoyed the solitude."

The men unloaded the Welles' portion of the wagon in the morning and drove it down to the Bates' cabin. Sabra stayed behind and put together food and supplies for Kade and Richard because they were heading up the mountain to check the cattle that afternoon. Kade thought that two nights would be enough to camp in the high country unless they found a big cat or grizzly causing trouble with the livestock. Kade hoped that Jim would let little James go with them and that they could take Jim's two hound dogs too. If there was a mountain lion in the area, having the dogs along would be good to tree a big cat. James might only be thirteen, but he was a resourceful guy and was pretty good handling the dogs.

Kade figured that James would be disappointed to hear that they wouldn't be meeting any wagon trains in the future, so going on a hunting trip might make it up to him. Kade would leave Army with Jim and Matthew to help with the haying. And finally, on the way back to the cabin before leaving, Kade and Richard would stop off at Tom's cabin. Kade wanted to introduce Richard to the old mountain man and tell Clara the good news that Sam was found and would soon visit.

CHAPTER 10

The Courtship of Martha - 1875

S am rode up the river and could see the two cabins coming into view. Hay fields, both cut and uncut, lay along both sides of the rushing water. Around the cabins were small, cultivated fields, garden truck, it seemed in most of them. Sam let his horse water at the river and then started across. Toward the east, he saw men in the fields, one using a horse-drawn mowing machine and the other with a team pulling a dump rake, dragging the hay into windrows. They were quite a distance away, so Sam just crossed the river and headed for the cabins. He was pretty sure this was the right place, but it wouldn't hurt to make his presence known.

As he came close, he saw a figure in the nearest field, scooting on the ground between the plants. He could see it was a woman, and she was weeding as she knelt on the ground. With her back to him, she didn't see him until she heard the jingle of the horse's bridle. She looked up and sat back on her rump, watching him approach. She did not have a smile of welcome but didn't appear to be alarmed either. At her side lay a pistol, but she didn't make a move to use it. As Sam got closer, she simply sat and watched him.

"Ma'am," Sam asked politely, "this here be the valley the Welles live in?"

The woman nodded, then pointed behind her. "They are that way," she said, not elaborating at all. Sam could see she was not an old woman. With her sunbonnet tight on her head, though, he couldn't even tell what her hair color was. Her face was plain but not unpleasant. She wasn't a girl, but she wasn't far out of youth. Her gaze was serious.

"I am looking for the Grissom cabin," Sam went on. "It's that way too?"

The girl studied Sam before saying, "You are Samuel, Clara's son." It wasn't a question.

"Yes, ma'am, that I am."

"She's been waiting for you," the woman stated.

"Reckon that makes two of us," Sam grinned. "I been watchin' for Ma for a long time. Jest looked in the wrong direction."

"Go up the valley some and look to the west," the woman told him. "You will see the cabin. There is a beaver pond there. I am glad for Clara that you made it." The woman still did not smile. "Your ma is pretty special."

Sam thanked her and rode on. *Strange,* he thought. Nary a smile and that gal jest sat there as still as could be. The only part of her that moved was her mouth and the one arm as she pointed up the valley. She didn't seem unfriendly, nor wary or afraid, but so still and emotionless. Sam glanced back once as he rode away, and he saw the woman had not resumed her work. She still sat motionless as if waiting for him to leave. *Yup, strange.*

Clara and Tom were sitting in the front of the cabin when Sam came into sight. Tom's rheumatism bothered his legs the most, but his hands, gnarled as they were, still held a knife and he was whittling on a piece of wood. Tom liked to work with wood. Clara was knitting. This is how they spent much of their days, sitting in the shade or the sun, depending on the day, watching for any activity that went on.

When they sighted Sam, Clara was instantly alert. She had waited a long time for her son to find her. But the minute she saw the figure, she knew this was him. Sam had filled out since his early teenage years with broad shoulders and muscled arms. He rode his horse with his rifle cradled over his saddle like most mountain men did. But when he looked up the hill toward her, Clara could see the same little boy in the man. Coming toward Clara was her long-lost son. Putting her knitting down, she rose and started to run.

Sam was enjoying himself. His mother hadn't changed except to be happy. Sam liked Tom, liked the way Tom teased his mother, liked the way the two of them were together. It made Sam feel good to see his mother happy. Lord knows she deserved it.

Sam also enjoyed being in this valley. He had gone hunting with Kade and Richard several times. Otherwise, he spent much of the day helping Kade and Army load and unload hay wagons. They had two big wagons, refitted prairie schooners outfitted with rails to help hold the hay as it was piled higher and higher. At first, Jim, Matthew, and their sons loaded one wagon, while

Kade and his crew loaded the other. Richard drove for them sometimes which allowed all three to pitch hay. When Thomas, Lathe, and Jackson came home and were added to the mix, a third wagon was utilized. With three crews and wagons, the stacks were hauled into large hay corrals in record time. It was hard work, but Sam enjoyed these men. Half of the time, they were joking, half of the time they were running little competitions to see who could load their wagon the fastest. Work wasn't work when it was fun.

Thomas, Lathe, and Jackson had returned two days before. The cattle had sold well, better than expected. The next morning, Kade walked down to talk to Jim and Matthew and settle accounts. Sam had walked along. When they reached the Bates' cabin, Sam saw the same woman he'd seen when he arrived. She was sitting in the shade on the porch. Kade introduced her as Martha, Jim's oldest girl. Today, Martha wasn't wearing her sunbonnet, and Sam noticed she had golden hair with a touch of red in it. It was pulled severely back into a bun. Sam waved Kade on without him.

"I'll jest set here and wait for you so's you can talk your business," Sam said, "an' I'll visit with this nice lady while I wait," he looked at Martha. "May I set ma'am?" he asked.

Martha nodded but didn't speak. Sam sank onto the bench and gazed across the fields toward the river. He could just see the diamond-like glisten of the water as it tumbled down over rocks. He could hear the water faintly from the porch.

"This is mighty peaceful," he commented. When Martha didn't reply, he let it go. He was getting the idea that this was not a chatty woman. After a spell, he tried again.

"It was good to see Ma again. Hard to believe it's been over twenty-some years."

Martha thought about that. "I am sure Clara was happy to see you."

"That she was. Well, guess she still is," Sam laughed at that. "I like her man."

"Tom and Clara have been like grandparents to all of us kids here," Martha told him. "We grew up not having any other grandparents. They just sort of adopted us."

"So, you been here all yer life?" Sam hoped he could keep her talking.

"No, I was about four when my folks came here. My real pa was killed on the Oregon Trail, and Mama married Jim. Jim's been a good father to me. I have a hard time remembering my real father anymore," she said seriously.

"You're lucky. My pa was a mean, sour man," Sam said. "I couldn't wait to run away. Wish't I could've made my ma run with me, but that isn't a woman's way, I suppose," he paused, and the silence settled comfortably around them before he continued. "I was jest a kid anyway. I couldn't have supported Ma, and she had no way to support me. Reckon it was meant to be." Again, they sat silent, listening to the river. Finally, Sam began again.

"So, what do you do for fun here?" Sam asked. "When yer not workin'?"

Martha didn't respond right away. It was like pulling teeth to get this woman to talk, Sam thought. But he had lived alone so much that the silence was not uncomfortable to him. He could wait. Finally, Martha answered, "Some of the kids go to the river. The current is too swift here to swim, really, but they play in the water. It is cold, but on a hot day, kids don't care. Then the fellows hunt, and when we were all younger, the others would play games. Sometimes we get together and sing in the evenings, or read, things like that. My ma taught us reading and arithmetic in the winters. All the kids came to our cabin for school."

"So, do you swim?"

"No," the answer came quick, and Martha didn't elaborate.

"What about games?"

"I was older than the rest," was all she replied. She was shutting down to these questions.

"Well, aren't they still your friends?" Sam asked.

"They are all much younger, except Jake. Jake was younger but only by three years. I guess Jake and I were friends." Martha thought about that before she added, "He understood."

That was a strange thing to say, Sam thought. He wondered what it was that Jake understood between them, but he didn't pursue it. Maybe she harbored secret feelings for Jake who was now married to Anna.

They sat for a while without talking until Sam finally continued, "My pa didn't believe in laughing. He didn't allow games or dancing or singing unless it was hymns. We lived in a community, and everyone worked. There was no joy there," Sam glanced over at the serious woman beside him. "You ever smile, Miss Martha?"

"Sometimes, I suppose I do," she answered, but there was no accompanying smile.

"I hope you don't think that a smile is a bad thing, like my pa thought," Sam watched her out of the corner of his eyes.

"Well, no," she said slowly, "not a bad thing. I like it when people smile and laugh. I just don't get around to it a lot myself." She thought some more, then added, "I don't do so well with strangers."

Sam grinned at her. "Well, this is the second time I have spoken to you," he said. "And now we have been properly introduced. Are we still strangers?"

Martha ducked her head, but Sam saw a hint of a smile light on her lips before she answered, "I don't know you so well yet."

Just then, Sam heard a woman in the cabin call for Martha. Martha's head came up, and she called back, "I am out on the porch, Mama."

"I need your help." Sarah Bates called out. "Would you come in?"

A stricken look flitted across Martha's face, and Sam wondered if Martha was enjoying visiting with him so much that she didn't want to go inside. When she stood up, though, he knew he guessed wrong. With her back to him, Martha murmured, "It was nice visiting with you," as she moved awkwardly off. For when she stood, Sam saw that she stood lopsided. Martha's right leg was shorter than the other, and it made her lean as she stood and limp as she walked. And her right arm was crooked, slightly twisted, and locked in a slightly angled way. Now Sam filled in the unspoken words. Martha didn't swim in the river or play games with the other children when she was young, not because she didn't want to, and not because she was older. Martha didn't do these things because she couldn't. Martha was disabled, and he could tell by her body language that this shamed her.

Martha was friends with Jake because he understood. Jake understood what it was like to be different.

Two days later, Sam came riding up to the Bates' cabin mid-afternoon. It was a warm afternoon, and the haying crew quit early and went on to other activities. Sam borrowed Tom's old quiet gelding and saddle and leading it from his own horse, Sam rode right up to the hitch rack in front of the cabin where he tied up and went to the door. Like most cabins, the door was open, and he peered inside as he knocked. It was Sarah who came to meet him.

"Afternoon, ma'am," Sam greeted her. "I brought a nice horse with me thinkin' I might get Miss Martha to come for a ride with me."

Sarah was surprised at this request, but she smiled and answered, "I think that would be very nice for Martha." Turning, she called inside, "Martha, there is someone here to see you."

When Martha entered the room, Sam repeated his request. He saw Martha stiffen, then look wildly at her mother.

"Mama, I can't."

Sam jumped in, "It's a gentle horse. I wouldn't let you get hurt."

Sarah also spoke, "You know perfectly well you can ride a horse, Martha. It would do you good to get out in the sunshine. Now, you go get out of the house for a bit."

"But . . ." Martha began.

Sam strode into the room and taking the elbow of Martha's crooked arm in his hand, he propelled her gently toward the door. "I will take good care of your daughter," he assured Sarah as they passed. "I will not keep her late."

Martha would not look at him as she fastened her bonnet on and hobbled toward the horse. Sam held her elbow firmly, and by supporting her lame side, her limp was not so defined. He noticed that she had no trouble mounting the horse without his help. *Horses she must be familiar with,* he thought.

They rode in silence for several minutes. Sam led the way toward the hills, away from the sound of the river. He wasn't sure he would get her to talk, but with the noise of the river, she would have to speak loudly, and he was pretty sure that was not going to happen. He knew she was embarrassed about her deformity. But hiding it wasn't going to change things. She intrigued him. She was so sad, so serious. He thought if he could only see her smile a bit, that would be good.

"So, were you born with a limp, or were you in an accident?" he asked. *Get it out of the way,* he thought. *Acknowledge that he saw what she didn't want him to see and then toss that burden away.*

She rode in silence a few strides before answering, "Accident. The same that killed my father."

"How old were you?"

"I was three," she murmured. She glanced quickly at him and then away. "I don't remember it much except for the days of pain. There weren't any doctors with our wagons, and I broke both my leg and arm. They never healed right."

It was time to change the subject. "I found this deer trail up this sidehill a few days ago," Sam said. "Are you game to climb?"

Martha, glad for the change of subject, looked up the hill and nodded. Cueing the horses, they started up the hill. When they reached the top, there was an open meadow that looked down over the river. An ancient tree lay slanted across the ground, and to this, they rode. Sam dismounted, and going to Martha, he held up his arms to her.

"What?" she made no attempt to dismount.

Sam reached up and, taking her by the waist, he swung her off the horse and over the log so that she was sitting on it facing the land below. She squealed as he swung her but when she settled safely on her perch, Sam saw that she was smiling.

"Now, ain't that pretty?" Sam commented.

"Yes," Martha replied, composing herself solemnly. "It is a pretty view."

"I wasn't talking about the view," Sam tweaked her chin. "I was talking about your smile." And he was rewarded with a quick smile before she looked away.

They sat for a long time quietly, Martha on the log and Sam settled on the ground, using the fallen tree for a backrest. As they sat, they spoke only a little, Sam usually pointing out things in the distance. As the sun started to sink toward the west, shadows played out in the valley. The mountains were like that, coming into shadow long before the day was done. A valley might be dusk while a mountain top still enjoyed sunshine. They saw some deer come out on the river bottom, going cautiously to the river. Sam pointed them out to Martha, but she had seen them already. There was nothing wrong with her eyes.

When the shadows touched the river, Sam rose. "Reckon I better git you back before someone comes a' lookin' for you," he said. He helped her stand, then taking her by the waist, he lifted her and stood her on the log. "Wait here and I will get your horse." She waited, balanced crookedly on the log, for him to bring the horse alongside her, then she easily swung herself on its back.

They rode in silence on the way back, but it wasn't uncomfortable. Sam had lived much of his life alone. He didn't need to talk, and Martha seemed content as well. Sam watched her as they rode, and noticed she was drinking in the sights around her. They rode close to the river for a while, and just before they turned away from it to head to the cabins, she started a conversation.

"When I was thirteen, I was out here with the other children," she pointed to a point where the river rushed over boulders, the water roaring. "I slipped and fell in."

"It's deep there," Sam noted. "Can you swim?"

"No, I never learned, and I remember I was so scared," she pointed to a spot in the river. "I think if I had only known how to do it, the current would have helped pull me there," she pointed again. "I could have stood up there, but I couldn't get my legs under me to move that way. I was caught under that angry water. Then, all of a sudden, these arms came around me and pulled me up," she smiled at the memory. "It was Jake. He was just a skinny ten-year-old, but he grabbed hold, and he wasn't going to let go. Even then, he was strong. We both went under a couple times, but he wouldn't let go. He pulled me out, and we lay gasping on the edge. The other kids just sat and stared at us. Thomas and Jeremiah were the next oldest, and they were six that year. Will was five. The rest of the kids were too little or not even born yet, so they weren't out with us. I remember Will was crying. Funny, the things that we remember."

"What did your folks say?"

"We never told them. Jake threatened the younger kids that he'd tan 'em if they told. I think Jake was afraid that our folks wouldn't let us go to the river anymore," Martha paused. "I never got close to the edge again."

When they returned to the cabin, Sam rode right up to the front step and helped Martha dismount. She stood still while he mounted again and watched him. "I thank you for the ride," she said politely.

"It was a mighty pleasant way to spend a hot afternoon, ma'am," Sam told her. "Thank you for coming with me." Turning his horse, he rode off, leading Tom's horse behind him. *It was a good afternoon,* he thought to himself.

Hay was the main crop of the farm families, bought and paid for by Kade. The growing season was too short for most traditional crops, but some thrived. Sugar beets were good food for animals and humans. Sam was pretty sure that some of the rows he rode by held sugar beets. Then he recognized broccoli, cauliflower, cabbage, and onion plants. He couldn't see what else there was, but Matthew and Jim still had some work to do to bring in the other crops. It wouldn't take long for the garden truck to be harvested after the haying was finished. Already the young folk were looking forward to their annual harvest frolic. Now they would just wait for the rest of the crops to be harvested, and for Jake and Anna to return.

Three days later, the haying crew quit again in midafternoon. The haying was done. More than enough hay had been brought in and piled up. The stacks would sit now until winter when the hay would be loaded up on wagons mounted on runners. Over the course of the winter, the horses and cattle would be fed daily.

Sam walked home from that last day of haying, sweaty and dusty. He stopped by the pond and stripped off his shirt. Swirling it in the water, he made a half-hearted effort at cleaning it, then used it as a washcloth to mop the sweat and dust off his body. Finished, he threw the shirt over a branch and walked up the hill to the cabin where Tom sat whittling on a block of wood.

"Ya know yer ma will collect that shirt an' wash it proper when she gets back from Sabra's, don't ya?" Tom asked.

"I think she's trying to make up for all the years I been gone," Sam laughed. "I could hide that shirt and she'd find it. I'll just make it easier for her if I leave it on the branch."

Tom grinned, "She likes doing it. She finds time on 'er hands now that she don't make the cheese anymore."

Clara had one milk cow when she first came home with Tom. She knew how to make cheese then, and over the years, Tom built a small cabin for her cheese making, connected to the main cabin by a dogtrot. Now there was a new cheese house down by the creek near the Jorgensen's home where the younger folk, taught by Clara, made cheese. Clara's little cabin only housed tools and odds and ends. It was here that Sam had thrown down his blankets for a bed in a corner and hung his few extra clothes on the pegs of the wall. He had lived too long alone to bunk in with his mother and Tom. He went to his things now and pulled on a clean shirt, washed, and neatly hung by Clara. As he left the cabin, Tom called to Sam to join him.

"Tenny, ya think any of sticking in this area?" Tom asked.

Sam thought about that before answering, "I reckon I ain't thought 'bout leavin' or stayin'. At the moment, I jest don't feel like ramblin'."

"Yer ma is some younger than me," Tom continued. "I don't see myself outlivin' her. Would be some easy on my mind iffen you were to stick, or mebbe jest drop by often." Tom looked across the valley toward Kade and Sabra's cabin. "I know Kade an' Sabra would always watch over Clara. Well, they all would, but to know you'd look in on her from time to time would be a comfort." Tom shaved on the block of wood. "She's been happiest she can be with you here."

Silence fell over them as they sat, each in his own thoughts. After a while, Sam spoke, "Tom, she's been a right bit happy for nigh about twenty years, I think. I kin see that in how she talks and laughs and how these people talk about her, an' you too. But I'll keep an eye on her, you kin count on that." Sam rose from the stump he was perched on and said, "You mind borrowin' me yer horse again? I'd have him back by dark."

Tom grinned, "Goin' courtin' agin?"

"Courtin'?" That surprised Sam. "No, jest takin' that sad girl out fer a ride. Hell, man, I'm old enough to be her daddy!"

Tom laughed at that, "You'd a been a young daddy. Yer only 'bout fifteen years older than Martha."

"I had my first woman when I was fourteen," Sam grinned. "Almost didn't know what to do with her, but there ya have it, could happen."

"Shit, Tenny, you must a been a scrawny little shit then; how'd you get a woman?"

"I ran errands for a widow woman jest before I headed west." Sam smiled, remembering. "I slept a while in her barn. Guess she was lonely. Nice woman, not old, but homely as a . . . Hell, I wasn't that scrawny."

Tom chuckled at that, "Take the horse. I don't have much use for him these days."

Sam rode his horse and, leading Tom's, started down the valley. He saw his mother come out of Sabra's and start for home. Sam changed directions and went to meet her.

"You want a ride, Ma?" he asked.

"No," Clara replied, smiling at him. "I like the walk. It's not far. Tom will watch for me. You goin' riding?"

"I won't be late," Sam replied, nodding, then smiling, he reined his horse away.

As he left Clara, he looked up at the Welles' cabin, and having another thought, he rode up to the door. Molly came out and saw him and called to Sabra, who came to join them outside.

"You have any pretties in those trade goods you and Kade keep," Sam asked. "Ribbons, maybe?"

"I am sure we do," Sabra answered but decided she shouldn't ask why. That Sam had taken Martha for a ride one day was common knowledge in the community. That he sat here on a horse leading another was a pretty strong hint that he was going there again. "Let's go and look."

There were several bolts of ribbons, and Sam asked for a strand of blue ribbon. When he tried to pay for it, Sabra just shook her head. She'd write it down, she told him. He'd been doing a lot of work harvesting hay. He could settle up with Kade later.

This time, when Sam rode up with the two horses to take her riding, Martha did not argue. She just nodded solemnly and limped out to the horse. They rode for some time without speaking, but neither was uncomfortable in the silence. Sam chose to ride in the direction up the valley, passing the Grissom and Welles' cabin, and then Jake and Anna's. When they got to the farthest point of the valley before the wooded hills rose above, there was a beaver pond. Sam reined over to the edge of the trees and dismounted.

"This here be a pretty place, looking down this valley," he said, reaching up to help Martha off her horse.

"I haven't been up here in years," she replied. "I used to ride more and came up here with the other kids when Kade and Tom brought home the trading cattle. But I haven't done that for a long time now." Martha found a stump to perch on. "It is a pretty place."

"Miss Martha," Sam changed the subject abruptly, "why on earth do ya wear that sunbonnet so tight around yer head? There ain't enough sun to scorch ya at this time of day."

That surprised Martha, and she had no answer, "I . . . I don't know."

Sam walked over to her, and kneeling in front of her, he untied her bonnet and pushed it off her face. "Yer hidin' behind it, that's why," he said bluntly. "Don't do that." He sat back on his haunches, surveying her. "An' take your hair down. Pretty hair like that needs to be free."

"No!" Martha was incredulous. "I'm no girl anymore. I shouldn't wear my hair down."

"Miss Martha," Sam spoke patiently, "take yer hair down, or I'll take it down for ya," he was firm but gentle in his tone. "Ya got hair like the evening sun going down behind the peaks. It needs to be free."

They had a stare-off for a few moments. When it looked like Martha would not move, Sam reached forward, but she jerked away. "All right, all right, just wait," she said hastily. She reached up and began to take the pins out of her hair until it tumbled down over her shoulders. "There. Are you satisfied now?"

Sam surveyed her, "You should be 'shamed of yourself, Miss Martha, fer hiding that pretty hair under that ugly bonnet an' then tying it up like a hogtied calf," he said, but he smiled, softening his words.

"Well," she sniffed, "a woman my age can't go around with her hair just flying away."

"Yer right 'bout that," Sam agreed. "So's I brung you somethin' to tie it up with." He drew the strand of ribbon from his pocket. "This here matches yer eyes. Now pull that hair here . . ." Sam reached and touched both sides of her head, pulling the hair that was above her ears back to lay behind her head. "And put the ribbon here," he touched the back of her head. "Like I seen yer sisters do. Let it lay off the back of ya."

"Mr. Tenbrook, I can't do that!" she looked at the ribbon he still held.

"Ya want me to do it for ya?"

She shook her head.

"You do it, or I will," he said firmly.

Martha shot him a frown, but she combed through her hair with her fingers until she got the tangles out, then drew the sides up and together in the back. When she was ready, she put her hand out, and Sam put the ribbon in it. Martha tied her hair with a bow on the top of her head.

"There now, that looks pretty," Sam commented mildly. "I don't want to see that poor hair corralled again. Jest ain't fair to do that. It's too pretty to keep hidden."

When Sam helped Martha off her horse just before dusk in front of her home, he reached up and gently stroked her hair. Then looking at her sternly, he said, "I better see that blue ribbon at the frolic." Then he mounted his horse and rode away.

Martha's family noticed the changed hairstyle and the ribbon, but nary a one commented on it. Martha still went through the days as solemn and quiet as ever, but every morning, the blue ribbon was in her hair.

Jake and Anna came home two days after the haying was finished. Jake had a mule loaded with pelts he had gotten in trade. It had been a profitable trip for him. Anna was beginning to show the coming of the baby, but she was happy and felt well. She had enjoyed the trip. They had stayed a week with the tribe before going on to Jacob's cabin. Anna felt comfortable with Brown Otter's people, having lived so many years with the Pawnee, and both Jake and Anna loved being in the high mountains again. But Twin Peaks and these people were their people. It was good to be home.

Jake told Kade and Sabra that there was a new settlement started near the hot springs the mountain men called Steamboat. It was less than a day's ride from the mountain cabin. Only a couple houses had been built, but the settlers seemed to think more would come. Jake had been able to do some trading with the newcomers.

North of the Steamboat community, a mining town had been established at Hahn's Peak, but Jake had no interest in going there. He had had enough trouble just getting the oxen to the Indian agency.

Jake, Anna, and the Utes had run across a small cavalry troop traveling along the Overland Trail, south of where they left the others. There had been a few tense moments when the soldiers first thought that the Indians had attacked a wagon train and stolen the oxen, and then when they saw Anna and realized that she was a white woman, the soldiers tried to rescue her. With Anna vehemently protesting, the soldiers finally listened to Jake, and it was then that one of the soldiers recognized Jake as the "mixed-blood trader" that came to Ft. Laramie.

"What would you have done if they hadn't recognized you, Jake?" Molly asked, wide-eyed.

Jake smiled fondly at his little sister, but his eyes turned cold as he said, "We would have shed some blood, I'm thinking. That wouldn't have helped the Utes, so I'm glad we didn't get to that point."

Now with everyone home and the bulk of the crops in, they could have their harvest frolic. Outside Jim's cabin a big table was set up and the women cooked for a couple of days making all sorts of dishes. The menfolk that weren't still in the fields scoured the hills for fresh meat, and there was mule deer, pronghorn antelope, rabbit, grouse, and even a mountain sheep bagged for the meal. By the time the women brought pies or cakes and added them to the table, it was a feast for sure.

With the addition of Army, who had a harmonica, they had three musicians. Sabra, with her piano, and Matthew, with the fiddle, played the rousing tunes, but Army played a good, slow tune on his instrument.

The dancing started just as the sun went down. The young people traded partners often, but it seemed as if Thomas and Beth and Jackson and Molly paired up the most. Army was a shy young man and seemed to dance mostly with Jim's youngest girl, Bonnie, and Matthew's youngest daughter, Rachel. Army felt more comfortable with them; he was tongue-tied with the older girls. Will, Jeremiah, and Lathe just cut in on them all, keeping everyone laughing and scurrying for another partner. Even young James danced with whichever girl he could grab.

Sam watched the festivities, took his turn with the younger girls, Rachel and Bonnie, and cut in a few times to dance with Clara and Sabra. But he couldn't help noticing Martha sitting quietly at the edge of the firelight watching the others have fun. After a while, Sam walked over to Army.

"Why don't you get that little harmonica out and play us a slow tune?" he asked. "We need to slow it down a bit."

Army agreed and stepped up to Matthew, telling him to take a break, something Matthew was more than willing to do. Taking a stool, Army played a soft, slow tune, and the couples took to the dance area, glad for a chance to catch their breath.

Sam walked over to Martha. "Would you honor me, Miss Martha?" he asked, taking her hand, and pulling her up.

The startled girl looked up at him and pulled back. "No!" she exclaimed. "I can't dance!" She looked mortified at the thought.

But Sam did not let her hand go. "You can do this," he soothed. "Jest let me help you."

Martha's face registered her alarm, but her voice lowered to a fierce whisper, "No! I can't do this!"

Sam held her hand firmly, not allowing her to move away from him or sit back down. He reached out and tipped her face toward him. "Trust me, Miss Martha," he soothed. "Jest give me a chance."

She could see he wasn't going to give in, and she didn't want to make a scene. She just stared at him, frightened.

"Now you put yer little foot right here on top of mine," Sam told her, indicating her short leg. When she at first didn't move, he went on, "Put your foot on mine, Miss Martha, or I'll do it for you."

Hesitantly, Martha lifted her foot and stepped on his foot. It was all the height she needed to stand straight. She looked up at Sam.

"Good girl," Sam smiled. "Now, the tricky part is to keep it there. But we are going to go slow." And with his strong arms around her, keeping her steady, they swayed and shuffled around the edge of the dancers until they got a rhythm going. Just before the song ended, Martha looked up at Sam with almost wonder in her eyes.

"I'm dancing, aren't I?"

"You bet you are," Sam replied. "An' in case you don't notice, this little crooked arm of yours jest fits me fine." He touched her arm that went to his waist.

"Think you been just made for this," he was rewarded with a shy smile.

No one stopped dancing to watch, but all eyes had been covertly following the strange couple. Jim noticed first when Sam pulled Martha up and was instantly alert. He had been having a pull on the jug with Jake, but seeing his eldest daughter shrink in horror as she was being pulled out to dance, he set his cup down.

"That is just about enough of that," he murmured angrily, starting toward Martha and Sam.

But Jake reached out and stopped him, "Uncle Jim, let it be. Let Martha fight her own battle."

"She's scared," Jim said, "can't he see that?"

"Course she's scared," Jake went on. "She's been afraid and ashamed her whole life, and you been letting her hide away because of it. Time that quits, and I think you are seeing the man who can help her," he took a breath. "Hell, Uncle Jim, I've been fighting my whole life. What kind of man would I be if my pa took on all my battles? Time you let Martha fight her own too. The only one she's got to fight against is herself. She sure as hell ain't happy the way she's been."

Jim looked uncertain, but he saw Sam tilt Martha's head up and speak to her. He saw Martha step onto Samuel's foot, straightening her body. The couple slowly began to move and finally, a smile came on his daughter's face.

"How'd you get so smart?" Jim asked Jake.

Jake just laughed, "I come from good stock," he said and went to find Anna. Dancing a slow song sounded good to him too.

The frolic went on until long after midnight. The whiskey jug was getting low by the time it broke up.

Throughout the evening, the music varied between fast, foot-stomping tunes and slow melodies. And after a while, Jake cut in on Sam.

"Martha, you have to show me how to do that," he said with a smile. He could see she wasn't sure about getting a new partner, but he had been her friend a long time, so she tried. They had a couple false of starts, but when Jake laughed and said, "Let's try again. I'm sure I can do it too." Martha relaxed.

After Jake, Martha had several partners and there was lots of laughing until they picked up a rhythm. But in the end, it was Sam who came to rescue her, saying, "I taught her everything she knows. My turn, boys."

The frolic was a success, more so this year than ever before, with the happy smile on Martha's face. By the time the dance broke up, everyone was bloated with food and drink. They all had sore feet, and this year, Martha did too.

Three days later, Thomas rode back up the valley after talking to Jim Bates. He had spoken to Jim about him and Beth. Thomas and Beth had an understanding. They wanted to get married. The problem was that Beth was only seventeen and Jim would not allow Beth to get married before she was eighteen. Jim and Sarah also wanted a preacher to perform the wedding, either at their settlement or in a town. So, Thomas and Beth had almost a year to wait. Thomas was a bit disappointed that they had to wait, but he knew it wasn't that long. And he could see Beth all the time anyway. Thomas could wait, he knew. As he rode up toward home, Thomas saw Sam coming from his home leading an extra horse. As they passed, they both grinned at each other. Thomas knew the extra horse was for Martha.

Sam rode up to the Bates' cabin with the two horses. Sarah had seen him coming and was on the porch, but Martha, not confident that Sam was coming to see her, waited until her mother called her before going outside. Sam noticed though that she was still wearing the blue ribbon.

"Come riding with me, Miss Martha," he said.

Martha nodded and mounted the old gelding. They rode off along the river a piece before Sam suggested they ride back up to the overlook where they rode the first time. Martha was content to ride, and Samuel didn't try to start a conversation. They rode quietly until they climbed to the top. Then, as he did the first time, Sam took Martha by the waist and swung her over the log, setting her gently upon it. Martha giggled as she flew from horse to log, but quickly composed herself.

Sam turned back to his horse and rummaging in a pack on the back of the saddle, he came up with a bundle. "Kin ya take off your shoe, Miss Martha?" he asked.

That surprised Martha. "Whatever for?" she asked.

"Now you know better than to ask," Sam smiled at her. "Jest trust me."

This time Martha smiled back at him. "Or what, you will do it yourself?" she asked, and Sam gave her a wicked grin. So, bending over, she started taking off the shoe from her good foot, but Sam stopped her.

"Not that foot, goose," he chided her. "The short foot."

Martha gave him a funny look, but she did what Sam told her until her foot was out of the boot she wore. She looked up inquisitively at Sam, who suddenly looked a little nervous himself.

"I been talking to Tom, and we had this idea. Now I got no idea if this will work, but we figured we could try. Tom's good with wood, so's he whittled something for ya an' I made you a moccasin shoe. If you think it might work, we might have to do some more whittling, but we got to try it on you first."

Sam moved around in front of Martha and knelt by her foot. Sam had a moccasin with him, but it was heavier than normal. When Sam slipped it on her foot, there was a thick piece of wood within the moccasin. Soft rabbit fur covered the piece of wood to cushion her foot. The moccasin was tall, and Sam drew out some leather straps and bound the moccasin to her foot and lower leg tightly.

"This may be too tight, but we kin change that, I reckon," he paused, feeling around her foot, "an' Tom can work on the wood if it irritates. Now stand up." He offered her his hand, pulling her up.

She stood slowly, feeling her body come up straight instead of lopsided. She stood, getting her balance.

"Kin you walk in it?" Sam asked.

Martha tried. She wobbled some, but after a few steps, she looked up at Sam and nodded. Then a radiant smile lit her face. "I'm not crooked," she whispered.

"Honey, you ain't never been crooked to anyone 'cept yerself. But you look good standing up straight," Sam smiled. He had hoped this attempt of his and Tom's wouldn't backfire and insult Martha.

Holding on to Sam, Martha moved slowly around the clearing. "Well, I might not win any races with this," she said, "but it feels good to have my hips level." Then she blushed deeply, realizing she spoke to him about a part of her anatomy that women just didn't mention. Sam, seeing her discomfort, laughed outright at her. Slowly they moved together until Sam steered her back to the log where Martha sank on it gratefully.

"I have to thank you for this. I never thought I'd stand straight . . . or dance," she said simply.

Sam just ducked his head and moved away to look at the view. Her thanks embarrassed him.

"Mr. Tenbrook, why are you doing all this?" Martha startled him with her question. "I mean the rides and the ribbon and this moccasin shoe?"

"Honey, surely you know when a man is courtin' you?" he replied, coming to the realization himself that he was doing just that.

"Courting?"

Sam smiled at her surprise, then sobered. "Miss Martha, I don't reckon I took ya riding the first time for no other reason than it was a challenge to see if I could make ya smile," he said solemnly. "But when ya did smile well that changed the whole game. I wanted to see that smile agin and agin. Then when we were dancing, an' ya put that crooked arm around my waist, well, girl, that jest felt mighty good." Sam took a breath, thinking through his words before continuing, "Martha, you are quite a bit younger than me, nigh unto fifteen years younger. You can do better'n me, an' I wouldn't blame you a bit. But I am here a' askin' an' if you'd a mind to answer, well then . . ." he drifted off, thoughts unfinished.

"What exactly are you asking, Mr. Tenbrook?"

"Well, I guess I'm asking for a yes," Sam was flustered. He hadn't expected to get to this spot today. For a man who had been so sure of himself when he was telling her to change her hair or dance with him, this was a mountain he had trouble crossing.

"Exactly what would I be saying yes to?" Martha pushed, too unsure of herself to believe in what was happening.

"Well, I reckon I'm askin' that you . . ." Sam was stammering now, "that you, if you was to want to . . . well we could . . ." he turned away from her. "Hell, woman, we could get married," he finished strong but stood with his back to her, looking over the river bottom.

Martha stood up, caught her balance, and carefully made her way the three steps to him, reaching out to touch his back. As he turned to face her, she said, "Yes, yes, yes," and smiled up at him.

Sam's smile lit his face, mirroring Martha's. They stood looking at each other for a moment until Sam leaned down and gently kissed her.

They rode most of the way home in silence. When they were almost there, Sam spoke, "Reckon I'll find your pa and speak with him."

Martha nodded, but then she voiced a concern she had thought of while they rode. "Samuel," she said, using his Christian name for the first time, "we'd stay here, wouldn't we? I don't think I could go live anywhere else . . . with strangers."

Sam grinned wickedly before replying, "Well, I mought like a cabin of our own. Don't think I want to bunk in with yer folks. I reckon we could fix up that little cabin next to Tom's for now an' build us a bigger one next year. We kin pick out a spot that pleases you, but I do like to have some privacy."

"Oh, Samuel," Martha actually laughed. "I didn't mean live with Pa and Ma. I want to stay in the valley, though. We can surely start in the little cabin this year."

Sam reined in his horse so he could say his piece before reaching the cabin. "Martha, I don't have much, but I think I kin throw in with Kade an' make a living. I got some money from guiding them Englishmen. I told you back there in the clearing that you could do better 'n me. But if yer still a mind to take me, I promise you can live yer life out here in this place. I might have to ramble some if it comes to that to make a living for us, but if I do, I'll always come back here to you."

"I don't want someone better," Martha said simply. "You make me feel good. You make me smile. What is better than that?"

"Well, you have to promise me you won't quit smiling," Sam told her with a grin. "I ain't living with no sourpuss!"

Martha smiled back at him. "I promise," she said.

Beth was worried about telling Martha that she had gotten a proposal. Beth was ten years younger than Martha, and here Beth was engaged already. Beth loved her older sister, but Beth didn't want to be an old maid like Martha, either. She loved Thomas and wished her pa would let her get married right away, but he said eighteen, so that was next spring. They could plan for a summer wedding. There was no budging Jim on that, and Sarah agreed.

The women were preparing supper when Martha came in the door. She walked slowly, for the moccasin shoe was a bit clumsy. It was Bonnie who looked up and saw Martha first. Her mixing spoon clattered to the floor as she stared in surprise.

"Martha, you are walking straight," Bonnie blurted, drawing everyone's attention.

Martha just stood and smiled. There were no words for her joy. Sarah and Beth came to her, and they all sat down. Martha showed them the moccasin shoe that Tom and Sam made for her.

"I can't move fast in it," she told them. "But it feels so good to stand up straight." Martha looked at her mother. "That's not all. Samuel asked me to marry him. He's out in the barn talking to pa."

"Oh, Martha, that is wonderful!" Sarah hugged her, then she straightened, thinking, and said softly. "Oh dear, your poor pa."

"Why, what is wrong with pa?" Martha was confused.

It was Beth who answered, "Thomas just left from asking Pa for my hand," she laughed. "You know how Pa hates change. Sam will be the second man asking for a daughter in one afternoon! Poor Pa!"

The girls laughed, and waited for their father to come in. There was a lot to talk about at supper that evening.

While Beth and Thomas had to wait a year, Martha insisted that she and Sam marry soon. Sarah and Jim wanted her to wait until they could find a traveling preacher or a missionary to perform the ceremony, but Martha would have none of it.

"Uncle Matthew has led us in Sunday worship for as long as I can remember," she stated, "so I want him to marry us."

"But Martha, that won't be a legal marriage," Sarah protested.

Martha was adamant. "You never think of Sabra and Kade or Tom and Clara or Jake and Anna as anything but married. You know they never had anyone perform a ceremony. I don't want to wait. I am old enough to make my own decisions, and it is up to Samuel and me to decide. I want your blessing, but I am going to get married."

In the end, Jim and Sarah gave them their blessing. They only asked for a few weeks to make a wedding dress for Martha and get together some things she would need as she started her married life.

That was fine with Martha. The next day Sam came to visit, and he and Martha talked over the details they wanted. They decided that they would wait two weeks, Matthew would marry them, and they would live in the cabin next to Tom and Clara's. Soon it would be time for the fall gather, so the wedding would be over before the men had to go up the mountain.

A few days after all these marriage proposals stirred up the settlement, Thomas and Kade were working with some of the colts in the corrals. Jake had taken a colt out alone and was gone for a few hours.

"Pa, I know you went up to check the cattle with Richard, but that was weeks ago. And we won't gather for another three weeks, so I was thinking that maybe us young folk could go up camping a few days and check things out; you know, do some hunting," Thomas paused. "Jackson and Richard are heading out right after the wedding so we thought it would be fun to get up to the high country once more before they leave." Kade thought about that and nodded. "That wouldn't be a bad idea. Jest you and Jackson?"

"Well, actually, pretty much all us young folk."

Kade looked at Thomas suspiciously, "All us young folk? Spell it out, boy."

"Well, we were talking at the frolic about going hunting, and everyone wants to go. You know, like a camping trip. Even little Rachel wants to go. We'd take care of the younger ones, Pa, you know that."

"Yer talkin' bout all the kids, boys and girls. Am I gettin' this right?"

"Well, yeah, but we got the line cabin the girls could sleep in, and us guys will pitch a couple tents. We won't go off and leave the young kids alone; we'd always have some older ones around." Thomas had a feeling his pa wasn't thinking this was such a good idea.

"So, let me get this straight, you and Molly, the four Jorgensen kids, and the four Bates kids, or is Martha going and making it five?"

"No, we asked Martha and Sam, but they think they have too much to do here," Thomas added. "But Army would like to go if you can spare him. Oh, and Jake said he and Anna are staying put until the fall gather. We were thinking we'd be gone two nights, so we won't be gone that long."

"Son, do you think this is wise?" Kade asked.

"Pa," Thomas was a bit disgusted at that. "We've been raised in these mountains. You never worried about us going off in them before."

"Ain't your mountain skills I'm worried about."

"Pa?"

Kade dismounted and tied his horse. "Thomas, you asked for a girl's hand just a few days ago, and now you want to take her up into the mountains for a camping trip? And her Pa don't want her married 'til next summer."

"Pa, there are going to be all the kids there. Hell, you know you can trust me."

"Thomas," Kade spoke firmly, "I know you are responsible. But I remember being young once. Takes a powerful, strong man to keep his hands off a woman if he finds himself alone with her. Going camping in the mountains ain't especially a place where a bunch of randy young men with a bunch of girls is thought to be a good idea. I got nothing but respect for Jim Bates. I would hate for you to have to go speak to him that waiting a year isn't going to be possible. And then there are Molly and Catherine to think about too. They are almost grown up. Maybe too grown up."

"Pa, we all grew up together," Thomas was serious. "You think we would let anything happen to any of the girls, or any of the guys either? I gave Jim my promise to wait. I'll wait. And Jackson is a good man. He won't hurt Molly. He knows that Jake or I would kick his ass if he did. Molly is not that dumb anyway. We might not get to do this again, leastwise not all of us. It's happening already with Jake married and Martha soon to be."

Kade knew what Thomas said was true. They were all grown or almost grown. They had all been raised right. He nodded, "If you can get the other fathers to let the girls go, Molly can go. But I am trusting you older men to keep them all safe, in every way."

"We will, Pa. You know we will," then he grinned wickedly at Kade. "And just think, you will have two days without us. Think what you can do with that."

"Yeah," Kade grumbled, "Jake and I will be riding extra colts that you and Army should be helping us with."

Thomas laughed at that, "That's not all you'll be riding."

Kade gave him a shrewd look, "You sassin' your father, boy?"

"Oh, shit Pa, you think us kids don't know why you send us up the valley or over to Tom's when you come home from your travels? I have no idea how you kept your hands off Ma when you were young 'cause you sure can't now when you're old!"

"Well, your ma is a pretty handsome woman . . . and I ain't that old!"

"Hell, Pa, we think it's cute, but you aren't fooling anyone," Thomas laughed at his father's discomfort.

"You mean you and Jake know . . . not Molly?"

"Pa, you taught us kids to watch for every sign, every sound, to always know our surroundings. Molly knew when she was twelve. She's as good as any of us," Thomas started to strip the saddle off his colt.

Kade watched his son take the saddle to the barn, then turned to his horse to unsaddle. Under his breath, he muttered, "Shit," before pulling his saddle off and following Thomas to the barn.

Sabra and Kade stood in front of the cabin watching the young folk ride away. It was just past dawn, Sabra's favorite time of the day. Eleven of the settlement kids were grown or almost grown, and the two newcomers, Army and Jackson, were riding in a group. Thomas and Lathe were riding young horses that were cutting up some, not accustomed to riding with so many other horses. Kade could hear the laughter and light banter between the kids as they rode.

"I have no damn idea how they talked Jim and Matthew into this," Kade mused. "Well, maybe Matthew isn't so hard to sway," he thought about that, "'cause he has the fear of God instilled in those girls, but Jim? That's a different story."

Sabra laughed, "I was a bit surprised about Jim, too, but I know Thomas went down and talked to him. Thomas can be pretty persuasive sometimes," she looked up at Kade. "Let's go in," she whispered, reaching out and pulling his shirt from his trousers, her hands moving up his back.

Kade groaned, "That gawd damned Thomas."

"Kade Welles, why are you swearing at our son?" Sabra stopped what she was doing and looked up at him.

"Sabra, my love, they know."

"Who knows . . . knows what?" she began, then looked out at the young folk riding up the valley, "Oh," she breathed, her fingers moving again inside his shirt. "Thomas? Jake too?" When Kade nodded she whispered, "But not Molly?"

Kade looked down at Sabra and grinned, "Apparently since she was twelve."

"Well, damn . . ." Sabra caught herself, but Kade laughed outright at her use of profanity. "How?"

Kade watched the riders grow smaller. "They are mountain grown, Sabra. We never shielded them from the horses and cattle. And we taught them to be so gawdawful watchful. Didn't think they'd use it against us."

"Well," Sabra thought about that, watching the riders in the distance, "they are way down the valley now," she slipped her hand lower into his trousers, "we can go in now."

"You are jest as bad as them, woman," he laughed and scooped her up. She was such a little woman, but for all her years, she still had her figure and his heart. They headed for the cabin.

From way down the valley, they both heard the war-hoop and shout, "Yee haw, boys, pay up!"

"That gawd damn, Thomas," Kade breathed as he slammed the door behind them.

The kids rode in two days later with a mountain lion pelt and stories of campfires and pranks and bleary eyes from lack of sleep, but Thomas swore there was no messing around.

"Jeremiah and Will were both sworn to watch their sisters," he told Kade. "Hell, I wasn't going to wreck a friendship," he laughed. "I can wait 'til next summer. And I kept Molly or Jackson in my sights the whole time," he sobered then and looked seriously at Kade. "I wouldn't shame you, Pa."

"No, you'd jest bet on your ma and me," Kade grumbled.

"Well," Thomas grinned wickedly, "easy money, but the only ones who would bet were Army and Jackson. The rest knew better."

The wedding plans were well underway by then. Clara and Samuel were cleaning out the little cabin. Tom was making a wedding present with some help from Samuel too. They were building an off-the-floor bed carved from pine and aspen trees with rope springs. Clara made a good straw tick for it and Sabra brought over a handmade quilt that she had been working on. She had started it for Molly, but she would have time to make another one. Molly was too young to marry if her pa had any say in it.

In the wagon of goods that came from St. Louis was a cookstove for Jake and Anna. Jake insisted that the new couple take the stove since Sam's cabin had no fireplace in it.

"Anna does fireplace cooking really well," Jake remarked, "and never has used a stove, so she doesn't care. We can order another one next year or go to Laramie City. Thomas said they have stores there that have supplies like that."

The stove was installed in one corner, the bed in another, and Samuel fashioned shelves and pegs for their belongings. This cabin didn't have a wood floor, but they put down skins that were warm and made the small room look cozy. Next summer, he could split logs and lay a floor unless they decided to build a new and larger cabin somewhere in the valley. There was one window that overlooked the valley. Clara had the glass shiny clean for the newlyweds.

In the goods sent out from St. Louis was new material for the men's trousers. Denim, it was called and was a stiff, tough fabric. Clara and Sabra were busy sewing new pants for their menfolk, wanting them to wear new clothes for the wedding. And Sabra had also seen two women on the last wagon train riding in split skirts. She was intrigued by them and sewed herself an outfit and one for Molly too. Kade even approved of these outfits and was relieved to know the women would retire their knickerbocker riding outfits.

Sarah and Martha had taken some pretty blue material and made Martha a dress to be married in that would also be a serviceable dress for special occasions. Sarah had preferred a yellow fabric, but Martha had been firm. It had to be blue. It had to match the blue of her eyes, the blue of her first ribbon. The two weeks were busy and passed quickly.

The wedding was held in the late afternoon. Because of Martha's handicap, they decided not to have a dance. The ceremony was first, held on the porch of Jim and Sarah's cabin. Then they feasted, and finally, just about dark, Army brought out his harmonica and played some soft slow tunes so the bride could dance with her new husband and her father. Then amidst cheers and whistles, the couple mounted horses and made their way to their new home. It was a fine celebration.

Martha was overwhelmed at the little cabin. Sam lit a candle and set it in the window, and she looked around the room.

"Oh, Samuel, an off-the-floor bed, and it is so pretty with that quilt!" she breathed. "And a cookstove!"

"The bed an' linens and such are from Tom and Clara and Sabra, but I helped some," Sam was proud of the room. "An' I made the shelves fer ya. We can pack the rest of yer plunder up tomorrow an' bring it here. But the things you sent home with Clara are on the shelf already." He led her over to the bed and they sat on it, feeling the comfort of it. Sam leaned over her, tipping her head up to his and kissed her.

"Samuel?" Martha whispered when Sam let her go, "I'm not sure what I'm supposed to do?"

"You nervous, girl?" Sam tweaked her chin.

"Yes, I guess I am," she replied.

"Well, you can relax, honey. Ain't nothing going to happen tonight."

A confused look came into Martha's eyes. "I don't understand."

Sam just laughed and said, "Reckon enough time has gone on, I kin blow out the candle." Sam took Martha's hand and pulled her up. "We gotta git outta here."

"Where are we going? Samuel, what is going on?" Martha might not be experienced about weddings and wedding nights, but she knew that leaving wasn't right.

Sam blew out the candle, then pulled Martha out the door and shut it behind them. "Honey, we are soon going to have some company. Reckon I don't want to be surprised with my pants down."

"Company? Who?" realization came over Martha. "They are going to shivaree us, aren't they? Like with Jake and Anna?"

"Yup, and I got plans."

"How did you know?" Martha asked.

"I smelled apple pie, and there weren't no apple pie on the table tonight," he smiled at her in the gloom. "And if you looked closely at Sabra and Kade's cabin, there is a wagon behind it with Sabra's piano on it. They let us git away far too easily for a wedding night. They be a-comin'; they was just waiting for the candle to go out."

"Are we going to run away?"

"Hell no, it's going to be a fun time. I'm not missing that, and neither are you," Sam laughed, "but they're getting a surprise too."

Sam led her a short way into the woods and found a spot to sit on the ground. "We'll jest wait for them here," he kissed her again then and pushed her gently to the ground. He traced her face with his fingers, then moved to her dress and started to unbutton it. When he got to her waist, he folded back the dress, revealing her chemise. He touched the flimsy material, tracing the mounds below.

"Samuel, what if they come?"

Sam laughed at this. "That's one reason we are out here," he murmured, intent on what he was doing. "I'll hear them long before they git here. You don't have to worry 'bout that. I'll git you put back together before they come." He pushed the chemise down, slipping the straps off her shoulders until first one, then the other breast popped out into the moonlight. "We picked the right time fer our wedding," he murmured. "Everyone should get married when the moon is full." He leaned over her until his lips found her flesh. He played with her, until he felt her moan with unconscious pleasure.

"Honey, see," he whispered, "you don't have to be nervous; yer body will know what to do." But he pulled back then. "Reckon we best quit before we cain't," he said regretfully. "They're comin'."

Martha sat up in alarm, "Where?" She pulled at her clothing, covering, and buttoning up.

"You got time," Sam laughed at her concern. "They are just leaving Kade's, but when you get put together, let me check you for grass an' twigs."

They heard the jingle of the harness first and then whispers and chuckles as the people approached. In the gloom, Sam could make out Jake and Anna riding across the bottomland to meet the wagon and walkers. Leaving the animals below, they came quietly up the hill, carrying pots and pans to beat together as noisemakers.

As they ringed the cabin. The noise started, laughter and catcalls and war-hoops enough to raise the hair on their heads. Tom and Clara came out of their cabin and joined the fun. When no one emerged from the cabin, William tried the door and found it open.

"They're not here!" he called out, and everyone grew quiet.

"'Course we're not there," Sam called out from the trees. "Ya didn't want us to miss the fun, did you?"

First surprise and then laughter rang out as Sam and Martha came out of the woods. "Ya didn't think you could fool this old mountain man, did you? We been waitin'. Thought you'd never come."

It was a great shivaree, even if they hadn't rousted the married couple from their bed. The music went on all night. The food came out by midnight, and the jug was empty by daylight, signaling time to go home. Sam and Martha stood together, waving to family and friends as they rode away. Sam looked fondly down at his new younger wife.

"Now, girl, it is our time," he whispered. "Time to try out that new bed."

Martha smiled and looked up at him, "Anna said that after their shivaree, Jake was asleep on his robes before she got the door locked."

"Sweet thing," Sam grinned, "Jake's jest a pup, don't know how to hold his liquor." He squeezed her to him as they moved inside. "And it wasn't Jake's first night with his woman neither. I been watching my drink. I'm not goin' to miss my wedding bed." He kissed her gently, then turned and latched the door.

CHAPTER 11

Laramie City – Summer 1876

Kade rode drag on the herd. He and the boys took turns on that so none of them had to breathe in the dust all day. It wasn't that bad though. It was late June, and the grass was still green on the plains. There was some dust, but it was not choking. Here and there they came on small groups of longhorn cattle, still thin from the winter. It wasn't hard to keep their cattle separated as they passed. He had a big crew on this drive.

He surveyed the collection of people and animals ahead of him. Most of the settlement was on this trail drive. Thomas and Beth were going to be married in Laramie City while they were there. The young couple rode together, slightly ahead and to the right of Kade. Jim was driving the light wagon with extra wagon seats for Mattie and Sarah and any of the girls who wanted to take a rest from riding. Matthew drove one of the heavy wagons as he and Jeremiah were going to pick up a big saw and extra supplies. Jeremiah thought he would start a sawmill. People were moving into the area, and he felt that a sawmill would be an added income as well as a help to the valley residents. Jeremiah was courting a schoolteacher from the mining town a two-day ride from them. He was thinking about his future in more ways than one. The wagons came behind the herd a little way back to let the dust settle.

Sabra and Molly rode on the south side of the herd. From a distance, they could be twins. They sat their horses the same, walked the same, and they had the same beautiful smile. Molly was seventeen this year. Last fall, she had moped for quite some time when Jackson rode away with his father, bound for England. There had come one letter in mid-winter when a traveler brought it to them from Laramie City. There were no promises in it, only tales of travel and passage home. Kade was relieved. He liked Jackson but had no desire to see his daughter go so far away as England. Surely, she could find a beau here. And for a while there this winter, he thought maybe Lathe or Will might be harboring courting thoughts when the young folk gathered. If Molly took to Lathe or Will, she would always be here. Kade would like that. But when Thomas teased Molly about the boys once, Molly had been indignant.

"For goodness sakes, Thomas," she exploded. "They are Jake's cousins, and they are practically brothers to me. We are just joshing. It doesn't mean anything."

"Well, I'm marrying Beth," he retorted. "Why is that different?"

"Because you love Beth," Molly explained, "and I don't love Lathe and Will, at least not like that. That's why it's different."

Well, Kade liked the precedent that Jim put on Beth. No marrying until eighteen. If Kade could stick with that, Molly had another year at home before going off with anyone. Funny how he never thought about losing a son when the son married, but with his daughter, well, that was different.

The rest of the young folk were all on horses. It looked like a herd of cattle being hounded by a herd of young folk. Almost everyone was riding along on this trip because of the wedding. And what a thrill for the younger generation who had never been to a town. Big doings for them.

There were a few from their valley who were missing on this trip. Sam and Martha were back in the valley tending to the garden plots and chickens and pigs, even milking the cows. Martha gave birth to a baby boy in May. She hadn't wanted to make a trip to Laramie City anyway, wedding or no wedding. Martha loved her sister Beth, but having a handicap made Martha shy around other people. She did not want to go to a town. And for the first time in her life, with a new baby and a husband who adored her, she was truly happy. Having the baby so soon before the trip made staying home so much easier.

Clara and Tom stayed home too. Tom was slowly fading. On the good days, he mostly sat outside his cabin, knife in hand, whittling away on some piece of lumber or building something out of wood pieces. If his legs were crippled now, his sense of humor and memory of the old days were still strong. The best way to pass a lazy afternoon was to go and visit Tom, and everyone in the valley eventually found their way there at one time or another.

Army had drifted off just after Christmas on a mild January day. They didn't need help anymore, but Kade was willing to keep Army on anyway. He was a good man, honest, strong, and skilled. But Army wanted to ramble, so ramble he did. Kade told him to return in the summer if he needed a job. They had a lot of hay to put up, colts to ride, and cattle in the high country to check. But summer was upon them, and Army had not turned up again.

The Welles family had been down to Mattie and Matthew's the day Army left. Army had grinned and told Kade he might just come back. Then he had chucked Mattie's youngest, Rachel, on the chin and told Kade he had to come back and marry this little gal when she grows up. Little Rachel, who was barely fifteen, had grinned and punched him back, but Kade wasn't so sure Army wasn't telling the truth. Rachel was a cute little thing, and even at fifteen, you could see she would grow to a handsome woman. Time would tell if Army would be back.

There had been lots of changes in a year. Anna and Jake had a baby girl in December, the week before Christmas. Jake had brought Anna to his mother at dawn one day, bundled up against the cold. She was having pains. Sabra had told them to come home when it was time, and she would have Molly's room ready. Jake and Anna only had a one-room cabin. In December, there had to be a place for the menfolk to wait. It was too cold to sit outside. That was a wise move, as Anna had a long labor. For almost two days she struggled to have the baby. Clara, Mattie, and Sarah all came and took turns helping with the long delivery. By the time a healthy girl child was delivered, Jake, rigid with fear for his wife, had sworn off all future relations with Anna, swearing he would never touch her again.

It wasn't something to joke about at the time, but Kade had a suspicion that vow wouldn't last. So, until little Kestrel made her debut, Kade kept his silence. He sat with his son, offering what little support he could, and remembering other times when it had been he who sat, silent and brooding, waiting for a child to be born. The first child was the worst, though, for both mother and father, that he remembered vividly.

So here he was, a grandfather in his early fifties. Relieved and weary, Sabra called Jake in to see his new daughter and then sank into Kade's lap. "I am so glad that is over," she told him, laying her head on his shoulder. "I was getting really worried."

"Well, I am glad you didn't tell us before now," Kade commented dryly. "Your son has already sworn off ever touching his wife again."

Sabra glanced up at Kade and laughed. "That won't last. He might not be your blood son, but he's your son, all right. There will be more children, and hopefully, they will be easier ones."

Kade looked now for Jake and Anna and saw them riding on the north side of the herd, side by side. Jake was carrying little Kestrel. Anna rode in the wagon some of the time, letting the baby sleep on her lap, but she was more often on horseback beside Jake. Anna was a shadow, Jake's shadow. Her life was complete only when she was with him. Kade thought that might be a burden for this son of his who had spent so much time alone, trading with Indian villages or living alone in the mountain cabin, but Kade was wrong. The young couple complemented each other. It was good to see your children grow strong and straight and find that person who fills the empty spaces of their life. Jake had found his mate. He hoped Thomas and Molly would be as lucky.

Jake had at first tried to beg off from going on this trip. It was Thomas' wedding, he told Kade. There was always trouble when he showed up, always someone wanting to pick a fight. Jake didn't want to ruin his brother's wedding week, but Thomas would hear none of it. Thomas insisted that Jake be his best man. If there were a fight, they would all fight.

So here they were, nearing Laramie City with 464 head of four-year-old and five-year-old steers. This was the left over five-year-old cattle from last year and the four-year-olds; the whole crop of steers this year, ready for market. Last year, the buyer felt the Welles' cattle was superior to the longhorn cattle which were wintered on the plains. *And superior they should be,* Kade thought. Unlike the cattle grazing the open range who fended for themselves all winter, the Welles' cattle had hay and the shelter of the mountains and trees. These were cattle that came from the east, and over the years, the ranch had bred and raised a hearty, beefy animal. They were building up quite a herd and settling accounts between the Bates, Jorgensens, and themselves. No more selling the animals one by one with a succession of wagon trains until they had most traded or sold. Now it was one drive to a town. This year, that drive was not just to market the cattle. This year, it would also be the wedding trip of Thomas and Beth.

When they were a couple of miles out from town, Kade sent Thomas and Lathe in to find the cattle buyers. Thomas and Lathe had swung the deal the year before and had done well. Kade would stay out with the cattle.

It was time to let the boys take over much of the business. Thomas had been the son most interested in the cattle. Jake was more involved with the Welles' horses and traded on the side when he traveled. It was fitting that Thomas handled the cattle deal.

"No sense me getting in there," Kade told Thomas. "Not sure I will be the one bringing them here in the future. You might as well step up and take over. Jake will stay out here with me, and Will and James too. When you know where to put them, we will bring them in."

The women and wagons would also go ahead and get rooms at a hotel. They had lots to do in town, making wedding arrangements and buying clothes and supplies. The families would be in town for over a week, and the women were excited. It had been over twenty years since any of them had been to a town. Everyone, men and women alike, had a list of what they wanted to look for, and these cattle would bring enough money for expenses and still leave quite a chunk in the bank.

While all the families in the community had ordered things sent out from St. Louis since they had first settled in their valley, the excitement of looking at items and making decisions in person on what to purchase was almost thrilling. For twenty years, they had relied on letters back and forth to Joe and then had to wait for goods to arrive a year later. Walking into the general store would be almost an aphrodisiac to the women. There were barrels of flour, cornmeal, beans, and rice. Coffee and tea, sugar and spices, molasses and syrup, and real soap could be purchased. And best of all, the women could see and feel the fabric choices before buying. The men would stock up on window glass for the new cabins and additions to the old. They could see new farm equipment and leather goods. The newly married couples were looking at adding some plates and cups and silverware. Then there was tinned food, vegetables, and fruits to stock up. There was so much to see and do.

Thomas and Lathe found the same cattle buyer from the year before and had no trouble selling their herd for top price. While Thomas talked details, Lathe rode out and led in the herd. They hadn't lost a single head coming. The counting and sorting did not take long. Putting up their horses at the livery, the men found the hotel where the women had registered. That is when the first trouble started. As the men came into the lobby, the clerk came out and stopped them.

"Hey, you," he said, indicating Jake, "you can't be in here."

"And why, exactly, can't I?" Jake asked politely, but there was steel in his voice.

"We don't register rooms to Indians," the clerk replied.

"I am afraid you have already registered a room to me," Jake told him; then going to the register on the counter he swiveled it around to show the man. "Right here, see it says 'Mr. and Mrs. Jake Welles.' I am Mr. Welles."

The clerk looked confused. "But . . ."

"So, this is what is going to happen," Jake spoke carefully. "Either I stay here with my wife, or I leave with my wife. But if I leave," and here Jake pointed to all the other names on the register that belonged to their party, "then all these people leave with me. Do you want to tell your manager that you had seven rooms rented, but you turned them all out because you did not like me?" Jake paused. "I can guarantee that if you want me to leave, we all leave."

The clerk looked uncertainly at Jake, then at the men who ringed him, and he could see they all meant it. "I will have to talk to the manager," he stammered.

"No, you make the decision right now," this time, it was Thomas who spoke, anger in his voice. "Mr. Welles is my brother . . . their cousin," he indicated Lathe and Will. "He stays, or we all go with him."

The clerk bit his lip, then saw his way out. "Well, if he's kinfolk then, I guess it's all right."

As the men climbed the stairs, Kade looked at the others and grinned, "We won't mention this to the women. I could see Sabra heading down to the lobby with fire in her eyes. No one messes with the kittens of a mountain lion." And they all laughed at that.

The next order of business was to wash the trail dust off. The women had all ordered baths brought up to their rooms, but the men took clean clothes and went to find the public bathhouse. Kade and Jake made the supreme sacrifice and got their hair cut. While not short by any means, it was trimmed and neat, hanging halfway to their shoulders. The men were all in clean clothes by suppertime, but they made a strange group in the hotel dining room. The Jorgensens and Bates sported boots or shoes, having ordered footwear from St. Louis every year. While Sabra and Kade and their children had leather boots that they wore in the winter, none of the Welles wanted to wear the heavy things in the summer. They never had summer footwear sent out from St. Louis. All summer, they wore moccasins. It was first on their list to get proper footwear, but that would have to wait for the next day.

"Ma," Molly whispered as they neared the dining room, "We are going to look funny wearing our moccasins."

Sabra just smiled at this. "For a girl who didn't mind wearing knickerbockers, this seems like a small thing," she said. "Just hold your head high and walk in that dining room like you own the place. I just dare anyone to say a word." And that is what they did.

Shortly after they were seated, Molly leaned toward Sabra again and whispered, "Well, we got the best-looking menfolk anyway!" Sabra had to agree with that.

In the morning, the family groups went off in search of new clothes, boots, and the supplies they wanted. After lunch, Thomas and Sabra went with Beth and her parents to check out churches. The Bates wanted a preacher, if possible. The town was young, and no denomination had been established yet in the booming city, but they found a church that doubled for a school in the winter. Sabra was nervous, not having stepped in a church or talked to a preacher since being insulted by one when Jake was a baby. This was Jim and Sarah's deal, so her only concern was that Jake would be accepted.

Jim explained to Preacher Forsythe that they were in town wanting their children married in a church. He also mentioned that the best man, the brother of the groom had a quarter Indian blood. Finally, he explained that Jake was his cousin and second cousin to Beth.

The preacher didn't bat an eye. "I see no problem," he said. "Should there be?"

Sabra met Jim's eyes, tears welling in them. They had found a preacher. The wedding was set for the day after next, a Saturday. Everything seemed to be falling in place.

While Sabra was at the church with Jim and Sarah, Kade and Jake were waiting at the train station. Kade's brother, Joe, and his wife, Katie, were scheduled to arrive that afternoon. It had been twenty-seven years since Kade had seen his brother. They corresponded yearly, mostly through Sabra's letter writing. Joe and Katie had accepted Sabra and Jake into their home when Jake was only a baby, and they had given Sabra not only refuge but friendship. Every year, when Kade or Tom or Jake went to Ft. Laramie, Sabra would send letters back, keeping the couple up to date on their activities. Every year, there would be letters waiting at the fort for them unless someone had traveled through and stopped by with mail for them. Joe had money Sabra and Kade invested, and in the early years, they had used some of that money to expand their herd of cattle and horses and for necessary supplies. Now it appeared that they would live off their cattle and invest profits as well.

Joe and Katie were the first to get off the train. Kade recognized them right away. Katie was still as attractive as ever but in an older, statelier way. Joe hadn't changed much but for gray in his hair and a little bit of a paunch to his stomach.

"Damn, brother," Kade joshed Joe as he clapped him on the shoulder, "you need some exercise."

Turning to Katie, he held out his arms and gave his sister-in-law a big hug. "You are still as pretty as ever," he said. "How'd my brother get so lucky?" Then turning, he introduced both Joe and Katie to Jake.

"You met this man years ago, but he's grown up now," Kade smiled. "Sabra, Thomas, and Molly are off doing wedding things this afternoon. They will see you for supper."

Joe offered Jake his hand, "We have heard a lot about you over the years. Good things all."

"Jake, you are as handsome as your mother has said you are," Katie exclaimed with a smile. "Give your Aunt Katie a hug."

Jake smiled and went to her and pulled her in. "I have you to thank, you know," he whispered in her ear. "You gave me the best father a man could ask for. Pa told me the words you said to him when I was a baby, and he used the same words on me. You are one smart woman," Jake leaned back and looked at her, then kissed her on the forehead. "Thank you, Aunt Katie."

Katie smiled up at Jake. "Some things a woman just knows," she said softly. "We just have to get you hard-headed men to listen." Here, she smiled affectionately at her brother-in-law.

Kade took them back to the hotel where they found that the wedding party was back, going over details.

"Joe and I are going off for a drink," Kade told Sabra. Then looking at the others he asked, "Anyone else want to come?"

Jake, Thomas, and Lathe were not anxious to stay in the hotel, and Jim was more than ready to let the women take over the wedding planning. The six of them strolled down the street where they found the most popular hangout for cowboys, the Bucket of Blood Saloon.

"This here was a right wild place about ten years ago," Kade told the others. "It was owned by the first marshal, a guy named Long, but he was a crooked son of a bitch. I heard tell," Kade surveyed the room around them, "that he killed thirteen men before he got lynched himself. Not sure who owns this place now, but it has settled down some. This town had a rough reputation a few years back."

The men sat, catching up on years that had passed, and the stories flew back and forth. Jim had only met Joe once, back when Joe brought Sabra to visit her old home when Jake was a baby. But he enjoyed watching the two brothers together. Joe, the lawyer, and Kade, the mountain man turned cattle rancher, so different, yet so much alike. They had the same easy way about them and the same laugh. Thomas and Jake, raised on stories of their uncle and letters from Katie, enjoyed finally meeting this uncle they had heard so much about.

"So, what kind of wedding things are being planned?" Joe asked when there was a break in the conversation.

"The bride's parents and Sabra went to check out a church today," Kade explained. "Sabra asked me to go with, but I didn't figure I had much to offer in that department, so I begged off. Then I think they were going to get some fancy clothes."

"A church, huh?" Joe looked surprised, "I didn't think you'd ever get Sabra back in a church."

Kade looked at his brother curiously. "I'm not sure what you mean," he said slowly. "Sabra lives by her Bible teaching. Mattie's husband leads a meeting every Sunday for whoever wants to go," he looked a bit sheepish. "I seem to find a lot of things to do on Sundays, but sometimes I've gone with Sabra, and the kids all did when they were growing up. Why wouldn't she go in a church."

Joe gave his brother a hard stare before saying, "She never told you."

"Told me what?"

Joe glanced between Kade and Jake, deciding how much he should say after all these years. Kade saw Joe's hesitation.

"Spit it out, Joe. What didn't she tell me?"

"When you brought Sabra to us all those years ago, when you were just a little baby," Joe nodded to Jake at this. "Sabra went to church once with Katie and me. She left Jake with our maid," he hesitated before going on. "The minister noticed her in church and came to visit in the afternoon. He was not a real young man, but not old either, and he was unmarried," Joe shrugged. "Sabra was out in the back yard, watching her horse and Jake," again Joe glanced at Jake. "You were sleeping in the shade of a tree. When the preacher saw you, he got pretty abusive. He said some pretty mean words to Sabra. I imagine it shattered any hopes he had that this pretty little woman might be someone he could court."

Joe left it at that, but Kade would not. "What exactly did he say to Sabra?" he asked, and there was a hard note to his voice.

"It was a long time ago," Joe said, "and I wasn't there. Just words. Katie told me about it."

"Joe," Kade was serious, "what did he say to her?"

Joe glanced nervously at Jake and then back at his brother. "I'm not sure of the exact wording, but basically, he told her that living with Blue Knife was a terrible sin and nothing good would come from it," Joe looked apologetically at Jake. "He called Jake a child of the devil."

Jake just grinned at that. "Well, hell, I've been called way worse than that," he laughed. "That isn't so bad. Might at times have been true."

"There are times I have called you the same thing," Thomas laughed, punching his older brother on the shoulder.

But Kade sat silent and brooding before speaking, "Not to yer ma. To her, it was the worst thing a preacher could have said to her. To her, it was the worst thing she could have heard, especially from a man of God," Kade stared out the window before he began to talk again. "When we decided to marry, I told her I would bring her out, to a town or a fort, where we could get married proper. She just said her God would find her in the cabin. She said that she'd had enough of preachers. I figured she just didn't want to travel or wait to marry. It was winter then," Kade looked at Joe. "No, she never told me. But I guess I know now why she wanted me to go with her to see a church for this wedding. She's never been in a church since. She needed me with her today, and I let her down."

"Well, the church visit must have gone over well, didn't it, Uncle Jim?" Jake asked. "Everyone came home and seemed happy about it. No harm done, Pa."

Jim nodded as well, "The preacher didn't bat an eye about Jake being best man. It's all good, Kade."

They changed the subject then, talking about old times and present times, catching up on the two decades where the only contact between the two brothers was in letters.

They were just about ready to leave when seven dusty cattle punchers came in the door. With spurs singing, the cowboys walked up to the bar and, leaning against it, they surveyed the room. Their eyes fell on the six men, five dressed head to foot in brand new store-bought jeans and boots, and the sixth one in a suit. They took Joe's suit and the new sets of clothes on the others to mean that dudes had come to town, freshly dressed in new cowboy clothes. Then the cowboys spied Jake among them, and that's when the fun started.

"You must be newcomers to our cattle country," one of them spat at Joe, "since you ain't got no more sense than to drink with a fucking half-breed." The others with him laughed.

Jake went rigid. Rising, he stepped forward into the cowboy's face. The cowboy, taller and broader than Jake, did not back away. "I can't deny I'm a breed," Jake said levelly, "but I am not a 'fucking half-breed.' My name is Jake Welles. You call me that."

The cowboy stood up straight. "I'll call you anything I want," he challenged.

"Try it," there was no backing down in Jake's tone, "if you think you are man enough. Otherwise, get your ass out of my way."

That was when the cowboy threw the first punch. Jake ducked it easily and came back with a fist that caught the man solidly on the chin, snapping his head back and putting him staggering back against the bar. Jake grabbed the man by the front of his shirt and propelled him out the door, sending him flying off the boardwalk and into the street. The other cowboys jumped to defend their friend, and the whole Welles' crew entered the fray. They were all bloody before it was over, but they had taken most of the fighting out onto the street. It was over when the seven cowboys stayed down, and the four Welles and Lathe and Jim stood gasping but upright, leaning on the hitching posts.

"The women are gonna be plenty mad about this," Kade mused, grinning at his brother. "Hopefully, the groom won't have a black eye."

Joe looked over at the three young men with them and grinned. "They look kind of pretty to me," Joe said. Then he clamped his hand on Kade's shoulder and said, "Damn brother, I haven't had so much fun for thirty years. I've missed you."

One of the cowboys, rising slowly, looked up at Kade, "Who the hell are you guys?" he asked.

Kade looked back and grinned. "We brought that herd of cattle in yesterday. We are from the Twin Peaks ranch in the mountains southwest of here. Reckon you might want to remember that the next time you run acrost us."

The cowboy just grinned. "Hell, man, we took you for dudes. Can I buy you a drink?"

Kade looked over at his sons, "We got us a wedding, day after tomorrow. Think I better get them cleaned up before their women see them," Kade smiled at the cowboy. "Another time, but only if that includes both of my sons," he said, nodding at Jake and Thomas. "We don't cotton none to any exclusions."

The cowboy just nodded. "I don't cotton fighting him again, or any of you, for that matter," he said, grinning at Jake. Then he stuck out his hand to Jake. Jake studied the man a moment, then took the hand, offered in friendship and apology, and they shook.

It was wedding day. Kade and the rest of the men sat lazily in the hotel dining room most of the day, playing cards and reading the newspapers. They were given strict orders from their women to stay away from saloons for the day. They didn't look too worse for the wear, but the women didn't appreciate the black eyes. Luckily, Thomas only had a small cut on his eyebrow and a bruise on his temple. Joe and Lathe had black eyes. Jake, who had the most men pitted against him, only sported a bruised cheek and cut lip, and most of the swelling was down. Kade had a cut down the side of his face and some bruising, but Jim had come out without more than a split lip. Like little kids, they'd just look at each other and grin when the women weren't around.

The wedding was scheduled for late afternoon. The wedding party would return to the hotel for a wedding dinner. Jim and Kade had hired some local musicians for a street dance in front of the hotel. Thomas had made it very clear that there would be no shivaree in a strange town.

"Catch us at home if you must," he told the rest of the men, "but that kind of thing here could bring on a lot more than a fight. I don't want Beth to be doing anything more than dancing." And to this, the others agreed. Laramie wasn't their town. If the dance got rowdy, they could go to bed.

It was almost time for the women to come down when a strapping young cowboy, spurs jingling, came to the dining room door. He surveyed the room, devoid of women, and the group of men sitting lazily at tables.

"Damn, I heard there was a gawdawful Indian here but just couldn't believe it," he said, but there was a smile on his face. It was Army, decked out in blue jeans, boots and hat, neckerchief at his throat.

Jake who recognized him first, stood and met Army as he approached. The poor desk clerk, watching from the lobby, began to look for a hiding place, expecting a fight to break out, but was surprised when the dark-skinned man put out his hand to the vulgar cowboy, and they shook warmly.

"Where the hell did you come from?" Jake asked as the others stood up to greet Army. Kade introduced Joe to Army, and they all returned to their seats.

"Well, I been working for an outfit not far out of town," Army told them, shaking hands with them all. "Funny thing that happened night before last," Army pulled up a nearby chair. "I was just thinking it time to hit my bedroll when part of the crew came staggering into the bunkhouse. The foreman sees these men come in, and they were some beat up and bloody. Boss says to them, 'What grizzly you boys run into?' and they tell of meeting this Injun and a bunch of dudes. Buster is a pretty good guy, and he got to telling the story that Bull, the one with the big mouth, started spoutin' off to this half-breed. Buster says this Injun ain't so big, so Bull figured he'd be an easy mark, and he was sitting with these dudes in brand new cowboy duds and another guy in a suit," Army looked over at Joe. "That must've been you?" When Joe nodded, Army continued, "Anyway, Bull thinks this would be fun, and when the Injun gets in his face, Bull takes a swipe at him an' the next thing he knows he's near got a broken jaw and is sprawled out on the street. Buster says he was all for calling it quits then, but oh no, the rest gotta jump in and defend ole' Bull, so what's a guy to do?" Army laughed at that. "Buster says they got in a few licks, but the dudes turned out to be cattle ranchers from the mountains southwest of Laramie and that's when I pricked up my ears. I said, 'You catch a name?' and he says, 'yeah, some Welles.' So, I ask, was the Indian called Jake Welles? An' he says, 'Yeah, that sounds right.' Buster says this Welles guy wasn't a big man, but he'd learn never to fight someone with such big shoulders. He said Bull missed that fact."

Army leaned back in his chair and looked at the men around him, "I reckon I can tell by the looks of you jest which ones were in there with Jake."

"Well, there were seven of them, so what's a guy to do?" Kade grinned.

"So that would make," Army counted the bruised faces, "six of you?"

"Well, maybe five and a half," Kade looked at his brother. "Joe here is sorely out of practice." Joe just grinned. By the looks of his eye, Joe had been right in the middle of that fight.

"So's, I said to the boss," Army continued his story, "I'll draw my pay tomorrow. I got another job," he looked over at Kade. "I hope that offer of a job still holds. It seems I find myself unemployed." When Kade nodded, Army continued, "The boys asked where I was going, and I told them I was going to run down that outfit that beat them up. I told them they picked the wrong hombres to mess with, and that mountain outfit had the prettiest women west of the Mississippi. So, here I am a' lookin' for a job."

"Boy, you are always welcome in our outfit," Kade told him. "But we will be almost a week before we head out of town. Thomas gets married today."

"No shit," Army exclaimed, looking at Thomas. "I figured you and Beth would have gotten married the day after her birthday!"

They sat companionably catching up on the last few months before they heard the women coming down the stairs. The men stood up and moved to the lobby to meet the women. Faces lit up when the women recognized Army, but it was little Rachel who rushed to him, squealing with joy.

"You came back!" she exclaimed, hugging Army.

"I told you I was coming back to marry you," Army laughed, hugging her back.

Rachel pulled back and looked at him indignantly, "I am still only fifteen; I can't get married yet."

"Well, darn," Army replied. "Well, I heard tell there's a dance tonight. Reckon I can at least get a dance?"

"I don't know," but the little girl smiled impishly at him. "We will just have to see about that."

The wedding was a splendid affair. Beth looked beautiful in a pale lavender dress, and Thomas wore new jeans, a shirt, and a vest. The young couple had eyes only for each other. Jake was the best man, and Beth's younger sister Bonnie was the maid of honor. The church was filled only with the families from the valley, but even then, almost half the church was filled.

By dark, the wedding party had eaten, and the musicians were warming up their instruments. Jim and Kade bought kegs of beer which were sitting on tables in front of the hotel. News of a Saturday night street dance had spread, and cowboys and townspeople were gathering. Molly and Catherine, eyes sparkling with excitement, came out from the hotel to watch Thomas and Beth take the first dance. Soon, both girls were claimed by young men and joined in the fun. Army had claimed Rachel, then Bonnie, then Rachel again. The street filled with dancing couples, and the beer flowed.

Jake and Anna stood leaning against the hotel, watching the festivities, and taking turns holding the baby. As much as Jake liked to dance, he wanted to keep a low profile. This wasn't Ft. Laramie, where, with one incident, his reputation was cemented for a year. He did not want to have Thomas and Beth's wedding dance ruined by a brawl. So, he stood with his arm around Anna, leaning against the hotel wall. They got long looks from some bystanders, but there was no trouble.

It was Jake who first recognized the familiar figures coming down the boardwalk toward the street dance. He pushed himself off the wall, squeezing Anna's arm and directing her attention to the two men approaching. She also recognized them and smiled.

"Wait here," he said. "I'll be back."

Jake went over to meet the men as they came up on the outskirts of the dancers.

"Richard . . . Jackson," he said, offering his hand to each, "you are a sight for sore eyes!? What the hell are you doing back here? You lost?" he asked.

If bystanders wondered what well-dressed Englishmen were doing shaking hands with an Indian, well-dressed though he was, no one said anything. But many eyes followed them as they made their way back to Anna and the baby.

"Let me find Pa," Jake said after the men had warmly greeted Anna and admired little Kestrel. "I know he is going to want to see you." Just as Jake was turning to leave, he saw Jackson scanning the dancing couples. The streetlights were dim, so it was hard to distinguish one couple from another. "Hey, Jack, maybe you better come with me," Jake was smiling. "I think someone would be pretty angry at me if I don't get you over to say hello."

They found Kade and Sabra dancing at the far edge of the crowd, and nearby was Molly. She was dancing with a tall, lean cowboy and laughing up at him as they moved with the music. But when her eyes rested on Jackson, Molly stopped still with surprise, and then a radiant smile lit her face. Molly looked up at the cowboy and spoke a few words of apology before turning to Jackson and throwing herself in his waiting arms.

Richard and Jackson were back in America on business. Jackson had decided on the business he wanted to invest in, and it was the cattle business on the western plains of America. The two had been in Denver and Cheyenne talking to cattlemen and making arrangements for a shipment of cattle to be brought up from Texas the next summer. Another rancher in Cheyenne would take Jackson under his wing for a year to get started and learn the ropes. Richard needed to get back to England and would be leaving by the end of the week. Richard had hoped to get out to visit the Welles' ranch before he left, but time was going too fast. So, Richard was glad that he had heard about this wedding dance being held in honor of some mountain rancher's son. When the story of the saloon fight reached him, Richard hoped the story was about Jake and his family.

The music and dancing went on until well after midnight before the crowd started to thin. When the musicians put their instruments away, the crowd dispersed. The hard-core drinkers left for the nearby saloons, the cowboys for their bedrolls or bunkhouses, and the rest to homes or hotels. It was a wedding and dance to remember.

As Sabra and Kade climbed the stairs, Kade had a surprise for her. Stopping on the landing, he turned her to him.

"You wish we would've had a wedding?" he asked her simply.

Sabra smiled up at him, "Well, back when we were married, I didn't have many friends, and what you had were scattered a long way away. I don't see how we could have had a wedding. No sense in wishing for what couldn't be."

Kade changed the subject. "Jake and I saw the preacher tonight at the dance. He seems a good sort."

"I know," Sabra was serious. "I liked him. I . . . well, I just liked him."

"Jake and Anna decided that as long as we are here, they would get the baby baptized. You up for church in the morning?"

Sabra was surprised, "Really? I never thought of suggesting that. I just wasn't thinking of doing things in a church. But yes," she found the idea pleasing, "I'd like that."

Sabra was both nervous and excited to be going to church the following morning. She dressed carefully. Unlike the wedding where only their own party attended, there would be a whole congregation there today. Sabra liked the preacher. He had been a traveling preacher for many years when he was younger, ministering to outlying settlements and Indian villages alike, so he welcomed Jake into the church. But that wouldn't mean a congregation would do the same.

Sabra was not dumb. She knew that Jake had confrontations when he went to the fort every year. Jake never told her about these, but she knew. He talked to Kade about it, and Kade talked to her. Kade probably told her watered-down versions, but they also had visitors in their valley. Often, someone, like Sam or Army, would come, and the men would laugh over something they had seen or heard at the fort involving Jake. Even this week, the men never told why they got in a fight in the saloon, but she could put the pieces together from what the men didn't say.

As Sabra, Kade, and Molly descended the stairs to the lobby, she was surprised to see all their party waiting there for them. Jake, Anna, and the baby were ready to go. Mattie and Matthew were all decked out in clean dress clothes, waiting with their two sons and two daughters. Jim and Sarah stood with Will, James, and Bonnie while Thomas and Beth stood close together near them. And by the door stood Richard, Jackson, and Army. Even Army had found clean clothes and was scrubbed and smiling.

"Oh, my," Sabra breathed, "everyone is going." Her eyes filled with tears of gratitude for these people. They would stand with Jake. They were his family, and by close friendship, her family as well.

They did cause a bit of a stir coming into the church. People scooted around so that there was enough room for them to sit together. Sabra noticed one man had an Indian woman with him, and no one seemed to care. She started to relax. It had been twenty-seven years since the last time Sabra attended a church service. To her, it was like coming home.

The minister preached a good sermon. He was not a "fire and brimstone" preacher, but instead talked of forgiveness and love. The service brought Sabra back to her childhood and going to church with her mother. Good memories she had pushed away over the years.

When it was time for the baptism, the preacher called the Welles family up. Beth and Thomas were going to be the godparents, but the preacher also wanted Kade and Sabra to come forward. The minister took little Kestrel and gave her to Beth to hold. The baby was good, not even crying when the preacher dripped the baptismal water on her forehead. But when the baptism was over, Beth did not give the baby back to Anna; instead, she and Thomas stepped back from the front, leaving Sabra, Kade, Jake, and Anna still standing before the minister.

"Now we have another special thing this morning," the preacher announced to the congregation. "Both of these couples were wed in civil ceremonies since there were no churches near them. So, they have asked to have their vows renewed this morning."

Sabra's eyes widened, and she looked up at Kade. He smiled down at her. "You did this?" she whispered.

"For you," he replied simply. Sabra answered him with a smile filled with joy.

It was a very abbreviated wedding ceremony, with first Kade and Sabra, and then Jake and Anna repeating the traditional wedding vows. But as Jake's turn ended, Sabra saw him lean over to Anna, and she heard him whisper, "And I will not sell you."

There were many congratulations for the two couples. Apparently, everyone knew what would take place during the service. Only Sabra had been surprised. The hotel dining room was crowded that day as they all went for a celebratory meal.

It wasn't until after the meal, when they were back in their hotel room, that Kade pulled out the wedding certificate that the minister had given them and showed it to Sabra.

"I like that preacher," he told her. "If we lived here, I would go and listen to him again. He talks straight and doesn't judge."

On the wedding certificate, where it said, "Date of Marriage" the minister had written "November 23, 1849" and this was followed by "Renewed Vows: July 2, 1876." Sabra read these dates and looked up at Kade.

"He put down our first date as if it was real." There was wonder in her voice. "You did this too."

"Sabra," Kade said seriously, drawing her close to him, "I made my vows to you twenty-seven years ago. They were enough for me. We didn't need no preacher, no government official, no paper to make them more real. But this here today, this was the right thing to do, for you and for our children and even for our friends. And this was right for Jake and Anna too. But I wouldn't have done it lest the preacher accept that we were already married. I drew the line at that, and he didn't fuss." Then he added sheepishly, "I might not have the first date exactly right, but it was about that time."

"So is Jake and Anna's written like this too?" Sabra asked, pulling away and looking up at Kade.

Kade nodded, "Jake didn't know the date he and Anna first said their vows either, but he figured that any late July day would work." Kade grinned then, and reaching out to pull Sabra to him, he whispered, "Molly went off with Jackson. Jackson rented a buggy, and they are going out for a drive. Come wife, we have a wedding afternoon to celebrate," Kade smiled down at her. "And we won't get shivareed."

As they lay in the bed later that day, Sabra had a thought. "I suppose everyone knows where we are, why we disappeared?"

"Probably," Kade murmured, nuzzling her neck. "But I don't suppose today we are the only newly married couple enjoying a lazy Sunday afternoon. We can try to be respectable by supper."

CHAPTER 12

Fourth of July – 1876

With the Fourth of July coming up, it was decided that the Twin Peaks families would stay in town and take part in the festivities. There was a new buggy coming on the train on the third, ordered by the four families. It had two rows of seats and could seat four easily. The buggy would come partially assembled so before they could drive it home, the men would have to get it ready to travel. Jim, Kade, and Matthew thought it was time to get a comfortable carriage for the women or the young people to use. It would have runners that could be used in the winter for sleighing. There were beginning to be ranches and settlements nearby, if one or two days away was "nearby." The young people, especially, thought that having a buggy might be a good thing. Jeremiah, for one, was seeing a schoolteacher who was a two-day ride from them, teaching in a mining town. Times were changing.

The Fourth of July celebration included horse races in the morning, a picnic in the afternoon, and fireworks at night. None of the young people had ever seen fireworks, so they were excited to stay over. The plan was to spend the fifth assembling the buggy and leaving for home on the sixth.

Jake and Molly each had a horse to race on the morning of the fourth, so the whole clan was up and out to

the track at the edge of town long before the races began. Jake's horse was the same one that Molly had raced
the summer before on the Oregon Trail. Blue was a year
older and even stronger. Molly had been ecstatic to find
that there was a race just for women. She knew her father would never let her race against men when Jake
and Thomas could ride, but he didn't voice an objec-
tion to her riding in the women's race. Molly was riding
Rascal, the young gelding she had trained. As Sabra had
suspected, this gelding would not be sold. He had become Molly's personal mount. Kade had looked over the
competition and knew that neither race would be easy,
but he had faith in their horses. He wasn't disappointed
either. When the races were finished, Jake brought his
horse in a neck ahead of the closest competition, and in
the women's race, Molly led by a length. Side bets put
money in everyone's pocket, and the reputation of the
fine Welles' horses grew. They would have buyers next
year for the dozen or more that they would want to sell.

The picnic began at noon. Sponsored by the busi-
nesses and the town council, along with donated beef
from nearby herds, it brought in a crowd from town,
homesteads, and ranches. For a frolic of any sort, people from outlying ranches and homesteads would travel
upward of one hundred miles to take part. Cowboys,
farmers, and townspeople rubbed elbows all afternoon.
There was also a contingency of Native Americans who
joined in the fun. There were foot races and games of
strength and a small band to entertain the crowd. In a
nearby corral, cowboys gathered to ride some broncs or
to show off with roping exhibitions. Throngs of people
ambled from food to fun all afternoon. For the Welles,
Bates, and Jorgensens, it was a great time to be in town

and take part in the festivities. Only the oldest of them remembered Fourth of July festivities from long ago homes in the east.

Late in the afternoon, Jake and Anna were leaning against a corral watching a cowboy saddling a blindfolded horse when a runner came from town. The young boy was carrying a stack of papers, grasping one in his hand.

"Extra! Extra!" the young boy called, waving a sheet of paper over his head. "News just in off the telegraph! Massacre in Montana!"

Jake tossed the boy a penny for a sheet, and he bent over it to see what was so exciting while the boy handed out many more. As he read, Anna nudged him for the news.

"Cheyenne and Sioux banded together and had a battle with a regiment under Custer," Jake said, still scanning the paper. "This isn't good. Sounds like the soldiers were wiped out," Jake looked around. "Let's find Pa. I don't like this."

"Is that close to here?" Anna was worried.

"No, but it was almost a week ago. There's a powerful lot of warring Indians out there somewhere, and none of them are my Ute people," Jake took Anna's arm, and they headed toward the picnic grounds. "Don't think we want to chance running into any of them."

They found Kade and Sabra, who had little Kestrel, also reading a news sheet.

"What do you think of this?" Jake asked Kade.

Kade looked seriously at Jake, "Maybe nothing. This happened a long way away. But says here there were over a thousand Indians fighting there. They gotta go somewhere. They can't stay together long because they can't supply themselves like an army can with supply wagons. You know, if there are a thousand warriors, there are double that with women and children along, not to mention the several thousand horses they'd have with them. So out there somewhere is a whole passel of Indians, probably going in a lot of different directions right now. And they can travel a long way in a week," Kade thought a minute. "Think we better get that buggy ready to roll this afternoon so we can head out first thing in the morning. See if you can round up Thomas and Army, and I'll go find Jim and Matthew."

Leaving Kestrel with Sabra, Anna walked off with Jake. "Should I start getting us packed up?" she asked.

"Yes, I think so," Jake replied. "We can pick up the supplies we bought at the mercantile in the morning before leaving. But get us as organized as you can so we can leave as early as possible."

A disturbance caught Jake's eye. At the edge of the crowd on the outskirts of town, two Pawnee men were leaning against a hitch rack, watching the people while two more were slouched against the boardwalk. Six mounted cowboys were addressing the Indians, swinging their lariats menacingly.

"You red sons of bitches think you can come back here after killing our soldiers?" one cowboy growled. "We should just string you up as a lesson."

The Pawnee men just watched the cowboys, faces showing no emotion. When he got no response from the Indians, the cowboy swung his rope, settling it over the neck of one of Indians and onto his shoulders. Jake, anticipating what was coming next, pulled his knife from its sheath and leaped to catch the rope as it tightened around the Indian, dragging the man away from his perch. Anna instantly knew there would be trouble, and looking wildly around, she glimpsed Jackson and Molly visiting with a group not far away. Anna raced to them.

"Molly!" she panted. "Trouble!" With those two words spoken, Anna turned and ran back toward Jake.

Jake slashed hard on the rope, and it cut loose, leaving the cowboy and horse heading out with the remnant dragging. Jake turned and went to the Pawnee and took the rope off, helping him to his feet. By then, the cowboy and his five friends had turned their horses and were descending on them.

"Get them out of here," Jake whispered urgently to Anna. "You too."

Anna turned and spoke to the Pawnee in their native language. With gestures and words, she impressed upon them that they should leave. They were startled that a white woman was speaking fluently in their native language, but they listened, and when she hurriedly finished, they slid away without a word. Anna turned back to Jake. She was more afraid of what might happen next with Jake than what would happen to the Indians.

"That was a dumb thing to do, breed," the ringleader said.

Jake looked at the cowboy mildly. "They are Pawnee. The news said it was Cheyenne and Sioux in the battle. Pawnee had nothing to do with this."

"Hell, they're Indians. What difference does it make?"

"Makes a lot of difference," Jake replied evenly. "Maybe if people would know that a lot of our problems wouldn't happen."

"So, what kind of Indian are you? Maybe you should be swinging?" another cowboy spoke up, riding his horse up close, crowding Jake.

"I'm the kind you better not tangle with," Jake spoke quietly, but his eyes were cold, and his gaze held the cowboy's. He did not give ground, and he did not put his knife back in its sheath.

"And if I decide I want to tangle?" the first cowboy growled. "You ruined my rope."

"Wrong place to put a rope," Jake still spoke calmly, but his gaze was direct. "Here's what you need to know about me. I'll shake your hand in friendship, or I'll cut your throat if you push me. You decide."

"I'll vouch for that," an English voice spoke up. "I've shaken his hand. Don't think you want to pick a fight with him." It was Jackson coming up to stand beside Jake.

"He's my brother. Fight him, you fight me," Thomas came up beside Jackson.

Suddenly many other voices were calling out with, "he's my cousin" or "he's my friend" or "he's my son." The group of men standing beside Jake grew to twice the size of the mounted men facing him.

"Boys," it was Army who spoke last. "You know me, so listen up. These are the 'dudes' that banged up the Triple S hands. You don't want to mess with them. I'm standing with them too. What you think you are doing is not going to solve anything."

Tension hung in the air for another moment as the cowboys assessed the crowd around them. Then they made a decision, and backing their horses up, they turned and headed out of town. The men around Jake began to relax and started to smile at one another.

"You just can't seem to stay out of trouble, can you?" Uncle Joe slapped Jake on the back. "Here, I had to come to your defense again."

"Hell, you had so much fun the first time," Jake grinned, "I figured to give you another chance."

Uncle Joe sobered then and said to Jake, "What you did was the right thing. I'm proud to call you nephew."

Army, though, looked at Jake, assessing him before asking, "So would you cut his throat?"

Jake was thoughtful, but when he answered, he didn't smile. "Well," he said, "let's just say I'd hope it wouldn't come to that."

Most of the crowd dispersed. The excitement was over, and with the news of the massacre, the celebration ended. The Welles' camp gathered and made a plan. They would assemble the buggy that very afternoon and they would watch the fireworks that night. The town was sobered by the news of the massacre, but the fireworks would still go off. The young people especially wanted to see fireworks, never having seen them before. Then, first thing in the morning, the mountain families would load their supplies and head home. The vacation was over.

CHAPTER 13

Desperate Stand – 1876

T he haying crew had been cutting hay for a week already and had hauled in loads for two days, stacking them behind the Bates and Jorgensen cabin at the mouth of the valley. They had not seen a trace of any Cheyenne or Sioux, neither on the trail home nor at the settlement. The Welles, Bates, and Jorgensens had traveled as fast as they could coming home, posting guards at night and everyone on alert during the day. Kade didn't want to be caught on the prairie if they met hostiles.

Now they had been home for eight days. Kade was beginning to relax, but he knew that until the army sent out soldiers again on regular patrols, there was always a chance that some of the warriors from the Custer fight might wander south. It was a slight chance, but still worrisome.

"Stay together," Kade had cautioned everyone after getting home. "Keep your rifles handy, and don't go out alone and be exposed."

"You think there is a chance that some of them bucks from that far up north will really find us here?" Sam asked when the families returned.

Kade looked around at the family and friends grouped around him as they began to unload supplies. "Finding us would be somewhat like finding a needle in a haystack," Kade answered. "But it can happen. There are goin' to be young braves that tasted first blood and liked it. I can't see that every one of them would just ride back home and go back to reservation life. I reckon there are some out there that are jest plain looking for coups."

Kade looked at Matthew and Jim as they hauled out barrels of flour from the wagon. "We run two wagons, a buggy, and how many horses in from the plains on our way home? We been following the river, and that would leave a trail as plain as a road to any Indians that cross it. Nothin's to say they won't get curious to see where all those hoofprints go," Kade looked back at Sam. "It's a slim chance that any band of hot-headed warriors would get here. But if any would, they would be thirstin' for more scalps. I don't aim to give 'em any."

So, for a week now, the haying crew kept a good watch, rifles at the ready on a sling under the hay wagon. The women had stayed near the cabins in sight of the men. Old Tom sat outside of his cabin every day, watching the valley and across to Kade and Sabra's as well as the new cabin below the barn of Thomas and Beth's. Tom's old joints might be stiff and sore, but his eyes never failed him. He sat with his old Hawkins and a newer Winchester Carbine beside him.

This 1866 Winchester was the first to carry the new Winchester name. The Winchester Arms Company was started by Oliver Winchester who had bought out the Henry Company. Kade had given the rifle to Tom in 1870 as a Christmas present. While Tom still favored his old Hawkins, this new rifle could fire several shots before having to be reloaded, a definite advantage over the old Hawkins. Tom might be riddled with rheumatism, but he would sound a warning if he saw anything amiss from that direction.

On this eighth day, the hay crew had a load of hay on both wagons when the second wagon came out of the river and hit a rock just right so that it cracked the wheel. Half the men stayed and helped Jim get the wheel off, and the rest went on and unloaded the first wagon.

"Can you fix it, Jim?" Kade asked before going off with the first load.

"If I can't, I'll bring out a new one. But I'll try to fix it first, and that will take some time," Jim replied, contemplating the wheel.

"Think the boys and I will ride some colts then. We can start back on the hay tomorrow. We will be just back in the valley. We won't go far. Keep your eyes open," Kade surveyed the fields and the crippled wagon by the river. "Wait 'til morning if you get the wheel fixed, and we can all go out together and mount it."

Jim just nodded as he, Jeremiah, and Matthew struggled with the broken wheel. "Sure, see you in the morning," he didn't look up as Kade and his crew headed to the hay lot.

Kade, Jake, and Thomas rode back down the valley toward home. They were riding four-year-old colts, but the ride had been a relatively easy one. Kade wanted to stay close, so they did no mountain climbing or riding into the trees. Instead, they worked the young horses on various skills that would make them more valuable when they sold them. The men worked the horses on collection and lead changes, roping and dragging logs in preparation for roping cattle, and standing ground tied for extended lengths of time. Jackson was due in any day, and he was going to bring some hands with him. Jackson wanted to buy a string of horses for his newly started cattle business, and he wanted the best.

The three riders came together and headed home. The day was warm but not hot like on the plains. They still had hours of daylight left, but after bucking hay all morning and early afternoon, it wouldn't hurt to kick back early. As they came closer, they noticed the horses tied up below Tom's cabin.

"Looks like Tom is having a party," Thomas remarked. "Think we should stop?"

Jake grinned, "A party at Tom's in the afternoon means a nip of whiskey and some damn good stories. I'm game."

Kade just grinned, still surveying the countryside. As they approached, he saw that Lathe, Army, and young James had joined Tom and Sam in the shade. Sure enough, the whiskey jug was sitting beside Tom, but it was too early for any serious drinking. *That was just as well,* Kade thought. He didn't want anyone drunk these days, not until the snow fell or they got word that all hostiles were well out of the area.

Tom was finishing a story as they walked up the slope and the rest were chuckling. A comfortable silence fell over the group as Kade and his boys settled themselves. It was James who broke the silence.

"Grampa Tom, is Clara and Martha inside?" he asked.

"Nah, they walked themselves over to Sabra's before you came," Tom smiled mischievously. "They figured someone would come wanderin' up this afternoon an' Clara said iffen we was goin' to sit around tellin' lies, she was goin' to leave."

Quiet settled again until James spoke once more.

"Grampa Tom, if you ain't going traveling anymore, who's going to teach me about women?"

That brought a laugh from the group, and Tom's eyes twinkled with mischief, but it was Lathe who answered.

"Twasn't Tom who taught me."

"Waugh boy!" Tom guffawed, "yer teacher was a student of mine."

Jake hung his head and grinned, and Lathe colored slightly. Young James didn't catch on and looked around the group. "You Uncle Kade?" he asked.

Tom laughed at that. "Old Kade is too good a man fer that. His pup ain't, though," Tom grinned at Jake. Looking back at James, he said, "You need to go with Jake one summer. He can teach you all he knows. Yer too young yet."

"I'm not that young," James protested. "I'm fourteen now, almost fifteen. I seen those girls in Laramie City. They looked pretty good to me."

"Don't let yer pa hear you talkin' like that er' you'll never get to go with Jake," Tom laughed. "Jake's takin' after me, an' bein' a bad example to you innocent young men."

Silence settled around them again until Tom, seeming to think about something, asked, "James, you got any idea why the good Lord above give a woman two breasts?"

This was going to be good, Kade thought, smiling inwardly. Tom was up to something and Kade, for sure, knew enough to keep his mouth shut right about now.

Wide-eyed, James shook his head but answered tentatively, "Reckon they'd be lopsided with one?" That brought some laughter.

"Wal, I guess that would depend where one was placed," Tom reflected. "But no, don't reckon that is it. You see, when a young man and woman first get together, them breasts are a mighty fine thing fer a man to have. But then along comes a young'un. That jest upsets the whole plan," Tom stopped and puffed on his pipe, waiting. The older men knew better than to say anything, but James rose to the bait.

"What do you mean?"

"Well, here is that little bitty baby takin' a man's pleasure away. So, what's a red-blooded man to do but share."

"How's that?" James asked, clearly confused.

"Wal, here comes the new father and sees his young wife sitting in that brand new rockin' chair, baby to her breast and iffen he jest kneels down next to her, he can jest pull that rockin' chair to him, and baby is content on one side, and he can pleasure on the other. That wouldn't happen lessin' a woman had two," Tom finished.

Samuel colored deep red at this. "Hellfire," he whispered under his breath, "I thought we closed the door."

"Son, you didn't close it soon enough," Tom retorted, and the whole contingency burst out laughing.

"A man learns lots when he jest sits around all day," Tom mused. "Seein' a lot of horses tied up at cabins during all hours of the day around here lately. Doors close pretty quick sometimes." This brought a blush from Thomas and Jake, but they knew better than to say anything.

"Course, I been watching those doors closin' durin' th' day fer nigh onto twenty-seven years now. Some things jest don't change."

Kade grinned at Tom. No sense in denying the obvious. Damn old man anyway. Kade knew enough to keep quiet, but Sam hadn't learned his lesson yet and spoke up.

"Well, at least we got a reason to close our doors, old man," Sam teased. "An we don't go to bed two hours afore the daylight leaves us."

"Wal," Tom replied, unperturbed, "there be nothing nicer than crawling into bed and watching the light fade over those two twin peaks."

Sam, instantly catching on, groaned and hung his head, knowing he had laid himself wide open. But James, not understanding, had to comment. "Grampa Tom, there ain't peaks out your window, just a mountain ridge."

Kade grinned. *Bless the innocent boy*, he thought. Tom fixed an eye on James.

"Boy, I got the best woman a man could ask for. She takes care of me and loves me, and there is nothing like lying in bed with her an' taking pleasure in her mountains. I jest wish you the same joy someday."

Sam groaned again. "That is my mother you are talkin' about," he moaned. "Shit, how did we get on this subject?"

Tom just put his head back and laughed heartily, the rest joining in. Then after a bit, Tom sobered and said, "I see my darlin' and yers, Tenny, starting fer home, so guess this subject is closed."

Kade, also, had noticed Martha carrying the baby, and Clara leaving his cabin across the meadow. They walked carefully down the slope in front of Kade's cabin and started across. Martha was wearing new shoes, brought home with them from Laramie City. One of the shoes had a built-up sole and fit better around her foot than the raised moccasin that Tom had made her. She still walked slowly, but she walked more easily now, with no leaning toward her shorter leg. The men sat quietly for a few minutes watching the two women as they ambled slowly across the meadow toward them.

It was then that shots began, far off from the river direction. First there were two shots, then a pause and three more rounds followed in rapid succession. There was a pause then more volleys were heard. Kade and Jake were up and heading to the horses at the first sound, the rest following behind. They knew instinctively that there was trouble.

"James!" Tom called sharply, "Take your horse an' get Clara an' Martha. They cain't run. Bring 'em home."

James nodded, and kicking his horse into a run, he went after the women. The rest of the men already mounted, headed toward the cabins and the river beyond them at a dead run. There was trouble out there in the river valley from the sounds, and most of the men were up the valley.

Kade was the first to reach the cabins. He saw Matthew and Jeremiah spread out in front of their cabin, sheltering behind the upright supports of the wood fence, guns up and shooting. Sarah was also at the fence, her rifle in hand. Mattie and Catherine must have been at Sarah's as they stood on Jim and Sarah's porch waiting with Bonnie and Rachel, rifles with them. Kade had the fleeting thought that all his days of hammering it into these people that the women should also be comfortable with firearms had not been wasted.

Kade dismounted on a run, leaving his horse to ground tie by the cabins. He joined Sarah, who was resting her gun on the fence, looking for a target.

"What? Sarah?" Kade asked, voice clipped and eyes searching for trouble.

"Jim and Will went out with the wheel to put it on!" Sarah pointed out toward the river. "I heard the shots and looked out, and I saw one of them fall!" Sarah's voice rose, "Oh God, I think it's Jim."

"Did you see how many?" Kade didn't need to elaborate. They both knew marauding Indians had found them.

"When I heard the first shot and looked out," Sarah was near panic, "I saw maybe a dozen off to the east, and there were more moving along the river, but I couldn't see how many. The hay wagon is blocking my view."

Off in the distance, Kade could see that at least a dozen horses were being held by an Indian, which meant that the riders of those horses were somewhere out in the tall grasses. As he studied the landscape, Jake and Thomas came up beside him. They, too, were scanning the fields, looking for movement. On the one hand, the harvested hayfields closest to the cabins made it difficult for any Indians to get close enough for easy shots. On the other hand, the settlers themselves would be exposed if they tried to reach Jim and Will, who were out by the river.

"Sarah," Kade turned to her, "go back to the cabin. Get yourself and the others inside. They're out there and will be coming closer in the grass. Take out the glass or break it and be ready to shoot. We don't know how many are out there or if they will circle around behind. You watch all ways, front and back. The boys and I will worry about Jim and Will. Now go."

Sarah looked out toward her husband and son and back to Kade and nodded. Just as she turned, Kade added one more warning. "Sarah," he said softly, "if things go bad here, remember to keep the last bullet. Remind the girls," Kade saw from the stricken look on her face that his meaning sank in. They had talked about this long ago when the farm families first came. Always keep the last bullet for yourself if it came to that. Sarah hesitated, then nodded and made her way back to her cabin.

"Pa, I can get out there," Jake said, his voice calm. "We need more rifles out there with Jim and Will. We are too far away here to be very useful."

"Son, they'll pick you off before you get there," Kade replied. "I 'spect they are scattered in those uncut fields. We got to hope they move, an' we can see that."

"You forget I spend my summers with Brown Otter," Jake said, surveying the land. "We don't sit around all day smoking a pipe. I can get out there."

Kade realized what Jake was thinking. The Utes were known for their fine horsemanship. They had perfected the art of riding off the side of their horses, shielded from their enemies by the horse's body. Jake was good at that, having spent many a summer riding with the Utes and participating in their games and races. Never before had he used the skill in a battle, though. It was dangerous and risky.

"They'll pick off your horse," Kade argued.

"It's a good horse," Jake replied. "They'll want it. I don't think they'll shoot it. I'm going to try."

Kade didn't like it, but Jake was right. They needed rifles out farther. And they would be unprotected trying to get out there on foot. While Jake went to his horse and got ready, Kade pulled down some of the fence boards so that Jake could ride directly from the yard toward the hay wagon without going around by the gate. It would be a shorter way to get to Will and Jim. Then Kade watched the tall grass while he waited for Jake. Kade saw the grass move across the river and for just an instant, he saw a form moving. He sighted on the spot and shot. The grass waved abruptly, but no figure came up out of them. Kade thought he had hit one. How badly hit was anyone's guess.

Jake spurred his horse into a run before leaving the yard, jumping the fence logs laying on the ground. Immediately, he slid off to the side. Using a repeating rifle, he fired under the horse's neck. Jake didn't hope to hit anything, but it could possibly keep the Indians from popping up to get a good aim at him.

The rifles barked along the fence line, trying to give Jake cover. Kade watched his son as he headed out. When Jake was halfway to the wagon, Kade took off on a run. There was a boulder out in the field. It would offer Kade protection to shoot from and get him a bit closer to the enemy. Kade hoped the Indians would be so busy watching Jake that they would miss his run. He knew that if he was sighted, he had a good chance of getting hit himself. Shots rang out, but he didn't feel anything whistle close to him. Just as he dove behind the big rock, he saw Jake's horse, almost at the wagon, go down. Jake lost that gamble; his horse was shot out from under him. Kade saw Jake roll twice and then scramble back to his dying horse. He had another rifle secured there. He needed the protection of the horse's body, and he needed the firepower. Jake himself did not appear hurt as he dropped behind his horse. He sighted over the horse and returned fire, then unstrapped the extra rifle and hauled it back to him.

Kade watched the grasses, trying to see movement. It was a still day, not a breeze blowing, so nothing moved unless it was moved by man. Jake must have seen something because he fired. This time Kade saw a brave jerk up and then fall back. That was one down for sure. They waited. The Indians were more cautious now.

Tom watched James bringing Clara and Martha across to him. James got Clara on the horse first, then handed up the baby to Clara and got Martha on behind. Then grasping the horse's mane, James urged the horse forward at a slow lope, lunging along beside it. He brought the women right up to the cabin and helped them dismount.

"Clara, bring me my other rifle an' yours too," Tom ordered. He moved his chair to a stack of wood and used the woodpile to shoot behind and to rest his rifle. Tom was never far from his old Hawkins, but he had the Winchester in the cabin. Although she was never a good shot, Clara had an older rifle, and Tom wanted that close by also. Tom looked at Martha, thinking, "Martha, get your gun and get in my cabin, leave the front door open so you can hear us, but watch out the back window." As the women went as ordered, Tom looked at James.

"Boy, straight up from here is a cliff that overhangs some. It will shield you from above, an' there is a passel of rocks below the overhang that you can get behind . . ."

"Tom, I ain't gonna hide!" James interrupted him.

"James!" Tom's voice was harsh, startling the boy. "Listen to me now. You take yor horse an' tie him to the south of them rocks in the trees. Take him as far as possible but where you kin still see his head from them rocks. Then you get back to that slide. You watch . . ."

Tom suddenly stopped talking, watching the distant sidehills. Anna was sneaking through the edge of the woods, little Kestrel in her arms, heading for Sabra's cabin. Above her crept a brave. Tom propped his rifle upon the woodpile. The Indian was slightly above and back of Anna, and at the moment, Tom didn't have a shot. He also knew Anna had no idea she was being tracked.

Suddenly, the brave leaped down on Anna, grabbing her hair, and pulling her around. One arm grasping the baby, Anna tried to fight him off. The Indian jerked her back off her feet and threw her to the ground. Even at that distance, Tom could hear the baby squalling. The Indian towered over Anna and raised a war club above her.

"Stay down, Anna," Tom whispered, almost to himself, and squeezed the trigger. Anna stayed down, and the bullet found its mark. The man jerked once, straightening, then he slumped to the ground, dropping the club as he went down. Anna was up then like a rabbit, and, gathering Kestrel in her arms, she ran for Kade's cabin.

"Rifle!" Tom held out his hand to Clara, and she put his other rifle in it, taking his Hawkins to load. Tom sighted and fired again, and a man tumbled out of the trees.

"Holy shit, Tom," James whispered, "I didn't even see him!"

"Load those, Clara," Tom spoke levelly, "an' James, git your horse up the hill an' tied up an' git in them rocks an' keep down. Iffen they sent runners up that ridge behind Kade's, there's likely gonna be some comin' this way. I figure they came along from the river, so it'll take 'em longer to get on this side of our meadow. But they'll likely come. Watch yer horse's head. When they come, that horse will tell you iffen they be comin' straight at you or up above you. Watch where the horse looks. Then signal to Martha. She won't be able to see the horse," Tom stopped a moment. Shots rang out from behind Kade's cabin. The cabin was in the way, and Tom couldn't see what was going on behind it. He knew that Sabra, Beth, Molly, and now Anna were in that cabin. Some or all were shooting out the back or side windows. But the worst of it was that he knew he couldn't help them now.

"If they come at you, there will probably be more'n one. Hold your shot as long as you can. Now go, James," Tom barked, "an' don't come down until someone tells you to."

James went. Grabbing his horse's reins, he climbed the slope behind the cabin, dodging trees until he disappeared behind the cabin. Tom and Clara could not see his rock hideout, but Tom knew the terrain and knew that Martha could see that far from the back window of the cabin. It was a waiting game now, Tom knew. He hoped he was wrong, and that James was keeping watch up there for nothing, but in his gut, Tom knew that more trouble was coming.

Kade wasn't sure how much time had elapsed. He could hear Jake talking with Will. He recognized Will's voice, but he couldn't hear what Will and Jake were saying. Kade watched for movement, but for the moment, all was still. Then he heard more shots that sent ice through Kade. They came from up the valley. Kade looked back at Thomas and Samuel at the yard fence.

"Our women an' Tom!" Kade called to them. "Go!"

He didn't need to bother. Thomas and Samuel knew immediately that the danger had spread. They were racing to their horses while more shots rang from the direction of the upper meadow homes. Kade was not a praying man, but he prayed then, silently, and urgently, praying that his family was safe. He saw movement, sighted, and fired. Two for sure.

Kade watched the grass, intent on seeing something unnatural. If he could see a flash of a gun, he could aim in that vicinity, but the Indians were not standing up, asking to be shot. Without question, though, they still were there. It was a waiting game. The attackers had sent braves up the valley to scout, probably through the higher ridges; this Kade was sure. The ones out here, lying hidden by the river, were waiting to hear from the scouts. The Indians probably thought they might get the braves in a position to surround these cabins. Then they ran into Tom and the women back there. Kade hoped that Thomas and Samuel would be in time to help.

"Kade!" Matthew shouted at him, "more Indians coming!" Matthew pointed downriver, and four braves were coming at a dead run. At the distance they were, Kade couldn't see the riders well, but as he studied them coming, he recognized the lead horse. It was a horse Jake had traded to Brown Otter.

"Give them cover," he called back to Matthew, "It's Brown Otter. Draw attention away from them!" Kade took the repeating rifle and sent off shots, kicking up dust in several places, hoping that he could get Brown Otter as close as possible before the enemy realized they were being flanked.

It worked. Brown Otter was near the river before an attacker heard the running hoofbeats. Kade saw one rise up out of the grass and turn around. Kade was ready. He squeezed off a shot, and the man fell. Kade saw Brown Otter slide off the side of his horse and then, three strides later, abruptly rise back up. Brown Otter raised a war club and it fell on a buck that stood up to meet him. The man on the ground slumped over as Brown Otter continued, horse at a full run.

He galloped through the river and again sank to the side of his horse, heading for Jake. Before the warring Indians could regroup, Brown Otter was off his horse and taking refuge under the wagon with Will and Jim. The other three Utes attacked the Indians on the ground, and as the attackers rose to fight the Utes, Jake, Kade, Will, and Brown Otter came out of their hiding places and gave the Utes firepower. The war party broke and ran. Heading for their horses, they mounted and headed out. The three Utes took up the chase but only for a short distance. There were still more than a dozen braves heading out when the two groups merged in the distance. The three Utes knew better than to follow that large of a force.

Kade heard more shots ring out from up the valley. Jake was on the run toward the cabins. "You get Jim, Pa," he called as he ran by Kade. "I think he's hurt bad. I'll go check on home."

Kade was torn, but he knew that Jim needed immediate help. Anyway, Jake was faster. He'd make Jim's cabin where Kade's horse waited and be home long before Kade could get there. Brown Otter also was on the run. His horse had stopped running between the wagon and the cabin and stood ground tied while Brown Otter approached it. Brown Otter leaped on the horse and followed Jake. Together the two brothers disappeared behind the cabins.

Tom heard the shots across the valley stop. The cabin door never opened, and no renegade Indians came into view. Tom hoped that meant that the women's shots had found their mark, leaving the women safe inside. But he kept scanning the distance, watching for movement. He saw nothing. Then he heard shots behind him. James and Martha were shooting.

"Clara, get in the cabin," Tom ordered.

"No," Clara said simply. "I'm a terrible shot, but I can load. I'm staying right here next to you."

Tom never quit scanning the slopes, "Promise me iffen I get hit, you get inside. And stay down."

They waited. Shots came sporadically from the back of the cabin, but Tom could see no one there yet. Tom knew he had a fourteen-year-old boy in the rocks and a young woman in the cabin; he just hoped he and Kade had trained them well.

"Tom, look!" Clara pointed.

Down the valley rode Sam and Thomas, coming at a dead run. As they neared Thomas and Beth's cabin, they split. Thomas stopped at his cabin, and finding Beth gone, he rode on to Sabra's. Sam came on toward them. Tom signaled to Sam to watch the woods. Sam reined in his horse at the bottom of the slope and took cover behind some trees. He watched the woods for movement. Then the shots started again. They were closer. Tom knew that both Martha and James were shooting, but he could see nothing with the cabin in the way. Clara knelt between Tom's chair and the wood pile, but Tom was exposed from the side and the back. He didn't move fast enough or steady enough to try to change his position. Tom just kept scanning the distant hills, as well as his front yard. But he knew the shots were coming closer.

Clara heard the shot from the woods as it whistled nearby. She immediately knew that Tom was hit. His body jerked, then collapsed, almost falling from the chair. Clara reached up to steady him and caught him looking down at her kneeling on the ground next to him.

"I been happy with you," Tom whispered faintly, drawing a painful breath.

"Tom, don't leave," Clara moaned.

"Tell James he did good," Clara almost couldn't hear the words Tom whispered so weakly. Blood bubbled up from Tom's lips. But he struggled to smile. "Tell Kade it's been a hell of a good ride with . . ." Then the life went out of him, and his body relaxed. Clara knew he was gone.

Fury rose in Clara. Taking her rifle, she aimed at an unseen foe and started to fire. Clara was not a good shot. This was no exception. She did not hit a thing except trees, but it distracted the two enemies hiding in the woods. They didn't know she was a terrible shot. As the Indians retreated, looking for better cover, Sam sighted them. He dropped the first and wounded the second. The second Indian disappeared into the woods and was gone.

Sam raced up the hill, but even he could see that he was too late for Tom. Quickly he assessed the situation, going to the cabin to find Martha trying to comfort the baby yet still holding the rifle and keeping watch out of the window.

"Oh, Samuel," she cried, "I think James is hit! He's in the rocks up the hill!"

Sam took off at a run. He found James, bleeding and weak but alive, straining to stay upright. James leaned on the rock and still had his rifle ready. He had a wound on his face where a bullet grazed him, and a leg wound from a shot that ricocheted off the granite. While the bloody face wound looked bad, Sam knew it was the laceration on the leg that was more serious. Sam scooped the boy up in his arms and headed down the slope.

"I can walk," James protested. Sam knew better. James was losing a lot of blood. Then rounding the cabin and seeing Tom slumped in his chair, bloodstains covering his chest, James cried out, "Oh God, not Tom! Tenny, not Tom!" Sam just kept running.

Sam laid the boy on Clara's bed and told Martha to start cutting off the pant leg. "We gotta see how bad that is," Sam said. "It's bleeding powerful bad." Then leaving James to Martha, he went out to his mother.

"Ma, you can't help Tom anymore," he said gently. Clara sat silently beside Tom, tears running down her wrinkled face. "James needs you now. I need you to come help us with him. You know more 'bout carin' fer wounds." He took Clara's arm, helping her up. When she looked up at him, he said simply, "You go see to the livin'. I'll see to Tom."

CHAPTER 14

Hard Good-Byes – 1876

Jim was dead. Will said it was almost instant. When his father was hit, Will dragged him under the wagon before returning fire. He thought Jim was aware of Will being with him for only a minute, and then the life just went out of him. Will had a crease in his forearm that bled quite a bit at first but wasn't deep. Matthew had wood slivers stuck in his neck from a close bullet that ripped through a fence post. Rachel caught a bullet that shot half of her ear off as she looked out a window. Brown Otter had ridden back to tell Kade that Jake and Thomas were with the women at Sabra's. He didn't elaborate on whether they were hurt or not but went off to join the other three Utes.

Kade helped get Jim's body into a wagon and then headed for a horse to check on his family. Brown Otter hadn't gone inside Kade's cabin, so he had no other information for Kade. Kade mounted and, putting spurs to the horse, he headed home.

When Kade rode up to the cabin, Thomas stood out front with a sobbing Beth held close.

"Anyone hurt?" he called to Thomas as he dismounted and made for the cabin.

"Ma and Anna are working on Molly in Molly's room," Thomas called, "but she's . . ." he never finished. His father had already disappeared inside.

Molly was lying in her bed with her eyes closed, covered with blood. Kade's heart turned to stone at the sight of his daughter lying so still. But Sabra looked up and saw him and spoke quickly.

"Keep your eyes closed, Molly," she cautioned, then turned to Kade. "It's not as bad as it looks. Molly didn't have the glass out of the top of the window and a bullet shattered it and splattered glass all over her. I think this will all heal. But we have some little bits by her eyes to get yet."

The words eased Kade some. He came to the bedside, took Molly's hand, and squeezed it. "Molly girl, I'm so sorry."

"Pa, it's not your fault. I have to learn to duck," Molly, eyes still closed, gave a weak smile. "Ma says it won't leave scars, or at least not bad ones."

"You're in good hands, honey," Kade whispered to her. "I got to go check across the meadow now."

Kade went outside. Jake had come up to stand with Thomas. He had saddled a fresh horse and was going to head over to Tom's, but seeing his father at the cabin, he waited beside Thomas and Beth. Beth had quit crying but was standing close to Thomas, leaning into him.

"Pa," Thomas spoke quietly, "I think they got Tom. I saw Tenny laying him out. Nobody is working on him."

Pain flitted across Kade's face. He stood and looked out across the valley. He could see the still form of a body lying there, but no one was out with it. The cabin door was open, but there was no movement that they could see in the yard.

"Pa," Thomas said quietly, "Anna said they were Cheyenne."

"Anna was trying to get here and had one attack her. She recognized him," Jake added. "He was from the village that had her. He was one of the bucks that abused her. She has some scars from him, bite marks. She said he knew her. Called her the bad name the Cheyenne gave her. I don't reckon she minds him being dead."

Jake looked across the valley. "Tom made the shot from his yard. That is a powerful long shot."

Kade looked across at Tom's yard. "Tom is the best shot I have ever seen. You boys haven't known him for his fightin', but he's probably the best man I ever stood beside. He always told me he'd sit there and watch over us. Reckon he did."

They stood silent for a bit, each with his or her own thoughts. Then Thomas asked, "Pa, you think the Cheyenne are gone, or will they regroup and come back?"

"Shit, Thomas!" Kade exploded, "I had no goddamn idea they'd come today, or I sure as hell wouldn't a been sittin' tellin' stories. How the hell do you think I'd know what they're goin' to do next?"

He turned suddenly to his horse and mounted, leaving Thomas, Jake and Beth stunned at his outburst. Kade turned his horse away and moved off a short way before stopping. He didn't turn back, but he spoke low, "Excuse me, Beth, I shouldn't have spoken so in front of you." Then he pivoted the horse to look back at Thomas, "I'm not mad at you, son. This has just been . . . I just should've known." Kade cued his horse for a lope, and he moved off toward Tom's.

❧

Jake, Thomas, and Sam took night watch for the upper valley cabins that night. Will, Matthew, Army, and Jeremiah split the watch for the farm family cabins. Brown Otter and the other three Utes made camp below Jake's cabin. Here, they would watch the north end of the valley.

One of the young men that Brown Otter had with him was his son, Swift Hawk. Hawk, as Jake often called him, had visited a couple of years earlier, and Jake knew him from summers spent in the mountain, but now Hawk, at nineteen, rode with the men. Jake knew that Brown Otter was concerned about his son's place in this new world with their lands encroached upon by whites. Many of the young people of the tribe were becoming lazy on the reservation, where the government provided annuities to the people. Brown Otter had known Jake was in Laramie City and thought it would be good to ride over and see if the family was back. Maybe Otter and Hawk would ride to the mountain cabin with Jake. Otter wanted to get Hawk off the reservation.

Clara had cleaned James' wound. The boy had passed out shortly after Sam got him in the cabin, so Clara and Martha had been able to get the bullet out of his leg while the boy was unconscious. They bandaged his leg and cleaned his face. Sam was going to transport him to Sarah's house before he lost daylight. James had lost a lot of blood, but Clara felt the wound would heal. Tom's body would rest in the cabin until they buried him the next day. Clara would sleep with Martha that night.

Kade mounted his horse and left shortly after checking with Sam. He told Sam he was going to track the retreating Indians until he lost the light. He wanted to make sure that they were not regrouping to return. Sam had offered to ride with him, but Kade had bluntly turned him down.

"I don't want anyone else leaving here right now," Kade said grimly. "The more guns here, the safer everyone will be. I won't go more than a few miles, and I'll turn around before it gets plumb dark."

When Sam told Jake and Thomas later that Kade had ridden out, they both were worried. They knew their father was not the same calm and steady man they knew. Losing Jim and Tom was affecting Kade in a way that was more than grief for good friends. Kade was a driven man right then.

"I'll ride out after him," Jake said, "and I'll probably meet him coming back. You take first watch, Thomas, and Sam can take the second. Sam, come and get me, and I'll take the third."

Jake met Kade well after dark, about three miles east along the river. Kade was on his way back. Jake heard Kade's horse loping, coming at him, so he called out. He didn't want his father to suspect an ambush. Kade answered and pulled his horse down to a walk as he rode up to Jake. Jake could hear the horse puffing, loud and labored. As Kade came into view, Jake saw the horse was lathered, white flecks against the dark coat.

"How far did you go?" Jake asked.

"I was about six miles out when it got dark," Kade replied. "I turned around then. I saw no sign they were stopping or turning back."

Jake thought about that. There hadn't been much light left when Kade rode out. Kade had pushed his horse hard to go that distance and back in that amount of time. The horse looked it too. Welles' horses were strong and had staying power, but this horse had been ridden to the top of his endurance tonight.

"It's all quiet at home," Jake told Kade. "We don't have to rush back."

They rode in silence the whole way home. Whatever thoughts were going on in Kade's head, he didn't want to share them. Jake knew this wasn't his father's usual disposition. After his outburst at Thomas that day, Jake had a feeling that his father was not in the mood for talk.

When they got back to the corral and unsaddled, Jake was surprised to see Kade catch another horse up and start to saddle it.

"You fixin' on riding out again?" Jake asked.

"I'm just going to be in the area," Kade answered.

"I'll ride with you."

"No," Kade's voice was sharp. "You get some rest so you can do a night shift. I won't be far."

Jake watched his father fade into the night. What the hell was his father up to? He knew that Kade was tired. The day's events had taken their toll on all of them, but Kade was taking this hard, too hard. It was as if he just couldn't be still.

It was shortly after dawn when Jake, Thomas, and Sam were up and saddling. Among the three of them, they had seen or heard Kade many times during the night.

"What the hell is he doing?" Thomas had asked Sam when they changed shifts in the night. "I hear him up on the slopes. Sounds like he's dragging something."

"He's looking fer the dead," Sam answered. "I think he's draggin' them over to the burial ground."

"The dead Indians? In the dark?" Thomas was surprised. "How can he find them in the dark? How does he know where to look?"

"He was asking about where the shots came from around here," Sam mused, "and he has a good idea out on the hayfields where some of them fell. I reckon he can most likely smell them. If he gets close to a body, he'll know by how his horse acts."

"Shit," Thomas said. "We could go out in the morning, and all of us help him haul them in."

"I don't think he wants help right now. But when he starts digging graves in the morning, we better be ready. We may have one hell of a big grave to dig for those Indians," Sam peered into the dark. "I've been hearing a lot of crashing around in those woods."

During Jake's shift, he saw Kade come in and change horses again. When the dawning light was just a glimmer coming over the mountains, he saw Kade return once more and stop at the barn. Kade came out with something, mounted his horse, and rode off again. Jake suspected his dad was going to start digging graves. He went and woke Thomas, and before they both were saddled, Sam came to join them. Taking shovels, they rode out to the river valley. They stopped by the cabins first. Army was on the last shift and came to meet them.

"Kade ever go to bed last night?" Army asked.

"He hasn't been in all night," Jake answered. "You see him out here too?"

"I seen him out in the moonlight, riding the fields. He was bringing in the bodies, weren't he?" Army asked. "He jest went by here a bit ago, and I think he had a shovel."

"We're heading that way," Thomas said. "Pa can't do it all himself. He's gonna collapse soon."

"I doubt your Pa will collapse," Army commented, "but he's gonna be powerful tired. I'll roust the boys and we'll come help."

By the time Jake, Sam, and Thomas arrived at the burial ground, Kade had begun to dig. The bodies of the Indians were piled haphazardly at the bottom of the hill. Kade had started to dig a grave up the slope. There were four small graves of still-born babies scattered near the top of the rise. One was a baby of Jim and Sarah's, and beside this grave is where Kade was starting to dig.

"I can do this myself," Kade grunted as he threw out a shovel full of dirt. "Go dig something to roll them other bodies in."

"They can wait," Jake replied evenly. "We are going to help you. Jim was my blood relative. Tom was Thomas' namesake. It's our right."

Kade looked hard at his sons, then shrugged and continued digging. When Army arrived, he had Jeremiah, Lathe, and Will with him. Kade glanced at the young men coming up the slope and then studied the mound of bodies lying down below.

"I'd like to get them in the ground before any of the women might wander up," he spoke more calmly now, gesturing down the hill. "Put them in one hole, jest big enough for them all." Kade looked at Will, "This here should be your dad's grave. You want to stay and help me, and the rest can get started down there. We'll do Tom's last."

Satisfied to leave Will with their father, Jake and Thomas led the group down the hill. As they approached the pile of bodies, it became apparent that Kade had drug the men in by their legs, arms stretched out behind them. He had simply pulled them into a pile and took the rope off their feet and left them wherever they ended up.

"Sweet, Jesus!" Jeremiah breathed as they came close.

Thomas was surprised to hear blasphemy coming from Jeremiah. Matthew was a righteous man and his children, save Lathe when he was out of earshot, seldom even cussed, but they never, Lathe included, used the Lord's name in vain. As Thomas came closer though, and saw what Jeremiah saw, he had a fleeting thought that Jeremiah was not using blasphemy but was rather looking for support from his Maker. Thomas looked over at Jake, taking strength from his older brother's quiet composure.

"Holy shit," Army murmured. "He scalped them."

They all stopped dead, staring at the Cheyenne. There were eleven bodies, and each one had been scalped.

"I didn't think your Pa ever took trophies," Jeremiah said, looking at the bodies. "Tom once said Kade never liked to do that."

"That wasn't trophies he was taking," Jake replied slowly. "That was revenge."

"Fuck, that's not all," Lathe was shocked. "He cut off . . . oh, shit, that one there." Lathe pointed at one brave that lay off to one side.

The Indians were dressed in breechcloth and shirts, or some had leggings while some went shirtless. But on the far side was one buck who was naked from the waist down. His private parts were missing, along with his scalp. Besides that, the skull of the brave was horribly mangled, face smashed, especially around the mouth and jaw. A war club lay on the ground beside the dead man.

Thomas looked at Jake, trying to stay calm like his brother. This was a side of his father he never thought he would see. Jake saw Thomas watching him.

"That was for Anna," Jake said grimly. "Reckon he figured he'd save me from doing it." The others cast glances between them at that statement, but no one commented more.

"Why the head?" Lathe finally asked, barely in a whisper.

"It's the Indian way," Jake replied, eyes on the dead man, "to mutilate the part of the dead that did harm," Jake hesitated. "He was from Anna's village where I got her. He abused her, raped her. She carries scars, bite marks of his," Jake looked away then. "Let's get them in the ground," he said, dismissing the subject, and they all began to dig.

Even with so many men digging, it took a while to get a hole big enough for eleven bodies. It wasn't like they cared how laid out the Indians were so as soon as it was big enough, they rolled the bodies into the pit. Brown Otter and Swift Hawk had found them by then and helped put the bodies into the grave. Brown Otter's black eyes glittered when he saw the mutilation of the one brave, and he caught Jake's eyes questioningly.

"Pa got to him first," Jake remarked quietly.

"That is good," Brown Otter told him gravely. "You do not come from our generation that does such things. You are from two worlds, but you do not need to do this thing."

"I thought last night that maybe he pulled them all in so I wouldn't know which one," Jake was thoughtful. "He did this for Anna, but for me too."

They had the bodies in the grave, and the hole filled when Kade came down the slope, leading his horse. Without a word to the rest, he took a lance off his horse. It was a Cheyenne lance. He put one end on the ground and stamped on the middle of the lance, breaking it into two pieces. Reaching to the off side of his horse, he untied a leather string and pulled it up over the horse. There hung eleven bloody scalps, all in a row. Fastening the string to the top of one piece of the lance, he thrust the lance into the mound of dirt, driving it in as far as he could. He left the other piece laying on the grave, and without a word, leading his horse, he returned up the slope to resume digging Tom's grave.

The men stared at the lance with the scalps dangling from it. Army broke the silence. "Is that some kind of Indian headstone?" he asked.

They stood, contemplating it. It was Brown Otter who answered. "It is not a headstone," he hesitated. "It is a warning."

They thought about Brown Otter's words for a while before Lathe asked, "What do you suppose he did with . . . the other?"

No one answered at once, then Jake said quietly, "Let's just hope he threw it away." Turning, Jake left the mass grave and headed up the slope toward Kade, the rest following behind.

With all the help, the grave for Tom was soon ready. No one had spoken about what had just taken place, what they had seen. The events of the last twenty-four hours were taking a toll on them all. When they finished, Kade went to his horse before finally breaking the silence.

"What time is the burial?" he asked no one in particular.

"Ma and Clara wanted to bury them about noon," Will answered. "Aunt Mattie and Sabra have a meal for us after that."

Jake looked at the sun. It was midmorning now. That would be about two hours until they would gather for the final good-byes. They had no way to preserve the bodies. They had to get them in the ground before the day heated up.

Will looked up at Kade, who had mounted his horse. "Kade," he paused, watching to see if Kade was listening, "Ma and Clara both want you to help carry them," he didn't need to elaborate. Everyone knew what Will meant.

Kade looked down on the young man, his eyes sunken hollows in his face. For a minute, Jake thought maybe his father would not reply to that, but when he did, his words surprised them all. "I don't reckon I deserve that honor," his words were choked. Kade looked at his two sons. "I'm goin' to clean up," he said. "Tell yer ma I'll be back in time." Without another word, he reined his horse and rode away.

"Yer Pa ain't taking this well," Lathe commented when Kade was out of earshot. "I ain't never seen him like this."

"You aren't the only one," Thomas replied, staring after his father as he rode away.

The men made their way to Jim's cabin. Sam got help from Thomas and Jake, and they brought Tom's body down with the light farm wagon and laid him beside Jim in the front room. Jeremiah and Will fashioned a casket out of lumber for Jim, but Tom would be wrapped in buffalo robes.

"He wouldn't want to be shut up in a box," Clara had said. "Lay him on some carrying boards an' wrap him up in the skins. He'll feel better in that."

So, the two bodies were there, waiting to be sealed away from the world. The families moved in and out of the house quietly, waiting for the sun to make noon. Sabra came in to talk to Sarah and saw her two boys.

"Have you seen your Pa lately?" Sabra asked. She knew Kade had been out all night and at the burial plot this morning, but Sabra had not talked to him since the day before when she had been dressing Molly's wounds.

"Pa went home to clean up," Thomas told her. "He said he'd be back, but he's not acting right." He told his mother and Sarah about the Indian bodies, leaving out the revenge for Anna. Then he looked at Sarah and Clara. "Will told him you wanted him to help carry them to . . ." Thomas choked then before going on, "But he said he didn't deserve it." Thomas looked back at his mother, "Pa just ain't right."

Sarah lifted her head at that, "What do you mean he doesn't deserve it?"

It was Jake that answered, "He's taking this like it's his fault."

"That is just plain foolishness!" Sarah exclaimed. "Why would he think that? And why would he drag all those bodies in and do such things?"

The answer came from the doorway. Brown Otter stood there, not sure if he was welcome to enter and view the bodies. "He brought you here. Long time ago but it was him that brought you," Brown Otter stopped, seeming to cast around for the words. "He worked all night for what your religion calls . . ." he looked at Sabra, "what is word for being sorry for sin?"

"Penitence," Sabra replied softly.

"Yes, he worked all night for penitence. He search for enemy. But I think," Brown Otter looked at Jake, "enemy inside him now."

It made sense, they realized. It wasn't just grief for his two friends, or the pain of the injured, that drove Kade now. It was the heavy burden of guilt.

Sarah stood and went to Brown Otter, "You are wise. You know us better than we do." She reached out to the man and took his hands in hers. "I never thanked you yet. We are grateful. You are always welcome in my home."

Sarah turned to Thomas, "We will need to hitch the buggy up. James wants to go to the burial ground, and he can't walk. But I need the buggy first, so will you bring it here now?" Sarah looked at Jake next. "Will you drive me up to your Pa?" she asked. "I need to talk to him."

Jake tied up the team by the barn and helped Sarah down. "I'll catch a horse and ride back," he told her. "Pa can drive you back."

There was hidden meaning there, and Sarah caught it. Kade would not deny the widow of his friend. If he had decided to forego the funeral, Sarah would make him bring her back. In Kade's present state of mind, nothing was a given.

Sarah went to the open front door and looked in, letting her eyes adjust. Kade was cleaned up and sat at the table off to one side. She studied him for a moment. He sat slumped in a chair. She could see the weariness in the man. It was like a burden sat on his shoulders, weighing him down. On the table beside him sat the whiskey jug, and he cradled a cup in his hands. But it was the fact that he hadn't noticed that she stood there that told her the most about his state of mind. Kade was somewhere else in thought.

"Kade," she said softly.

He was startled to see her in the doorway. He lurched to his feet, still holding the cup.

"Sarah," he stared at her through haunted eyes.

"I think I need a sip of that too," she said, nodding to the jug.

Kade nodded, and without a word, he got a cup and poured a small amount of liquor into it. Sarah took the cup and took a sip. She shuddered visibly and looked at Kade, "How do you men drink this stuff?"

Any other time, Kade would have smiled at that, but he just contemplated the question and answered simply, "I think it's somethin' we get used to."

"Must be," Sarah answered before taking another sip. "The second swallow goes down easier. I think my throat is numb."

Silence settled around them for a moment before Kade blurted out, "Sarah, I am so sorry."

Sarah looked at him levelly. This was the type of opening she wanted. "Just exactly what are you sorry for, Kade Welles?" she asked severely, looking him in the eyes. "Are you sorry you brought us out here twenty-five odd years ago?" She took a breath before continuing. "Or maybe you are sorry you brought us to this place where we raised our family in the beauty of these mountains? Maybe you are sorry for being the best friend, save Matthew, that my Jim ever had? Or are you sorry you helped us survive all these years and brought us away from being scrounging dirt farmers to a living that made us all well off? Are you sorry that Jim loved this place like no other? What exactly are you sorry for?"

Kade just stared at her, letting her words sink into his grief and whiskey-fuzzed mind. "Sarah, this shouldn't have happened," his words came out strangled. "I should've been ready instead of sitting up at Tom's laughing and listening to stories."

"Shame on you, Kade Welles," Sarah retorted, her voice harsh, "for taking this burden on by yourself. You taught us when we came here what we needed to know to be safe. We have been here all these years. We all have that burden, not just you. Jim was wrong to go out with only Will. Will even reminded him you said to wait. But Jim made that mistake, not you! It wasn't you."

Kade stood silent, just watching her. Forgetting the strength of the drink, she tossed down the last swallow and choked.

"How do you men stand this . . . stuff?" she struggled to find the words, tears welling, spilling from her eyes.

In two strides, Kade reached her and folded her into his arms. She sank against him then and let the sobs come. Awkwardly he patted her back, holding her tight. When she regained her composure, she moved away and looked up at him.

"Now, I will not accept any more of this," she said, her voice firm again. "Jim and Tom deserve being honored by their best friend. You will help carry them. Now I need you to drive me back."

Sabra knew the minute Kade and Sarah drove up that whatever Sarah had said to Kade had worked. Kade helped Sarah down and joined his sons and the sons of Jim and Matthew. Quietly, they carried out the two bodies. Sabra watched Kade. There remained the weariness, the grief. His eyes were sunken, but they were not haunted. Gone was the unleashed anger that had driven him. Kade was hurting, but he was coming back.

They walked, family by family, behind the wagon bearing the two bodies and the buggy. Will drove Sarah, the injured James, and Rachel. Bonnie, unhurt, walked with Martha, Sam, and Clara. Behind them walked Matthew and Mattie and their children. Kade, Sabra, and Molly, her face still swollen, cut, and bruised from the glass wounds, walked together and the boys and their wives followed. Brown Otter, Swift Hawk, and Army walked beside Jake and Anna. The other two Utes had returned to the reservation that morning.

Solemnly the procession wove its way to the two graves on the hill. The casket and the robe-wrapped body were taken off the wagon and set down beside the graves. Just before Matthew began to speak, riders were sighted coming along the river. The men found their rifles in the wagon and stood waiting to see if these were friend or foe.

There were four riders, and when they got closer, Jake's keen eyes recognized Jackson first. "Friends," he said simply. "Might as well wait for them." He walked down the slope to meet them.

It was Jackson and three cowboys. Jake recognized the one as Buster who shook hands with him after the fight in Laramie City. Briefly, Jake filled them in before leading them up to the waiting families. Nodding to Matthew, the funeral began.

Matthew spoke words from the Bible. *He should have been a preacher*, Sabra thought. But she knew his farming soul couldn't leave the land. He found God in the sunrise and all the growing things as well as the Book. When Matthew finished, he looked at Kade.

"Would you like to say anything, Kade?" he asked.

Kade looked down at his two dead friends. They lay, one in the open casket and the other covered by the buffalo robe. Kade searched for the words before beginning to speak.

"Here lie the two best friends a man could ever hope to have. Both brave, honorable men. One a farmer, hunter, business partner and friend; the other a trapper, mountain man . . . jest the best man I ever had the privilege to ride with. We traveled together for a long time, one longer than the other. I ain't regretted a minute of it. They brought out the best of us . . . of me. This is a hard good-bye," Kade stepped back. He had no more words.

☙

The bodies were in the ground, covered, and the procession started back to Matthew's where Sabra and Mattie would set food out on tables in the yard. Jake noticed that Molly had not looked at Jackson. She ducked her head, letting her hair fall over her face. *Even in grief,* Jake thought, *a girl worries about her appearance.* He saw Jackson look curiously at the pretty girl, wondering why she didn't greet him.

Jake went to Jackson. "She got a might cut up in the fight," he said quietly. "Might leave some scars on her face. Not bad but . . . you know girls."

"She got shot in the face?" Jackson was alarmed.

"No," Jake clarified, "glass from the window. Ma don't think it will be much for scars, but Molly's face is a bit swollen and looks rough right now."

Jackson nodded, looking toward Molly, who was walking toward the cabin ahead of them. "Thanks, Jake," he said in his English accent, "I don't believe it makes a difference to me."

He strode on, catching up with Molly. Taking her arm, he pulled her out of the line of people. Jake watched his sister. She wouldn't look up at Jackson. Jackson gently reached out and lifted her hair off her face. He traced her face, his fingers gently moving around the cuts. Jake saw him lean over and whisper something to Molly. She sobbed then, and he folded her into his arms. The rest left the young couple there and walked past. *Healing comes in many ways,* Jake thought. Molly was beginning to heal.

Sabra and Mattie put out food on long tables, and the families and visitors sat around eating and visiting all afternoon. After eating, the young people gravitated to logs while the older couples stayed at the table. Jake and Sam seemed to be the two who fit both groups. They moved with their wives to the steps of the porch, where they could interact with both groups, young and old, as they lounged. The stories of Tom and Jim went around, letting them laugh while remembering the good times.

Army sat with Rachel, his arm over her shoulders. He was eight years older than Rachel, but Jake didn't think the age difference would be an issue. Army, who last year teased the girl that he would come back and marry her, had already spoken to Matthew about his intentions. It didn't look like Matthew had the same feeling that a girl had to wait until she was eighteen to wed. Jake suspected that Army and Rachel would marry next year. When the fighting was over the day before, and Army heard that Rachel was injured, he had rushed to the house and found Rachel with a bloody rag clutched to her ear. He had picked her up and sat with her in his lap, rocking her back and forth as she cried.

Brown Otter sat next to Jake and watched his son join the young people, sitting beside Lathe. The two boys were the same age, nineteen, and seemed to enjoy each other's company. In the past, when Brown Otter had come to visit bringing Swift Hawk, Lathe and Hawk spent time hunting together. Hawk was comfortable around Lathe. Hawk didn't talk much around the rest of the young people, but they would tease him or ask him questions enough that he was included. He was warming up to these "white cousins," distant relatives though they were.

"I always used to say you walked in two worlds," Brown Otter commented to Jake, watching Hawk. "I used to think that was a bad thing, not being one or the other, but I was wrong. You have choices. My way of life is ending. I don't like the reservation life. I don't like it for my children. I am too old to change. My place is with my people. My woman knows no other life. So, we will stay with our village. But I want my children to have a choice."

Jake contemplated Brown Otter's words. "It is hard to be an Indian now," he said. "The white men will keep coming. If our community of white people weren't here, the other whites would still come. We don't really want them to come either, but it is going to happen."

"I remember as a boy, when our father lived with your mother," Brown Otter said, "she would read us stories about the white people. The people in the cities that she read about were as numerous as the stars in the skies. Our father would question her about those things." Brown Otter stopped for a minute before continuing, "I know my father knew our way of life would someday end. He told me I must learn the language of the whites. I think our father could have lived the white life better than me."

That intrigued Jake. "Why?" he asked.

"You forget that our father grew up living with Jacob, our grandfather, for almost fifteen years before going to live in the village full time. When Blue Knife took my mother as his wife, he lived with her in the village. He visited Jacob less then, but he still went to Jacob's cabin," Brown Otter leaned back, remembering. "When

I lived with your mother, before my father came for me, I learned her ways. We worked with the horses, played with the little children, and even hunted together after my grandfather was killed. It was very different for me, but I liked her. I liked her laughter and her music and the stories she read from her books.

"When my father came, she changed at first. She was afraid of him. She was like a captive. But she learned that my father loved her. When she learned not to be afraid, she even loved him under the robes."

Jake stifled a grin, "That is probably more than I need to know."

Brown Otter chuckled and looked at his half-brother, "You have too much white blood in you. These things are hard for you to talk about. In the village, it is just part of nature; not something to hide," Brown Otter grew serious again. "But when your mother became happy again, she made the music and read the stories and laughed. Our father liked that. If he had lived, he would still be in that mountain cabin with your mother. He was content there.

"Other than that year I spent with your mother at the cabin, I have lived all my life with my people. It would be hard for me to leave the village for good. I don't like it on the reservation, but I don't want to leave my people, either. I want more for my children. I want them to have choices. I want them to understand the white people. They still have a little bit of white blood in them."

The two brothers sat for a long time, listening to the conversations around them before Brown Otter brought up another question. "Will you go to the mountain cabin this summer still?" he asked.

"Yes, but I am not sure when I will get there," Jake replied. "We are short two men now . . . three actually with James laid up . . . so I need to stay for the haying. But I am thinking I may get Lathe to come with me. We will only be there a few weeks. I want to start another room on the cabin. Settlers are coming into that area, and I want to make my claim on that land. I don't want to lose it. If there are new improvements, it will be harder for a claim jumper to try to take it from me. I don't worry about it in the winter. The snows keep people out, but in the summer, I need to make that place mine. I am thinking of going next summer with Anna and Kestrel and staying longer. We have talked about it. Anna agrees. That is our special place."

Brown Otter nodded, thinking, "Kestrel," he commented, "your little falcon. She will be a pretty little bird."

Jake smiled at that, "If she takes after her mother, she will be. I already have Beautiful Bird, so we decided she would be our little falcon. Maybe we call her White Kestrel?"

"I will leave Swift Hawk here when I go," Brown Otter changed the subject again, "and you teach him how to put up hay like a white man. Then you bring him and Lathe to the mountain when you come. Stop at the village, and we will go on together to Jacob's cabin. We will make the cabin walls go up faster that way. I, too, do not want to lose that place to other white men. But it is not my people's land anymore."

"I'd like Hawk to stay," Jake agreed, "and we will come to the agency when we are done with the hay. I think Lathe would like to visit the village again too,"

Jake smiled at that. "He made some friends last time I took him there."

Sabra sat next to Kade at the table and felt his body start to sag against her. The sun was going down, and the shadows were lengthening. Sabra knew Kade was exhausted. She had cornered Jake earlier and made him tell her the whole story.

"What else, Jake? What else are you not telling the women?"

"Maybe you should just leave it, Ma," Jake replied gently. "You don't have to know."

"Your father and I have never had secrets," she said. "I can't help him if I don't know. And Lord knows your father needs some help right now."

Jake gave that some thought and then relented, "The Cheyenne who attacked Anna knew her. He had raped her in the village. He also bit her so hard that she still has a scar on her left breast. She told me that the man who Tom shot was the man who hurt her. I mentioned it to Pa after the fight was over yesterday. I know now I shouldn't have said anything," Jake sat quietly, watching his mother. "You know Pa scalped them all. But that one, he took a war club and ruined his face. And he cut off . . . the other offending part." Jake looked off into the distance, thinking. "Mother," Jake seldom ever called her that, "if Pa hadn't done that, I would have. It sounds pretty bad, but I would have. Maybe I have more of Blue Knife in me than I thought."

Sabra sat quietly for a moment before speaking, thinking over her response. "Then I am glad your father did it for you," Sabra told him. "Some things I didn't want you to grow up to know . . . or do."

Sabra remembered that conversation with Jake as she sat with Kade. She nudged him. "I think it is time we go home," she said quietly.

Kade nodded, and they got up, saying their good-byes. Side by side they walked back to their cabin. Sabra did not make conversation. She didn't feel that Kade had the energy to talk.

It wasn't even full dark when they got home, but Sabra knew that the only place Kade needed to go was to their bed. He was physically and emotionally drained. She was loath to leave him alone until he drifted off to sleep, so she undressed and crawled into bed, spooning against him, waiting for his body to relax around her.

But relaxation didn't come. She could feel him behind her, willing himself to sleep and not finding the peace he sought. His body remained rigid.

"What are you thinking, Kade," she finally whispered, the shadows gone now leaving the cabin in darkness.

"Oh, hell, Sabra," he retorted wearily, "I know Sarah was right; I know I am not to blame, but I keep thinking over and over again how I could have changed this."

"With that many hostiles coming against us, you could not have kept us all from their bullets," Sabra retorted. "Tom was ready. He had plenty of time to prepare, and we still lost him. Maybe Jim would be alive, but others might be dead," she stroked his arm under her head. "You have to let it go."

"I know, but . . ." he broke off.

Sabra rolled toward him and pushed him onto his back. She began to stroke his chest, moving gentle fingertips along his muscles.

JOHNY WEBER

"God, Sabra, I'm exhausted," he murmured.

"I know," she replied, "so go to sleep."

"I can't. I just can't shut my mind off."

"So, what are you seeing?" she asked him gently.

"Everything. Tom and Jim lifeless, Molly bloody, James unconscious, Rachel . . . all of them. And I keep seeing that fu . . . that face as I . . ." Kade stopped abruptly.

"You have to stop. If you hadn't done that, Jake would have. You kept him from that. Let it go now." Sabra felt rather than saw Kade glance at her in the darkness, trying to discern if she knew. "I know," she said simply.

Sabra sat up and pulled her nightdress off, climbed on, and straddled Kade. He groaned again, "Sabra, no."

She put her fingers to his mouth, shushing him. Then she kissed him, but she was not gentle. She ran her fingers through his hair, pulling hard, bringing his mouth to hers. She brought her knee up between his legs, pushing into him. Then she moved her lips to his neck. Her hands moved down until she found him, and she grasped him with both hands, roughly. He groaned, and she felt him grow hard despite his weariness. Still, he did not move to touch her.

"Sabra," he murmured, "not tonight."

She bit him then, her teeth found purchase on his shoulder, and she knew she bit hard enough to hurt him. That aroused him from his lethargy. He grasped her around the waist and threw her off him and onto the bed beside him. He reared up, and getting on top of her, he entered her with a violent thrust. She met him, thrust for thrust, her fingernails raking his back. Somewhere deep in Sabra's being, she knew that Kade had to hurt, had to be hurt now. It was fast and furious lovemaking, almost savage. All the pain and grief and fear of the last twenty-four hours was released in both of them. It was over almost as quickly as it started. Emotionally and physically spent, Kade slid off Sabra, and she spooned back against him again.

"I'm sorry, Sabra," Kade whispered. "Did I hurt you?"

"Go to sleep now, Kade," Sabra whispered back. "I bit you first, remember?"

"You did," he said thoughtfully. "It hurt."

She didn't reply to that. She listened to his breathing and felt his body begin to relax. He was asleep almost immediately. *A woman,* she thought, *when she had that much grief and rage and pent-up emotion in her, would find a private place or someone she loved and would break down and cry.* She would sob until she was spent, releasing the grief. A man, a man like Kade, would not let himself do that. He needed something else to find release. Kade needed a woman's body, her body. He needed pain to take the pain away. He would sleep tonight, and tomorrow he would wake up and begin his journey back to himself, and to her.

CHAPTER 15

Jacob's Cabin – Summer 1877

Jake rode, enjoying the river bottom and the cool air of the mountains. They would be at the mountain cabin in a couple of hours. He looked back at Anna and Kestrel and knew they would be ready to stop. Leaving the agency the morning before, Jake and his family had been riding for almost two days.

Kestrel was a good traveler, though. At a year and a half, the little girl loved being on horses with her mom and dad. She rode for hours without complaining. She mostly babbled and pointed and petted the horse, but she was learning words and got her meaning across when she wanted something. Because Anna was still nursing, there was always a snack close by while they rode.

But he saw the weariness in Anna this trip. She wouldn't admit that hauling a baby was hard on her, not after the trouble they had had last summer between them. Jake had found out that mild and meek Anna was almost vicious when she was angry. He could grin about it now in the remembering, but at the time, they had had one hell of a fight.

Last summer, after losing Jim and Tom, he stayed to help with the haying. It cut his mountain trip down to a three-week window between haying and fall gather. He had toyed with not going at all, but Swift Hawk was with them, and Lathe wanted to ramble. Jake thought the three of them could make tracks faster if Anna and the baby stayed home. They would meet Brown Otter at the agency and then go on to Jacob's cabin and start building a new room on the cabin before heading home. With three or four days each way to travel, he would have barely two weeks to put some improvements on the cabin. He needed to make improvements so that the place looked cared for and lived in for at least part of the year. He thought he had explained his reasons to Anna, but she was upset to be left behind. He thought when he returned, she would be over her anger and welcome him back. He was wrong.

Each day Jake was gone, Anna seemed to get more and more upset. Kade told Jake that he had checked on Anna one morning a week after Jake left and found Anna throwing all of Jake's things out onto the yard. She was going to burn them. Kade got her settled down that time, but he caught Jake when Jake rode home and told him to watch his scalp. Jake's little woman was on the warpath.

And she was. At first Jake could not understand her rage. He was safe; he was home. He thought if she were worried about him getting hurt, as she had that time on the Oregon Trail when he was shot, she would relax once he was home. But she wouldn't look at him, wouldn't let him touch her.

"Anna," he finally raged back at her after experiencing hours of her sharp tongue, "what the hell is the matter with you?"

She had turned on him then, body rigid with anger. "How many squaws you take without me?" she spit the words at him. "You buy any?"

Jake was incredulous. Where did she get that idea? It took him a few moments to even think of an answer. He tried to speak more calmly, "Anna, you know I don't want any other women. We made our vows."

"You left me!" she still raged. "You go to village. Only reason to leave me was to have more squaws."

"I left you because Kestrel is so little, and the trip would be so fast. I tried to explain that to you," he was exasperated at her reasoning. "I wasn't gone that long."

"You gone three weeks!" she screamed at him. "You can't make it three weeks without a woman in your bed!"

"Woman, I made it a hell of a lot longer than three weeks before I bought you," frustration made Jake mad again, and they stood shouting at each other, waking the baby.

Finally, Jake stormed out of the cabin. Going to his corral, he saddled a horse and brought it to the house. It was well after dark now, and he knew candles would be out in the cabins, but he was fuming. He was going to settle this now.

Taking up the baby, who had gone back to sleep, he headed for the door. Anna, suddenly alarmed at this turn of events, rushed out after him. He easily mounted the horse with the baby in his arms.

"No!" Anna cried, "don't take her!"

"Then get the hell up here with me," he growled at her, "or I'll ride off without you."

Anna mounted behind him, but he wouldn't give her the baby. She rode, trying not to touch him and too angry to ask him what he was doing. They rode down to

Matthew's cabin. It was dark and quiet as everyone was in bed. Jake rode right up to the porch and dismounted, still holding Kestrel. He knew that Anna would stick with him and not run off if he had the baby. He pounded on the door.

"Lathe," he shouted to the dark cabin, "I need to talk to you."

It took a moment before Lathe came, shirtless, to the door rubbing his eyes. "What the hell, Jake," he said quietly, "you're going to wake up the whole family."

"Step out here then," Jake lowered his voice, "I need you to tell Anna something."

Lathe came out. He had hurriedly pulled on his denim pants but was barefoot as well as shirtless. He looked at Jake holding the baby and then at Anna questioningly.

"Tell Anna how long we stayed in the village at the agency," Jake commanded Lathe.

"One night," Lathe replied, then added, "unfortunately."

"And who did I sleep with that night," Jake said tightly.

"What?" Lathe asked, surprised at the question. "You slept in Brown Otter's tepee. You didn't sleep with anyone. What is this about?" Then realization came over Lathe. He looked between the man and woman, seeing for the first time the stiffness and anger between them. Lathe started to laugh.

"You mean Anna thinks you . . ." Lathe laughed harder. Anna began to look uncertain, and Jake just stiffened more. "Oh, Anna girl," Lathe said when he caught his breath, "you got this man hogtied to you." Lathe turned and went back up the steps to the porch, still chuckling. "You woke me up for this?"

As Lathe went back into the cabin, Matthew stepped out. "Jake," he said as he stepped off the porch, "I think you need to go home and let the rest of us get back to sleep." He walked closer and lowered his voice, "I think you need to work this out together." Then Matthew lowered his voice even more and whispered to Jake, "A good fuck helps." With that profound statement, Matthew turned and went into the cabin and shut the door.

Jake just stood there, looking after Matthew. He knew it wasn't the words that shocked him as much as them coming from Matthew, the settlement's man of God. Finally, he turned to Anna.

"Can we go home now?" he asked.

Anna nodded her head. Jake gave her the sleeping baby and climbed up behind her this time. They rode silently for a little while, and then to test the waters, Jake's free hand began to explore his wife. She did not pull away from him. By the time they had passed Kade and Sabra's cabin, Jake had simply laid the reins over the horse's neck, letting it wander its way toward home, and had Anna's dress unbuttoned and open. They didn't make it into the house but instead laid the baby in fragrant grasses near the corral. They both learned how good it was to make up after a fight.

Now this summer, they were spending at least a couple of months at Jacob's cabin. Jake had no intention of leaving Anna and Kestrel behind this time. Lathe was riding in the lead in front of the small herd of horses they were bringing with them. They would finish the new room on the cabin and start another cabin for Lathe in the upper meadow where Sabra and Jake's grandfather used to hide extra horses. Jake and Lathe each had six young horses to train when they weren't building cabins. And Brown Otter would come in a few days, bringing his family. Jacob's cabin was not on the reservation, but no one would find the Utes there or care if they did. While the land was off the reservation, the Utes still ranged upon these slopes to hunt. Brown Otter wanted to get his family away from the agency for the summer. Jacob's cabin would be the place.

Lathe was so much like Jake. He liked the high mountains where the hunting was still good. He was riding colts now for the Welles and stayed as far away from farming as he could. Of all Jake's cousins, Lathe was the one who would have followed old Jacob if they had lived during the same years. Eight years younger than Jake, Lathe had developed into a strong, lean man. He had restless feet like Jake. Moving back and forth from the low valley of their folks to the high mountain cabin seemed to satisfy the rambling nature of both men. Lathe liked the Utes and had gone to Brown Otter's village with Jake long enough to be accepted by them. There were a couple of comely women who Lathe particularly liked and their husbands liked the gifts Lathe brought. In late summer, Jake and Lathe would go back home for the last half of the haying when the ranch needed more help, helping haul the stacks into the hay corrals. But until August, they had over two months to ride and work in the high elevation. Thirty years earlier, Jake and Lathe would have trapped these mountains together. Now they packed four-year-old colts in to ride the high slopes.

There were five cabins now in the area around the hot waters. Steamboat Springs, the people there were calling the place. The first family to settle, the Crawfords, thought a town would grow quickly and hoped that soon there would be a post office and railroad coming to the area. Jake hoped that didn't happen. The countryside would be filled with settlers when the railroad arrived. Jake, Anna, and Lathe had stopped briefly and visited with the Crawford family as they passed through. The Crawfords seemed like friendly people and didn't appear to mind Jake's mixed blood. If they wondered how he came to have a white wife and white cousin, they didn't ask. They had admired the horses that Lathe and Jake had with them and offered a meal. But Jake wanted to make tracks, so they moved on. Jacob's cabin was calling to him. He wanted to be home.

Three days later, Brown Otter and his wife arrived with Swift Hawk and Hawk's younger sister, Kasa. They raised their tepee on the other side of the barn, where they could get water easily from the little stream that ran through the corral. Brown Otter's wife, Snowbird, was already a friend of Anna's and the two women got along well. Brown Otter had two daughters. The eldest daughter was married and stayed with the tribe. Brown Otter's younger daughter was Kasa, which meant Dressed in Furs. Kasa, which was easier to say than Dressed in Furs, was sixteen. When Jake had visited the village the year before, Kasa was still a gangly teenager, shy around him and giggly when he observed her with other young women. But Jake had known her since she was a young'un, and she was a favorite niece to him. This year she had filled out and had a more serious demeanor.

A pretty girl with big dark eyes, she was quiet when she was around the adults but would bustle around the fire helping Anna and Snowbird with their chores.

The days settled into a routine of sorts. The men worked on the cabins in the morning and rode, hunted, or fished in the afternoons. Jake and Lathe had six horses each to ride, so they usually rode three a day. Swift Hawk sometimes rode with them. When he did, Jake and Lathe could ride longer on two horses. Swift Hawk was good with the horses and quickly learned the ways that Jake wanted the horses handled. Jake had been taught not only by his father and mother but by the skill of the Utes. The Utes were well known for their horsemanship skills and good horses. The combination turned out horses that were getting a reputation of being the finest animals. From Ft. Laramie to Laramie City, the Welles' horses were becoming well-known.

One afternoon, Jake rode home from the high ridges and came upon Lathe and Kasa. The girl had been out searching for greens and spring berries, and Lathe came upon her and stopped to visit. Jake reined in for a few minutes, visiting, and then moved on. He had another horse to ride. He wasn't far when Lathe caught up to him. They rode in companionable silence down the mountain until they came out on the meadow.

"I'm not sure how to make this place make money for us," Jake commented, looking down on the cabin and tepee nestled on the far side. "But I just can't seem to leave it. It keeps calling me back."

Lathe surveyed the scene then looked at Jake. He just nodded. This place was part of their heritage, with its high peaks around it and its bubbling streams and beaver ponds. Neither Jake nor Lathe had met their ancestor, Jacob, but Jacob's cabin kept calling them home. During the next four weeks, the new room on Jacob's cabin was finished. It was a small room that would give Jake a place to leave his trading plunder and cured skins. It wasn't that they needed much space, but Kestrel was toddling around now, and she got into everything. They had already caught her once in his packs playing with some trading needles and scattering his things. He was glad to get his gear shut away from her.

Lathe liked the upper valley, so he chose a spot and was putting up a small cabin there. The men had a path cleared through the fallen timber between the upper and lower meadows so that they could ride right into the upper meadow now rather than clamber by foot over the fallen butts of trees, long brought down by beaver. It would never be a permanent home for Lathe, but rather a summer cabin where most of the living would be outside. Lathe did not want to bunk with Jake, Anna, and the baby. The walls were almost up on Lathe's cabin, and he was anxious to move his few things into it.

Many times during that month, Jake would come out on a clearing or the meadows and find Lathe and Kasa together. Jake wondered about that. He didn't see any intimacy between them, but they seemed comfortable with each other. He knew Lathe enjoyed a woman when he visited the village. But Lathe never talked about settling down, and he never went with Jeremiah to the mining town where Jeremiah's sweetheart lived and taught. Growing up so far from other young people was lonely sometimes. Lathe was twenty now, starting to make his own way. But he never voiced a desire to find a wife or settle down to one job.

⚬

Finally, the walls for Lathe's cabin were finished. The rafters would be next, and then they would make a roof out of bark for this year. After putting the final horse away one afternoon, Lathe headed toward his cabin.

"I'm going to move my packs inside the walls," he told Jake. "I can sleep in there as well as out here in the yard unless it rains. I can set a tent in the corner. We should get the roof on this week."

"I'm kickin' back then," Jake said, going to rescue Kestrel from falling in the brook, "or chase after this little devil. See you later for supper."

Lathe surveyed his cabin. It was small, but it was all he'd need. He didn't cotton sharing a cabin with a married couple. They could share a campfire along the trail, and he could play with little Kestrel, but when the darkness came, he wanted to be off by himself. He knew he cramped Jake and Anna's nights when he was close.

This would be a good cabin for the summers. He knew he would follow Jake here for as long as Jake came. This high mountain meadow grew on a man and his own cabin would give him privacy.

As Lathe came out of the cabin for his last load, he saw Kasa approaching. She had a basket over her arm with greens and berries in it. She had been out scavenging the surrounding hills.

"You heading back?" Lathe called to her.

Kasa smiled at him and held up her basket, "For supper."

"What have you got there," Lathe went up to her, peaking in the basket.

"Berries and wild onions," she replied, and, plucking out a berry, she held it to his mouth.

It was sweet, and Lathe rolled it around his mouth, then peered into the basket and plucked out a wild onion. "I like these too," he said.

Kasa laughed at him and took it away. "For supper. It makes your mouth stink now."

"What do you care if my mouth stinks," he teased her.

"I care," she frowned at him. Then looking at the cabin, she asked, "You move things in?"

"I'll have to put up a tent if it rains, but the walls are done," Lathe answered. "Come look at it."

Kasa was impressed by the little cabin. For the moment, Lathe only had a pile of robes in one corner for a bed, and his personal supplies piled up in another corner. There was no fireplace in this cabin, for it was only meant for summer living. Lathe knew he would take his meals with Jake, so there was no need to build extras he didn't need.

Kasa plucked another berry out of the basket and pressed it to his mouth. Her fingers lingered on his mouth, tracing his lips. She looked up at him and smiled shyly. "Nice mouth." Then her fingers traced his face and moved into his hair. "Nice face," she whispered.

She stood close, looking up at Lathe. He could smell the sweet woodsy smell of her, berries and grasses and the mountain breeze. Without thinking, he leaned down and kissed her, and she met him, kissing him back. Gently he pushed her down to the ground upon his robes. They lay for a while, wrapped together, lips exploring. Lathe felt Kasa pull his shirt from his trousers, fingers moving underneath and up his sides. The sensation sent tingling throughout his body, and he knew he was close to losing control. Somewhere in the depths of his being, he fought the urge to let go. Kasa was his cousin's niece, a distant relative of his own even. He pulled back from her.

"We can't do this, Kasa," Lathe whispered.

"Why?"

"Have you laid with a man before?" Lathe asked.

"No, but I am grown. I am ready."

"That's not the point," Lathe told her. "It isn't the way this should happen."

"But you are ready," she said softly. "I feel you."

She was right about that, Lathe thought, but he couldn't go back and face Jake and tell him he just bedded his niece. He had to have more honor than that.

"A young girl needs the first man to be special," he said. He wasn't sure that was exactly what he meant, but it was what he could come up with.

"You are special to me," she answered him, her fingers still touching his back.

"I can't just take you here," Lathe struggled to find words for what he meant. "It's not right to do that to you."

"You mean not hurt me; no, not spoil?" she questioned.

"Right," he agreed, "I can't spoil you. You will find a man to live with, and that man is the one who should . . ."

"Roll over," Kasa commanded, interrupting. She pushed Lathe away from her. She shoved him hard so that he lay on his side, his back to her. He didn't question. *It would help him to get control if he turned away,* he thought. He was wrong.

Lathe felt Kasa moving closer, curling up behind him, leaning over his waist. She laid her head on his side and reached down and started to unbutton his jeans.

"Kasa, don't . . ."

"*Shhh*," she commanded again. "I won't be spoiled this way."

Lathe groaned when her hands found his erection. She knew what to do too. Never had he experienced this sensation when he had lain with a woman in the village. There the sex had been straightforward and intense. This was entirely different, yet similar, at least in his response. Somewhere deep in his being, he wondered if this was a betrayal of Jake, but he pushed it from his mind. With her first touch, he was lost to her. When he felt the bliss of release, he shuddered and lay back, breathing deeply.

"Where did you learn to do that?" Lathe asked Kasa softly, his fingers tracing her face tenderly.

Kasa smiled at him. "Tepee very small," she said simply.

Holy hell, Lathe thought. *It must have been.*

He looked up at the blue sky above and remembered something from his childhood. There had been visitors to the valley, old trappers who rambled the mountains yet. They had stopped to visit Tom. It was always fun to have visitors, and the boys had joined the circle around Tom's cabin. Lathe had been about eight then, so Jake would have been sixteen. They had all been sitting and listening to stories until the visitors were ready to leave. As Kade and the boys walked the visitors down the slope when they were leaving, one mountain man looked over at Jake, then addressing Kade, asked him how long he had packed a squaw. Kade had replied that he had never packed an Indian woman. Glancing at Jake, Kade said that Jake was Sabra's son by her first husband and that he had adopted him. Kade didn't elaborate on who the first husband was or what the circumstances were. He just left it there. But one of the visitors didn't let it drop.

"I hear tell that livin' with an Injun jest makes a white woman that much better," he had grinned at Kade, "hear they learn things. Reckon, you know?"

Kade turned, and in one smooth movement, he hit the man hard enough to lay him out flat. Then without another word, Kade walked away. At the time, Lathe had not understood what the man had said that made Kade so mad. He never asked anyone either. Now Lathe understood, and though he still knew better than to ask, he too wondered if it was true. Tepees were very small.

Jake sat leaning against the cabin with a sleeping Kestrel stretched out on his legs and watched Lathe and Kasa walking down from the upper meadow. They walked together, Kasa carrying a basket in one hand. Jake noticed that they would touch hands as they walked, almost secretly as if they were making sure the other was there. Now and then, one or the other would sneak a glance at the other, little smiles breaking out on their faces like they shared a secret joke. *This was different*, Jake thought, than what he had seen in the chance meetings he had come upon when out riding. This could mean something. At the tepee, Kasa turned off and went inside.

"Where's Otter and Hawk?" Lathe asked as he came up to sit in the shade beside Jake.

"They went fishing," Jake replied. "They should be back soon. Anna is over at Snowbird's. They are doing something there, but there's a roast sizzling on the fire. Should be ready soon."

"Hmmm," Lathe replied, finding a place against the cabin to sit. "I'm not starving. I can wait."

They sat in companionable silence for a while. Jake figured if he waited long enough, something would come out if Lathe had anything on his mind. He didn't have to wait too long.

"Jake," Lathe started tentatively, "did you ever regret being . . . you know, mixed blood?"

"What's to regret?" Jake asked. "It's not like I could change it."

"Well, maybe regret ain't right, but did you ever wish you weren't?"

"Wishin' for things you can't have don't make sense. Waste of time," Jake replied. "It's what you make of yourself that counts. But that's not what you are really wanting to know, is it?"

"Well, hell," Lathe sighed, "you look at Kestrel here, and she's got a pretty light complexion. Between you and Anna, you got a heap of white blood in her. So, you think she's gonna have a rough time of it?" Lathe still wasn't really at the crux of it. He tried again, "You think ever about how your young'uns are going to be? How they are going to be treated when they grow up?"

319

"I would think most fathers that love their young'uns wonder that," Jake replied thoughtfully, "but it isn't a mixed-blood question, it's just a father question. Hell, look at Martha, growing up crippled and never being happy until she met Sam. You think only mixed bloods have problems? It isn't so." Jake looked at Lathe, and suddenly he knew where this conversation came from. "So, are you wondering what your kids might have to go through if you were to maybe take an Indian girl for a wife?"

Lathe shot him a quick glance, "Well, yeah, I sort of am."

"Look, Lathe. You can't make the way for your children easy or hard. You just have to raise them up so they can deal with their problems. And this feeling that breeds are bad is only held by some. It's changing. Hell, I heard tell of some town way up north that got a half-breed mayor. Now, who would have thought that would happen? But it did. Being of mixed blood just isn't something to worry about. Train up your young'uns to know how to be proud of themselves. Teach them how to live."

Lathe digested this and sat thinking. Finally, he spoke again. "You know, Kasa and I are related, aren't we? But it's pretty distant, ain't it?"

Jake laughed at that. "Yes, very distant. Kasa's great grandfather was Jacob. Jacob was your ma's uncle, so he's your great uncle. I don't reckon you are going to have to worry about that." Jake had a pretty good idea where this conversation was leading now.

"So, if I were to want to ask for Kasa, how do I go about that? I mean, do I go and talk to her father?"

"You are going to want to offer Brown Otter a bride price for Kasa," Jake told him. "If he accepts it, you can marry Kasa. If we were at the village, there would be a ceremony, but if you do it out here, he might just send her to you."

"Bride price?"

Jake laughed, "Yes, bride price. You give what you think the bride is worth to her father. Like two or three horses, maybe with new blankets laying beside them."

"Oh," Lathe was disappointed. "I don't have any of my own horses here."

"You got wages coming, and probably some on Pa's books too," Jake grinned. "If you want, I could sell you a couple horses." Jake paused a moment before asking, "This seemed to come up sort of sudden. You sure this is what you want to do?"

Lathe thought about that before answering, "I do. I been sort of talking to Kasa here and there for a month now, and we enjoy each other. I keep watching for her, things like that. And this afternoon, well, I kissed her, and I just didn't want to let her go. I guess I'm either going to have to marry her or leave here before we do something we shouldn't."

Jake laid his head back and laughed at that. "I do remember the feeling," he said. "So, here's what I'd suggest. You take that blue roan stud we brought with us and one of the sorrels and tie them up to that tepee after dark. If Brown Otter accepts that, he probably will send Kasa over tomorrow. If not, then you either can add more to the pot, or you give up."

Lathe was surprised, "That roan is the best one! You want to let him go?"

"Well, he's for sale anyway. You might as well be the one to buy him," Jake paused. "It won't be any cheaper to give him three horses that aren't as good!"

Jake was starting a fire in front of the cabin the following morning when Brown Otter came out of the tepee to find the two horses tied up to his tepee stakes. Otter looked across at Jake, and the two brothers grinned at each other. Brown Otter leaned into his tepee and spoke before coming over to inspect the horses. It didn't take Kasa long to emerge. Brown Otter spoke to her, and her face lit up. Turning, she took off at a run on the path to Lathe's cabin.

"If we're going to have a wedding feast tonight," Jake called to Brown Otter, "reckon we better go hunting for some fresh meat."

Brown Otter nodded, "I can try out new horses," he added gravely.

It was midafternoon when Otter, Hawk, and Jake rode through the upper meadow leading a packhorse laden with fresh elk meat. There was no movement around the roofless cabin, but a cured skin hung over the doorway. Jake looked at the father and son riding with him and grinned. Riding over to the cabin, he side-passed his horse close and pounded on the walls.

"Anyone in there?" he shouted. "You can't live under the robes forever."

There was silence for a moment, and then Lathe replied sleepily, "We can try."

"We got meat for supper," Jake told him. "If you two aren't down to eat soon, you best get ready for a shivaree 'cause we'll be coming for you."

A giggle came from inside before Lathe answered, "We'll be there, damn it, give us a little bit."

Jake rode with Anna and carried Kestrel. They were almost home. It was warmer in the lower elevation, but the mountain breezes still whispered and cooled them. It was mid-August. Time to return and help finish the haying. In another month, it would be almost time to go into the higher slopes for the fall gather. But before that, there were weddings. Molly and Jackson, for one, were getting married. There would be a lot to do in a month.

Jake studied Lathe riding ahead of them and Kasa, off to the side. Lathe had gotten quiet today. Even when they stopped for a quick lunch, he was morose, not wanting to talk. Jake was beginning to suspect that Lathe was not so comfortable arriving home with his new Indian wife. Now they were only a few miles from home. Jake thought maybe it was time to have a visit with his young cousin.

Nodding to Anna, Jake rode forward to ride beside Lathe. "So, cuz," Jake started, "the marriage already on the rocks or something else bothering you?"

Lathe looked at Jake, surprised, "No, we're fine. Why?"

"You've been riding off by yourself most of the day, looking like you are going to meet a hanging party,"

Jake replied. "Something is bothering you. I see it and I'm sure Kasa sees it."

"Well, hell, Jake," Lathe sputtered, "I guess I never thought about having to go back to Ma and Pa and tellin' them I got myself hitched while I was gone."

"You think your folks will not like Kasa," Jake asked, "because she's Ute?"

Lathe shot Jake a guarded look before answering, "No, I don't think that. They might be surprised, but guess you paved the way for that. They will be all right with Kasa," Lathe got thoughtful before continuing. "No, but me sleepin' with her before getting married ain't goin' to sit well with Pa, and Ma pretty much goes along with what Pa thinks."

Jake laughed at that. He knew his uncle. Matthew was a stickler on some things, and this could pretty much be one of them. "So, here's the thing," he told Lathe. "You got to tell your folks right off that you got married the Indian way while you were there with Kasa's folks. Tell them you did that for Kasa's sake. Then you have to tell your Pa you want him to marry you the white way. You can ask him to do that right away too. I think that might just make him and your Ma easier in their minds," Jake grinned at Lathe. "Otherwise, you can just about figure you two aren't using the same robes tonight."

Lathe grinned at that. That was his thought too.

"Speaking of sleeping," Jake continued, "you got any place picked out in your mind to camp when you get back? You can't very well share the bedroom with Jeremiah."

"I figured we'd just set up a lean-to somewhere for now," Lathe said. "Maybe we can sneak enough time to get a cabin of sorts up between haying and weddings and fall gather that would hold us for the winter. We can get a permanent place next summer."

"Well, here's an idea," Jake responded. "I just built that small room onto my cabin before leaving for the summer. We haven't moved anything into it yet. It still needs some chinking but wouldn't take much. You and Kasa could take that for the winter. Kasa would be close to Anna this first winter, and that might be a comfort to her. You can pick out a cabin site and work on it when you have time."

Lathe nodded, "I'd like that. I think Kasa would feel more comfortable near Anna too. Coming to the ranch is going to be a big change for her."

"It's settled then," Jake said, looking over at Kasa. "When you get things settled with your folks, you come to my cabin, and we will get you moved in. But you better go talk to your little woman. I think she is scared you are mad at her the way you've been acting today."

Lathe nodded at Jake and reined his horse over beside Kasa. Jake watched as Lathe talked to her, reaching over, and touching her hand. Just before Jake turned back to ride beside Anna, he saw Kasa flash Lathe a radiant smile. *Ah, for young love,* Jake thought.

"I think Lathe is feeling better now," Jake commented to Anna. "He was worried about his folks knowing he's been living with Kasa without his Pa doing a ceremony." Jake smiled at Anna, "Glad I never had to worry about that."

"I think," Anna said slyly, "you had other things to worry about when you brought me home."

Jake laughed, "Yes, I did at that, but it all turned out good." He put Kestrel, who was coming awake, to his shoulder. "And look what a little falcon we have now that is all ours."

Anna smiled fondly at the sleeping toddler. "Maybe a little eagle will be your next present," she said, "but he will come in February, not December."

Jake shot her a quick glance, and then, side passing his horse close to her, he reached over and laid his hand on her belly, "Here? Now?"

Anna laughed, "You see everything around you, but you don't see what is in front of you. You see the deer in the thicket, but not me. I thought you would see I am growing."

Jake smiled at her fondly, "I see now," he whispered. "I am glad."

CHAPTER 16

Three Weddings and a Necktie Party – 1877

Kade and Sam rode into sight of the cabins leading a packhorse each, loaded with fresh meat. They had found some mountain sheep today to add to the bounty that had already been brought in. There would be a powerful number of people here by the next evening, so there were a lot of preparations needed. Jake and Thomas had been hunting too, but they were busy working with the colts.

It was the second week of September. Fall gather would start before the end of the month. But before the men headed up the mountain, there was going to be one hell of a frolic. There were going to be three weddings, and every cowboy or settler within one hundred miles would be coming to help in the festivities.

First, Molly was marrying Jackson. He had spoken to Kade for Molly's hand the fall before, after the funerals. Jackson had spent the last year visiting big ranches on the nearby plains. He had bought cattle the summer before, hired a half dozen hands, and staked out a section of river valley about fifteen miles north of the Welles' settlement, closer to the prairie but still in the foothills. Here Jackson started to build his ranch. With his own and investors' money, he built an owner's house, a foreman's house, a barn, and a bunkhouse all during the summer. All summer long, Jackson had wagons traveling back and forth between Jeremiah's sawmill and his building site, hauling the lumber needed for a four-room home with a full front porch. It would have two bedrooms, a kitchen, and a parlor. Molly had been busy all summer gathering the dowry that she would need to begin married life in such a large home.

Buster, the cowhand who was in the fight in Laramie City the summer before, was now Jackson's foreman. He had been riding back and forth to the settlement with Jackson all winter and was sparking Catherine. They were also going to get married and take up residence in the foreman's home. The same age and best friends, Molly and Catherine were excited to be living next to each other in their new married life.

As if two weddings at the same time wasn't enough, Army was going to marry Rachel. At sixteen, Rachel was the youngest settlement offspring to marry, but she was a mature young lady. She and Army had always had eyes for no one else. Army built a cabin that summer just up the river valley from Matthew and Mattie's where he too could stake a homestead. Here they would start their life together.

Along with these three weddings and Lathe's marriage to Kasa earlier in the summer, the settlement just kept growing, and that would probably continue. Jeremiah's schoolteacher wanted to teach one more year, but Jeremiah was serious about the woman. Will, at twenty-three, was corresponding with a woman from Missouri. Who knew what would come from that? Bonnie, at sixteen, was still too young by Sarah's standards to marry, which was all right since she had no beau yet, and James, at fifteen, was noticing the women, but that was it. The way the country was starting to fill up, there would be opportunities for these young folks.

As word of the three weddings at one time spread throughout the countryside, Kade knew they would have a lot of people coming in to dance the night away. Married couples, single men, and the few single women who were available in this unsettled land would travel days for the chance of a frolic. A wedding feast needed to be planned that would last into the early morning hours, and then they would have breakfast.

Sabra watched the dancers from the swing on Matthew's porch. She had no idea what time it was, but she knew it was well into the early morning hours before dawn. It had been a wonderful day. Three weddings, one her precious daughter, and all so happy. Soon, she and Kade would spread some blankets on Sarah's floor and get a few hours of sleep. Let the young people keep the frolic alive. When Jackson and Molly decided to sneak away, they would go to Molly's old room for their first night together. There they could sleep much of the day away before emerging fully married.

As she sat, she saw Kade leave a group of men and move off, out of the dim light cast by many lanterns. When he didn't return, she realized where he had gone. He was going to the burial ground to talk to Tom and Jim. She knew he did that occasionally but never asked him about it. She knew Kade missed his two friends, men he had asked council of for many years. This was his way to keep them in his life. But maybe tonight it was time to join him there. Sabra rose and made her way around the edge of the dancers and into the darkness.

Sabra knew Kade heard her coming long before she got close. In the gloom, she saw his silhouette against the night sky. She went and slipped her arm around his waist, standing close beside him. After a pause, she whispered, "They would have loved today, especially Tom. He'd be sitting on the porch telling stories all night."

Kade smiled, remembering, "Tom would have been in his glory. Damn, I miss that old man."

"Our daughter is so happy tonight," Sabra said, changing the subject. "Hard to believe she is old enough to marry, much less go off and manage her own home. I am going to miss her."

"She won't be that far," Kade replied, "but I'll miss her too. We've got horses stout enough to make it to visit her in half a day's time. We will just have to do that."

They stood silent then, each in their own thoughts. Molly was the last of their brood to leave the cabin. It would be a lot quieter now. But the boys were close, their cabins within walking distance. Molly was moving to Jackson's ranch headquarters, and before settling into housekeeping, they were going overseas, back to England to meet Jackson's mother and other relatives. Molly was excited about the trip, but Sabra worried that the people would look down on her.

"You think the people in England will be good to Molly?" Sabra asked Kade.

"I talked to Jackson about that when he told me they were planning a trip," Kade replied. "He'll take care of her. He plans to spend a week in New York and buy her all the fancy clothes she will need," Kade pulled Sabra close. "You have taught her well, honey. Your year of finishing school served you well in motherhood. She knows how to act," he hesitated, then added, "and she's tough enough to tell someone to go to hell if they cross her. Reckon if she can stand straight and proud, rifle in hand defending her home, she can take on some Englishers. She'll do alright."

"I almost wish we could ride with them to Laramie City and stand with them when they repeat their vows," Sabra murmured, "but I am not up to another trip right now."

Jackson had told them that he and Molly would seek out the preacher that married Thomas and Beth and have him marry them again. They would get a marriage paper that way. Jackson was ready to face his people with his mountain bride, but he felt his mother would be more comfortable in her mind to know that her son was married by a proper preacher. She didn't need to know that the vows with the preacher happened a week after the wedding.

"Are you bringing the herd in closer this afternoon still?" Sabra asked.

The four-year-old steers had not been sent to the mountain pasture with the cows and calves this year. Instead, they were cut off in the spring and pushed west along the river valley about ten miles, far enough to keep them from the hay fields. Here they summered, along the river on the rich grass there. A week ago, the herd was gathered and bunched up and brought about five miles closer. This afternoon when a few men finally wakened, they would ride out and bring the herd closer still to graze the cut hay fields and riverbanks, around the rocks and trees on grass that hadn't been harvested for hay.

When Jackson and Molly, Buster and Catherine, and the rest of Jackson's hands headed for home the next day, they would push the herd with them. They would combine the Welles herd with the Crowden herd and take them all to Laramie City to sell. This year, only Jeremiah would go from the Welles' camp to represent their herd. Jeremiah's sweetheart had come for the weddings, and Jeremiah would take her home on the way. There was more than enough help from Jackson's ranch to take the herd to Laramie City. The fall gather would begin before Jeremiah returned. They needed the rest of the men here at home for that.

"I figure I can get some boys woke up and ready after the noon meal and head out. Probably let the newlyweds sleep," Kade squeezed Sabra knowingly. "I reckon maybe we better go make ourselves a bed somewhere. Sleep sounds good about now."

"You are getting old, Kade Welles," Sabra teased him. "It wouldn't be sleep that you'd be wanting before."

"I am not that old," Kade protested, pulling Sabra to him for a kiss. "But we jest don't have our own cabin at the moment."

Sabra laughed at him, "No, but in the old days, you'd probably be lying with me here on Tom's grave."

Kade squeezed her to him, "You are a wicked woman to even think that." But in his heart, Kade knew she was probably right.

Jake was enjoying the ride, even if this young stud was testing him just about every mile. He was on a four-year-old they thought the ranch might keep for a herd stud. A deep dark bay, they had let the young stud cover a couple of mares in the spring to test the foals he would get the next spring. Then the stud had promptly gotten cut up badly, so he had spent most of the summer in the corral being doctored. Now he was healed and feeling his oats. After two or more months with his companions in the small meadow, the colt was loathe to leave home. The Welles' horses were seldom barn or herd sour because they were ridden so much by themselves that the animals soon learned manners, but this colt was a big strong stud and had sat too long being lazy while he was recovering. He had enough spirit to buck, enough strength to buck hard, and he had kept Jake watching him all morning.

Now Jake had just turned toward home with a small package of cows and calves in front of him. These came down from the high slopes early and found their way to the river bottom. Sam brought some in a few days earlier and told Jake and Kade that there were probably more out along the river. So, Jake went looking today. He thought it would be a good ride for the young stud. But now, turned toward home with the slow walking cattle in front of him, the horse started his cutups all over again. *This horse needed some serious miles put on him,* Jake thought, *and this slow walk behind this package of cows just wasn't doing the trick.* He had hours to go to get home, so he would have to put up with the horse's antics and correct him as needed.

Jake heard a faint sound from behind him and turned, scanning the river bottom. There in the distance, he saw riders coming. To his knowledge, no people were living that direction closer than a two-day ride. He watched the rider's approach. As they came closer, he relaxed. By the formation of the riders and the color of their uniforms, he could see they were military. Probably a small group of soldiers out on patrol. It had been rumored at the wedding that the soldiers were out a lot this summer. After Custer's massacre the summer before, the government had resupplied the forts and sent soldiers out to keep a presence on the plains. There had not been any soldiers who came into the mountains before though, although it wasn't surprising to find them in the area either. Jake let the cows slow and graze while he waited for the troops to reach him.

The young stud moved nervously as the riders came close. There looked to be a dozen men in the group. *Soldiers always made noise,* Jake thought. They always had the sabers and metal that clanked. It spooked his horse, and he had to fight with the horse to settle him down. The stud kept Jake's attention and when he got the animal under control, the soldiers were close and divided up into a formation that encircled Jake. Jake looked for the leader and nodded to him.

"Just passing through, Captain?" he asked.

"Where the hell you think you are taking those cows, boy?" the captain asked him belligerently.

Jake bristled at the words and the tone. "My name is Jake Welles. I am not your boy. And I am taking these cows home to our ranch. They have strayed."

"Git off yer horse," the man ordered, pulling a pistol, and pointing it at Jake, "You ain't goin' anywhere. Time you thievin' Indians be stopped." The rest of the troop also pulled guns.

"These are my cows," Jake replied mildly, "and I am taking them home. Ride along with me and see."

"You'd like that, wouldn't you?" the officer replied. "You got a bunch of bucks around the bend ready to jump out and ambush us like you ambushed Custer last year? Now git your ass off that horse!"

Jake was starting to get angry, but he reined in his retort and tried to speak reasonably, "Custer was fighting Sioux and Cheyenne. I'm part Ute. I had no part in it, and neither did my people."

Jake knew that two troopers had moved closer to his horse behind him, but he kept his gaze on the officer. The captain was the man who he needed to convince. Suddenly, the stock of a gun struck him on the side of his head. It hit him hard enough to make him see stars, and he had to grab hold of the saddle horn to stay on the horse. Then just as suddenly, he felt hands reach up and grab him, pulling him from the saddle.

"When Captain gives an order, breed," a voice growled behind him, "he means do it."

Jake shook his head, trying to clear his mind. He suddenly had the feeling he needed help. He still held the reins of his horse and jerking his arms free suddenly from the soldiers that held him, he stepped close to the horse. In one quick fluid movement, Jake jerked the headstall off the horse and lashed it with the bridle. Nervous already and wanting to go home, the lashing only served to cause the horse to wheel and bolt, nearly running over a soldier on foot. There was no headstall for the nearest soldier to grab, and the horse made its' get-a-way unobstructed.

"That was dumb, breed," the captain remarked. "Now you got nothin' to ride." He turned to a soldier and commanded, "Tie him up and let's get going. We'll settle this in the morning."

They tied Jake's hands in front of him and looped a long rope between his wrists. Mounting their horses, they turned back the way they had come and started off at a jog. Jake had no choice but to follow on foot or be dragged, tethered as he was to a soldier's horse. He just hoped that his obstinate stud horse wouldn't stop and graze on its way home. He had the distinct feeling he was in real trouble.

It was almost nightfall when the soldiers stopped. Jake was spent by then. They had ridden at a jog most of the way, slowing to a walk at intervals to rest the horses. Jake had kept up for what seemed like hours until finally, he knew he needed to stop moving, his lungs were screaming for air. Watching for what looked like level grassy ground, he had grasped the rope with both hands, hoping to cushion his tied wrists. He had no trouble feigning a stumble and sinking to the ground. It hurt his arms, hands, and wrists to drag, but there were few rocks in the area and, if he kept his head turned upwards, it gave his lungs a chance to rest and catch his breath. He dragged first on his belly, then twisted to his back. His hair filled with dust and dirt from the horses ahead of him. He tried to keep his face from dragging but wasn't always successful. He felt himself dragged over rocks and branches hidden in the grass, things that cut. He couldn't help that. His lungs needed to rest. He felt rather than saw his shirt tear as he went over things in the grass. When he couldn't stand the pain in his arms and hands anymore, he was up on his feet again, jogging behind the horses.

When Jake recovered his feet after the second time he went down, a young trooper rode up close to him. "Grab hold of the mane," the young man said quietly. "Let the horse help you." Jake looked up at the soldier gratefully and did as instructed. It helped, and the others did not prohibit this. Still, when they stopped for the night, Jake was more than ready. He knew if he went down a third time, he wouldn't have the strength to get up again. He was coming to the end of his endurance.

At their stopping place, it was apparent to Jake that this was where the soldiers had camped the night before. There were remnants of a campfire, and the grass was trampled down by the soldiers' feet and the horses' hooves. What set them to ride the river valley from the west and then turn around and take him back here was not evident at once. There was water all along the river valley that they rode. The difference here were only the trees; one old monster that survived years of mountain storms.

After cutting Jake loose to relieve himself, they bound his hands behind him and tied him in a sitting position to the giant tree. It felt good to sit after the grueling run, and he tried to ignore the hurts his body felt. The restraints were uncomfortable, and he knew by morning he would be sore from these and from sitting in one position too. His mouth was dry, and he was hungry. He was not offered water or food when the soldiers ate, but the same trooper who had helped him along the trail brought him a cup of water after the sun went down and helped him drink. The captain objected at first, but the soldier was brave enough to stick up for Jake.

"Captain, it don't hurt to give him a cup of water. We got plenty of that," the young soldier said.

Shrugging, the captain remarked, "Just don't waste any food. He won't need it after the sun comes up."

Jake didn't want to ask what was meant by that, but it became apparent when one of the troopers came up to the big tree and threw a rope over a high branch. At the end of the rope was a hangman's noose.

"You're fucking kidding me," Jake spoke then, low and angry, "You're going to hang me for gathering my own cows?"

The soldier gave him a grim look. "We've hung some for less'n that. We call it hangin' fer Custer."

"Captain," the young trooper spoke up, "what if this man does own those cows? Shouldn't we find out? He might be innocent."

"He's Injun," the captain replied shortly. "He's hangin' at daybreak."

The young stud made it home by late afternoon. Matthew noticed him trot by while working outside. He knew that a saddled horse coming home without its rider was not a good sign. Saddling a horse of his own, Matthew rode to Kade's. Kade had already caught up the horse and was down at Thomas' cabin.

"What's this mean?" Matthew asked Kade.

"Nothing good," Kade answered. "Jake's not going to let a horse get away from him with no bridle. I'm thinkin' the horse was turned loose. His cinch is still tight, and the rifle is in the scabbard. If he threw Jake, there would be a bridle and reins draggin'. We're going out to look for Jake. Would you find Sam, Army, and Hawk? They were going up the valley riding some colts.

Thomas and I will gather saddle horses and get ready. We'll bring a couple candle lanterns. This horse has come a piece, and we might lose the light before we find anything."

"I'll ride with you," Matthew said, "and I'll get Will, Lathe, and James. They are around here somewhere. I'll have Mattie gather the women, and they can all stay together in one cabin until we get back."

The men rode hard until they lost the light. They had found the spot that riders had intercepted Jake. They saw the scuffle that had taken place and where the stud horse's hooves had dug into the sod when he wheeled and turned. Hawk was an excellent tracker for his twenty years, and Sam and Kade had more than twice that in experience. But when they lost the light, the going became much slower. They put two men a half-mile or more ahead in the dark. If the tracks turned off the river valley, someone would ride ahead and get the lead men. But the lead men were there to see campfires before anyone could see their lanterns.

They took turns riding and walking, holding the lanterns low to watch for signs. For the number of horses in the group they were following, it wasn't hard to track them. They also saw the moccasin tracks of a man on foot. The first time they came to where Jake had been dragged, Kade's face got hard, the muscles in his neck taut. He knew what was going on by what he saw on the ground. They had seen Jake's moccasin tracks for miles and knew he was the one on foot. Kade could be grateful that Jake was not in his cowboy boots which were harder to run in.

But when the tracks showed a second dragging, it also showed a few drops of blood on blades of grass.

They found a piece of cloth from Jake's shirt, blood-stained and filthy, caught on a rock. The men knew they couldn't stop until they found Jake. They knew Jake was in trouble. Kade pushed as hard as the horses and men could take until dark, the men sometimes riding and sometimes running beside their horses. Kade knew the animals could rest after dark when the going would be slower. No one complained.

It must have been about three hours before daylight when Army came riding back from his spot in the lead.

"Campfire ahead," he told them. "Hawk stayed up there to watch. You better put out them lanterns."

The men rode on quietly then. When they reached Hawk, they all dismounted.

"What do you think?" Kade asked the young Ute.

"I think we leave the horses here with most of the men and go closer," Hawk answered quietly. "The horses in that camp will give us away if we take our animals closer."

Kade looked at his friends, thinking. "Hawk and I will go ahead. Stay here and get some rest, and we will be back."

What Hawk and Kade saw when they got closer was a campfire with several bodies sleeping around it. It was a soldier's troop; they could tell from the several soldiers awake and standing guard. In the flickering firelight, they saw Jake tied in a sitting position to the tree. He was alive. But hanging from the tree, almost indiscernible in the dark, they saw the shadow of the hanging noose.

"I'm going back for the others, Hawk," Kade whispered to the young man. "If I send Lathe and Army to you, can you three skirt the camp and come up behind them? When it is first daylight, the rest of us will come in. I don't know how their stick floats, so I'd rather not move in the dark. But if you see them make a move before that with Jake, you let us know. Fire a round if you have to."

Kade made his way back to the others then. They were waiting, hoping this was where they would find Jake and that he would be alive.

"They got Jake tied to a tree," Kade told them. "It's soldiers, maybe a dozen or so. They got a watch. They also have a hanging noose in a tree," Kade looked at the group, his voice tight. "I don't know if this is a troop of renegade soldiers or what, but I want you to all know this right here and now. I don't damn well care if they got the president of the states with them. If they are fixin' to hang my son, and if it comes to it, I'll shoot to kill. If you have a problem with going up against soldiers, you'd best turn around right now. I won't hold it against you. I haven't lived in the states for most of my life. If this is what the calvary wants to do, then they got a war right here with me."

The men exchanged glances, but it was Matthew that spoke for all of them, "If it comes to fighting with soldiers for one of our own, we fight," Matthew's face was grim. "We are all with you on this. Just tell us what you want us to do."

Jake dozed little during the night, thirsty, uncomfortable, and sore beneath the tree. He was hungry, and he hurt from the run and the dragging. His wrists where he was tied were bloody and raw. He couldn't see his hands, tied as they were behind his back, but he felt them swelling around the ropes from being dragged. His arms and his feet ached. He knew he had a deep cut on his back from when he was dragged over something hard and sharp. He was filthy from dragging, his whole body feeling gritty. It was hard to get comfortable against the tree when his back was so bruised and raw. But with a hanging noose above him, he thought that discomfort was a small thing to worry about.

He tried to estimate in his mind how long it may have taken the horse to get home and then how long it would take Kade to follow. For he knew his father would be on his trail. Of that, he had no doubt. What he doubted was whether Kade would make it in time. *Damn stud horse gave me trouble all day,* he thought. *He had better have kept hightailing it home when I turned him loose.* Because if the horse didn't, if the horse stopped to graze, there wasn't time. Jake knew he had traveled too many miles with the soldiers for his pa to make it here if the horse dallied on the way home. He knew the dark would slow his father down, too. It wasn't a comforting thought, not with a hangman's noose above him.

He thought about his run and when he let himself down to be dragged. He heard the soldiers laughing at him. "Looks like a damn fish on a line," one had remarked, and they had laughed. He didn't like being laughed at. He never let things like that go by, but today he had no choice. One had mocked him when they let him relieve himself. "Reckon that there pecker of yer's done poked its last squaw," one soldier told him. Jake had the Indian desire to cut the man's tongue out, but that too was out of his control now. Between his anger, hunger, discomfort, and worry, Jake didn't sleep much that night.

The camp came awake slowly. The camp cook threw more wood on the fire and started coffee boiling. It smelled good to Jake, but he knew it wasn't for him. The sun was not over the mountains yet, but the peaks were bathed in sunshine when the captain gave the order.

"Go untie the Indian and let's get this done," he said. "I'm hungry."

"Captain," it was the young soldier again, "you shouldn't do this." The young man looked over at Jake. "He could be telling the truth."

The captain straightened and walked over to the young soldier slowly. It appeared he might be thinking over the trooper's words until he reached the young man. To the young soldier's credit, he stood his ground, holding the officer's gaze. Then suddenly, the officer lashed out at the man, hitting him solidly in the face. The soldier reeled back, losing his balance.

"Say another word, and I'll see you court-martialed when we get back," the officer snarled. Then he turned to the others and barked out orders again, to bring a horse and cut Jake loose.

Jake met the young man's gaze and nodded slightly. The man had tried. Short of taking a rifle and going up against eleven other men, the young soldier was help-less to do more.

Jake felt his bonds to the tree come loose, but his hands remained tied behind his back. He needed help to stand, and then he had to lean against the tree for balance to let the blood flow to his legs again. He had prayed on and off during the night. Silently and fer-vently, he had asked his Maker to bring him help. As

Jake stood there, trying to get his balance, he made one more silent prayer for help, remembering Matthew's teaching about the hours before Christ's crucifixion. Christ had asked God to be spared from what was to come. Christ had finished the prayer with, "They will be done." In his mind, Jake reluctantly echoed those words of Jesus.

But Jake also decided that he would not go to his hanging meekly. He knew that tied as he was, he had no chance of getting away, but he was determined that he would shed some blood before they put that noose around his neck. He wasn't going to his death without hurting someone, be it with his feet or his head. But first, he had to get his balance and get his legs working again.

It was then, as he stood there, waiting for a horse to be brought up and for what was to come, that he saw the riders in the distance. They were coming toward the camp at a nice, collected lope, not hurrying, but not slow either. They all rode with their rifles cradled in front of them, old mountain man style. He knew without seeing who would be in the lead. Jake wasn't in the clear yet, but his heart leaped. He might still die, but it wouldn't be by a noose, and it wouldn't be alone.

"Cap, there's riders comin'," a soldier said, alerting the rest.

The captain turned and, taking up a rifle, went to the front of his men to meet the riders. The rest of the soldiers stood watching and ready.

Kade rode before the other men, his eyes taking in the scene. He saw Jake standing now, leaning back against the tree, feet straddled for balance, arms still tied behind him. He saw the blood on Jake's face. He saw the tattered, blood-stained shirt and ripped denim trousers. He knew just by looking at Jake that he had had a bad time of it.

There were twelve soldiers. Ten of them stood armed with the officer. One stood off to the far side, nose bleeding, not far from Jake. Kade saw one soldier with the horses throwing on a saddle. He smelled the coffee, heard the river rippling nearby, saw the sunshine coming over the peaks and the hangman's noose starting to catch the light. His eyes took it all in before he pulled up and spoke.

"Peers to me, you boys are fixin' to have a necktie party," Kade spoke amiably enough unless one knew him well. Then you would pick up the unleashed anger in his voice.

"Found this breed out stealing cattle," the officer said. "Hangin' might be too good for him, especially after what his kind did to Custer last year."

"Was the brand on the cattle two inverted V's?" Kade asked. "Almost look like an upside-down W but not connected?"

"Yup, that was the brand," the captain agreed, beginning to relax, thinking these men may be after a thief too.

"That is the Twin Peaks Ranch brand," Kade said slowly, "and he's one of the owners of Twin Peaks. He wasn't stealing; he was bringing them home," Kade looked around at the soldiers, still speaking calmly. "Be obliged if you turn him loose."

The officer looked at Kade, anger in his eyes. "No breed is gonna be an owner of a ranch," the officer growled. "He's got to pay for Custer. I ain't letting him loose. He's an Injun."

"He had nothing to do with Custer," Kade's voice changed now and was tight with anger. "When are you soldier boys going to start thinking with your heads?" Kade's rifle came up, pointing now toward the soldiers. Then his voice turned low, and there was steel in it, enunciating each word, "Now turn him loose, or I'll do it myself."

No one knew which soldier shot first. It was a stupid thing for them to do, for each rider with Kade was also ready. With the first shot, every rifle of the Twin Peaks Ranch spoke. The young soldier in the back dove for Jake and pulled him down. Unsheathing his knife, he cut Jake's bonds, and together they rolled out of the line of fire. Hawk, Lathe, and Army stood up from their hiding places and began firing as well, catching the soldiers in a crossfire. It wasn't a long fight. Bullets grazed Kade, Will and Thomas, but other than that, they came through the battle unscathed. The soldiers weren't so lucky. Within minutes, caught in a crossfire with Hawk, Lathe, and Army behind them, the soldiers all laid dead save the young man with Jake.

Dismounting, Kade let the rest of the men check the dead. Instead, he went to Jake and helped him up, seeing the bloody swollen wrists, the torn, filthy shirt, grass burn marks, and cuts on Jake's face and torso. "You alright, son?" he asked, his voice tight with emotion.

"I am now," Jake choked, his relief so great he struggled to speak.

"What about this one?" Sam asked, indicating the soldier getting up by Jake.

"Leave him," Jake told them. "He tried to help."

"He'd be a witness to this," Sam said solemnly, just stating a fact.

Jake looked at the young man. "That a problem for you?" he asked the young soldier.

The young man looked at Jake steadily before answering, "Not for me. I jest mustered out of the army. Don't think it was for me. Think I'm going lookin' for a job now."

"If you want a ranch job," Kade told him, "you got it." Then looking at the carnage around him, he said, "These army boys should have some shovels with them. Think we better get them and their saddles and bridles in the ground and get the hell away from here. Turn their horses loose. We got an extra for Jake. Keep back one army horse for this man," he said, indicating the young soldier.

Kade turned back to Jake as the others went in search of shovels. "Shit, son, that was cutting it too close. We almost didn't make it in time."

Jake nodded, rubbing his wrists. "When did that stud horse get home?"

"A couple hours before dark."

Jake nodded at that. "That horse has a gawd awful disposition, but he saved my life. I'll never sell him," Jake wavered then, trying to get his balance. Kade put an arm out to steady him. "Reckon, I might be a bit hungry and thirsty," Jake murmured. "I just need a minute."

Kade reached out to Jake then, and pulling him close, he held him in a big bear hug. "God damn, I was worried," he spoke low. "When I saw that noose, I was . . . hell, the only good thing was there was no neck in it yet."

"Pa, you weren't the only one worried," Jake pushed back and looked into his father's eyes. "I wasn't sure if that horse would make it home in time. I knew you'd come, but I wasn't sure if there was time. I sure as hell didn't want that rope around my neck, and I damn sure didn't want you finding me in it when it was too late. Damn, it was good to see you riding up the river. God damn awful good."

Army rummaged around in the soldier's packs and came up with cups. The coffee still simmered on the ashes of the fire, and he poured some for Jake and Kade, bringing it to them.

"You want the soldier boy to help us bury the dead?" he asked.

"No," Kade answered shortly, "he had no part in this. He don't need to bury his own. It's enough he didn't raise a gun to them or us."

Jake took the coffee and went over to look at the dead. The soldiers had stripped him of his knives and revolver after they hauled him off his horse. He meant to have them back. He rolled a couple of the soldiers over with his foot until he found his hardware. He put his revolver in his waistband. Strapping on his knife sheath, he held the knife in his hand, flexing his fingers around it. He stared at the dead faces, remembering their laughter, his helplessness, and his anger.

"Jake," Matthew came over to him, "what are you thinking?"

Jake was startled that Matthew had come up without his noticing. He glanced at Matthew before speaking.

"I swore yesterday if I got out of this mess, I'd cut their tongues out," Jake said slowly. "But now that they're dead, I wonder if it is worth it. Revenge, that is."

"I don't know if revenge is ever worth it," Matthew retorted. "I know your pa has had trouble in his mind with what took place after the Cheyenne found us. He and I've talked about it several times. Hard to get things out of your mind after a deed is done." Matthew thought about that a minute before continuing, "Guess it might make a difference if you believe the Indian way that the body goes to the next life mutilated."

Jake thought about that. "Listened to you too much growing up, I reckon," Jake said softly. "I know the Ute creation story about Sinawav, the Creator, and Coyote. Brown Otter taught me the legends when I first met him. He taught me the other stories too. But I guess I believe what you taught more. I reckon maybe our God will sort it all out himself." Jake took a breath, looking again at the dead. "Maybe I don't need to help him." Making the decision, Jake returned his knife to its sheath, nodded at Matthew, and turned. He was hungry. There had to be food around in the packs.

They buried the dead along with all the army tack and weapons. While the men dug the graves, Kade talked with the young soldier.

"What was your mission supposed to be?" he asked.

"We were sent out to do reconnaissance. Just to make our presence on the plains known. But Captain had his own agenda. I was the only new recruit with them. The rest had ridden with Cap before. They were pretty much of the same mind. We came upon a little band of six Indians about a week north of here. He just shot them all. Said they needed to pay for Custer," the young man shook his head. "I didn't sign up to just kill people for no reason."

"What's your name, son?" Kade asked.

"Luke Brode," he answered.

"The offer of a job is open," Kade told him. "Or if you just want to mosey, you are free to go. This here," Kade gestured around him, "is forgotten as soon as we get them in the ground. Up to you."

"I'll take the job," Luke replied. "If you go to this length to protect your own, you must be a good outfit to stick with. Don't reckon the subject," Luke also gestured around him, "will ever come up again, but if it does, I reckon I must 'a hit my head and wandered these mountains for days before your crew picked me up. I have no idea where the rest of my unit is."

Kade slowly nodded his head. "I reckon that could happen," he said. "Now, I need you to help me up. Seems I caught some lead, and it is stiffening me up some."

They rode for several hours to put distance between themselves and the new mound with the grisly contents underneath the sod. But when the sun was high in the sky, Kade called for a halt.

"These horses are mostly spent," he said, "and me along with them. Think we better lay up an hour or so and let the horses rest." Kade looked around at the men and horses before going on, "Lathe and James, let the horses rest a bit and then take that army horse and the horse we led for Jake and make tracks for home. Those two horses had the least work before today, and you two are the lightest of us. Let the women know we are safe. Bring back the buggy with Clara and Sabra. I might need Clara to dig out a bullet. We can start toward home in a couple hours when the horses are some rested and meet you along the way."

Thomas and Jake were instantly alert. "Thought you were just grazed, Pa," Thomas said.

"Didn't figure it would give me much problem until we got home," Kade replied, "but I might have that wrong. We should have learned something from Jake's incident a few years back on the Oregon Trail. And we don't have a damn drop of whiskey along with us either."

It was a long afternoon. Lathe and James left shortly on the two horses that still had some bottom to them. The rest of the men laid up for a couple of hours, dozing, and then mounted again, riding slower this time. Just about supper time, they sighted the buggy coming to meet them. Lathe was driving, and Sabra sat beside him with Clara in the back. The women brought food with them but were mostly concerned with both Jake and Kade's condition. It was Kade that needed immediate care. Clara had whiskey and some medical tools with her. After dousing Kade with whiskey, both for his wound and for pain relief, she cut out the bullet. Kade was right that it wasn't severe, at least not after the bullet was out. But it hurt like hell and sapped Kade's strength. Half-drunk with whiskey, Kade relented and rode the buggy home with Clara and Sabra. It was two hours after dark when they returned home, and home never looked so good.

Jake rode alone to his home after passing his folks' cabin. He had maybe two hours of sleep that afternoon when they stopped to rest the horses and a few restless hours during the night. He was bone-weary tired. As he approached, he saw Anna waiting for him in the yard. The cabin, lit behind her with candles, was a welcome sight. He pulled up in front of her and stripping his saddle from his horse, he simply turned the animal loose. There was no rain in sight tonight, the saddle could lay where he dropped it until morning.

"Don't touch me," he said quietly to Anna, "I'm filthy. I'll go down to the creek and wash."

Even in the dark, Anna could see the tattered shirt, the dirt, the scrapes, the blood, and the bruises. Anna reached out and took his hand, "No, you come with me. I have water waiting for you."

Jake didn't protest. He had no strength left to protest. The last thirty-six hours had sapped him. He followed his wife inside.

"Lathe come up and talk to you?" Jake asked.

"He told me. I've been waiting. Take your clothes off and leave them," Anna told him softly. "I'll take care of them later. Then sit there," she pointed at the rocking chair. Tom had made the rocking chair for them before Kestrel was born. Anna had it turned, back against the table. There was a basin on the table and water heating. Anna took up a pitcher and, getting Jake to lean back with his head over the basin, she poured warm water over his head, running her fingers through his shaggy hair. He felt the soap and closed his eyes, feeling the comfort of it, the filth and sweat washing away. The tension began to leave his body. When Anna rinsed his hair, she threw out the water and poured clean water. Taking a rag, she began to wash him. He sat, naked and limp, eyes closed, letting her move around his face, his back, his chest, and down his body. He leaned forward and felt her wash out the gash on his back, gently digging out dirt.

"This is deep," she said softly, touching a clean rag to his back as he leaned forward. "It is filled with dirt. It will hurt digging it out."

"Hurt is good," Jake murmured. "Means I'm alive."

It took some time to get the wound cleaned. There were other smaller cuts and Anna gently cleaned them out as well.

Many times, she changed the water. Jake was too tired to respond, only moving as she told him so she could reach all of his body. He simply sat or sometimes stood, letting her clean his cuts and scrapes. Instinctively, Anna knew he didn't need her to question him. She felt his body sag. Finally, she reached his feet and sinking down she took them in her lap and began to wash and then massage them. That was when Jake finally began to talk.

"I used to hear Tom and Pa talking about 'seeing the elephant' in the old days. It was something like getting experience, but there was always a cost to it. Sometimes seeing the elephant was good, sometimes bad, but it always came with a price," Jake stopped talking for a moment, thinking through his thoughts. "I saw the elephant, and I hope to hell to never see it again."

Anna did not comment; she just kept working on his feet. She had a feeling he wasn't finished talking yet. It would come out if she gave him time.

"When I was running, I knew if I could just keep going, eventually, Pa would come. There was no way he couldn't track that many riders," Jake opened his eyes briefly, then closed them again. "When they laughed at me when I was dragging, I tried to shake it off. I figured I could make that right when Pa found us. But when they tied me to that tree, with the hangman's noose above me, I didn't know if Pa would make it in time."

Anna stood up, went behind Jake, and began massaging his shoulders and down his arms, working around his cuts and bruises. She waited for what would come next.

"I saw that damn noose all night," Jake opened his eyes and tipped his face up to see her behind him. "Anna, that's not the way I want to die. I can stand with a rifle to my shoulder, fighting my way, and I'll give my life up easy enough that way, but to dangle there at the end of a rope, that just ain't no way to die," he closed his eyes again. "I didn't want Pa to find me like that. I didn't want to die that way, but I didn't want Pa to see me that way either. I didn't want him to come home and tell you that's how I died. I know it would do something to him. Something worse than when Tom and Jim were killed."

Jake raised his hands to his face, rubbing them over his eyes. "Anna, I prayed that night. All night. I asked for lots of things. I asked for you to be comforted, I asked for a way out, I asked for Pa to make it in time. When daylight came, and they were cutting me loose, I just told God to do what He thought best. I wasn't giving in, I meant to fight as long as I could, but I knew that short of a miracle, I was helpless. I knew I was going to hang. That was my elephant. I was going to hang, and I was helpless," Jake took a deep breath. "And then there was Pa and the rest, coming across the valley. And I reckon maybe God made a decision," he looked again at Anna. "Bird, if I could have gotten to my knees right then to give thanks, I would have. But damn, I knew if I got down, I'd never make it up again. And I needed to be standing for whatever was to come," Jake hesitated. "Maybe we need to go some Sundays to Matthew's."

Anna rose and stood in front of Jake and pulled him up. "Are you hungry?" she asked. When Jake answered no with a shake of his head, she led him to the bed and lay down beside him. Cradling his head against her and running gentle fingers through his damp hair, she whispered, "It is over. Now you go to sleep. I prayed the whole time too. God answered both of our prayers. The elephant is gone."

She felt his arms tighten around her, and they lay that way, Jake feeling the comfort of being still seeping into his body. Finally, Jake murmured, "I love you, Bird. I am so damn glad to be home."

CHAPTER 17

Fatherhood - 1878

J ake rode behind the horses, but they were pretty trail broke by now. He glanced behind him, and the light wagon with Anna, Kasa, and the children in it was coming along at a nice slow jog. Behind it rode Bonnie. Jake had been surprised that Bonnie wanted to come with them. She was seventeen this summer, and after the wedding festivities the summer before, a slew of cowpokes kept drifting in to visit her. Some men came once, some a couple of times, but none came more than that. Bonnie was simply not interested in any of them. She laughed with them on Sarah's front porch, she took walks with them, or occasionally she took a saddle horse and went for a ride with one of them, but if they showed any interest more than just friendly, she shut it down right away. She was not interested. She was the last of the settlement girls who was unmarried, and it appeared not to bother her at all.

"Let me come with you to the high mountains, Jake," she had implored him as the snow began to melt this spring. "For a few months, I can get away from all these callers."

Jake had grinned at his young cousin. "I'd think you would like all the attention," he said.

"Well, it is sort of a compliment," Bonnie replied, "but I just don't want to marry yet. I don't see what the rush is."

So, Jake had relented if Sarah agreed to it. Bonnie was a help, especially now with little four-month-old Sabra Lark in the family. Anna had given birth to the little baby in early February. To Jake's relief, the labor had been quick and relatively easy for Anna. He had thought he wanted a boy this time, but when Jake saw little Lark, he knew that if he never got a boy, he would still be satisfied.

"There is nothing wrong with girls," Jake told a worried Anna. "We just have the most beautiful little girls. And maybe we can try again?"

Kasa was big with child now. Lathe was unsure if they should travel that summer, but Kasa had been insistent. She wanted to go to the mountains where her mother would be with her when it was her time. So, Lathe had relented, wanting to go himself.

Between the two little ones and Kasa's condition, it was decided to bring the light wagon this year. Jake was pretty sure he could get the wagon to the mountain cabin if they stayed along the river valley. It might take them a little bit longer to get there, but it could be done.

First, they had gone to the White River Agency to see if Brown Otter's village was there. They found the Indian village there, but Brown Otter was out on a hunt. They stayed two nights in the village until Otter returned. Then Jake was ready to leave.

The atmosphere at the agency was not good. The promised supplies had been late to arrive again. This had happened repeatedly over the past few years, and the Indians were anxious and angry about it. Trying to find enough game to feed the village to tide them over was difficult with the reduced land the Utes were allowed to hunt and the encroaching whites on the prairies. Brown Otter and some men with him had brought home meat, but Otter wanted to wait a couple of days to see if the supply train would come. Then Brown Otter and Snowbird would head for the mountains to join Jake and Lathe at Jacob's cabin.

Jake looked toward the front of the horse herd, watching his lead riders. Moving horses was different than pushing cattle, especially when the horses weren't wild. Cattle needed riders on each side to keep the herd bunched and riders behind the herd to push. A horse herd needed a leader which was a rider on a horse, and a pusher which was a rider behind to keep the horses moving. Horses familiar with each other usually stayed together. Occasionally, the rider following behind may have to help turn the bunch, but usually, trail broke horses would follow the lead rider.

Today there were two lead riders. Jake watched Lathe and James ride together and could see them laughing. Jake knew Lathe was razzing the young James. This was James' first trip out of the valley other than the trip to Laramie City when Thomas and Beth got married. Now at sixteen, James was keen to go with them. James had deviled Jake all winter to be allowed to go with for the summer. When James heard that his sister was going, he was even more anxious to go.

"Jake, I'm sixteen," he had argued. "You rambled when you were sixteen, and if Bonnie goes, I should get to go too."

Jake had just grinned at the youngster and told him to get his ma's permission, and he could go. Sarah didn't

JOHNY WEBER

want to have a pouting boy around all summer so, here
James was, riding off at the front of the herd with his
older cousin. *At least,* Jake thought, *it wasn't me that
corrupted this boy.* Lathe did that all by himself. James
crawled out of a tepee the first morning with a whole
new appreciation for the Indian way of life. Like Lathe
the year before, two nights at the village wasn't enough
for the young stud, but two nights was all he got. Now
Jake knew that Lathe was helping James relive the experience. James had a new swagger in his step.

Jake pushed before him almost seventy head of
horses. Twenty of these were two-year-olds, too young
to start riding any more than lightly, but the trip and
the mountain slopes would toughen the young animals.
The men could work with them some, saddling and doing groundwork, but mostly they would just get them
off the grass of the home valley for the summer. There
were 30 three-year-olds and 15 four-year-olds and a
few seasoned saddle horses like Savior, the stud horse
Jake was riding now.

Savior was the stud Jake rode the summer before
when he almost found himself strung up. Naming
the young horse and vowing never to sell him, Savior became his main saddle horse when Jake needed
a seasoned mount. With more riding, he became
a trusted saddle horse but was still somewhat un-
ruly when he was around mares. It was good to get
the horse away from the valley. All the horses they
drove before them were geldings or young studs.
Savior, like young James, was just going to have to
suffer alone for the summer.

With this many horses off the home pastures, the
grass there would hold out longer. There were enough

four and five-year-olds at home to keep Kade, Army, Sam, and Luke busy between haying and checking on the cattle in the high country. Before Jake returned in August, Kade would take some of the five-year-old finished horses to Laramie City or a fort to sell. There was value in good horses that were as well trained as the Welles' horses.

Will and Matthew had their farming fields already planted by the time Jake left, and Jeremiah was busy most of the time cutting lumber at his sawmill. There would be more building going on this summer. Thomas and Beth were already talking about adding another room to their cabin. Beth was expecting this fall. Sam and Martha had a second son just before winter broke, and they were about to burst out of the two small rooms of their cabin. The news from Jackson's ranch was that a baby was due before mid-summer. It wouldn't be long before he was an uncle to several babies. *Pretty damn soon, they would be calling Twin Peaks a town instead of a ranch,* Jake thought. *Well, maybe not really a town, but they certainly were filling up the river valley with cabins and young'uns.* And with Jeremiah, Will, Bonnie, and James still unmarried, there were bound to be more cabins built soon, especially if Jeremiah's schoolteacher finally accepts Jeremiah's proposal. Jake had a sneaking suspicion that there would be another wedding this fall, and that might be why Jeremiah was so intent on stockpiling more lumber.

So many changes had come to his homeland, and so many yet to come. Like Kade, Jake regretted the influx of more people, but he found he felt differently about his own people multiplying. Jake knew they could never go back to the wild country he knew as a child, meeting the wagon trains on the Oregon Trail. He was glad he had Jacob's cabin to go to in the summers. For a while each summer, he could live in nature far from a lot of people. But he knew this wasn't going to last either. These mountains would fill up just like the lowlands. Like the Utes, life as they knew it was ending. As Kade once told him, "Adapt or die." Jake guessed he would have to adapt.

They had been at Jacob's cabin for three weeks now. Jake and Hawk brought the horse herd into the corral by Jacob's cabin and cut off the horses they would work with that day, turning the rest out to graze the lower meadow. At nightfall, they would drive all the horses into the upper meadow by Lathe's cabin and barricade the pathway between the two pastures. They never had to worry about the horses wandering off that way. There was only one way out of the upper meadow. They hadn't sorted long before James and Lathe joined them. Each picked out the horses that they would work with that day and would go off in their own directions. The two-year-olds never left the corrals or the meadow near the cabin when the men worked with them. The three- and four-year-olds were ridden off for hours, usually alone, as the young horses needed to learn to be away from the other horses.

Kasa still had not had her baby, and Lathe was nervous about it, not wanting to be far away from her. Jake left him to work with the two-year-old colts in the corral. For now, Hawk, James, and Kade did all the long distant riding. Sometimes they hunted while they rode, bringing home fresh meat. Some days they took off for an afternoon to go fishing in the river. Hawk had spent the winter with Jake and after a few days with the tribe, he wandered up to the mountains to help ride the colts. He didn't like the reservation life, and he enjoyed riding the good horses that the Welles' raised. He was fitting in well. James and Hawk camped together in a canvas tent next to Lathe's cabin.

Brown Otter was glad to see his son adapting to the white ways. As much as he hated to see his son leave his village, he knew that the life Hawk was learning to live at Twin Peaks would be a better life for him in the long run. With his half-Ute uncle and his sister, Kasa, Swift Hawk was not alone in this new life. After all, even the Bates and Jorgensens were distant relatives. Hawk was even learning how to read and write a little from Bonnie, who had been teaching Anna. Anna, who had been so young when the Pawnee captured her, could not remember any learning. Bonnie had offered to help Anna learn the basics. Hawk had watched the two women several times as they did their lessons in one cabin or another during the winter months, and, finally one day, he had asked to join them. Bonnie admitted it was just a beginning of what Anna and Hawk could learn, but it was a beginning.

On this day, there was little conversation between the men as they saddled horses and went on their way. Jake knew the younger men understood their jobs. He would see them eventually when they had ridden their last horse. When the corral was empty, they were done for the day.

♢

It was afternoon when Jake headed home, having ridden three horses this day. The second horse had tested him a lot but the horse he was finishing now was a four-year-old and would soon be an exceptional horse. He was sure-footed, intelligent, and willing. Jake decided to ride him on the high ridges, along some narrow trails that could be dangerous with the younger horses. He was surprised then to come upon one of their horses tied up below the ridgeline in the trees. As he got closer, he recognized Hawk's saddle. Jake glanced around him, but he could not see Hawk. Tying up his horse next to Hawk's, he wandered up to the ridgeline. Somewhere around here was Hawk. Jake was curious to see what the young Ute was up to.

Jake stood at the high ridge, looking over the crest. He could see the flat-top mountains in the distance. Always impressive, they rose like a fortress on the western horizon. But what caught Jake's attention was the two bodies lying on a ledge about thirty feet below and off to the side from where Jake stood.

Hawk and Bonnie lay on their sides, facing each other, smiling and talking, oblivious that they were being watched. Between them lay a basket with berries that they were eating from while they lay. Jake was relieved that they were wearing all their clothes. He wasn't sure why he cared, but he did. He wasn't sure he wanted to go home and tell Sarah that her daughter got herself married the Indian way while on his watch.

Jake studied the two handsome young people, one dark-skinned and one fair. There was a familiarity between them, but Jake didn't think there was intimacy. *How had he missed this?* He had never caught a glance or a touch between the two in all the months that Hawk had lived with them. But these two were clearly easy with each other. Just the way they lay together, talking and laughing, comfortable together, told Jake this wasn't the first time the two had been alone. Now he had to decide what to do about it.

While Jake stood, trying to decide if he should fade away or scramble down the slope to confront the two, Bonnie tossed a berry up in the air, and Hawk dove for it, trying to catch it in his mouth. Jake heard peals of laughter come from Bonnie. The movement caused Hawk to glance upward, initially to catch the berry, but instead caught sight of Jake. Hawk went still, and Bonnie, seeing him go rigid, looked to see what he saw. Bonnie, too, went still, staring at her older cousin. Neither Hawk nor Bonnie moved, not to be closer together nor to jerk away. They simply looked at Jake.

Jake studied them again for a moment, then giving a slight nod, he turned and faded away. It was up to them to come to him now. He knew they would seek him out, one or the other. Jake wasn't sure when, but they would come. And then he would find out what intentions they had for each other.

Jake turned his horse loose and headed to the cabin. He heard Anna calling to Kestrel just as the little girl came scooting out the cabin door, her fat little legs pumping. He reached down and scooped her up, holding her high in the air as she giggled.

"I have her, Bird," he laughed.

"Good," Anna retorted, "I am going to nurse the baby, and she is always running off. You watch her for a while."

Jake grinned, and taking his daughter, he went to the shade of the cabin and sat down on the ground, leaning back against the logs. He remembered Tom's teasing the day of the attack and smiled fondly. *Damn, that Tom.* He knew them so well. Yes, if it had been Kestrel that Anna was nursing, he would have been in there, getting his own pleasure, as Tom put it. But now, with a two-and-a-half-year-old learning to talk, it just wouldn't do to have her watch her pa playing with his wife. There was no muzzle on what a toddler would say. She would be worse than Tom. Instead, he teased the little girl, hiding twigs and pinecones under his legs, making her dig around to find them.

It wasn't long before he saw Hawk riding through the trees. Jake didn't think it would take Hawk long to return. He wasn't surprised to see Bonnie riding double behind Hawk. Now that they were found out, there was no need to come in separately. Jake wondered which one would come and talk to him. He hoped it was Hawk. A man needs to own up for his actions. A white man should know that, but he wasn't sure if Hawk would think the same way. He knew his nephew, but some things just didn't come up, and this was one of them.

Jake wasn't sure what was bothering him. He had no difficulty last year when he had learned that Lathe wanted to marry Kasa. Now, why was he unsettled about finding Hawk and Bonnie together? Was it because he knew that Sarah still stood by the rule that her daughter must be eighteen to marry? Jake wasn't Bonnie's father, but with Jim dead and Sarah days away at home, Bonnie had been entrusted to him. It was not a thing to take lightly. He would just have to wait to see who came to him and what they had to say.

Jake watched Hawk unsaddle his colt and turn him loose. Bonnie stood by the corral fence waiting, and then they both walked over to Jake. Jake was surprised that they came together, but it pleased him also. It was the right thing to do, neither running from this. Kestrel, seeing the young people that she loved, ran to them, and Hawk picked her up and carried her back with them on his shoulders. The two young people were solemn, but walked with purpose, not as if they feared the outcome. It was Bonnie who spoke first.

"So, now you know," she said simply to Jake.

Jake looked at the two steadily before answering, "Exactly, what do I know?

"We," Hawk paused, searching for words. He spoke good English but sometimes struggled to find just the right words, "Like being together."

"Nothing wrong with that," Jake commented mildly.

Hawk shook his head, "Not just like. We want to be together."

Jake looked at Bonnie then. "And you?"

"We sort of have been meeting on and off all winter," Bonnie admitted. "We like to be together."

"Nothing wrong with that," Jake repeated. They were being pretty vague. He looked at the two of them, waiting for them to say more. He watched them grow uncomfortable, not knowing where to go next. Jake thought he'd help them out.

"Exactly where do you think this 'liking' is going to go with you two?"

The two young people looked at each other before Hawk answered, "We want to marry."

"You know your ma's rules," Jake told Bonnie.

"I know," Bonnie replied, glancing at Hawk. "We know. We will wait."

"Then why are you hiding?" Jake asked her gently. "Why are you sneaking?"

"We didn't know if," Hawk began but stopped, thinking, "we weren't sure how people, your people, would . . ." he couldn't find the words, but Jake knew his meaning.

"That would sort of make us all hypocrites, wouldn't it?" Jake asked. "Considering where I came from?"

Bonnie suddenly became animated, "Exactly, that is what I told Hawk, but he was afraid he'd be sent away if you all knew. So, we kept it a secret."

"Were you expecting ever to tell anyone?" Jake hid a smile.

"Well, we thought that when I was eighteen, we'd say then," Bonnie said.

"Honey," Jake spoke softly, "don't you think it might be nice not to spring this on your ma all of a sudden? Might be nice to let her work into this slowly? Losing her last daughter is going to be hard on her. It hasn't been that long since she lost your dad." Jake looked at Hawk sharply, "And do you understand how important it is to Sarah that Bonnie does not have to get married before she is eighteen?" He hoped they both caught the hidden meaning in that question.

Hawk grinned at that, "Yes, I know. Bonnie is very clear on that."

"Then I'll trust you two to do the right thing," Jake told them. "But you have to tell your ma, Bonnie. She needs to know. I think you will find that she will accept it."

Jake looked at Hawk again, "You might want to let your father in on this. He and I don't have secrets, so it's either you or me."

Hawk nodded, "I will talk to him."

"There's another thing you both should think about," Jake stood up then, taking Kestrel from Hawk. "You come from different places, different customs. One of you is going to give up a lot if you stay together. Which one of you is willing to do that?"

The two young people looked at each other, but neither of them spoke. Jake went on, "Kasa gave up her way of life for Lathe. Some think it is a woman's place to go where her husband goes," Jake looked at Bonnie. "If you two think that way, are you willing to go to the reservation and live? You see yourself living in a tepee in the village?" He turned to Hawk, "Or are you willing to live the white man life off the reservation? You two better think of some of those things before you go any farther with this liking." Jake turned and left them, taking Kestrel, and going into the cabin. He had said his piece. But there was a lot more to think about here than simply wanting to be together. The young don't always think that way until it is too late.

Nothing more was said that night. Anna had supper for them all, but soon after eating, Hawk, Lathe, and Kasa headed toward the upper meadow, driving the horse herd before them for the night. Jake wasn't sure how much longer Kasa could go before this baby came out. She looked like she was going to explode, but she insisted she felt fine. Lathe hovered over her continually, nervous as a bluetick hound that had just lost a scent.

When Brown Otter and Snowbird left the fire to head back to their tepee, Otter turned and spoke to

Jake, "Maybe tomorrow morning we do some hunting before you start on your horses?"

Jake nodded. The hunting would be best at dawn. But Jake knew it was not hunting that was on Otter's mind. Jake knew that Hawk had talked to Brown Otter, and now Otter wanted to discuss this news with Jake. Hell, Jake felt like a father to more than toddlers. *How did he get into this?*

The two brothers were miles from the cabin when the sun finally reached the river valley. They left just as the sun was kissing the mountain tops, but the meadows were only shadows.

When they came upon a young moose, grazing in the swamps around an oxbow of the river, they bagged the meat they would bring back. They skinned the animal, packed the meat onto a packhorse they had with them, and started slowly toward home. So far, they had not spoken about the young couple, but Jake knew that the subject would come up. They were halfway home before Brown Otter broke his silence.

"Swift Hawk tells me you saw them yesterday," he commented.

"*Hmmm*," Jake replied. "I did. They were not doing anything wrong, just lying and talking and laughing, eating berries. But they told me later that they want more."

"What do you think?"

Jake exhaled slowly, "Hell, I have no idea. I can't figure myself out, much less them. Why did I have no reservations last year when Lathe wanted to take Kasa, but this year I am uncomfortable in my mind when I find Hawk and Bonnie together? Shit, she isn't even my daughter. I don't even know why it concerns me."

"What do you see when you see them together?" Brown Otter asked.

Jake was surprised at the question, "What do I see? I see them. What should I see?"

"You see your mother and our father," Brown Otter's gaze was direct.

"I never knew my father," Jake protested.

"You see a red man and a white woman," Brown Otter continued. "You see your mother and our father in your mind. You have always known the story of your parents, but now you see them. Did they bring happiness into your life or pain? Will Hawk and Bonnie bring happiness or pain?"

Jake thought about that. Maybe Otter had hit on something. They rode in silence a while. Finally, Jake had his own question. "What do you think?" he asked.

Brown Otter smiled at his younger half-brother. He knew that Jake couldn't answer the question yet, so Jake threw the question back. Otter knew this question would come. He knew his answer.

"Twenty years ago, when my son was born, I never thought that I would ever want my son anywhere but in the village with us. I dreamed of his marriage to a Ute girl and them living in a tepee in the village. I saw him hunting with me, fighting beside me. I would teach him the ways of our people. He would be a warrior. These are the things I thought of then," he finished.

"You have done well raising him to do those things. Hawk is a good hunter, fearless in battle. I have seen these things. He is a man to be respected."

Brown Otter nodded. "But today, our young men sit in the village much of the year by the agency and drink the white man's liquor when they can get it. They wait for the supply trains to bring them food. There are no Arapaho that come to steal our horses. We do not need to be watchful, ready to fight. The old men are not satisfied, and the young men are becoming lazy."

Brown Otter rode for several minutes before continuing, "I do not see a future for my son in the village. I do not want him to leave, but I do not want him to stay. He likes to ride the horses you have. He is learning about the cattle. If he went to your valley, he would have a good life. Not the life I dreamed that he would have. Not the life we love. But twenty years ago, I didn't know we would lose our land, our hunting grounds. If he and Bonnie are right for each other, then I accept it."

Jake rode quietly, thinking of what Brown Otter had said. Finally, he started to speak.

"My mother never says a bad word about Blue Knife. She won't let anyone else either. What did she have to give up when Blue Knife took her for a wife?"

"She gave up little. In the beginning, she gave up control of her own life. But it was Blue Knife that gave up his way," Otter answered. "Once Sabra learned not to fear Blue Knife, she went on with her life, here in these mountains, doing what she had always done. My father gave up our people for her. He knew she would have to change if they returned to the tribe. He didn't want her to change."

"So, will Hawk give up his way? Will he be content to live the life we live if he marries Bonnie?"

"He already has. He talks of returning with you. I think the little bit of white blood that flows in his veins is strong. If he still wants Bonnie next year, he will never leave her," Brown Otter looked at the river that they rode beside. "He will live your life."

"Then I have no reservations about this," Jake said. "I will speak to Bonnie's mother when we return. Hawk will have to speak to her too. But I know Sarah. She will accept Hawk."

"If you accept him, they all will. They look to you. Someday when Kade is gone, you will lead them all," Otter was serious.

"Me? No," Jake was surprised. "Matthew and Sam are older than I. Thomas is Kade's blood son. They would lead us."

Brown Otter smiled at this. "Matthew leads you to your God, but he is not a leader of men. Sam is like Tom. He likes fun. He is smart about the ways of the mountains. He will give you guidance; he will stand at your side. But he is not a leader. Thomas looks to you for strength. He will follow you. He already does. You will be a leader like both of your fathers. You already are."

They rode quietly from there. Jake mulled over Brown Otter's words, wondering if it were true. He never thought of himself as a leader, but he also knew he was comfortable in his own decisions. He had made his way for years now, within the valley and out. When he acted, he was confident he was doing the right thing. But to be a leader of others, well, that was just not something he thought much about.

When the two brothers rode into the lower meadow, they found both Jacob's cabin and the tepee empty, the cabin door closed, no fires, and no women and children. There were no horses in the corral, waiting to be sorted and ridden.

"Either the boys are taking the day off," Jake commented, "or something is going on."

"Trouble," Brown Otter said, "or Kasa is having the baby."

Jake glanced at his brother. "I'll hang the meat," he said. "You go and check, and if there is trouble, signal me. Otherwise, I'll be along directly."

It was not trouble. Kasa was having her baby. When Jake rode into the upper meadow, he found a nervous Lathe pacing in front of his cabin. Bonnie, Swift Hawk, Brown Otter, and the children were with him. Kestrel came running to her father, and he scooped her up, putting her on his shoulders.

"How long?" Jake inquired of Bonnie after turning his horse loose.

"Couple hours," she answered. "Anna just nursed the baby. Would you keep her, and I'll go back inside?" Bonnie handed the baby to Jake before continuing, "I think it is going alright," Bonnie glanced at Lathe, noting that he was listening.

Jake took the baby from Bonnie, noticing that Lark was already dozing. Looking around, he eased down in front of the cabin, leaning against the wall. Lark continued sleeping on his lap as he settled. Kestrel climbed off his shoulders and snuggled into his legs, playing with the fringe on his buckskin pants. Brown Otter came and sat down beside Jake and took out his pipe. This was a day for women's work. The horses could wait a day.

Lathe continued his slow pacing, not knowing what to do with himself. Jake remembered when Kestrel was born and how scared he had been for Anna. But Kestrel had taken much of two days to appear. Lark had been much easier, but still a father is worthless on the birthing day, unable to help. He wasn't sure how much help he could be to Lathe either, but he would sit here anyway. Maybe his presence alone would give the young man some comfort.

"How did Molly take to England last fall?" Brown Otter broke the silence.

Jake smiled at his brother. Here was at least something to talk about while they waited. "She found it interesting, but I don't think she intends to go back there to live. I believe she told Jackson when they got home that if he ever thought he wanted to go home to England to stay, he could go alone," Jake laughed at this. "And I do believe she meant it. Jackson told me he wasn't going to test her on that."

Otter also smiled, for he too knew that Molly was a headstrong woman. If she said she wouldn't live there, she meant it.

"She liked Jackson's mother," Jake went on. "Of course, Molly knew Richard already, and he had apparently filled his wife in on the woman Jackson had married and Molly's family. So, she welcomed Molly." Jake paused, thinking, then went on, "Ma was really on Molly about manners and what she called etiquette. Stuff Ma learned as a girl in finishing school. I can guarantee you that I am very glad not to be a woman in England, or even back east, for that matter. I couldn't believe all the things that Molly had to remember. But Ma was determined that Molly would not go there and look like some dirt farmer from Missouri," Jake laughed at that. "Hell, Ma had Molly wearing gloves to protect her hands for months before the wedding. Ma said we may be mountain grown from the American west, but she wasn't going to have her daughter put down because of it."

Otter grinned, "I can see your mother with her back straight, telling Molly how to act. When she gets an idea, she pushes hard."

"So, I guess the trip went pretty well until Jackson and Molly got invited to another estate for a week of activities," Jake continued. "Molly had a picture of our whole family that we took at Thomas and Beth's wedding. Well, you can guess that everyone had to see her mountain family, and when they did, there I was, big as day and dark as an Indian," Jake grinned, looking sideways at Otter. "Guess that started some conversations. The only thing that would have made that worse was if we had been wearing our buckskins instead of our wedding clothes. Pa and I had cut our braids off, so that was a good thing, too."

Jake noticed that Lathe, who knew the story of Molly in England, had quit his pacing, and had hunkered down on the ground, listening.

"Didn't you say that they asked Molly how many people you scalped?" Lathe asked.

"That they did, and you know Molly. She's like a she-bear about her family. Jackson told me she stood up proud and looked directly at the woman who asked before telling her that her brother didn't ever scalp anyone, but her pa had. You can guess that stopped a lot of conversation," Jake grinned. "Jackson said you can't muffle Molly when she gets her back up, so she went through the battle we had with the Cheyenne, how she got hurt, and Jim and Tom were killed, and how Pa was so angry, he took revenge out on the dead Cheyenne by scalping them. She did leave out the rest, though, what Pa did, but Jackson said he was sweating hard by then, not knowing how far she'd go.

"Jackson said he figured they would never get another invitation after that, but instead, they had so many invites they couldn't go to them all. Guess everyone wanted to see Jackson and his 'mountain' woman. The next place they stayed had a shooting match where the men shot these discs that a servant would make fly up into the air. Well, of course, Molly went to watch with Jackson, but in her defense, other women went out to watch also. Molly told Jackson that the shooting wasn't that hard as the discs always went the same way at the same speed, and someone overheard her and asked Molly if she would like to try. So, she borrowed Jackson's gun and never missed."

Jake laughed then, "Jackson told me she told the others that it was much harder to hit game or even a man that was moving because you never knew which way they would go. Well, then, the story came up about our fight with the pirates on the Oregon Trail when I got shot." Jake had his pipe out by then and puffed on it for a while. "Jackson is a pretty good man. I think a lot of those civilized men in England would be embarrassed with his woman talking about such things, but Jackson said he was proud to have such a woman. Jackson also said that just between us, he never wants to go back to that life. I think the word he used was that it was stifling. I think Jackson is a westerner through and through now."

The men grew quiet, watching Kestrel play, going from one man to the next for attention. Lathe was still nervous, but he stayed seated, pulling out threads on his shirt. The day got warmer, and the sun rose higher, reaching its zenith. The baby finally woke and began to cry, and Bonnie came for her, taking her to Anna to nurse. Jake went for a chunk of meat, and Otter started a fire to roast it. The day dragged. Finally, when the sun was beginning to put shadows in the meadow, there was a baby's wail that came from inside. Lathe's firstborn, a son, had arrived.

They returned to the home valley in mid-August. The haying was well underway, and the home crew was glad to get more help. Jake did not talk again with Bonnie and Hawk about their plans. He hoped that they would do the right thing and speak with Sarah, and if they did, he would hear about it. He would talk to Sarah himself but wanted to wait for the young couple to make a move first.

It was three days after returning when Sarah asked Jake to stay back after the noon meal finished. Sarah and Mattie fed the haying crew the noon meal every day, alternating between their homes. This day they were at Sarah's cabin, and when the men got up to leave, Sarah asked Jake to hold back a minute. He knew the subject had come up.

"Bonnie and Hawk talked to me last night," Sarah began. "They told me that you knew they had feelings for each other."

Jake sat back down at the table, and Sarah slid onto the bench across from him. "I saw them together one day out riding," he told Sarah. "They were just talking, but, well," he hesitated, "I knew there was more than that. They came and talked to me, and I told Bonnie she needed to speak to you. I am glad she did."

"What do you think?" Sarah asked.

"Sarah, I am not sure it matters what I think. What do you think?"

Sarah looked away for a moment, then looked back. "I guess what I mean is," she stopped again. "I don't know what I mean, actually. I am not opposed to them being together, but ..."

Jake smiled at her. "You wonder if they will be suited for each other because their backgrounds are so different."

"There is that, yes," Sarah replied. "I've watched Hawk a lot this past winter when he was around so much. He seems to fit in; I like him, but what kind of expectations will he have for a wife? Will they fit in with what expectations Bonnie will have for a husband?"

"I talked to Otter about that," Jake answered. "He talked about my father, Blue Knife, and how he gave up the village and his people when he took my mother. Otter thinks that Hawk is like Blue Knife. He thinks that Hawk will adapt to our ways if he truly loves Bonnie. Otter thinks Hawk has already adapted. But, Sarah, can we ever be sure that the young ones that marry will always be happy, will always adapt? Don't we just have to let them make their own choices?"

Sarah studied Jake. "Oh, Jake, your father must have been a wise man to have such a wise son. And maybe Kade and Sabra have a bit to do with that too, but you're right, I have to let go."

"Bonnie won't be eighteen until next summer, so those two have some time to get to know each other before they start making any promises. It's enough, Sarah, that you accept Hawk now and let Bonnie and Hawk work things out. If it is right for them, they should know by next fall." Jake reached over and took Sarah's hand. "If you want an opinion, here it is. I think Bonnie is a smart young lady who will listen to her heart but use her head. And I think it might take some time for Hawk to learn all our ways, but he is a good man. I don't think he will hurt Bonnie. And if they truly love each other, they will work all the rest out."

CHAPTER 18

Where There is Smoke – 1879

Jake sat his horse on the ridge, looking out toward the mighty flattop mountains to the southwest. They were shrouded in smoke. The smoke was coming closer and thicker now, and the night before, when he had checked from the ridge after dark, he could see the faint glow of fire on the horizon. He hated to leave the high mountain so early; it was not yet August, but he knew it was time to go. The smoke was bad on the lungs, and on the worst days, it stung their eyes as well. He knew it couldn't be good for the children. And Anna was pregnant this summer. She thought the baby would be born in late October. The smoke couldn't be good for her either. Damn the fires, no matter how they started.

For it depended on who you talked to how the fires started. The whites blamed the Utes. And it certainly could be the Utes as they had burned forests for years for various reasons. Sometimes they started fires to drive game out, sometimes to drive an enemy out, sometimes just to cause trouble. But there were a lot of fires started this summer, and Jake didn't think the Utes were the cause of them all, if any. There was a strong case that the railroad started some, and campfires over by a mining camp were also a prime cause. And then several thunderstorms had gone through during the last thirty days. The lightning had been dreadful. Maybe all these were causes.

In any case, the fires, and there was certainly more than one, were coming closer. The air was filled with smoke and if the winds brought the fires much closer, it could be dangerous to stay and dangerous to leave. Fire could be so unpredictable. Jake made the decision. It was time to get out before the fires got any closer. He reined his horse and started back toward Jacob's cabin and his family.

Jake had just started to unsaddle his horse when he saw Brown Otter coming from the river valley. Otter had ridden along the ridges on the other side of the river to look toward the Rabbit Ear Rocks to see if there was any change in the smoke coming from the east. He was not sparing his horse much as he returned. That didn't look so good either. Jake waited to hear his report.

"I can see light from the fires just coming over the far mountain," Brown Otter told Jake, pulling off his saddle and turning his horse loose. "What about the south and west?"

"About the same," Jake replied. "I'm for heading out in the morning. Can't depend on the wind, and if it changes, one or the other of the fires will make it here. I'm thinking we got to make tracks and get the women and children away from this smoke."

Brown Otter nodded. "We will pack up and be ready to leave before the sun reaches us in the morning. I'll watch for Hawk to come in. He's still out riding, but I think Lathe is up at his cabin."

"I'll let Lathe know. When Hawk brings his last horse in, have him drive all the horses to pasture for the night. No sense in messing with them again today," Jake looked at the horses grazing in the meadow. Then turning, he went to his cabin to help Anna start packing.

It took all afternoon and into the evening to get all their supplies packed. They had a couple of pack mules if needed, along with the light wagon. In the wagon, the women made a bed for the children to sleep in during the day, plus plenty of room for packs of supplies. Kestrel rode her horse most of the day, but at three-and-a-half she still needed at least one nap during the day, if not two. But she was a "little Sabra" for sure, always ready to ride. She rode an older gelding that had been Molly's main ride when Molly was younger. At sixteen, the horse was perfect for the little girl. Then there was little Sabra Lark, who, at a year-and-a-half, loved riding with her pa. But Lark would tire after a while and be content to curl up on her mother's lap in the wagon or play on the bed in the back. Kasa and Lathe's little boy, Slade Layton, was just a year and not quite walking, but he still got around quickly if Kasa didn't keep a good eye on him. Slade and Lark could crawl right out of that wagon if they weren't watched.

Jake hooked the team to the wagon in the gloom of the predawn dark. The smoke was thick. They would be heading north and then northwest, so he hoped the air would clear up some as they traveled. He didn't want to go back to the agency, but the others all did. Kasa and Hawk's older sister was away with her husband when they went through in late May. So, they wanted to see her as well as visit with cousins and friends before they headed home. James had his hopes set on staying a few days, but he would have to settle for two nights as that was all Jake was willing to give.

The atmosphere in the village in May had not been good. He didn't expect it to be better now after a summer with the new agent. Nathaniel Meeker had arrived at the White River Agency in May and right away began pushing the Utes to change their lifestyle. He wanted them to plow up the good grazing lands and give up their horses. It hadn't sat well with the Indians in May. If the agent had continued his efforts, Jake was afraid that the village could be a tinderbox of anger. The rest of Jake's party wanted to stop, so stop they would, but Jake was firm that two nights was it.

Hawk was anxious to reach the Ute village at the agency, so he rode in front of the horse herd leading the way. Lathe, Brown Otter, and Jake trailed behind, occasionally moving a lagging horse up but mainly to keep them going. The wagon with the women and children followed behind. Sometimes Bonnie rode, but today she had climbed in the wagon at noon with Anna, Snowbird, and Kasa. They were almost at the White River Agency and the Ute village. The next ridge, where Hawk was nearing the top, would look down on the vast Milk Creek bottomland where the agency and tepees would be scattered. Jake watched Hawk lope his horse up the rise, then suddenly as he reached the summit he reined to a complete stop. The herd behind him split around him, not knowing where to go. The horses were ready to stop and drifted around him, some dropping their heads to graze, some going over the hill and out of sight.

"What the hell is he stopping for?" Lathe called to Jake.

"No idea," came the reply. "Let's ride up and see."

The three men reached Hawk quickly and looked over the bottomland. "Holy shit!" Lathe breathed. There below them, where the Utes always kept their vast and prized horse herd in a lush meadow, now lay plowed fields. The racetrack that the Utes used for games and races was gone. There were even buildings out in the middle of it. Jake glanced over at Brown Otter. Otter's face was not emotionless as it so often was. It was clouded with anger. This was not good.

Jake cast around the area for a place to take their horses. "We better run these horses up the creek some and settle them for the night." He turned to Brown Otter, "If you and Hawk want to ride ahead to the village, Lathe, James, and I can see to the horses. Have the wagon follow you."

Brown Otter just nodded to Jake, and he and Hawk started down the hill. Jake motioned to the women in the wagon to go to the village, and then he and Lathe took the horses off. This loss of the horse pasture wasn't his affair, but it certainly was for Hawk and Brown Otter. Let them sort it out first.

Morning brought little relief to the resentment that was evident in the village. Brown Otter and Swift Hawk had stayed out late, talking with the other men. The Utes were all angered by the actions of the new agent. There was unrest in the village. Agent Meeker was pushing for the Indians to farm the land. Jake could see his reasoning, although he disagreed with it. It was white man reasoning. It was the same reasoning that the government held. Make the Indian a farmer, and they could subsist on fewer acres. Reservations would become smaller, and the annuities of food and supplies would be fewer.

But the reasoning was not going to sway the Utes. They had been a hunter and gatherer society for too long. Their horses were too important to them to give up. Most of the Utes were refusing to do the farming, so the agent had his hired workers plow the fields. Meeker also wanted the Indians to give up their horses. Jake felt the Utes' anger and agreed with them. This was the Utes' homeland first. Jake had promised Hawk and Kasa that they would stay two nights. With the atmosphere in the village what it was, it might be a long two nights.

About midmorning the next day, a messenger from the agent came to Jake's wagon. Anna and Bonnie had a fire going and were starting a stew. The children were playing with Hawk's nieces and nephews at Otter's tepee close to them.

"Ma'am," the messenger addressed Anna and Bonnie, "the Meekers heard that you were here and ask that you come for tea. They don't get many white visitors and would enjoy your company."

Anna looked up at Jake, sitting in front of Otter's tepee. He nodded to her. "Yes, we could do that," Anna replied. "Now?"

The messenger nodded assent, gave them directions to the Meeker cabin, and took his leave. Anna looked at Jake.

"You will go with us?" she asked, hopefully.

"I don't reckon they want to visit with me," Jake replied.

"Please come, Uncle Jake," Bonnie implored. Jake and Bonnie both knew he wasn't her uncle, but often the younger kids called him uncle, especially when they wanted something from him.

Lathe, stooping, came out of the tepee. "Go where?" he asked.

"Bonnie and Anna got invited to tea at the Meeker's," Jake told him. "They heard there were white people here."

"I'll go," Lathe said. Then looking at Jake, he continued, "But Bonnie's right, you better come too."

Jake looked at the three of them. In his mind, he remembered what Otter had said, "You will lead them. They will follow you."

Jake sighed, "I'll go. What about Kasa? You going to get her?"

"She went off with her sister. Snowbird has the baby sleeping. I don't think Kasa would want to go over there anyway. There is too much bad blood right now," Lathe answered. "And who knows what tepee James is in," Lathe chuckled at that but then sobered before continuing. "Jake, maybe you can talk some sense into the agent."

Jake shrugged. He didn't think he would be swaying anyone's mind here, but he supposed it never hurt to try. The four of them walked over to the Agent's cabin, leaving the toddlers playing with some village children under Snowbird's watchful eye.

As they approached the Meeker cabin, Jake could see a table in the front, set with cups and saucers and small cakes. Jake felt Anna's hesitation. She was still not comfortable with white strangers, and she had little experience with parties. Going to Laramie City and having meals in the fancy hotel dining room had been a real learning experience for her. Jake knew she was more comfortable in an Indian village then she was with white strangers.

The agent came forward, offering his hand to Lathe. "Welcome," he said genially, "I am Nathaniel Meeker, and this is my wife, Arvilla, and my daughter, Josephine. We heard there were visitors to the village."

"Lathe Jorgensen," Lathe replied. "These are my cousins."

The agent nodded politely as Anna and Bonnie told him their names. Then the agent looked to Jake.

"And this must be your guide?" Meeker inquired, not extending his hand.

Jake offered his hand first, "Actually, I am Jake Welles. I am Anna's husband and Lathe and Bonnie's cousin."

The agent was surprised, but he shook Jake's hand, recovering quickly, and invited them all to sit down. Jake and Anna sat down together, and Jake found himself across from Josephine.

The Meekers were curious where Jake and his party were from and what brought them to the agency. Jake explained where they spent their summers and where the ranch was. As Jake suspected it would, the question came up on how Jake and Anna got married. Jake saw Anna glance up at him nervously, and he knew intuitively that she did not want these people to know about her past.

"I met Anna a couple years ago when I went back to Ft. Laramie for supplies," Jake explained. "We seemed to get along well, so we decided to marry. It has worked out well for us."

Josephine looked across at Anna, "Your parents didn't object?"

"Anna's parents had been dead for many years before I met her," Jake went on smoothly. "Do you think they would have objected, Miss Meeker?"

"It is just unusual," Josephine answered easily. "I'm sorry. I meant no disrespect."

"And your connection to the Utes?" Nathaniel asked.

"I have a half-brother, Brown Otter, who lives here when he isn't in the mountains with us," Jake answered. "We have just spent two months up by the Steamboat Springs. Perhaps you have heard of the area? There is a post office there now. We have a claim near there that used to be my grandfather's land. My grandfather was a fur trapper."

"I have heard of the area," Meeker replied, "But I have not been able to travel that way yet."

"Well, don't do it this summer," Lathe commented. "It is a little smokey here, but up in the high mountains, the smoke is thick right now. We usually stay longer but Jake thought we could get caught by fires if the winds change."

The conversation went on with Jake, Lathe, and Bonnie contributing. Anna would speak if spoken to directly, but she did not offer anything extra. Jake knew she was uncomfortable. She watched him like a hawk, doing what he did. He deliberately took his napkin and set it on his lap. She would follow his movements, using the silverware he did. But she would smile occasionally and nod at the Meekers when they asked her if she was enjoying the tea.

When enough time had elapsed, Jake looked at Lathe and mentioned they should check on the horses. The people around the table all rose.

"Thank you for the tea and cakes," Jake told the Meekers.

"Yes, it was nice," Anna echoed. Jake knew it was hard for Anna to speak to strangers, so he was pleased she had expressed her thanks. He smiled down at her.

As the others took their leave, Jake hesitated, turning back to the Indian agent.

"Plowing the land isn't going to make them farmers, you know," he said softly.

"They need to learn to take care of themselves," Meeker retorted.

"They know how to take care of themselves," Jake replied. "They have been doing that for centuries. They just don't know how to get rid of the people taking their land."

"The settlers will come," Nathaniel said. "I am just trying to teach them how to live."

"Yes, the settlers will come," Jake acknowledged. "But if the government would keep promises, we might be able to live in peace. All of us." Jake turned to leave, but just before he turned completely away, he said quietly, "No good will come of this breaking up of the land. They will not give up their horses and follow behind a plow. There will be trouble if you push too hard." He didn't wait for the Indian agent's reply.

CHAPTER 19

Death at Milk Creek – Fall 1879

Jake surveyed the foothills on either side of the river valley, watching for his riders. It was getting late, and he had seen no cattle for the last several miles. He didn't want to go farther. It was time to gather his riders and set up camp for the night. Jake signaled to Sam across the river to watch for Lathe, while scanning his side of the river hills for Luke. He and Sam, riding the flat along the river, would make more time than the riders in the hills. There were some scrub brushes in a bend of the river, and they could make camp there for the night. Jake waved to Sam, and they both rode for it, knowing Lathe and Luke would be watching for them as well.

They were just about a day's ride from the ranch, looking for strays that might have come down off the mountain early to graze on the river bottom. Sam and Jake had ridden the foothills this morning, trading off with Luke and Lathe in the afternoon. The horses climbing the slopes worked the hardest, so by switching, they were able to give the horses a rest. When they came upon cattle in the foothills, the riders would push them out onto the river bottom. Here the cattle would stay and graze for the day it would take the riders to turn around and head home, picking up these strays and pushing them back to the ranch.

Sam had a fire going, and Jake was starting to fry some deer steaks when the two younger men rode in. The nights were colder and the days shorter now, but it was October first, so that was expected. Traveling at this time of year meant bringing clothes for all types of weather. It could just as likely snow as it was to be hot. This night was chilly, but the weather had been generally mild.

"See anything in the last few miles?" Jake inquired of the other men after they had their horses hobbled for the night.

"Not for a long time," Lathe replied. "I haven't seen any sign of cattle up in the hills either. What about on the valley?"

"Nothing for quite a while," Jake answered. "In my way of thinking, if there are any cattle up ahead, they can just wander. I don't hanker to go on any farther."

Sam cast him a curious glance, but it was Lathe that questioned, "How much farther is it?"

"Depends on if you are riding or running," Jake hesitated, "or dragging. Don't reckon I have a good handle on the distance. I just know I don't want to go on."

The others left it at that. It had been a year since Jake had almost met the hangman's noose, and he didn't want to talk about it.

Shortly after the night settled into deep darkness, the younger two men turned in, but Jake and Sam sat up together, nursing along coffee by the fire. They sat in companionable silence for a while, each in his own thoughts until suddenly Jake began to talk.

"You would think after a year, I would quit having the nightmares," he spoke softly.

"You have them a lot?" Sam wondered.

"More than I'd want to have them, but not all the time. Just about when I think I am through with them, I get another."

"Do you feel yourself hanging?" Sam asked.

"No, but I see that damn noose, and then I see this faceless body hanging there," Jake said. "But the worst is that I see Pa sitting on his horse underneath. I see his face and his jaw is clenched, and his eyes are hard like he is in misery."

Sam thought about that for a bit. "When I was jest a young'un, I almost drowned. I had nightmares a bunch after that. I always felt the water coming over me and woke up choking. Reckon that is because I experienced that. You live the nightmare you went through. For you, it was seeing the rope and imagining the end."

"I keep thinking that maybe if I go there and see that big old tree, maybe I'd get over them," Jake was thoughtful. "But I don't want to do that either. Maybe next year."

"If you are like me, eventually, the nightmares will end. Give it time," Sam said gently.

The following morning, the men were up at dawn saddling their horses. It wouldn't take them quite as long to get home because they would all four ride on the river bottom where the going was easier on the horses. Still, the cattle would move slower, so they wanted an early start. They had ridden about three hours and had a package of cattle in front of them when Sam looked back, scanning the hills just in case they might have missed something. He saw a rider approaching coming at them on a high trot.

"Jake," he called, "a rider is coming up behind us."

Jake pulled up, letting the cattle drift ahead of him, and turned to wait for the stranger to catch them. As the rider came closer, they could see the calvary uniform and they could also see the horse was lathered. It was apparent that the soldier had been pushing it for some time. The soldier slowed his horse to a walk and approached cautiously.

"You've come a piece, soldier," Sam commented when he was close.

"That I have," the young man said, pulling his horse up. "I need a fresh mount. I have to get to Ft. Steele."

"What's the hurry?" Jake asked.

The soldier looked warily at Jake before answering, speaking again to Sam, "The Utes have attacked the command of Major Thornburg's at Milk Creek. There were 153 calvary and twenty-three militia from Ft. Steele with the major, and the Utes have them pinned down. Most of the horses are dead or wounded. I'm to ride for help."

"What was the cause of the attack?" Jake asked. "What was your mission?"

Again, the soldier glanced at Jake but spoke to Sam, assuming Sam was the trail boss because he was older and white, "We were sent to the White River Agency. There has been some trouble there, and the agent requested help."

"If you crossed Milk Creek with troops, then you were going onto the reservation," Jake observed. "That is an act of war according to the treaty the Utes signed with the government. Didn't your officers know that?"

"Mister," this time, the soldier spoke sharply to Jake, "I jest take orders. I don't ask." The soldier looked back at Sam, "I jest know they need help, so I was sent to get it."

Jake looked at Sam, then coming to a decision, he stepped off his horse. "Take this horse. He's a stud, hankering for home, and he will take you directly back to our ranch. Ask at the first cabins you come to for Kade Welles. They'll give you directions. Kade's my pa. He will give you a meal and a fresh horse. Have you eaten?"

The soldier shook his head.

"Lathe, you got any hardtack and jerky in your packs?" Jake asked, stripping his saddle off Savior. "Give this soldier something to get him home."

It didn't take the soldier long to get Savior saddled. "If you push this horse, he will get you to our ranch by midafternoon, or even earlier. Tell Kade I sent you and that we are coming in with cattle," Jake looked thoughtfully at the trooper. "You just might mention when you get to Ft. Steele that the Utes were just defending their lands. It is the army that started this war."

The young man looked hard at Jake, realizing now that this was the head of these men. "Are you Ute?"

"I am," Jake retorted shortly. "You can mention that to your superiors too. Remind them where you got a fresh horse."

As the young soldier rode off on the stud, Jake looked at the three men with him, assessing their horses. They were all riding Twin Peaks' horses.

"Luke," Jake said, "let me have your horse. You will have to make do with this spent one."

"I would have thought after your last run-in with soldiers," Luke said, dismounting, "that you wouldn't be wanting to help any. Especially when they are waging war on your own people."

"The thought did cross my mind," Jake said, "but that is what's so damned wrong with all that has gone on between the Indians and the whites. Be it Indians or whites that start something, the other side takes it out on people who weren't involved. I can't blame this soldier or the ones on Milk Creek for what happened to me last year. We aren't ever going to live together if we keep doing that."

Jake turned to Sam. "Take these cattle home and tell my folks and Anna that I went to the agency. I got to sort this out. I knew there would be trouble, but this will do no good for my people. I need to find Brown Otter. You better let Hawk know too. Be up to him what he does. But his folks are over there somewhere. I wouldn't be surprised if Otter was in the fight. I reckon Hawk will make tracks too."

"Jake," Lathe asked, "when you get there, who you going to side with?"

Jake looked at Lathe, then off in the distance before answering. "I have no damn idea," he said. "Hopefully, I won't have to choose." He looked back at Lathe, "Go talk to Anna. Tell her I will be all right. Tell her I'll be back."

Jake smelled the battleground before he saw it. The smell of dead and rotting horses and mules was overpowering. The soldiers had to be suffering from the stink. When Jake did come upon the soldiers, he skirted them at a distance and rode into the hills to the Utes who were pinning them down. The Utes had chosen a good place to ambush the soldiers. They were on high ground where they could shoot down upon the calvary just after the soldiers had crossed the boundary into the reservation. The Utes had shot the horses and mules right out from under the soldiers, leaving them stranded with their dead and injured animals.

Jake knew that someone in the war party of the Utes would recognize him. He didn't try to hide or sneak in. He just skirted the soldiers far enough that they had no shot at him and climbed the hills to the Indians. The first man Jake saw was Iron Wing. He came to meet Jake, accompanied by Jacks, a Ute chief. Jake stopped and dismounted. He cast around to see if Brown Otter were close, but he did not see his brother.

"You have them pinned down pretty well," Jake spoke to the two men in the Ute language. They both spoke English, but Jake felt he was accepted better when he used the native language.

"White soldiers are enjoying the smell," Jacks replied sarcastically.

"They got a runner out," Jake told them. "There will be more soldiers coming."

"It will take them time," Iron Wing said, "and when they come, we will see how many. Then decide what to do."

"Where is Brown Otter?" Jake asked.

Iron Wing looked at Jacks before speaking, "He was shot the first day. He was taken to the village."

"How bad?" Jake was concerned.

Iron Wing shrugged. "Maybe bad, maybe not. Sent him back to village."

"You come to fight with us?" Jacks asked.

"I come to see if I can help. Might fight, might not," Jake replied shortly. "But first, I want to find Otter."

"Village moved," Iron Wing told him. "It is away from the agency. Farther away. Agency not there anymore."

Jake looked sharply at Iron Wing and Jacks both. "What happened?"

"The agent and the other white men dead. Douglass and some others killed them. Burned buildings. We heard about it when we sent our wounded back."

"What about the agent's women?" Jake asked.

Jacks shrugged. "Not killed. Taken. Don't know."

Jake looked down at the soldiers, hunkered down behind dead animals. This battle would not come out right, no matter how justified the Indians were to defend their land. But the killing of the agent and his men was worse. And kidnapping the women was sure to raise the anger of the whites. Jake shook his head.

"I will go find my brother," he said. "I will see what is best for me to do then."

Jacks spoke once more as Jake mounted, "It was our right to protect our lands. We do not want another Sand Creek Massacre. The soldiers should not cross our boundaries."

Jake looked down at him. "You speak true. You had the right. But the whites won't take this well, especially hearing the agent is dead and his women gone." In English, he added, "There will be hell to pay."

It was about eighteen miles to the agency from the reservation boundary and another five miles before Jake found the first tepees. The log buildings of the agency were still smoldering as he went by, and the dead were still lying where they had been slain, but

Jake didn't stop. He wanted to find Brown Otter. He couldn't help the dead now.

When Jake found the first village, it was only a handful of tepees. The first person he saw was Brown Otter's married daughter. She came to him, tears in her eyes, and pointed to a tepee at the edge. Jake didn't question her, just went where she pointed. He opened the flap and went inside.

Brown Otter lay at the far side, Snowbird at his side. She was rocking and wailing softly. She saw him come in and turned her tear-soaked face to him. "He die this morning," was all she could get out.

While the women prepared the body, Jake dug the grave. If there had been time, Jake would have liked to find a cave to put Otter in. The Utes often used caves to bury their dead. The work gave him an outlet for his grief. He would bury his older brother, his link to the father he never knew.

Otter, twelve years older, was almost like a father to him in many ways. He was the man who taught Jake the ways of the tribe. For all his adult life, Jake had met Brown Otter every summer. It was hard to imagine a summer without spending it with Otter. *Senseless killings,* Jake kept thinking. *When would the senseless killings end?*

Hawk rode in on an exhausted horse the next morning. He took his father's killing hard. His first impulse was to go back to the battleground and take his revenge against the soldiers there, but Jake got him settled down.

"Your mother needs you now," he told the young man. "Those soldiers are hunkered down, waiting for reinforcements. When they come, the Utes will fade away. Your warriors won't fight a battle they can't win. Your father fought when there was a chance to win. Help me bury Otter. Then if you feel you have to go back, you go. But be smart. Don't die for revenge."

They buried Brown Otter at mid-morning, wrapped in a buffalo robe. When the grave was covered, Jake and Hawk walked back to the tepees. Jake turned to the young man.

"I am heading out to see if I can catch the band that took the white women," he told Hawk. "It is important for us, for the Utes, that they be treated well and released. I know how the whites will feel about this. It's the best way I can help."

"I am going back to Milk Creek," Hawk said. "I will use my head. I will not be stupid. But if there is more fighting, I must fight for my father."

Jake nodded. He was not surprised at Hawk's decision. He hoped that more fighting would not come about, but he could not tell the young man what to do. Hawk had to find his own way.

It wasn't hard to follow the retreating Indians that had the women captives. What took the most time, though, was following all the splits that they made. It appeared that they separated and camped in different places, then would come together again to continue traveling. They were generally heading south, and Jake suspected that they were heading to the Uncompahgre Utes in the south. The southern Utes had a well-known chief, Ouray, who had gained favor with the whites. Ouray was well-spoken and educated. He and several other members of the southern Utes had traveled to Washington, calling for peace between the whites and the Utes. Jake knew Ouray's sister was a wife to one of the Utes in the band he was following. It made sense that the fleeing Utes would head south to the southern Utes.

Jake had been on the trail about a week when he spied riders coming toward him from the east. He didn't like being alone and meeting a larger party. He watched them warily but continued forward. As they came closer, Jake recognized the army-blue uniforms of some of the riders. He leaned back and pulled his rifle from the scabbard and checked his pistol. He reached into his pack and got out his spare pistol and put it in his waistband. He knew he was in a precarious spot right now. Jake was Ute, and the Utes were suddenly at war. He didn't intend to be caught flat-footed again and facing a hangman's noose. They could kill him outright if that were the intention, but Jake wouldn't let himself be taken this time.

When the riders were almost to him, Jake reined his horse to a stop and turned to face them, rifle held across his saddle, ready. Three of the men were not in uniform, and one of these men rode forward.

"How," was all he said.

"Can I help you, gentlemen?" Jake replied easily. *Why did white men always say "how?"*

The man looked startled at Jake's English, "I . . . we are looking for some kidnapped women."

"Well, you're crossing their trail right now," Jake responded, gesturing ahead of him. "I've been tracking them for over a week now. I've been gaining on them, but they still are a way ahead of us."

"Why are you looking for them?" the man inquired.

"Let's just say that I think it is best for the Utes and the women if we find them unharmed and get them home safe."

"Are you from the tribe that did this?"

"Only part of the tribe did this. The rest are defending the reservation boundary to the north of here. I'm from a ranch about three days north of the reservation. But I have relatives that are part of the tribe. I never lived with them, just spent some time with them in the summers." Jake was feeling some better about this man who appeared to lead the soldiers. He was asking questions before giving orders.

"I have been commissioned to find the captives and take them to safety," the man said. "If you know the country, I would appreciate the help if you would be willing to ride along with us. My name is Charles Adams," the man said.

Jake eyed him and the soldiers that rode behind. "I would be willing," he answered. He reined his horse to the south again. "Jake Welles. We got hours of sun yet. Let's make tracks."

As they rode on, Adams asked Jake what had happened in the north. Jake told him as much as he knew about the Utes ambushing the soldiers when they entered the reservation.

"As for what happened at the agency, I have no idea. My guess," Jake said grimly, "is that Meeker pushed too hard. My family and I stopped the end of July and Meeker had plowed up their horse pasture and racetrack. Feelings were pretty hard then. The Utes were angry."

"Angry enough to kill the agent and burn the buildings?"

"It festered for two months since I spoke to Meeker in July. I told him then that no good would come from what he did," Jake sighed, thinking back to that day. "My sister-in-law said he made a decree that the head of each family had to be present to get their weekly rations. That would mean the men had to stay near the agency. That wouldn't set well either. I knew there would be some repercussions just from the plowing of the land, but I hoped that Meeker would be the one to change. Reckon that didn't happen."

"Did you talk to anyone who was at the agency when they were massacred?" the officer wanted to know.

"Not really," Jake replied. "The men I spoke with were at Milk Creek fighting. They didn't know there was any killing at the agency until they had some of their wounded sent back to the village. The two things happened about the same time but eighteen miles apart." Jake rode silently for a bit, then continued, "My sister-in-law had moved her tepee away from the village when her husband, my brother, went to fight at Milk Creek."

"You have a brother in the tribe?" the man asked.

Jake gave him a direct look before answering, "I had a brother, a half-brother, but he was killed at Milk Creek. He was a good man, just fighting for his way of life."

"I am sorry to hear that," Adams told him. They rode silently for quite some time before Adams asked, "You knew the Meekers, then?"

"Just met them once late in July. My wife and children and some of my cousins summer in the high mountains with me. We were driven out early by the smoke of the fires. We stopped for a couple nights at the village. Meeker heard white folk were there and invited them to tea," Jake grinned suddenly at the captain. "He got a surprise when I showed up with the white folk."

The captain smiled at Jake, "You have a white wife?"

"I have a white wife and white cousins. I am the only outcropping of the family. Long story." Jake turned serious again, "Maybe that's why I feel I need to try to get these women back. It hits close to home."

They rode for several days, the Indian sign before them getting fresher each day. Jake had the tracking skills, and with the extra riders, the tracking went faster. They could split and follow the different directions that the Indians took. As they gained on the village, though, they became increasingly more cautious. It was midday of the sixth day when they came upon two riders. Jake signaled to slow to a walk, and they approached cautiously.

The riders were Uncompahgre, southern Utes. Jake talked to them and asked if they knew how far ahead the village was. The Uncompahgre braves knew where the northern Utes were camped. They knew three different chiefs were holding the women, but they were all camped together at that time. These southern Utes also knew the consequences of the massacre at the agency could be devastating to all the Utes. They told Adams that they would ride to the hostiles' camp and let the northern Utes know of Adam's approach and that Adams just wanted the white women and children and not to make more war.

Just before noon of the next day, Jake led the way into the camp with Adams and his men behind him. The first Ute that they met knew Jake. Jake questioned this man and, at first, was told that there were no white women in the camp, but Jake caught movement in one tepee. A squaw was holding a blanket over the opening, but Jake saw a white face peek out over the top of the blanket. Suddenly, Josephine Meeker pushed her way out, coming right toward Adams. Adams dismounted and went to Josephine. They talked briefly and then moved away, hoping to find the tepee where the other women were held.

Jake did not go with them. He wasn't needed anymore by Adams. Adams would meet with some of the other chiefs, negotiating for the women's release. Instead, Jake reined his horse to the side and dismounted, going to speak to a Ute man, Blade Runner, whom he knew. He asked Blade Runner about the women and how they had been treated. When Jake finished talking to Blade Runner, he saw that Adams was with two Ute chiefs. Standing a distance away alone was Josephine Meeker, waiting for the other women to be located and released. Jake approached her slowly.

"Miss Meeker," he said softly, "do you remember me?"

Josephine turned to him, at first questioningly, before she remembered. "You came to tea in July," she said. "You had your wife and cousins with you."

"Yes, ma'am, I did."

"What are you doing here?" she asked.

"I came looking for you," Jake said simply, "I think you will be in good hands now. This man Adams is good."

"Why did you come?" her gaze was direct.

"Miss Meeker, I don't know what kind of treatment you, your mother, and the other woman have had, but I know you have had a bad time of it, if for no other reason than losing your menfolk so violently. But this retreat can't have been easy either," Jake hesitated, not sure how to say what he wanted to say. "Miss Meeker, I don't need to know what happened to you. I was told that you were kept by Persune and his squaws, and the talk was that Persune considered you one of his wives. I just want you to know that if you are a strong woman, and I have been told that you are, you will survive this ordeal. Sometimes white women don't think they can, but . . ." Jake let the sentence trail off.

"And you know this because why, Mr. Welles?" Josephine's voice was tinged with anger. "That is your name, isn't it?"

Jake looked steadily at Josephine. "You asked me when we were your guests how I met my wife," he said. "I knew at the time that she didn't want me to tell you about her past. But the truth of it is that I bought her from the Cheyenne when she was seventeen years old. Her family were all butchered along the Oregon trail by Pawnee when she was eight. An old Pawnee grandmother raised her until the old woman died, then Anna was sold to the Cheyenne. I came along about four months after, and she was starving. She had been beaten, burned, and raped. I traded one pony for her."

"You must have been kind to her," Josephine murmured, her eyes wide with surprise. "She seemed happy with you."

"Oh, I didn't buy her to be a wife," Jake continued. "I bought her because when I saw her haunted eyes, I knew that would have been my mother's fate if my blood father, my Ute father, hadn't taken her for his wife," Jake paused, watching Josephine recoil from this. "When we visited you, you assumed my father was a white man, a squaw man, didn't you? My father was not a squaw man. He was a Ute half-breed. He took my mother for his wife so she wouldn't be taken back to the tribe to be a slave to all. A prostitute. My mother is a white woman."

Josephine blanched, "Your wife and your mother? Both of them? Both taken?"

"Yes, both of them," Jake continued gently. "My wife and I fell in love. We made the decision to marry. My mother had no choice, but she never says one bad thing about my blood father, nor does she allow anyone else to either. He was good to her. When he was killed, she grieved for him. She married my stepfather after that, and they had more children. They have had a good life. Both my wife and my mother are strong, proud women. They are not ashamed. You should not be either."

Josephine contemplated this, then looked up at Jake. "Thank you for telling me this. It helps. I will tell my mother and Mrs. Price."

Jake nodded gravely, "Good luck to you, Miss Meeker." Then turning, he mounted his horse and headed north. He had done what he came to do. The women were safe and would be escorted home by Adams and his men. It was time to go home.

Jake made it back to where Snowbird was camped in half the time it took him to follow the Utes on their southern retreat. Without the detours he had to make as he followed several different routes of the Utes as they split apart and came back together, he made good time. He did not spare his horse either. It was near the end of October. Anna was expecting the baby at the end of October or early November. He wanted to be home with her.

The Utes at Milk Creek had faded away just as Jake had predicted they would when more troops showed up. Hawk was living with his mother and his mother's brother, waiting for Jake's return. Jake's horse was worn out, so he traded with Hawk for one of Hawk's fresh horses. Jake didn't even want to stay a night with them. He wanted to get on his way. The days were getting shorter, the nights colder. Hawk walked out with him to saddle a fresh horse.

"Are you staying here?" Jake asked his nephew.

Hawk looked thoughtful before answering, "I will for a while, but I will follow you soon. I think my mother will go with my sister and her husband. But I will wait to make sure."

Jake took a pouch from a thong around his neck and handed it to Hawk. "Here, give this to your mother. It isn't much but tell her if she ever needs anything to get one of the young men to ride for us."

Hawk looked at Jake's pouch, feeling the coins inside, before answering, "I will take care of my mother."

"That is good," Jake responded seriously, "A son should take care of his mother. But a man should help his brother's wife. Give it to her."

Hawk thought about that and nodded. Jake turned back to the fresh horse Hawk had provided him and tightened the cinch. When all was ready, he mounted and looked down at his nephew.

"We will watch for you," he said.

Hawk nodded before saying, "Tell Bonnie I will come. She is eighteen now. We have things to plan."

.◆.

Jake could see the cabins coming into view. He was ready to be home. He estimated it was still October, but he could be wrong on that. Time had a way of getting away from him when he was rambling. He worried about Anna being alone at this time. Hawk's little horse had a lot of bottom to it, and he had pushed it hard. Jake was glad he was almost home. Both he and the horse needed to rest.

Just as he rounded Sarah's cabin and headed up the valley, he saw two riders approaching him. From the tiny size of one of the riders he knew it was Kestrel which meant it was his pa with the little girl. Jake spurred his tired horse on faster.

"Daddy!" Kestrel called, coming to meet him, her little arms outstretched. He reached over and scooped her off her horse to sit facing him in his lap. She patted his chest and hugged him, babbling happily.

Kade smiled at Jake, "You made it back."

Jake nodded. He knew his father would not ask but would wait for Jake to talk when he was ready.

"Is Anna all right?" Jake asked first.

"She's resting today. Your ma has Lark, and this little imp thought she needed to ride Smokey. You can come for the girls later. Anna will be waiting for you now."

"Brown Otter was killed at Milk Creek," Jake was somber. "I helped Snowbird bury him. The agency men were killed, and the women kidnapped. I went after the women, but the calvary came along. The women are safe now anyway. Now I guess we wait and see what happens next. It won't be good for the Utes. There is going to be an outcry over this. It makes no matter that it was Meeker's own fault," Jake ended bitterly.

Kade regarded him solemnly, but before he could speak again, Kestrel broke in, "Daddy smell bad," she patted his chest. "Papa," she looked at her grandfather, "ride 'Mokie now. Ride, Papa, ride." She reached her little arms out to her grandfather.

Kade grinned up at Jake. "Guess I better make tracks before I get in trouble. And you better go wash. I'll look for you before dark, or I can bring the girls up too, but your ma will want to see you."

"I'll come for them later," Jake said. "I'll go see Anna and get cleaned up," he added, smiling at his daughter.

The cabin door was shut when Jake got home. The fall weather was much too chilly to leave it open. It didn't take Jake long to strip the saddle from his tired horse and put it in the lean-to. He knew it was past noon, but the sun was still high in the sky. Anna would be inside. He burst into the cabin, letting his eyes adjust to the dim light.

There in the rocking chair sat his wife, a new baby nestled in her arms, hungrily nursing. Jake stopped dead in surprise. His father, or more importantly, Kestrel, had not said a word. How did they muffle an almost four-year-old to keep this secret?

"When?" Jake whispered, going to Anna's side, and kneeling beside her, he looked at the little face greedily sucking.

"Two days ago," Anna smiled at him. "You have a son."

Jake had thought that it didn't matter. He loved the girls, but when she spoke, he knew it did matter. A man wants a son too. He just knelt there and smiled. Anna unwrapped the baby, letting Jake see his son for the first time.

"Did you give him a name?" Jake asked.

"In my heart, I call him the name you and I decided on, but I haven't told anyone," she answered. "And I didn't know what middle name you wanted. So, I just told your folks I would wait for you."

Anna wrapped the baby up again against the fall chill. As Jake watched, the baby's eyes began to close, although he kept sucking. Jake reached up, cupping Anna's face, and pulling the chair toward him, he kissed her.

"I missed you," he said. "Did you have a hard time with this one?"

"Not much," Anna replied. "Your mother and Martha were here." Anna looked teasingly at Jake before continuing, "And no man was pacing outside for me to worry about."

Jake sat back on his heels, watching the baby. Then he reached to his wife, his hand creeping under her blouse to her other breast. "I suppose it is too soon?" he whispered.

"There are other ways," Anna murmured. "Put your son in his cradle."

"I have to go wash up first," Jake said wryly. "Kestrel told me I stink. I think she's right."

"Put the baby in the cradle," Anna repeated. "I have water warming on the stove. I will bathe you."

Jake kissed her again. "I do love you, Beautiful Bird," he said, gathering the sleeping baby into his arms and carrying him to the cradle. Then looking back at his wife, he murmured, "Old Tom knew us so well."

⚘

The afternoon shadows were lengthening when the baby demanded attention. Jake looked at Anna, lying beside him on the bed. "I reckon he wants you, not me?" But he got up and went to the cradle, picking up the little bundle and bringing the baby to his mother. Then reaching for clean clothes, he quickly pulled them on.

"I'll go for the girls," he told her. "Pa said that Ma would want to see me too. So, I'll be a while."

He walked down the slope from his cabin, surveying the vast valley before him. At the far end by the beaver ponds, there was a large herd of cattle grazing. There was enough grass here in the valley until the snows fell, then they would start feeding hay. He had missed fall gather this year, but it looked like it went well.

In the other direction, across the narrow neck of the valley, he could see Sam and Martha's cabin. He heard the ax chopping and knew Sam was getting firewood. Jake knew he would have to work on doing that soon too. They would need a powerful amount of firewood to make it through the winter. He saw movement across the meadow and saw Sam carrying in a load. Jake lifted a hand in greeting, seeing Sam smile and nod to him. Tomorrow he would visit with Sam. Today was for family.

As he drew close to his folks' cabin, Jake saw Sabra and Kade sitting out front on a bench that Tom had made for them. They were watching the two little girls playing in the yard. He saw Kade say something to the children and gesture his way. Kestrel popped up like a jack-in-the-box, searching. When she spied her daddy walking toward them, she climbed a stump, waving her little arms at him. She was off like a light then, little legs pumping as she ran to greet him. He scooped her up and put her on his shoulders, where she clapped her hands and yelled to her grandparents.

"Daddy smell good!"

Little imp, Jake thought. *How did they keep her from telling about the baby?* He couldn't muffle her for anything.

Sabra Lark came toddling over to him when he got near, and he picked her up also. Finding a spot on the ground by his folks where he could sit, he let the girls play around him.

"Kade told me about Brown Otter," Sabra began. "I am so sorry, son," she said sadly. "I hate the thought of him being gone."

Jake nodded, "Maybe it is for the best. He didn't like the way things were going. He went down fighting. It was his way."

They visited quietly, Jake telling them about the events at the agency and at Milk Creek. "The Utes were in the right about defending their boundary at Milk Creek," Jake told them. "But being in the right isn't going to be enough. And the outcry about the killings and kidnappings at the agency is going to be fierce. I don't think any good is going to come of this. I wouldn't be surprised if the Utes get forced out again. When it comes to treaties, I don't much trust the government.

"I have been thinking," Jake continued, changing the subject, "that maybe Anna and I and the kids might stay here next summer. It gets harder and harder to haul little kids, what with three now. Anna and I thought maybe you two would like to spend some time up there at the cabin. Lathe and Kasa would go too, and James. It's been some time since you were up there. You need a break from haying."

Sabra looked at Kade, and they both smiled. "We might jest do that," Kade spoke. "We could take some horses with us to work and jest sort of enjoy the mountain."

"Did you name the baby?" Sabra asked, changing the subject once more.

Jake stretched out his legs, shaking two little girls off him before he stood up. "Yes, we had known a first name before I left if it were to be a boy, but wasn't sure what to put with it," he looked over at Kade. "His name is Kade Brown Welles. He's got a name to live up to, named after the two best men I have ever known."

Kade's smile spread across his face. He stood up and put out his hand to his son. "You have always made me proud son, but this is an honor. I know how Tom felt now when Thomas was born, and we gave Thomas his name and how Sabra felt when Sabra Lark was born."

Sabra stood as well and hugged Jake. "That is a fine name."

Jake smiled at them both, feeling contentment flow through him, replacing the sadness that he felt for the loss of Brown Otter and the plight of the Utes. Nodding to his folks, Jake turned, carrying his two toddlers, and went down the hill. As he descended, he glanced to the south and saw the two twin cabins of the Bates' and Jorgensen's. Somewhere beyond was the cabin of Army and Rachel, and below his folks' cabin was the barn with Thomas and Beth's home beyond it. Lathe and Kasa had built just up the valley from Jake's home. And soon, there would be another cabin for Hawk and Bonnie. *This was his community, his ranch,* he thought. *This was his family, his people. It was good to be home.*

ACKNOWLEDGEMENTS

Writing a book involves many more people than simply the author. It is because of all the people who have helped me in this journey that this work is produced. First, I want to thank my sister-in-law, Dayna Beckman for her painstaking editing. Dayna doesn't rest until she gets me to "get it right"! I thought I was pretty good with grammar, but I have learned tons about grammar and my writing through Dayna.

Next, I want to thank all my readers; the people who read, commented, and encouraged me along the way. Without them, I probably wouldn't do anything with my manuscripts except hide them on a shelf. Friends like Judy, Adele, Renee, Gene, and Patty (Oh my gosh, I hope I haven't forgotten someone) who read this story and gave me such good feedback. I am thankful for friends who read my first book and now meet me on the street, in the grocery store, or on social media and keep asking when the sequel would come out. They spurred me on to keep looking for the right publisher.

And finally, a special thank you to JuLee Brand of W. Brand Publishing who believes in this book and is helping me see it to fruition.

About the Author

Johny Weber is a retired assistant professor at Northern State University in Aberdeen, South Dakota. Since childhood, her life has revolved around horses. Marrying a rodeo cowboy, she moved with him to the plains of South Dakota where they both competed in rodeos and then turned to a ranching lifestyle. Her career in education began by teaching first grade and by retirement she was teaching graduate courses to teachers in a state-funded program. Johny and her late husband raised a son and daughter on the prairies of the Cheyenne River Indian Reservation. She now enjoys time spent with her children and grandchildren and traveling with her horse and dog to ride the mountains of the west in the summer and the deserts of the southwest in the winter.

Also available
Mountain Series
Book One,
Mountain Refuge

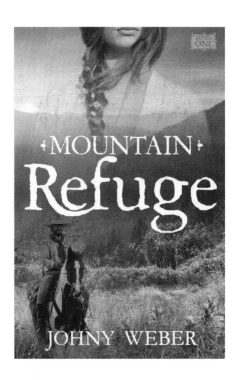